Step, Shuffle

DIE

Step, Shuffle
DIE

Cheryl Miller Thurston

ACKNOWLEDGMENTS

I would like to thank the following:

- Shirley Wilsey and Susan Malmstadt for their suggestions, ideas, and enthusiasm. Their help with this book was invaluable.
- Sally Nibbelink for reviewing tap dancing information.
- Annet Wollan for help with police procedural questions.
- Joy Kalamen for a suggestion I loved. (You know, which one, Joy!)
- My husband, Ed Armstrong, for his encouragement.
- Sally Nibbelink, Karen Kleber, and Randy Downing for making tap dancing classes so much fun over the years.
- Many of the readers of *Death By Accordion* whose kind words encouraged me to continue Ella's story.

Cheryl Miller Thurston

*"If you can walk you can dance.
If you can talk you can sing."*
-Zimbabwean proverb

PROLOGUE

I tend to obsess about things a little.

Okay, maybe a lot.

I was right in the middle of obsessing about the difficulties a certain 15-year-old was bringing to my life—and there were a lot of them—when a new obsession emerged: a murder. Who could have killed my best friend's one-time (literally one-time) lover?

It was a lot to obsess about. Of course, I never for a minute thought Sammie did it, even though much of America did. At least for a while.

I decided I had to find the murderer.

And that's when I discovered that a certain 15-year-old obsesses about things a little, too.

Actually, a lot.

CHAPTER ONE

May 18, 2019
6:20 p.m.

Step, shuffle, hop, step, around-the-world, stomp, clap.
Step, shuffle, hop, step, around-the-world, stomp, clap.

I threw in an extra stomp. How did I keep winding up on the wrong foot? Watching from her seat at the side of the dance floor, 15-year-old Cassie Sherman laughed, then quickly looked back down at her cell phone. I guess she thought a group of eleven adult women trying to tap dance was funny.

"Think it's easy, Cassie?" said the teacher, my best friend Sammie Russo. "Grab a pair of shoes from the Borrow Box and join us. Really." Her eyes held a challenge, and Cassie stood up.

For a moment I thought she was actually going to join us. Then she shuddered, evidently coming to her senses. "No, thank you," she said. Her words were polite but infected with a tinge of "Not even if you *paid* me!"

Sammie watched her for just a moment longer than necessary, and I wondered if her next words were going to be, "Get your butt out here. Now!" Sammie does not tolerate tap dance disparagement—even *implied* disparagement—but she must have decided Cassie's "No, thank you" was in the tolerable range, if barely. She moved on.

"Let's work on paddle and rolls now," she said. "We'll do them over and over, and pretty soon you won't even have to think about which foot does what."

She was right. After a while my brain relaxed while my feet carried on. Progress.

Now if I could just make progress regarding my attitude about Cassie, I thought. I glanced at the clock on the wall. Only a few more minutes and I'd be able to turn her over to her father. I couldn't wait.

I had learned of Cassie's existence only after I had started falling, hard, for Detective Dan Sherman. Okay, maybe I should have learned more about him before I started falling, but meeting during a murder investigation hadn't give us a lot of opportunity to share our life stories. I knew the important things—that he had kind brown eyes and a kind personality to go with them, a good sense of humor, a great singing voice, an approachable kind of handsomeness that made me want to ...

Never mind what I wanted to do. I had already done it—and before he told me he had married his pregnant girlfriend right out of high school. He'd been divorced for thirteen years, but his 15-year-old daughter was a big part of his life.

And now, mine.

Unfortunately.

As we finished stretching at the end of class, Sammie took my elbow and said, "Lock up. I've got to nurse. *Now!* My boobs are killing me." She gave a wave to everyone and hurried upstairs to her apartment above the dance studio.

"I hope the museum thing is a lot more interesting than *this* was," Cassie said after I'd changed out of my workout clothes and we'd stepped outside into the alley.

I didn't respond, just tapped the code into the key pad to lock the studio door. *You are the adult here,* I reminded myself. *Breathe. Don't engage.* I rechecked the lock, and then we started toward the museum.

I suddenly stopped, then turned around and went back to check the door again.

"Think the door was, like, going to unlock itself in half a block?" Cassie asked.

"Just being careful," I said, trying not to be snippy. I wasn't about to mention that I can be just a tad obsessive-compulsive.

Cassie watched me, and when I turned back around, she said, "Are you *sure* now? Maybe we should double-check five or six more times."

"It's fine," I snapped. *Was snapping better than being snippy?* I wondered, mad at myself for letting her get to me. *Breathe. Breathe.*

We headed down the alley and across the street to the Juniper Museum, where I was working as a volunteer for a special reception and lecture. Cassie's father would be joining us as soon as he got off work.

Except he didn't. Just as we walked in the door, Dan texted both of us. He was tied up at the police department and couldn't meet us until after the program.

"*Again!*" Cassie said. This wasn't the first time he'd had to bow out of plans because of police department demands. She flounced over to a bench and plopped down, arms across her chest, eyes furious. In just a moment, though, she apparently remembered her phone, and all was well. Or at least better. Her thumbs came alive.

Geraldine Betz, Sammie's mother and president of the museum board, watched the little drama out the corner of her eye and gave me a sympathetic look. I sighed and started helping her set out paper plates, platters of cookies, a bowl of punch, and cups for the coffee brewing in a large urn in the kitchen area.

There should have been three of us working. "Where the heck is Affinity?" Geraldine asked, arranging napkins beside the paper plates.

I shrugged. "Not a clue. She left tap class before we did, so I don't know how we beat her here."

"For someone who is so eager to volunteer for everything in town, you'd think she'd maybe want to show up on time."

People were arriving, so I picked up brochures and stood at the entrance to the special exhibit room. The sign read:

WHAT THE HECK IS A HECKELPHONE?
Musical Instruments from
Around the World
(The Heinrich Schmidt Collection is on loan
courtesy of Otto and Moriko Schmidt)

"I still think my name should have been a lot bigger," said Otto, approaching with a plate of cookies and a clear plastic cup of punch. He balanced the cup on his plate in one hand and hugged me with his other arm. The other five members of our polka band, the Streusals, gave me hugs as well. Yes, I know it's a little weird for someone my age to play in a polka band with six guys at least 40 years older than me, but so what? I love playing my accordion with them, and—let's face it—I don't get a lot of opportunities to play the accordion, the instrument my Polish grandfather introduced me to as a child.

The whole museum exhibit had been Otto's idea. He had inherited a musical instrument collection from his uncle, who had traveled the world with the United States Air Force Band for twenty years. Moriko, Otto's wife, wasn't thrilled with the legacy. Though she agreed to having a few instruments on display in their home, she drew the line at the four-foot-long heckelphone, an instrument something like an oboe but pitched an octave lower. The heckelphone was rare, one of only about a hundred known to exist. "I don't want to be responsible for it when I'm vacuuming," she said.

Otto had organized a series of talks and demonstrations featuring some of the more interesting instruments. Tonight's talk in the downstairs meeting room was to be about the hurdy-gurdy, an instrument played by cranking a wheel. In a few weeks the lecturer would be me, talking about and demonstrating the accordion.

Moriko nodded toward Cassie. "Dan didn't want her getting in trouble at home alone?" she guessed.

I sighed and nodded, then tried to be nice. "She did enjoy the bagpipe talk last week. I think."

"Everyone loved the bagpipe talk," Otto said. "What's not to love about bagpipes?" He finished off his remaining cookie and stuffed the napkin into his empty punch cup. "Let's go find good seats. We'll save two for you and Cassie."

I looked around idly as they all went downstairs to the lecture room. It was a good turnout. The exhibit room was already full, and I could hear kids exclaiming at the size of the didgeridoo and tapping (okay, pounding) on some African drums in the "Try me!" area.

Geraldine joined me and nodded toward Affinity, who had finally arrived. "She's worthless," Geraldine said.

Affinity mouthed a "Sorry!" at us and hurried to put her purse behind the reception counter. She had changed from the exercise clothes she'd worn to tap class into a short skirt that showed off her long legs. They were the perfect golden-tan color of someone who is either blessed with great genes or has found a perfect spray tan. My boring beige legs felt a little jealous.

Affinity gave a fluffing-her-hair shake of her head and moved to stand by the punch bowl. I guessed she was older than she looked—probably 38 or 39—and very attractive, though with a hint of trying too hard, maybe because of eyelash implants so thick and heavy that I wondered if they affected her balance.

"You know there are two of her," I said to Geraldine.

"What do you mean?" Geraldine said, alarmed.

"She's got a twin sister named Serenity who looks exactly like her. They're both in my tap class."

"Oh, lord. Is Serenity volunteering, too?"

"Relax. She doesn't even live here. She drives up from Denver every week to take the class and spend time with her sister and her aunt. She wasn't in class tonight, though, partly because this was a make-up night, not our regular one. Oh, and something about her having a sore toe."

"Thank God. Not about the toe, about her not

volunteering." Geraldine thought a moment. "What kind of parents come up with names like Affinity and Serenity?"

"Parents seriously into yoga, maybe?" We watched Affinity pour a few cups of punch and straighten the napkins. Then she stole behind the reception desk again, bending down a little to pull a compact from her purse and check her lipstick. She whispered something to the receptionist, a young woman hired to work afternoons and evenings. Then, suddenly, Affinity stood up straight. She poked the receptionist with an elbow and gestured with her thumb toward the museum double doors. My eyes followed.

A man posed in the doorway and looked around the room, waiting to be noticed.

People gasped.

I'm not exaggerating. They literally gasped.

Geraldine and I groaned.

CHAPTER TWO

Donald Sanders swiped a hand through his artfully messy hair and looked around the room. People didn't always recognize Donald's name, but they certainly recognized his face. He was a New York City actor and model who had grown up in Denver. He'd had minor roles in a number of movies but was most famous for the television beer commercial that makes everyone cry. In it, he plays a dad in a cowboy hat, tight jeans, and cowboy boots. He holds the hand of an adorable little girl with Down syndrome and walks her to a barn, where he opens the door to reveal a special birthday surprise—a pony. The little girl cries out, "Is the pony mine, Daddy? For *reals*?" The commercial has become as iconic as the old Mean Joe Greene Coke commercial where the little boy gives a football player a Coke. Or the "I'm the man you could smell like" Old Spice commercial.

Out came the cell phones. Women—only women, of course—asked for selfies, and Donald pulled the more attractive ones close. Very close. They didn't seem to mind. How often does a person get hugged by someone who looks like a Greek god?

I mean, really, the man was a total hunk.

"I can't watch this," Geraldine said. She escaped into the museum office.

After ten minutes of photos, Donald excused himself and went to talk to the receptionist, whose name I couldn't remember. Mary? Marie? Mallory? I'd only met her once. She was a young woman of about 22, quite pretty, and with a bust I'd estimate as 38D. Donald leaned over the desk and began speaking softly to her. She twirled a lock of hair around her finger as he spoke and had just reached out to touch his arm when someone approached to buy postcards. As she reluctantly turned to the cash register, Donald stood up, looked around, and—unfortunately—saw me. All eyes in the reception area followed him as he walked over. Even Cassie's.

I suspected they were all wondering why he'd picked me. I'm not exactly chopped liver, but I don't have the bust of the receptionist or the legs of Affinity. And it isn't only my legs that are beige; I'm kind of beige all over. Light brown curly hair. Light brown eyes. Light skin that never tans. Oh, I get a fair amount of attention from men, but not when women like the receptionist or Affinity are around.

"Bellella Polansky," Donald said, leaning against the table next to me and folding his arms.

Good friends and family mash together my first name, Belle, and my middle name, Ella, but most people call me Ella. Donald was neither a good friend nor family.

"Donald Sanders," I answered.

He seemed stuck then, conversation-wise, and just looked around the room, maybe to make sure people were still looking at him. They were.

Finally, he came up with something to say. "Did you hear my folks retired and bought a place here? Couldn't live with all the traffic in Denver anymore." Juniper is a little town about an hour and a half north of Denver, nestled along the Front Range of the Colorado Rockies. "Plus, they wanted a place with a three-car garage."

I guessed why—so they would have room for their own cars. Donald kept a red convertible Mercedes-Benz SLC parked in his parents' garage and another just like it in New York City. (The pony commercial had been lucrative. *Very* lucrative.)

"I hadn't heard," I said.

He nodded toward Affinity, who was now back by the punch bowl. "You know Affinity?"

I nodded.

"She lives next door to Mom and Dad. I ran into her at Starbucks earlier." He looked around the room again. People were still watching. I guess he decided he owed me an explanation for his presence. "I was doing stuff downtown. My car is parked in the museum parking lot."

I was surprised he hadn't said, "My Mercedes is parked in the museum parking lot."

Then he added, "You know, the red Mercedes."

I almost smiled but managed just to nod slightly.

He continued. "I started to get in the car …"

"The red Mercedes?" I almost said, but didn't.

"… but then I saw people coming in here and thought what the heck? Why not come in and see what's happening in downtown Juniper?"

Before he could say more, Affinity approached. "My turn now, Donald." She took his arm and led him over to a wall inlaid with mosaic tiles, a more attractive background than the poster-covered wall the others had used. She did have an eye for what would look good on social media. He put his arm around Affinity's waist, and the receptionist—Melissa, Margaret, Megan?—took their picture. Then they traded places, and he pulled the receptionist in front of him, his arms enclosing her in an embrace. He poked his head forward so that they were almost cheek to cheek. Affinity frowned but took the picture.

Donald started moving to the background music played over the speakers—a Muzak version of the country-western song "You Look So Good in Love." He turned the receptionist in his arms and started waltzing with her. She followed him effortlessly as everyone smiled at the impromptu little show.

Well, not everyone. Affinity wasn't smiling. I wasn't. And when Geraldine emerged from the bathroom, she wasn't, either.

"He went to see Sammie," I told Geraldine.

"Oh, lord. What next? I hope to heaven …" The lights flashed on and off, indicating that it was time to go downstairs to the lecture area. Geraldine had to introduce the speaker, so she hurried downstairs, giving Donald a curt nod as she passed.

As soon as the exhibit room emptied, I closed the door and arranged the flyers on a table at the entrance. When I looked up, Cassie was posing with Donald, smiling with her mouth closed, no doubt to avoid the flash of her braces. Donald's arm looped around her shoulders, his hand dangling far too close to her breast.

I jerked my head toward the door. "Time to go downstairs," I said. Cassie glared at me.

Donald gave Cassie a hug and let go. "I've got to go, too. I'm starving. Literally."

No, he wasn't literally starving. Yes, I know that language changes and the meaning of "literally" is changing to mean, well, not *literally*, but I have a hard time not hearing

Sister Dalmatia's voice in my head whenever Donald talks. Sister Dalmatia was one of the last nuns to teach when Sammie and I were in Catholic school, and her influence has been long-lasting. Literally.

"Nice to have ran into you, Bellella," he said, demonstrating once again that he could have used some of Sister Dalmatia's influence.

I didn't reply, just nodded and led Cassie toward the stairs.

"How do you know him?" Cassie breathed, looking back to see him talking to the receptionist again.

I sighed. "Long story."

Sadly, the hurdy-gurdy speaker, a professor from Denver, was not the audience pleaser the bagpipe man had been. Finally, at 8:15—a long forty-five minutes after he'd been introduced—he wound things up, and the audience members applauded dutifully, but without enthusiasm. The room emptied fast, probably because people were afraid he might start talking again if they lingered.

"*That* was fun," Cassie said. We helped stack the plastic chairs and move them into a storage closet, then trudged upstairs to the main lobby again, exhausted from boredom.

Adrenaline would soon change that.

Upstairs, we found the receptionist peering out the double glass doors of the museum entrance as sirens blared outside. Cassie and I edged in beside her to see what was going on, but she didn't take the hint and move over more. I noticed the tag of her cardigan sticking up and started to tuck it in for her. Then I realized the problem. "Your sweater's inside out," I whispered.

"What? Oh. Oh, thanks." She scooted over finally, pulling her sweater off and changing it around.

Looking across the street, we saw two police officers shining flashlights in the alley near Sammie's apartment. Without stopping to realize that I shouldn't drag a teenager into possible danger, I grabbed Cassie's arm and said, "Let's go. We've got to check on Sammie." I did remember to look both ways for traffic, though, as we jaywalked across the street and down the alley.

Cassie and I stood between the door to Sammie's apartment and the door to the dance studio, looking around. I was surprised to see a pizza delivery guy in the alley, too. It was the same one who had delivered a pizza for Sammie and me before Dan dropped Cassie off for class. Was Sammie's fiancé home now? Maybe he had ordered another pizza.

Just then the pizza delivery guy called to the police officers. "The guy I saw yelled, 'Call 9-1-1. Dance studio.' Maybe you should check the *dance studio*."

"We're getting to that!" Detective Mildred Kendrick snapped, approaching the door and frowning to see me. We had not exactly hit it off in a previous murder investigation. "Either of you know the code?"

Before I could tell her, she gave the door a tentative push and, to my surprise, it opened. I could see her feeling for the light switch, then flipping it on as she stepped inside.

"Holy shit!" she said.

Of course we couldn't just stand there and ignore a "Holy shit." Cassie and I pushed forward and peeked in before Mildred could stop us.

"Get back!" she said, pulling us back from the doorway. "You did not see that."

But we had.

A body lay on the floor, curled a bit to the side, eyes staring, unseeing, at the mirrored dance wall. A bit of blood crusted at his temple. He was nude from the waist up, wearing only jeans, a red sparkled bow tie around his neck, and a pair of tap shoes with bright pink shoelaces. His regular shoes were placed neatly by the mirror. *Manly shoes*, I couldn't help thinking approvingly as I noticed their solid, sturdy soles. I kind of have a thing about men's shoes.

Then I recognized the body.

It was Donald Sanders.

Cassie clutched my arm, and my brain short-circuited as I processed a number of thoughts at once. Why on earth was Donald Sanders in Sammie's dance studio—the dance studio I had locked up myself two hours earlier? How did he get in? Why was he wearing tap shoes? Where was his shirt? And most importantly, why was he apparently dead? There were no marks on his perfect face or torso. How had he died? Was this a murder?

My attention turned to Detective Dan Sherman, who had just arrived at the scene. As always, I wanted to throw my arms around him and kiss him. Or do more than kiss him. But he wasn't paying attention to me. He glanced briefly into the studio, then put his arm around his daughter and walked her farther from the crime scene, turning her away from the door. I followed.

"You should not have seen that," he said, hugging Cassie and giving me a glance that I read as ever so slightly accusing—a look that asked, "Why in the world do you have my daughter at a crime scene?"

"We heard sirens and wanted to check on Sammie," I said. I didn't add that it wasn't *my* fault he'd been called to work and left Cassie and me to attend the museum lecture without him.

Cassie's voice was shaky. "I just had my picture taken with him."

"What????" Dan looked at me as if he thought I might have turned the crime into an Instagram session. He quickly realized his mistake. "Pictures?" he asked more calmly.

"He was at the museum reception," I explained. "People took pictures with him."

Dan frowned. He clearly didn't understand, but he touched my shoulder in an apologetic gesture that was kind but more professional than I would have liked.

I had to tell him. "Dan, I recognize the body. It's Donald. Donald Sanders."

He looked blank.

"Famous model?" I added. "Actor? Dancing Donald?"

He finally caught on. "Oh, god."

"Who is dancing Donald?" Mildred demanded.

"Just a sec," he said, thinking. I could hear more sirens approaching and hoped one of them was an ambulance, though I was pretty sure it wasn't going to be any help. Finally, *finally*, Dan remembered to hug me. Then he turned back to Mildred. "You are going to have to take over as lead detective on this case."

She eyed me, then nodded, understanding. "Because you're personally involved with a witness. And it's her best friend's studio."

"I didn't witness anything," I said. "I just got here."

"So did I," Sammie's fiancé Sam said, apparently having

just arrived. Two policemen blocked him from joining us. "What the hell is going on?"

Dan held up a hand to him, gesturing "Wait." Then he turned back to Mildred and threw my best friend under the bus. He spoke softly, but I heard him. "When you question Sammie and her fiancé, be sure to ask about the baby. And her biological parents."

CHAPTER THREE

Things moved quickly then. All of us—Cassie, Sam, the pizza delivery guy, and I—were sent to wait separately in the museum. Sitting in the kitchen area with cold coffee, I looked out the door and saw the receptionist sitting at her desk, crying. Dan was in the office area with Cassie. I didn't know where the others were.

I tried to do yoga breathing to calm myself, but it wasn't working. I worried about Sammie. All that noise had to be keeping her baby awake, and Mildred, or maybe another officer, was probably in the apartment trying to question her at the same time. Not an easy situation, even without the more personal questions that were sure to come up.

An officer interrupted my thoughts. "Ella Polansky?" He sat down with me, first warming some coffee in the microwave. "It's going to be a long night," he said.

He was business-like but friendly as he interviewed me, taking down all I could remember about what had happened that evening, in detail. He wanted to know who all the "actors" were in the scenario, which I thought was weird. We weren't presenting a play. I told him all I knew, and I was glad when the curtain finally came down on our little scene together.

Dan was waiting for me in the lobby. "There's another problem across town I need to deal with. Can you take Cassie home and stay with her until I get there?"

"I don't need a babysitter," Cassie said.

"You've been through a lot. I am not leaving you alone."

"Of course I'll stay with her," I said. My voice was a little chilly, though. Thanks to Dan, police would be poking through parts of Sammie's life they had no business poking through.

Dan kissed us both and hurried off. Cassie and I finally stepped out again into the warm May night.

As we headed in my car to Dan's house, Cassie asked, "So how come you're mad at Dad?"

"Who said I was mad?"

She snorted. "Like it's not obvious?"

"Okay, it's because he pulled himself off the case. Now Mildred will be asking Sammie questions that are none of her business."

"Dad says everything is their business when it comes to murder."

"Digging up dirt isn't," I said without thinking.

"Dirt? Like what kind of dirt?" For the first time, she showed a real interest in something I said.

"I shouldn't have used the term *dirt*."

"Hmmm. You're usually so careful about words," Cassie said.

Once, just once, I'd corrected her grammar.

"Does Sammie have a secret past? Like maybe she was a stripper once? Or, like, maybe she screws around on Sam? She's so hot, she probably gets lots of chances. Or maybe she ..."

"No!" I snapped. "To all of those things."

"Usually *dirt* involves screwing around," she persisted. "And this is your best friend?" Her voice dripped judgment. "Or maybe, like, she's a *murderer*, too."

I'd had enough and decided to tell her the truth before she got wind of gossip. Stopping at a red light, I twisted in my seat to face her. "I'm going to tell you the real *dirt* and hope, out of a sense of honor you will keep it to yourself." I paused, wondering if I should define *honor.*

She was listening. She glanced at the light, which had changed. "You going to move or what?"

"I am, as long as you are listening carefully." I drove on. "Okay, Sammie and Donald Sanders ..."

"The dead guy," she interrupted.

I sighed. "Yes. They were old dance partners and danced together at clubs in Denver and other places for over ten years. It was always platonic. You know what *platonic* means, right?"

She made that tongue-against-her teeth smacking sound that generally goes with a look that says, "Duh!"

I wanted to be sure. "It means they did *not* sleep together. Sammie knew Donald was conceited and kind of a jerk in some ways, but he was a fabulous dancer. Like really fabulous. And the two of them were so beautiful to look at, too." I smiled, remembering. "They were amazing. Jitterbug, country-western, salsa, hip-hop, tango, whatever—people would clear the dance floor just to watch them. Really, just like in the movies. Sammie loves dancing more than about anything."

"Even her fiancé?"

"She didn't even *know* Sam then. Sammie and Donald danced together, period. Whenever Donald came to Colorado to see his parents, they'd go out dancing, and this went on for years." I took a breath. "One night last year, though, Sammie stupidly had way too much to drink. She normally doesn't drink much, but that night, for whatever reason, she did. People do stupid things when they're drunk."

"Like?"

"She slept with Donald. Even stupider, she didn't use birth control."

"That sure was doing more than dancing."

"*One time* it was doing more than dancing. And it wasn't smart." I didn't mention it, but *why* Sammie had slept with him after all those years was a mystery to all. Too much wine undoubtedly had something to do with it—that and the fact that she had been, as she put it, feeling "kind of restless." Maybe her biological clock had been ticking and secretly egging her on. No one, least of all Sammie, really understood her actions that night. "Six weeks later," I continued, "two things happened: Sammie realized she was pregnant, and shortly *after* that she met the love of her life, Sam."

"After she was already pregnant? *Awkward.*"

"Exceedingly. But Sam and Sammie fell in love. They broke up for a while when he found out, but he came back. He loves Sammie, and he loves the baby, and they are getting married in August."

"So what about Donald?"

"He wasn't remotely interested in being a dad and was happy to bow out of the picture. Legally. Sammie's mother set up a trust fund to support the baby long before Sam was even in the picture. She's quite rich, you know."

"Really? Why doesn't she, like, pick some better shoes then? Those cloggy things she had on tonight—hideous."

I ignored her. "This 'dirt' is no one's business. Sammie may have screwed up, but we *all* screw up sometimes."

Cassie was silent.

I continued. "I'll just say that I'm appealing to your sense of honor and leave it at that." I didn't know if it would work, but that was a tactic both my mom and Baba, my grandmother, had used on me occasionally. Honor. Leaving it to me. Appealing to my best self. It actually worked, for me, but I didn't know about Cassie. "Questions?"

"Um, no." She hesitated. "Okay, now I know."

"Let's move on then. This is between you and me." We were just getting out of the car at Dan's house when another car pulled up.

"He must have called Mom," Cassie said. "Geez. Like he thinks I'm going to fall apart or something."

"Hi, Ella," said Cassie's mom, a perfectly pleasant woman I'd met a couple of times. I wasn't sure how I felt about her, except for a teensy bit of jealousy. She had a connection to Dan that I could never be a part of. "Dan called me. I'm going to stay with her until he gets home. I'd take her to my place, but I know they have plans for tomorrow." Cassie was stalking toward the house. "Does she seem okay?" she asked me, her voice low.

"I think so," I said. "It's good you're here, though."

I said goodbye and left, a teensy bit hurt that Dan evidently didn't think I could be a comfort to his daughter.

CHAPTER FOUR

It was late, but I was still worried about Sammie. I texted her to let her know I was coming and drove back to the apartment. As I drove slowly by the alley, I realized that I couldn't get in that way because of the police.

The entrance to both Sammie's apartment and her dance studio are in the alley. It's not a dark, dumpster and graffiti-filled kind of alley, though. It is newly paved with pots of flowers at the back door store entrances along the block and a mural on one brick wall. Sammie's mother had spearheaded city council efforts to spiff up the older downtown areas of Juniper, and this was one of the more successful spiffs. Sammie's upstairs apartment runs above both the dance studio and her upscale secondhand clothing store, Second Chance. As she says, "You can't beat the commute."

The entrance to Second Chance is on the street, not the alley, so I parked around front and let myself in. (Same key code as the studio; Sammie doesn't like to remember numbers.) Quietly, I walked through the store to the vestibule that led to the apartment staircase.

A policeman stopped me, but I knew him. George looked around, probably to make sure Mildred wasn't nearby, and let me go upstairs. He knew I was Detective Dan's girlfriend. He also knew Mildred and I had no fondness for each other.

Upstairs, Sammie sat on the sofa, baby Isabelle in her

arms, Sam rubbing her back. Even with no make-up, extra pounds around her tummy, and a burp cloth over one shoulder, Sammie was beautiful. She has the jet black hair and dark eyes of her Italian-American father and the curves, ivory skin, and gracefulness of her mother. She also has a way with clothes, perhaps from long years of working a job where she had to look upscale on a small budget. Even in her pajamas, probably vintage silk, she somehow managed to look stylish.

I reached down and picked up Isabelle, as I did every chance I could get. Oh, how I love that baby! To be fair, I have a weakness for any baby, but Isabelle Bethany Russo is special. The first time Sammie placed her oh-so-carefully in my arms, I melted. I marveled at the wonder of this new little being, and I clutched at the hope that someday I'd be placing a baby of my own oh-so-carefully in Sammie's arms.

The name Isabelle, though? I wasn't a fan. I'm a kindergarten teacher, and a couple of years ago I had an Isabelle in my class who ruined the name for me forever. Actually, it was more her helicopter mother who ruined it, but the name was still tainted. At least Sammie and Sam hadn't carried on the cuteness of their own matching names and named the baby something like Samuella or Samone or Samitha. Sammie's brother often carried Isabelle around the living room, bouncing her and singing, "Izzie, Izzie, Izzie-Bee," and the nickname Izzie-Bee was growing on me.

"You okay?" I asked.

Sammie nodded.

Sam said, "I just got here. The police let me in. Finally."

Sammie reached for the diaper bag, pulled out a changing

pad, and, wincing, got down on the floor. Kneeling, I laid Isabelle carefully on the pad next to Sammie.

Instead of unsnapping the onesie and getting on with it, Sammie looked up at Sam and said, "Donald was here today. Earlier. Like this afternoon."

Sam raised his eyebrows. "Oh? What did he want?"

"He wanted to see Isabelle."

Uh-oh. Now I was worried. Had Donald changed his mind about allowing Sam to adopt Isabelle? Did he want to change the arrangements they had already made?

Sammie continued, changing the diaper as she spoke. "He said he *needed* to see her. Just once. Curiosity, I guess."

"He wasn't curious enough about her to want to be her dad," Sam said. He had wondered aloud to us, many times, "What kind of person couldn't love a baby, especially *Sammie's* baby?"

"It seemed like the least I could do," Sammie said. "Let him see her, I mean. He *is* the father. Biologically." She sounded a little defensive, maybe because I was staring at her.

I tried to keep my voice neutral. "So how'd it go?"

We waited. Sammie folded the wet diaper into a ball and handed it to Sam, who got up and put it in the Diaper Genie. She pulled the tabs open on a new diaper and slid it under Isabelle. "Turns out there was just one reason why he wanted to see Isabelle. He wanted to see if he was *really* her father."

That stumped me. "How did he plan to do that?"

"By looking at her. When I held her up, he studied her for a minute—of course he didn't want to pick her up himself. Then he said, 'Are you sure she's mine?'" She pulled a clean onesie up over the diaper. "He said, and I quote: 'She just doesn't look pretty enough to be our baby.'"

The look on Sam's face told me it was a good thing he hadn't been around when Donald said that.

Sammie continued, swaddling Isabelle as she spoke. "Donald said that with our genes, the baby should be a knockout and, again, I quote, 'She's not.'"

We both stared at her. "What did you do?" I asked.

"Well, I thought about whacking him on the head with a table lamp."

"And you would have been totally justified," I said.

Sam nodded.

Secretly, I did kind of understand why Donald had felt that way. How could two people as gorgeous as Sammie and Donald produce anything but a gorgeous baby? I looked over at Isabelle's face, covered with a rash of little bumps. Her wisp of nearly invisible hair. Her reddish face. Oh, she was beautiful in the way all babies are beautiful, but *beautiful*, by the strictly physical standards Donald undoubtedly used? Not yet.

"I told him that of course I was sure he was the father," Sammie said.

"So why did he sign the birth certificate, or the acknowledgment of paternity or whatever it was, if he had doubts?" I asked. Sammie had insisted on accuracy when it came to the birth. She was not going to start her baby's life out with a lie. Our Catholic school upbringing had obviously had an effect.

Okay, maybe not in all areas. The remaining-pure-until-marriage message hadn't taken hold, obviously.

"He didn't have doubts when he signed. It wasn't until recently that he started 'thinking.'" Sammie made little quotation marks in the air with her fingers. "After 'thinking' about it, he decided he should check out the baby."

"So did he want to un-sign the birth certificate?" Sam asked. "Is that even possible?"

"No. He said he believed me and that he hoped the beautiful genes would kick in later."

Sam just clenched his fists.

Sammie braced a hand on Sam's leg and pulled herself up off the floor. "There's one more thing." She took a breath. "He asked to use the studio tonight after class to practice some dance moves. Evidently his agent is negotiating for him to be on 'Dancing with the Stars,' and he thinks they might want him to audition in California next week."

I didn't like where this was heading. "And you said …?"

"I said okay, from 8:00-9:00."

Sam and I shook our heads.

She bristled. "I know how hard it is to find a large place with mirrors where you can practice a dance. *Really* hard. I couldn't think of a reason why he shouldn't use it, *this once*, so I gave him the key pad code so he could let himself in and I didn't have to go down and see him again." She added, as if to convince us, "I mean, really, the guy was in my life for ten years. It's not like he was a stranger."

"It's your studio," I said. I didn't add what I was thinking: *That sure didn't work out well, did it?*

Then the tears came. "He was going to my lawyer tomorrow to finish up the paperwork to allow the adoption. I don't know what will happen now."

Sam put his arms around her. "It's going to be okay. I promise. Isabelle is *our* baby now, and I am going to be her father. I will take care of both of you."

Sam can be a bit old-school, protecting his woman like a guy walking out of a 1940s movie. Sometimes Sammie just laughs at him and tells him to stop being John Wayne-ish. But sometimes, like tonight, she nestles into his arms like the weak little woman she is not.

It was after 1:30 a.m. by the time I got home and crawled into bed, exhausted. Then I couldn't sleep. For one thing, I was still annoyed with Dan. Most people, seeing Sam and Sammie with Isabelle, assumed that Sam was the biological father. No one corrected them. But now things might be different.

I couldn't get Donald out of my mind, either. So many people would be affected by his death. He was the biological father of Sammie's child, but Isabelle would never be able to meet him if she wanted to in years to come. He was the son of parents who, according to Sammie, were surprisingly nice. He was a tidy source of income for his agent. He was a thrill to women everywhere who ran into him and found themselves staring, open-mouthed.

No, I hadn't liked Donald much, but I was sorry he had died. I pounded my pillow and squashed it into one shape, then another. Purring, my cat Fluffles kept trying to nestle between my shoulder and my chin, but she finally gave up, giving a frustrated little grunt of a meow as she hopped off the bed and left the room. I kicked my blanket down to my knees, then in a few minutes felt chilly and pulled it back. When I tried to breathe deeply and count backwards from a hundred, in twos, Donald's face would insert itself between the numbers, and I'd have to start over. I remembered the stillness of his face, the utter stillness.

The sound of a key turning in the front door told me that Dan was letting himself in. "It's me," he called softly. He came into the bedroom and sat on the edge of the bed. "I came to check on you before I go home to Cassie. Are you okay, Bellella?" He rubbed my shoulder.

"No. I don't see why you had to excuse yourself from the case. You've never even met Donald."

"But I know about him and Sammie. That might color my interpretation of things." He took my hand. "Mildred will keep things private if she can, but the fact that Donald is Isabelle's biological father *is* relevant to the investigation. Or could be."

I thought a minute. "Only if Sammie did it. Or Sam. And they didn't."

"We don't know what is relevant and what is not. Yet."

I understood, really. "I'm just upset about the whole situation." One murder in my life had been quite enough, thank you very much. But now another? Only months later? It was too much. Too, too much.

"I know." He paused. "But here's one bright spot. I'll have more time for you since I'm off the case."

I nodded and smiled.

He kissed my forehead. "Now I'd better get home to Cassie. Try to sleep. I'll talk to you tomorrow."

He let himself out.

Fluffles came back and stood on my stomach, as if deciding where to go. I moved her to my side, and she kneaded the bed until she was satisfied, then curled herself into a ball. I lay there beside her, thinking. Tonight was just one more indication that a relationship with Detective Dan Sherman was not going to be a bed of roses.

Oh, there was plenty of "bed" involved. I smiled to myself. The "bed" part was good.

But there were other problems. One was Dan's job. Police work can be dangerous, and fear is a fact of life for anyone involved with an officer. Other complications came with the job, as well, like the ones evident tonight. It can't be easy to work in a small town where people know one another, secrets spill, relationships blur into work, and work carries over into relationships.

It also can't be easy to have your girlfriend turn up, again, at the scene of a murder.

But the biggest problem, hands down, was Cassie. We had not exactly bonded. Although I knew it was way too early for such ideas, I had already started imagining a wedding and a home together and even a lovely little baby for Dan and me. A teenager was definitely not part of my perfect picture.

CHAPTER FIVE

Dan called at noon the next day. "Let's put last night out of our minds for a bit. It's Sunday, and now I don't have to work today. Can I see you?"

"Yes." I smiled. I wanted nothing more than to see him.

Then he added, "We can go to Cassie's softball game."

My smile faded. Not again. This would be my third game since Dan had finally introduced me to Cassie. I sighed to myself and said, "Sure." If I kept trying with her, surely things would get better.

Cassie, as it turns out, is something of a jock. I am not. I have a hard time focusing on sports because my attention tends to wander. I'll find myself wondering, for example, who designs team uniforms, especially professional ones. Do they have to go to design school? Are they required to have experience playing sports themselves? Does someone try on a prototype and run around tackling or dribbling or whatever to test the uniform's functionality before buying? And what are bases on a baseball diamond actually made of? Who makes them? Is there a company that sells baseball diamonds? How would someone get into that business?

Needless to say, I could never think of anything to say to Cassie after a game. "I like the logos on your team shirts," didn't seem right. Generally, I kept quiet.

"You okay?" Dan asked when I met him on the porch

of my duplex. He wrapped his arms around me, and we just stood together, breathing, for a long time.

"I'm sorry I was being a little unreasonable last night," I said.

"I'm sorry about being right."

I swatted his arm and he smiled and pulled me closer.

"Do you know how Donald was killed yet?" I asked. "Or who killed him?"

He stepped back a bit. "We are not talking about the murder today. I am off the case, remember?"

I remembered. I pulled him close again.

"Are you coming, or what?" Cassie called from the car. Trying to be positive, I waved, and we joined her. She was sitting in the front seat, of course, so I got in back.

During the game, the incredibly long game, my mind wandered, as usual. How had Donald been killed? Who had done it? I stared at the field without really seeing anything.

Finally, I brought my attention back to the game, which had to be almost over. I looked up at the scoreboard.

It was only the fourth inning.

When the waitress came to take our orders at Red Robin after the game, I ordered the black and bleu burger.

"Perfect!" she said.

"Perfect?" said Dan. "Really? I was going to get the guacamole bacon burger, but maybe I should rethink that." He looked over at me, and I couldn't help smiling. He knows that I think "Perfect!" is tossed around far too frequently.

The waitress hurried to reassure him, "Oh, the guacamole bacon burger is great, too."

He looked up at her. "But it can't be *perfect*, if it's the black and bleu burger that's perfect. Surely you can't have more than one perfect item on your menu?"

The waitress looked confused and hesitated.

"He'll have the guacamole bacon burger," I said. "Medium."

"What was that all about?" Cassie asked when the waitress left.

"Oh, Ella thinks people throw around the word *perfect* too much."

Cassie frowned, not understanding but shrugging it off. "Weird," she said.

I smiled at Dan. I love the way he pays attention to my observations about language.

After that, Cassie pretty much ignored me, as usual. She talked to Dan. Dan talked to me. She answered when I asked her a question, careful not to be rude enough to get called on it, but not being exactly personable, either.

I tried a couple of times while we waited for our food. "Are you glad school's almost out for the summer?" I asked, mentally kicking myself for such a lame question, but I couldn't think of anything else.

"Yes. I hate school."

"You must like some subject."

"No."

I decided to appeal to her darker side. "Okay, what's the subject you hate the most?"

"English."

Of course it was. It probably involved actually using language. "What do you hate about it?"

"The teacher. Teachers suck."

"Cassie," Dan said, a warning in his voice.

"They do!"

"Cassie, Ella is a teacher."

"I know."

The waitress set down our plates and left. Dan reached over and touched Cassie's arm, stalling it in mid-air as she reached for a french fry. He waited for her to turn and look at him before he spoke. "You can't make blatant statements like that about a whole group of people. What if someone said, 'Softball sucks.' Or 'Teenagers suck'"?

I didn't think it was a good time to mention that I felt like saying both of those things at the moment.

Cassie saw the anger in his eyes and nodded her understanding. "Okay, some teachers suck more than others."

His hand remained in position.

"Okay, and some don't suck at all." She didn't exactly sound sincere, but Dan put his hand down.

"Pass the ketchup, please," I said, trying to change the subject. When I dipped a fry, I managed to plop some ketchup onto my white T-shirt. I dabbed at the stain with a napkin, but then my bra showed through the wet spot. Cassie noticed but hid a smirk and didn't comment.

I went back to eating, dipping my fries more carefully this time, and listening to more about the softball game. I was not going to attempt conversation again.

The music was loud, and I found myself tapping my toes to the rhythm of a hip-hop piece. I imagined trying to duplicate the percussion with beatboxing and, without thinking, pursed my lips to give it a try. Luckily, I caught myself and stopped. What would a 15-year-old think of a teacher who beatboxed at all, let alone at a restaurant? I didn't think Cassie was ready to hear that I sometimes beatboxed with a polka band.

I finished my burger and played another song's melody on an imaginary accordion keyboard in my lap, keeping my fingers well-hidden below the table, of course. I knew how to entertain myself.

I saw Dan nudge Cassie with his elbow. Something was being communicated between them, but I wasn't sure what. Apparently dragging a question from the depth of her soul, Cassie choked out, "So do you like teaching kindergartners, Ella?"

Ah, Dan had evidently taught her that it is polite to ask questions. Before I could answer, she went on. "It seems like it would be so boring. I mean, they, like, don't know anything."

"Actually, that's part of what makes it interesting," I said. "So much is new to them, and they get excited about everything. They aren't at all jaded." I was on a roll. I had been quiet too long. "And they are so funny. I'll be talking to them about, oh, the sound a 'p' makes—*puh, puh*—and one of them will pop up with something completely random like, 'It's better to say *tooted* than *farted*,' or, 'My dad tried to shoot my loose tooth out with a Nerf gun.'"

I saw a hint of a smile, but she quickly hid it. "What's *jaded?*"

"Jaded is when you don't get excited about anything. Everything bores you."

"Like I'm jaded about school."

"Evidently." I pushed my plate away and put my elbows on the table, leaning forward. "But I'll bet you aren't as jaded as you let on. There must be some class that is more fun than others. Art, maybe?"

"I made a vase last quarter, but it cracked in the kiln."

"How about music?"

"Mom makes me take band, so I play the clarinet. I suck at it."

"There are other verbs in the English language besides *suck*," Dan said. He set his glass of iced tea down a lot harder than necessary and then tried to keep the conversation going. "Ella is musical. She plays the accordion."

"I *know*, Dad. That's how you met. Somebody pushed an accordion off a balcony and killed someone. And it looked like it might have been Ella."

"I didn't do it," I reminded her.

She nodded. She looked like she had a lot more to say, but she didn't. We ate in silence for a while. Then Cassie said, "So who do you think killed Donald Sanders?"

"I told you, we are putting murder out of our minds today," Dan said.

"Okay, okay." She waved her hands in the air. "Erased. Gone."

We had no idea that, while we spoke, downtown Juniper was filling up with people who definitely had *not* erased murder from their minds.

CHAPTER SIX

I was running a bit late in the morning and didn't pull up the local newspaper on my phone, as I usually did. I hurried directly to school and was busy with kindergartners all morning.

"Did you hear?" the school secretary asked when I came into the office to check my mailbox at lunch time. Evelyn sits in the office with the radio turned low all day long and is eager to be the first to pass on juicy or interesting bits of information.

I shook my head. Whatever it was, of course I hadn't heard. I'd been teaching all morning.

"That guy who was murdered was probably killed with a blow to his head," she said. "Probably a tap shoe."

A tap shoe? I wondered if she knew Donald was *wearing* tap shoes when he died. I didn't say anything, though, because Mildred had asked Cassie and me to keep what we had seen to ourselves.

"But they're testing for drugs, too," she said. "No one knows what he was doing in your best friend's dance studio." She looked up from the papers she was collating and stapling, peering at me over the top of her glasses. Then she added, "Sammie Russo's," as if I wouldn't remember who my best friend was.

"And you know all this how?" I asked.

"Just what I've heard," she said. "You know, on the street."

I couldn't help it. I opened my eyes wide, hoping for an innocent expression, and asked, "When were you out on the street? I thought you've been here working."

She stapled a bit harder than necessary. "It's a figure of speech."

Maybe it was, but I happened to know that her brother-in-law was a clerk in the police department. I suspected the "street talk" was coming from him.

Evelyn went on. "I talked to my sister, and she said there are media trucks all over downtown. The murder's all over the Internet. I even saw it on Fox News this morning."

I hadn't thought of that. Donald is—*was*—kind of famous. And so good-looking. The media would love him. "Hmmmm," I said.

My phone blipped and I saw a text from Sammie.

Reporters ringing doorbell & waking I.

Waking I? Had motherhood affected her command of pronouns? Quickly, I realized that, of course, she was abbreviating "Isabelle."

I went to my classroom, closed the door, and called her. "Are they ringing the doorbell because the murder took place in your dance studio or because they found out you had a relationship with Donald?"

I could hear Isabelle crying. "I hope it's because of the dance studio. Do you know how to disable a doorbell? I can't reach Sam."

Sam is notoriously clueless when it comes to fixing things, so I wasn't sure what good that would do. I could hear that someone was really leaning on her doorbell. "Can you just yank it out of the wall?"

"It's too high. The ladder is downstairs. I can't get the ladder and hold Isabelle at the same time." She sounded frantic—odd, since she is generally so unflappable.

"Put her in the baby carrier and leave it in a safe place. Then go get the ladder."

"She's screaming."

"She can scream in the baby carrier as well as in your arms. You won't damage her for life. Just go get the ladder."

"But …"

She wasn't thinking clearly. Maybe there really is such a thing as the new mom brain fog I'd heard about. "Go! I'll listen to Isabelle and google doorbell disabling while you go."

I guess it comforted her to know I'd be "watching" Isabelle while she got the ladder, so she went. When she got back, I read instructions to her as my kids streamed into the room after lunch. Finally the ringing stopped, and I heard Sammie breathe a sigh of relief. "I'll come by after school," I said. "Gotta go."

I quickly shot Dan a text.

A tap shoe????? Seriously?????

I turned my attention to my kids. It was Spirit Week, and today was "Dress as Your Favorite Character Day," which would be followed by "Crazy Hair Day, "Inside-Out Clothes Day," "Pajama Day," and "Crazy Socks Day."

In my opinion, the kids have more than enough spirit in May without Spirit Week. In fact, one of my biggest challenges is channeling that spirit into appropriate activities when the end of the school year is so near. Dressing up just made the kids even less focused on school, and they were already unfocused enough.

I looked around at the costumes. Spiderman. Dora the Explorer. Batman. Peppa Pig. Thomas the Tank Engine. Ariel. Elsa.

So many Elsas. I counted six of them, some in the glittery turquoise gown from the original *Frozen* and some in the sparkly white dress over white pants from *Frozen 2*. Was the popularity of the *Frozen* movies ever going to wane? And why was not even one girl dressed as Anna?

Okay, I knew why. Anna isn't the glamorous one. But how is it that five-year-olds already recognize the glam factor and long for it?

As the kids gathered on the rainbow rug, I decided to do my part for future womanhood.

"I see that we've got six Elsas here. Who else is important in *Frozen*?" I asked.

"Olaf." said Claire.

"I hate *Frozen*," said Joseph.

"Sven, the moose," said Sylvia.

"Hans," said Victoria.

"Kristoff," said Alissa, smiling like a smitten teenager.

"How about Anna?" I asked.

They nodded. Yes, they knew her.

"I wonder why no one dressed up as her," I said.

"Elsa's prettier," said Emma, folding her arms in front of her to indicate further discussion was unnecessary.

"But Anna's pretty, too. And she's smart and brave and really saves the day in the first *Frozen*."

"Her dress doesn't have sparkles," said Emma. The other girls nodded.

"Well, if I was dressing up, I'd dress up as Anna," I said. No one said anything. I guess they thought it was my right to make dumb choices. No self-respecting five- or six-year-old would choose a dress without sparkles.

I remembered how much I'd loved my prom dress in high school. Those little sparkly beads at the bodice—so pretty. Did females have an innate love of sparkles? Or was that a sexist thought? And if we did have an innate love of sparkles, could that have some basis in evolution—like maybe that sparkly water was likely to be clearer and thus safer to drink?

Sparkles reminded me of Donald's sequined bow tie. I shuddered and pulled my attention back to the kids. Seraphina, my principal, could walk in at any moment, and she would not be pleased. I could just imagine her asking, "And how does this fit your learning target for the day?" Then she would look around to see if my target was posted, as required, for all the kids to see. Never mind that most of the kids could read only a few simple words. Seraphina is a firm believer in having learning targets posted.

I'd tried to reason with her once, pointing out that kids don't need to be able to say what a target is in order to meet it. For example, a learning target is *I can count to ten.* "Raymond can count to ten, but he can't say what learning target he has met," I told her. "Is it more important that he meets the target or that he is able to say what it is?"

Seraphina then talked at me for some time about "empowering students to take ownership of their own learning." I was supposed to think of learning targets as "a destination in a journey" with landmarks along that journey for kids to meet.

I'm pretty sure she would not have approved of "I will persuade the girls to appreciate Anna as well as Elsa" as a learning target, even if I'd posted it.

I decided to make my own personal learning target and post it inside my middle desk drawer: *I will demonstrate calm when Seraphina freaks out to find that, once again, I've got a connection to a murder.*

CHAPTER SEVEN

Despite Evelyn's warning about all the reporters downtown, I was still shocked at the number of them when I drove downtown late that afternoon. News vans filled the museum parking lot across the street from Sammie's apartment, and reporters lounged against lamp posts and even camped out in lawn chairs in the alley behind the apartment, presumably hoping for something to happen.

Street parking was impossible. I drove around and finally managed to snag a spot in the lot a few blocks away when someone backed out. I'd been in contact with Geraldine, and the plan was for me to meet Geraldine, her husband Jake, and Sammie's brother Derek at Whitney's bar and restaurant and then walk across the street to Sammie's apartment. We figured it would be easier to make our way through the reporters as a group. We were bringing both moral support and dinner.

Derek jumped up from a table as we entered and kissed me, then held my hand. "Hi, babe."

I stared at him. "I'm your boyfriend," he muttered. "Go along with it." He often changes his appearance, opting tonight for Gene Kelly-like pleated pants, a flowered shirt, a Panama hat, and dark sunglasses. He spoke softly, explaining. "I don't want reporters to recognize me. I work later and want to eavesdrop if they're in here." Derek is a writer, and he works as a bartender at Whitney's while trying to find an agent for his first novel.

"I have some pointers before we go over," Geraldine said as we gathered around a table. We listened attentively because that's what you do with Geraldine. She is known in town as the Pickle Queen, but it's not only because she inherited the fortune her grandfather made with his pickle factory. (*Betz are the best!*) It also has to do with how she generally gets her own way, no matter if it's a committee decision at the Catholic Church, a tax referendum she wants the city council to pass, or a vote for her in the upcoming mayoral race. She hadn't won that race yet, but I had little doubt that she would.

"Walk with your eyes straight ahead," she said. "Say nothing, not even 'No comment.' Any kind of reaction at all on our part will reward them and encourage them to keep after us."

"I'll protect us," Derek said in a fake macho voice. He whispered, "I've got my gun."

Geraldine pushed her chair back and stood up, glaring at him.

"Kidding, Mom. Kidding. Sit down."

She sat down. "I'm a little stressed already, Derek. I don't need this."

The waitress delivered two large bags of take-out food we had ordered. I picked up one bag and held it in front me like armor. Derek picked up the other and we all headed toward the apartment.

As soon as we turned into the alley and neared the apartment door, a reporter approached, shooting questions rapid fire while a photographer moved in close with a camera. Geraldine yelled, "Back off!" but they continued. In a flash Geraldine was standing toe-to-toe with the photographer, pushing her face against the camera screen. "I told you to back off!" she yelled. Derek and Jake each took one of Geraldine's arms and guided her through the sea of shouting reporters.

"Are you Donald Sanders' mother?" someone yelled.

"What was Sanders doing in the dance studio?"

"Is it true he was carrying on with one of the tap dance students?"

"What is your relationship to Sammie Russo?"

Jake tapped the key pad quickly to unlock the door, and we slipped inside. We trudged upstairs, feeling a little dirty from the verbal assault.

"Eyes straight ahead. Do not engage," Derek said, mimicking his mother as we entered the apartment. "She almost decked a photographer," he explained to Sam and Sammie, who had to smile.

"Slimy people," Geraldine fumed. "Just slimy." As we set out the food, she said, "We need a plan. Reporters are going to track down anyone with any kind of relationship to Donald Sanders, and I'm sorry to say that Sammie is exactly what they want. Beautiful woman. Beautiful baby."

"And living with such a handsome guy," Derek added.

"I didn't think you'd noticed," Sam said, giving Derek a little bow.

"Really, Mom. What can we do?" Sammie asked. "We can't control what other people do or think. And it's pretty obvious they're going to think I killed him. Why wouldn't they? He was found in my dance studio."

"Maybe we can point them in other directions."

"How?"

"I haven't figured that out yet. That's why we're here."

"Maybe a better idea would be to figure out who actually killed Donald," I suggested.

"Whoa. Listen to Bellella!" Derek said. "Last fall you wanted to leave everything to the police. We had to drag you kicking and screaming into clearing your name."

"I've evolved." I didn't want to think about last fall.

"By the way," he added, "the going theory is that a swing of a tap shoe, hard, against Donald's temple is what killed him. Bar talk I overheard at 1:30 last night."

"Oh, I'm sure *that's* reliable," Sammie said.

"No one dies from a tap shoe," I said. "A baseball bat, maybe. A tire iron, maybe. Not a tap shoe. Anyone who wanted to murder someone would be smart enough to choose a sensible weapon."

"This from the woman whose accordion was used as a murder weapon not long ago," commented Geraldine.

Sam interrupted. "I've got a little more detail to add to our small town murder mystery."

Derek hunched his shoulders and rubbed his hands together. "Ooooh. The plot thickens."

"Last night I was called into work to fix a problem, and I left as soon as Sammie came up to nurse Isabelle after class. My boss confirmed my alibi. I didn't get home until the police were in the alley, so I'm clear." He rested Isabelle on his lap so that she faced the table, then reached over her carefully to take a sip of his IPA. "That's the good news."

"And the bad news?" Geraldine asked.

"Sammie can't prove she was up here in the apartment taking care of a baby instead of murdering Donald downstairs in the dance studio." He looked around the room at all of us. "Surely you have thought of that."

The sad looks on our faces told him that we had.

Sammie said, "Screw the breast milk. I'm having wine."

"Sammie!" said Geraldine, shocked.

"I pumped earlier, Mom. I think my situation warrants one glass of chardonnay."

"She should be allowed a little chardonnay before she goes to prison, Mom," Derek said. Sammie smacked him on the arm as she went to get a glass.

My phone blipped with a text message:

Ready to plow through. Have door unlocked.

"It's Dan," I said, getting up. "He's outside."

"He can stay outside," Geraldine said. She wasn't pleased with Detective Dan.

"Let him in," said Jake, patting her hand.

Downstairs, I slammed the door quickly after Dan slipped in. "Just warning you—you're not very popular upstairs."

"I know," he said, kissing me.

When we walked back into the apartment, Isabelle was crying. Geraldine held her over her shoulder, bouncing her and repeating, "Hush now, sweetie. Hush."

Dan walked over and peered over Geraldine's shoulder at Isabelle. "Shhhhhhh," he said. "Shhhhhhh." Then he blew very gently in her face. Izzie-Bee shhhed.

"Someone still likes me," he said. "Isabelle smiled."

"Babies this small don't smile," Geraldine said. "It was gas."

Sam offered him a beer.

"No thanks. I've got a shift later." He sat down at the table with us. No one spoke.

He took a deep breath.

"Okay, let's talk about the elephant in the room," he said.

"We get it," Sam said. He looked over at Sammie and modified his statement. "Or *I* do. You had to do your job. It *could* be that Isabelle's paternity had something to do with the murder."

Dan nodded. "Like you or Sammie killing him to get him out of your life."

Sammie took a big gulp of wine and glared at him over the top of her glass.

Dan continued. "Hey, of course *I* don't think that. But better to get all this out of the way in the beginning. It would be worse if I—or you—withheld information like that and it came out later. You'd look even more guilty."

I took Dan's hand. I knew he was making sense.

"So my motive would supposedly be to get Donald out of my life completely?" Sammie asked.

"That would do it," Dan said. "Ella, you're the one who supposedly locked things up after class. Maybe you conspired to let Donald in."

I took my hand back.

"Come on. I'm just pointing out what Mildred— Detective Mildred—might be thinking. She's not discussing things with me. I'm off the case, remember?"

Isabelle started fussing again, and Dan didn't ask, just took Isabelle from Geraldine's arms. The baby curled on Dan's shoulder and closed her eyes. He kept one hand on her bottom and patted her gently. Isabelle loved Detective Dan. I admired her taste.

"So I heard that a blow from a tap shoe is what killed Donald," I said. "But I don't believe that."

"Ella doesn't believe in tap shoes as murder weapons," Derek explained to Dan. "Only musical instruments."

Dan smiled, which annoyed me just a little. "Who has access to this building?" he asked.

"Me," Geraldine said. "I own the building." She looked at Jake. "And as my husband, he has access, too. To all my properties."

"I know the key pad code," I said.

"Me, too," said Sam.

"And me," said Derek.

"Apparently I'm the only one who doesn't," Dan said.

Derek got up and picked up the black bag he'd carried over. "It's been fun, but I have to change clothes and get to work."

He went into the bedroom with his bag and emerged in boots, coveralls, a mustache, and a baseball cap on backwards over a black wig. He went to a utility cupboard in the kitchen and took out a bucket and mop. "*Hasta luego*," he said.

"Go out the front through the store, and I'll lock up after you," I said. "Not so many paparazzi there."

We went downstairs into the vestibule, and I unlocked the door to Second Chance. We walked through the store, and I let him out the front door. As I locked the door behind him, I heard a reporter say, half-heartedly, "So, are you cleaning up after the murder?"

"*No hablo Ingles,*" Derek said.

A few minutes later he called me. "Success. Act like you're a janitor who can't speak English and no one pays attention to you."

"Sad," I said, "but in our circumstances *Muy bien.*"

CHAPTER EIGHT

On my way home after our meeting at Sammie's, I stopped for gas at a nearby Kwik Mart. A teenager of about 16 was cleaning his windshield on the other side of my pump. "Pizza guy!" I said, setting my nozzle so that it filled automatically and then stepping to his side.

"I have a name," he said.

"I'm Ella," I said, holding out my hand.

"Blake. I recognize you," he said. "You were at the murder scene."

"I was, and so were you. The paparazzi after you yet?" He looked alarmed. "Just warning you. You were there that night, so they'll figure you must know something."

"All I did was call 9-1-1!"

"Really? Why?"

He sighed. "I'm sick of telling this."

"Just one more time?" I pleaded. "You brought us a pizza earlier that night. Why were you back there more than three hours later?"

He continued, maybe because we'd tipped him well that night. "When I got back to Blackjack's I, like, couldn't find my house key. Probably fell out of my pocket in the alley when I got hot and took off my hoodie. So I came back to look for it when my shift was over." He was watching the numbers on the pump carefully, and clicked off the gas lever at $10.00 even.

I pulled his attention back to the story. "And then?"

"I couldn't find it. So I gave up and was heading back to my car when I, like heard something and looked back. A man and a woman came out of the dance studio, and he had a hold of her arm. He kind of, like, yipped, like she'd stepped on him or pinched him or something? Anyway, it was weird because it was kind of a squeaky yip for a guy?" He took the hose out of his tank and hung it up. "And then he took her arm again, and they both hurried toward the other end of the alley. When the guy saw me, he yelled, 'Call 9-1-1. Dance studio.' So I did. Called 9-1-1. And then they, like, turned down the block and disappeared." He shrugged. "That's all I know."

"But you waited around for the police?"

"Yeah. I hung around to tell the cops what I saw, but they were busy looking around and, like, pretty much ignored me. So I yelled that maybe they ought to check the *dance studio*, since that's what the guy had yelled. I was a little sarcastic, I guess. That female detective seemed kind of like pissed off at me."

"I know her. She gets pissed off easily. So what did the man and woman look like?"

"I didn't get a very good look because the sun was setting and kind of in my eyes. About all I could tell was that the guy was tall, taller than her, and she was …" He looked at me. " … maybe taller than you. Maybe not. And he was a big guy … well, bigger than me."

That wasn't a big help, as Blake was only about 5'4". "Did you ever find your key?" I couldn't help asking.

"Yeah. On the floor of my car."

"Good. Listen, Blake, you live with your folks?"

"Sure."

"You might want to suggest that your family screen calls for a while. Reporters are going to find you."

"Why me?"

"You were there. When you get ambushed, I'd suggest just saying 'No comment' or, better yet, not answering at all."

He thought that over. "Thanks. What about you? Won't they come after you, too?"

"Undoubtedly," I said.

When I got home, my mother called. She hadn't been pleased to hear about my connection to another murder, but there wasn't a lot she could do about it.

"You probably ought to be prepared," she said. "Read Harvey's blog tonight." She was referring to Harvey Klump, the man running against Geraldine for mayor of Juniper. Geraldine always describes him as "a nightmare of a good old boy." His motto, as the owner of a construction company, is "Let no square of land go undeveloped."

Okay, it isn't. But it might as well be.

Klump had started a blog called "Inside Juniper" soon after he announced his candidacy. I never read it, but evidently many Juniper residents did. I reluctantly opened my computer and took a look:

I think the question must be asked: Is Geraldine Betz a suitable candidate for mayor of Juniper?? Or is she too closely involved with the local murder that has gained nationwide attention???

Donald Sanders died in the dance studio owned by Geraldine's daughter, Sammie Russo. Sources tell me he probably died from a blow to the head with a tap danc-ing shoe. Who had access to both the dance studio and tap shoes? That would be Geraldine's daughter!!! Some say she is the prime suspect in the murder.

If so, why hasn't Sammie Russo been arrested or even brought in for questioning???? Some say it is because her best friend is dating a police officer. Some say Geraldine exerted influence on the police department through her many connections. Is someone who uses her influence in such a manner a suitable candidate for mayor?

Some would say, NO!!!!

Furious, I called Dan. When he answered, I didn't even say hello. "Could you mention to Detective Mildred that Harvey Klump has a bug up his butt about all of us? And that he's full of you-know-what and ought to shut up?"

"So elegantly put. But I think she knows."

"Is she going to do something? Like issue a statement that he's a sleazy liar?"

"I don't think she's probably going to do that."

"Maybe you should suggest it."

"I'm leaving this to Mildred, Ella. The truth will out."

"The truth may out too late to salvage Sammie's reputa-tion. Or Geraldine's. Or mine!"

"In case you didn't notice, my reputation was besmirched as well," he said.

"*Besmirched.* What a good word." Sometimes I'm eas-ily distracted. "You just don't hear that very often. It's kind of old-fashioned …"

"Ella, I'm at work. I have to go."

"Wait. My instincts are good, right?"

"R-i-i-g-g-h-h-t-t."

I had told him, perhaps more than once, of my visit to Blockbuster Video with my mother when I was 14. We had been looking for movies to rent for my birthday slumber party when I saw a man enter the store and look around. He was around 30, dressed in jeans and a striped button-down collar shirt—very pale blue stripes, I remembered—and holding a jacket over one arm. For no apparent reason, I'd suddenly felt my stomach clutch and was overwhelmed with a sense of danger. I grabbed Mom's arm and said, "We have to get out of here. Now." I started toward the front, and she followed.

"Are you sick, Ella? What's wrong?"

I said the only thing I could think of that would really get her attention. "I'm going to throw up."

She hustled me out of the store.

When we reached the car, I said, "Drive. Please." Something in my voice made her listen.

We found out later that shortly after we left, the man in the button-down collar shirt pulled a gun from beneath his jacket and robbed the store.

"You have unbelievable instincts," Mom had told me when we heard the news. "Don't ever let anyone tell you different."

And I hadn't.

I wouldn't now, either. "R-i-i-g-g-h-h-t-t?" I imitated Dan. "You don't sound like you're convinced."

"Okay, yes, as far as I know you have excellent instincts," he said.

"Well, my instincts tell me that Harvey Klump is dangerous and up to no good."

"Noted." He hung up.

CHAPTER NINE

The next day at school, the press arrived. Thinking the first reporter who showed up was a parent, Evelyn let him in when he pressed the security button at the door.

"When he came in the office, he asked if he could get a comment from Ella Polansky about the murder," she told me during my lunch break. "Seraphina heard and told him to leave. He kept asking stuff until she said she was going to call the police. After that, I had to ask everyone their business before I buzzed them in." She puffed up in importance. "You wouldn't believe the stuff some of them made up. They'd say, 'I'm here to drop off lunch for my son.' So I'd say, 'And your son is …?' They'd say, ' … Uh … Johnny.' Not very original."

"I guess they've read too many 'Johnny can't read' stories. Or 'Johnny can't write in cursive.' Or whatever."

"Right. So I'd say, 'Johnny who?' And they'd make up a name like "Johnny Jones," and I'd tell them we have no Johnny Jones in the school." She looked around and made sure Seraphina wasn't listening. Her door was closed, and through the windows around her office we could see she was on the phone. "I got used to this, and when Matthew Miller's dad came to pick him up for his orthodontist appointment, I didn't recognize him when he said he was Ed Miller, so I didn't let him in."

"I'll bet Mr. Miller loved that." I remembered Mr. Miller

from when I'd had Matthew in class. Let's just say he was the kind of guy who would yell at a waitress because the ice in his glass was too cold and then not give her a tip.

"Um, no. I apologized a lot and let him in. I told him I was trying so hard to protect the kids that I overreacted. He seemed okay then." She looked nervously over at Seraphina's office again. She was still on the phone.

The outside door intercom buzzed. "They just keep coming," she said to me. Then, in the microphone, she said, "State your business, ma'am."

"I'm here to interview one of your teachers. Miss Polansky."

"I'm sorry, but she's teaching."

"I know this is her lunch break, so she should be available."

How did she *know* that this was my lunch break? What else did she know about me? I peeked out the window. It was a redheaded reporter I'd seen several times.

"Miss Polansky is not available," Evelyn said and shut off the intercom, looking satisfied and a little too proud of herself.

I decided it was a good idea to keep her on my side. "Great job, Evelyn," I said. I went back to my classroom feeling more than a little unsettled.

It was not a good afternoon. All the teachers in my school are required to have a Place of Peace where kids can go to feel safe and calm down. Mine was a little tent in a corner of the room—my POP tent. Unfortunately, while I was dealing with a melt-down from Colin because Mario was "looking" at him again, Brandon decided to crawl inside the POP tent with the pencil sharpener receptacle, dump all the shavings into a pile "like dirt," add pencils crosswise on top "like a campfire," and pile ripped strips of red construction paper on top "like flames." When I finished calming Colin and discovered the mess, my first thought was surprise that, for once, it wasn't the principal's son Nathan causing trouble. Then I pointed out firmly to Brandon that we do *not* use the POP tent for pretend camping and pushed the intercom button to see if the office had a hand vacuum I could borrow for the pencil shavings.

The rest happened in an instant: Emily tugged on my arm to tell me, "Brandon said the 'F' word."

An outraged Brandon yelled, "I didn't say the 'F' word! I said 'Shit!'"

Unfortunately, my finger lingered a little too long on the intercom button. As I found out later, Seraphina, the principal, had been at the front office desk trying to reason with Mr. Miller, who was complaining that his fifth grader hadn't received credit for a report on gorillas that was turned in five days late and included whole paragraphs copied from Wikipedia. After hearing Brandon's "shit" broadcast, Mr. Miller decided that standards at the school had gone down the toilet, and he would be "contacting the superintendent personally to lodge a complaint."

Seraphina was not happy. When I suggested later that maybe she should try to see the humor in the situation, she confirmed my long-held opinion that "sense of humor" was not a character trait she had been blessed with.

I eyed the POP tent. Maybe I should be the one crawling inside. Stress was getting to me, but it had more to do with murder than with kindergartners. How could we prove

Sammie hadn't killed Donald? Why the heck was Donald in the studio wearing tap shoes? Who was the man who asked Blake to call 9-1-1? Who was the woman with him?

Nothing made sense to me.

After work, as usual, I drove to Sammie's. I needed my daily dose of Isabelle cuddling, but I also wanted to see how Sammie was coping. Had Mildred brought her in for more questioning? She had survived the first round, but I was sure Mildred wasn't finished with her yet.

Reporters still lurked everywhere, so I had to park six blocks away. I braced myself and walked toward Second Chance, thinking I could pretend to be shopping and slip upstairs more easily through the store than trying to get past reporters at the alley entrance.

As I opened the door, the redheaded reporter I'd seen at school suddenly jumped out of a red Nissan. *A red Nissan for a redhead in a red shirt*, I thought. *How appropriate.* I noticed her sunburn and added, in my mind, *with a red nose.*

Her questions began, rapid fire: "Is it true Sammie Russo had been having an affair with Donald Sanders for ten years?" she asked. "Was she in love with him? Did he reject her? Did she decide to end the affair by killing him? Did her live-in boyfriend find out about her philandering?"

Philandering? I thought. She sounded like someone from my grandmother's generation.

"Did he find out about the affair and kill Donald Sanders?" she continued.

I walked into the store without answering, trying not to show a reaction to any of her questions. To my surprise, she didn't follow. I looked back and saw she was taking a picture of my license plate. Weird.

Sammie's older brother's wife, Bianca, had been running the store for Sammie since the baby was born. She raised a hand in greeting. "Glad it's just you. If it was another reporter trying to weasel information out of me, I was going to bash him with a handbag."

"I hope not one of the Louis Vuitton's." Sammie had built up quite a nationwide clientele selling upscale handbags through the Second Chance website.

"It's been a long day. I might have."

I went through the back of the store and up the stairs to Sammie's apartment. Geraldine was already there. I knew I'd have a hard time prying Isabelle from her arms, so I sat down.

"Your day about like mine?" Sammie asked.

"If it involved paparazzi and the word *shit,* yes," I said.

"It did. Not the word, but the real deal." She gestured toward the Diaper Genie.

Sammie turned to her mother, who was gushing lovey-dovey words to a fascinated Isabelle lying in her lap. "You said you had news, Mom. Can you stop with the goo-gah stuff for five minutes and tell us?"

Geraldine looked up reluctantly. "Okay. The museum was closed Sunday and Monday, so the cleaning gal came in early this morning to vacuum before we opened. Like always. But she found one of the musical instruments on the floor behind the display pedestal, like someone had knocked it off."

"A break in?" I asked, alarmed. I hoped none of Otto's musical instruments had been damaged.

"No evidence of that. We think it happened during the lecture Saturday night."

"I closed the door to the exhibit room before I went down to the lecture. Everything was fine then." The police hadn't used the room for interviews that night, either. "I don't think anyone ever opened it. What instrument was on the floor?"

"Just a sec. I wrote down what was on the display card." She reached into a pocket and pulled out a scrap of paper. She read, "'Double pipe nose flute used by the indigenous peoples of Taiwan.'" She looked up. "And there was blood on it."

Sammie was shaking her head. "This just gets weirder and weirder. A *nose flute?* "

"The receptionist must have seen something. Or done something," I said.

"Exactly. I grilled her as soon as she got to work."

I felt some sympathy for the receptionist. Geraldine can be fearsome when she grills.

"What she admitted—finally—was that Donald asked her to meet him in the exhibit area after everyone was downstairs at the lecture. Affinity had hightailed it out of there the second she'd put the food away, so they were alone. He told her she was 'so pretty' and maybe he could recommend her to his modeling agency. He thought the exotic setting with all those interesting instruments would look good and ..."

"... and the pictures would be even better if she was nude," Sammie guessed.

"Yes ... and yada, yada, yada, she finally agreed to pose quickly for only three photos, nude from the waist up, and where she could kind of hide behind the pedestals in case someone came upstairs. So she did that, but then he said she had a beautiful body and wanted to see more."

"Of course he did," Sammie said.

"I guess that explains why her sweater was on inside out when I came upstairs after the lecture."

Geraldine nodded. "He started coming toward her and, according to her, she got scared. No one was around, and she thought he was going to attack her, so she just grabbed the first thing she saw and smacked him with it."

"The nose flute," Sammie said.

"So maybe that's what killed Donald," I said, excited.

"No," Geraldine said. "She insisted that she didn't hit him that hard. It just cut him and drew a little blood. He was pissed off, though, and went in the bathroom to wash off. When he came out he told her there was no need to hit him, that he wasn't going to attack her. She was embarrassed about overreacting. So she says."

"And you believe her?"

"I do. Maybe it's because she didn't seem at all worried that the police might be looking at her for murder. She was more upset that the Donald's death might have ruined her chances with a model agency. Besides, I don't think one little whack from a little thing like her would kill anybody."

"Not *all* of her is so little," I said, thinking that the nude photos were probably pretty impressive, at least from a male perspective. "And maybe she hit him in just the right spot on the temple. I saw on TV once that just the right blow to the temple can kill a person."

"But doesn't death from that kind of blow happen instantly? He managed to leave on his own two feet, then walk across the street and down the alley and open the dance studio," Geraldine said.

Not to mention take off his shirt and put on tap shoes and a bow tie, I thought to myself, remembering my promise to Mildred to keep that quiet.

Geraldine continued. "No, I'm pretty sure whatever she did to him didn't cause him to drop dead less than an hour later."

"I assume you told Detective Dan all this?" Sammie asked.

"Of course not. He's off the case. I told Detective Mildred."

We all sat, silent. I wasn't sure what to make of all this. Suddenly Geraldine's cell phone timer buzzed, and she got up, handing Isabelle over to me. "Your turn. I've got a campaign meeting."

As I took advantage of my Isabelle time, Sammie invited me to stay for dinner. "Keep her entertained, and I'll make spaghetti. Sam could use a decent meal when he gets home, and so could I."

Happily, I complied, holding Isabelle while Sammie opened cans, diced tomatoes, and told me about her day: "Nursed. Changed diapers. Slept a little. Nursed. Changed diapers. Started laundry. Nursed. Changed diapers. Peeked outside at the paparazzi. Cursed a little. Then nursed. Changed diapers ..."

"Got it," I said.

Sammie left the sauce to simmer and took a load of clothes out of the dryer. Her phone started playing the Britney Spears song "You Drive Me Crazy," and she sighed. "Mom. Already."

"I'm going to kill him!" The voice on the phone was so loud I could hear it as I followed Sammie into the living room.

"What'd he do now?" Sammie asked, putting the phone on speaker and sitting down with a plastic laundry basket heaped with baby clothes. I put Izzie-Bee in her carrier and started folding. It's amazing how many onesies, blankets, towels, and burp cloths a baby can go through in a couple of days.

"Here's what he wrote today." Geraldine read aloud:

The question must be asked again: Is Geraldine Betz a suitable mayoral candidate for our fair city???

I have it on good authority that NUDE pictures of a female museum worker were found on Donald Sanders' cell phone, taken in the museum on the night of the murder!!!! The only female workers on duty that night were Geraldine Betz, a receptionist whose name was not readily available, and two volunteers—Ella Polansky and Affinity Knowles. From the description of the bodies in the photos, it's likely the photos are of one of the younger women."

She interrupted her reading to say, "Why younger women, not me? Now he's even insulting my body!"

"Not the point, Mom. Where is he getting this stuff? There has to be a leak in the police department."

"You heard him. He's getting it from 'good authority.' So there's more:

Some say the photos are rather lewd and involve a Sousaphone and a glockenspiel. Geraldine Betz was the museum board member in charge that evening. How could she allow that sort of thing to happen??!!!!

And who is the indecent docent who posed for the pictures??? Which woman is she??? And could she be the murderer??? Some say that this subject needs serious investigation, and I agree!!!

If it was a Nancy Drew mystery, we might call it, "The Case of the Indecent Docent."

I had stopped folding a tiny T-shirt as I listened. Was I actually being accused of posing for nude photos with Donald Sanders? Seriously?

"How can he call it 'The Case of the Indecent Docent?'" Geraldine asked. "There *were* no docents there the night of the murder. None were available, just volunteers and the receptionist. Our *docents* undergo training to provide accurate and important information for our visitors."

"Missing the point again, Mom."

"Okay, yes, the *some say, some say* garbage. Surely any reader can see through that."

She was quiet, so I leaned into the phone. "Geraldine, Harvey is suggesting that it might have been *me* who posed for naked pictures."

"Of course you didn't."

"I know that, but his readers don't know that."

"I was talking to Sammie. What happened to her?"

"I'm here, Mom. Folding baby stuff. Yes, Harvey's terrible. Yes, he's made terrible accusations. Yes, he's ridiculous. Stop reading his blog."

"I have to, to know what he's up to."

"Maybe you should start your own blog. Call it 'Thoughts from Geraldine.'"

"Could I call him a bastard there?"

"Maybe you could write '*Some say*' he's a bastard," Sammie said.

"Good idea."

"Kidding! Mom, calm down and don't do anything rash." Rash was kind of Geraldine's style.

"I won't."

"Really, Mom, I want you to win."

I glared at Sammie. "*That's* your takeaway from this? That you want your mom to win? What about the injustice of accusing your best friend of unspeakable acts?"

"They weren't unspeakable acts," Geraldine said. "They were nude pictures. There's a difference." She ended the call.

"There goes my job again," I said, sinking my head against a pile of the freshly stacked cloth diapers Sammie used only for burp cloths. "My principal is going to freak when she reads about naked pictures."

"You've only got to make it through a day or two until school is out. Surely the police department is going to have to issue something saying that Harvey is barking up the wrong tree." Isabelle started fussing, so I picked her up while Sammie went to get the next load out of the dryer. I kissed Izzie-Bee's sleepy face and cuddled her in my arms.

In a few moments, "Damn! Damn! Damn!" came from the laundry room.

"Uh-oh," I whispered to Isabelle. "Let's see what's going on."

Sammie had left a tissue in the pocket of the pants she'd washed, and white fuzz covered all the dark clothes in the dryer. She slammed the dryer door, startling Isabelle.

Then my phone rang, startling her again. I passed

Isabelle to Sammie, looked at the phone screen and groaned. Mildred. Reluctantly, I answered and listened.

"I'll be there," I said, then turned to Sammie. "Mildred wants me to come down to answer some more questions. Now."

Before Sammie could say anything, her phone rang. She passed Isabelle back to me and pulled her phone from the waistband of her leggings. "Seven o'clock will work," she sighed, ending the call. "She wants to question me. Again. Tonight at 7:00, here."

She kicked the dryer. I didn't think it was because of all the white fuzz. She stalked into the living room and punched a sofa pillow.

"Enough with the kicking and punching," I said. "It's probably best if you don't display a tendency toward violence."

Then I headed for the police station. No spaghetti for me.

CHAPTER TEN

Mildred turned on a tape-recorder, stated the date, and had me give my name and age. Before she could say anything else, I said, "I'd like it on record that I did not pose for any nude pictures with Donald Sanders."

"I know that."

"Why aren't you issuing a statement or something then? My reputation is being besmirched!" I'd decided I liked that word.

"As a matter of fact, I am issuing a statement to that effect at a press conference at 8:30 tonight."

That was good. I calmed down a bit.

"Now, Miss Polansky, would you go through what happened the night of the murder, starting with your arrival at the museum thing?"

"The special exhibit of musical instruments from around the world," I corrected.

She sighed. "Yes. The special exhibit of musical instruments from around the world."

I recreated the evening, probably in a lot more detail than she wanted. As I told her how, according to what I'd learned from the boring professor, the rosined rim of a wooden wheel turned by a handle is what sounds the strings on a hurdy-gurdy, not a bow, she stopped me.

"I think we're done with the hurdy-gurdy. What happened *after* the lecture?"

I told her about stacking the chairs and then going upstairs to find sirens blaring and the receptionist looking out the doors. "What is her name, anyway? The receptionist's?" I asked.

"It doesn't matter. Just tell me what happened."

"The receptionist's cardigan was on inside out, so I pointed that out to her," I said. "Then she—the receptionist—scooted over and … You know, it would be easier if I didn't have to keep saying *the receptionist*," I said.

"Her name is Mariah," she snapped.

"As in 'They Call the Wind Mariah?'"

"It's Mariah."

I realized that she didn't know the song, so I moved on, telling her about the rest of the evening and ending with the discovery of Donald's body. "He must have taken the tap shoes out of the Borrow Box. Sammie has collected bunches of old tap shoes for people to borrow if they forget their own. Or if they just want to try a class without committing to a series of lessons. She puts pink laces in all the shoes, to identify them." I remembered that Dan says you never know what information will turn out to be useful in a murder investigation, so I added, trying to be helpful, "She also has a couple of costume boxes in the closet with a bunch of sparkly hats and boas and stuff. That's probably where Donald got the bow tie. I guess you can't have too much glittery stuff in a dance studio. Everyone wants to be Elsa."

She looked puzzled.

"Elsa. You know. *Frozen?*"

"It's a movie, right?" She didn't sound sure.

"Two movies. *Frozen and Frozen 2.* Elsa sings the song "Let It Go," the anthem of five-year-old girls. "

"I've never seen either movie."

"But surely you've heard the song." I could understand not recognizing "They Call the Wind Mariah." It was an old song. But "Let It Go?" I began singing.

She listened for a minute, then frowned. "We are getting off track here."

I think she didn't want to admit she'd been living in a cave.

"What happened after you stood at the doors with the receptionist?" she asked.

"Then we heard sirens and saw police by Sammie's place, so I ran across the street with Cassie. I had to see if Sammie was okay. And you know the rest. You were there."

"Okay, what do you know of Mr. Sanders' attitude earlier that evening, when you were at the museum?"

"He was his usual self," I said. "Kind of lecherous … no, *lecherous* doesn't seem like the right word for a young guy like him. Seems better for old guys ... *Sexy* doesn't cover the kind of creepy factor. Though he was sexy." I twisted my mouth to the side, trying to think of the right word. I came up with *lascivious,* but I wasn't sure I could pronounce it properly, so I didn't say it.

"Let's move on. Was Sammie angry with Donald for not wanting to be a part of the baby's life?"

"Are you kidding me? Sammie knew Donald would be a rotten father. From the very first, she did *not* want him involved. At all."

She played with her pen for a moment. "Let's go back to when you left the dance studio to go to the museum. Did you lock the door behind you?"

I nodded, then remembered the tape recorder. "Yes. I checked three times, actually. It's not that I was being particularly careful. I always do that whenever I lock a door—re-check a lot. I'm a little OCD." I hurried to explain, in case she was clueless about psychology as well as pop culture. "Obsessive Compulsive Disorder."

"I *know* what OCD means. What time did the lecture at the museum end?"

"It was 8:15. Exactly."

"That's a specific memory."

"I remember because I got a text from Baba just as it ended. She likes to watch *Friends* reruns from 8:00-8:30, so I knew it must be commercial time halfway through the show."

"Baba?"

"My grandmother. She loves *Friends*. She texted, 'It's the turkey on the head episode.' You know, in case I wanted to tune in. That one *is* really funny. But I couldn't watch because we were putting away chairs."

"Got it."

"And then, like I said, we all heard sirens, went upstairs. I saw the recep ... saw *Mariah* at the doors, told her about her sweater inside out, saw the police in the alley, came over to Sammie's studio, and saw what we saw when you pushed open the door. Donald. Dead. Half naked and wearing tap shoes and a bow tie."

"You don't know that. The half naked and wearing tap shoes and a bow tie part, remember?"

"I remember. We are keeping that part hush-hush. But you've read Harvey Klump's blog? Clearly the information is out."

"I don't think so. He thinks a tap shoe was the murder weapon. He hasn't mentioned that Mr. Sanders was *wearing* tap shoes."

"Got it."

"Now I'd like you to go through what happened at the museum that evening, one more time."

I sighed. And then, I went through what happened at the museum that evening one more time.

On the way home I thought about Mildred and why she always annoys me so much. Part of it is that she's what I call a *slow reactor.* Slow reactors wait a little too long to smile, frown, answer, or respond in any way after you say something to them. Maybe they are just trying to be thoughtful in their responses, but the delay makes me so uncomfortable. I feel as though my words are going into a black hole, so I start talking. Some would say too much.

Also, Mildred doesn't have much of a sense of humor.

Or any.

As I turned into my driveway, I saw a sign planted in my front yard. "SLUT!" it read. I jumped out of the car, pulled up the sign, and angrily ripped it in two. Then I stomped on the wooden stake, breaking it. I took all the debris to the trash can in the back yard and called Dan.

"So you have to tell me. Did you really find nude photos on Donald's phone, like Harvey said? Geraldine said the recep ... *Mariah* ... admitted to posing for some."

"I'm off the case, remember?"

"You can still see case files. You aren't being quarantined or anything."

"True."

"So were there nude photos on his phone?" He didn't answer, so I went on. "Did his parents give Mildred his phone pass code? Or if they didn't know it—which they probably didn't—did she open it with facial recognition, even though he was dead? Does that work on a dead person?"

"You know I can't give out confidential police information."

"Someone sure is."

"I know. We're working on figuring out who."

"The school secretary's brother-in-law is a clerk at the police department."

"We checked that. We can't trace it to him. Not yet anyway."

"Are you going to keep trying?"

"Just so you know, Mildred is issuing a statement at a late press conference at 8:30 tonight. It will help clarify things."

"Maybe she'll clarify who put a *SLUT* sign on my front lawn." I told him what I'd found.

"Ella, be careful. Get Derek to come over and stay with you until I get off work. I don't think you should be alone."

"I'll be fine. I've got the pepper spray Baba gave me. And an attitude. What kind of person puts up a sign like that anyway?"

"I don't know. I really don't know."

Half an hour later Derek showed up. "No complaining. I don't work tonight, so you've got company."

"Dan called you."

"Live with it."

I poured us both some wine, and we sat down just before

8:30 to listen to the press conference. After a short introduction, we heard Mildred's voice:

"I am here to clarify some information that has been inadvertently leaked." She didn't mention Harvey's blog. "Some of that information is true, and some of it is not." I heard the sound of cameras clicking as she took a breath. "It is true that nude photos of a museum volunteer appeared on Donald Sanders' cell phone, and they were taken in the special exhibit area the night of the murder. We are investigating what relevance, if any, those photos have to the murder investigation. In light of allegations that have been made, however, I would like to state that these photos were most assuredly *not* of any of the women whose names were mentioned in a local blog."

I noticed her wording: *the photos were most assuredly not of any of the women whose names were mentioned in a local blog.* Harvey hadn't used the receptionist's name. *Mariah's* name.

Then shouted questions began. "Who appears in those photos?"

"What do the photos have to do with Donald Sanders' murder?"

"Do you have any leads in the murder?"

"Has anyone been arrested?"

And on and on.

"Let's hope that helps restore your wholesome reputation," Derek said after the press conference ended.

Before I could respond, my phone started playing "You've Got a Friend," Sammie's ringtone. "So how'd the interview go?" I asked her.

"Mildred thinks I did it."

"Not surprising. Did she *say* that?"

"No, but I can tell she's trying to find evidence to charge me. I make the most sense as the murderer, motive-wise. Maybe I wanted to get Donald out of the way so that Isabelle inherits."

"Isabelle doesn't need his money."

"No, but I'm not sure Mildred gets that. I had to go over and over what Mom has set up for her financially. I don't think she was convinced. I'm worried she's going to charge me."

"She has to have evidence to charge you, and she's not going to find it because you didn't do it."

"Have you never heard of those cases where someone is locked up for like 45 years because of something they actually didn't do?"

She had a point. "Okay, so we need to prove you're innocent. I just don't think we can trust Mildred to do it. I mean, I can understand never having heard of 'They Call the Wind Mariah.' It's an old song. But never hearing of 'Let It Go'? This is not a woman on top of things."

When I hung up, Derek was smiling at me in that irritating, know-it-all way he has. "So you think Mildred needs to know song lyrics to solve a murder?"

"Don't start with me. I just think we have a big advantage over Mildred for figuring out who murdered Donald. We've grown up here."

"And that's an advantage how?"

"With all the people I know and all the people you and my friends and relatives know, we've got connections to pretty much everybody in town."

"Maybe a bit of an exaggeration, but yes."

"Mildred moved here less than a year ago. How can she possibly know how things work? How can she know how intertwined small town connections can be?" He opened his mouth, I was sure, to ask me if it was possible Mildred also came from a small town. "She's from Chicago," I interrupted.

Maybe she was. Maybe she wasn't. I was making a point. "Our key to solving this is talking to people, using our connections and our knowledge of how this town works. People like stories. People like to talk."

"Maybe."

"Really, I just have a *feeling* this is our best approach."

"I know, I know. Your excellent instincts." There was a touch of sarcasm in his voice. Derek had heard the Blockbuster video story a few times too often.

My phone buzzed, and I looked down.

A text from Baba:

Parnella Tonight. Now.

I quickly turned on the television and flipped to *Parnella Tonight*. Parnella Dubois collects gossip and dirt for her popular national show. Across the bottom of the screen scrolled the words *Witness accuses Colorado woman in the murder of model Donald Sanders*.

Who? What witness? A little box at the side of the screen showed a pair of tap shoes with the words "Tap Dance Murder" above them. The case now had a logo? That seemed wrong. Just wrong.

A pretty blonde woman filled the screen. Her long, wavy hair was pulled over one shoulder and cascaded to the low-cut neckline of her dress. An interview was underway. "And the beautiful woman was arguing with the man I recognized as the guy from the adorable commercial with that little girl and the pony. Donald Sanders. Anyway, the beautiful lady *hit* Mr. Sanders with something. Hard. It looked like a shoe."

"Who was the woman who did that?" Parnella asked, looking concerned.

"I identified her in a photo later. I was told it was Sammie Russo." She paused. "I'm pretty sure she's the daughter of the woman running for mayor of Juniper. Geraldine Betz."

"Tell us what happened next."

"When she hit him, Donald Sanders went down. She must have hit him in just the right place."

"A blow to the temple can kill someone," Parnella interjected.

"Right. I think that must have been what happened. Anyway, then another man came out of the door next to the dance studio, and he yelled, 'What did you *do*?' He seemed mad. But after a minute of thinking, he dragged Donald into the dance studio."

"And then?"

"And then the two of them, the lady and the man, went back in the door next to the studio, like nothing happened!"

"Did you try to go in and check on Donald?"

"No." She started crying. "I was scared Sammie Russo and that man would come after me!" She sniffed. "But maybe I *could* have done something for Donald. I did take a CPR class once."

"Our viewers are going to want to know, Miss Wisteria,

why you didn't at least come forward right away with this information."

She sniffed again and used a tissue to wipe delicately around her eyes, careful not to smear her mascara. "I was just so, so embarrassed at my … my cowardice … how I didn't help Donald. I didn't want the whole world to know how awful I'd been." And here she began crying again. "And now it's happening anyway. Everyone knows." Through her tears, she bucked up and looked right into the camera. "But, in the end, I *have* done the right thing."

"Yes, you have. Thank you, Miss Wisteria." Parnella turned to the camera. "To recap, we just had an exclusive interview with a young woman who says she witnessed someone she has identified as Sammie Russo assault murder victim Donald Sanders. The man who reportedly helped her hide the body in the dance studio may have been Russo's fiancé, Sam Quillan." An icon cartwheeled down the screen and turned into a picture of Sammie and Sam together. Then another twirled down and became a picture of Sammie and Donald together. "We have been informed by anonymous sources that Sammie Russo was once Donald Sanders' longtime girlfriend. We'll be back later with more news about this shocking development."

"She was not his girlfriend!" I said to the television. The show cut to a commercial.

"Her tears were heart-wrenching," Derek said, wiping away a fake tear. I ignored him and called Baba.

"We missed the beginning, Baba. Who the heck is this woman? Where did she supposedly see this?"

"She's visiting family in Juniper. Said she stepped outside a restaurant for a smoke and saw it all." Here Baba imitated her breathy voice perfectly. "She was so, so embarrassed to admit she smoked, too. But smoking helps her, you know, keep her weight down.'"

"This is so, so bogus."

"Of course it is."

"I'm calling Dan."

There was no answer. I called Sammie. She answered with, "This is so, so bogus!"

"It's late but I'm coming over."

"Of course you are. Hurry up. Sam is working tonight. I need company."

"You're off the hook," I told Derek. "I'm going to Sammie's."

"Not alone, you're not."

"I don't need protection."

"You might need reining in, though."

I let him drive.

Sammie was holding Isabelle over her shoulder and patting her vigorously when we walked in. Isabelle burped. "Okay, so how do we prove that damned woman is lying?" she demanded.

"Step one is to sort out whoever the heck she is," I said. "I didn't see the whole interview. Did you get her name?"

"Willow. Willow Wisteria."

"You're kidding," Derek said.

Sammie shrugged.

"What family is she supposed to be visiting?" I asked.

"They didn't say. I assume the restaurant she was visiting was the Saturn, since it's the only restaurant on the block."

I sat down and googled *Willow Wisteria* on my phone.

"She's an actress," I said, looking at her website. "Not a very successful one evidently." I read more. "She was in a commercial for something called Effermalia … no idea what that is . . . Oh, and get this. I read aloud: *She was smitten with the acting bug when she played Sandy in a non-musical version of an Iowa high school production of Grease.* Doesn't she mean 'bitten,' not 'smitten?'"

Sammie nodded. "And what in the world is a *non*-musical version of *Grease?*"

"Pretty terrible, I imagine," Derek said.

I continued looking at the website. "She was in the movie *La La Land.*"

"That's impressive."

"Not so impressive." I turned the screen to show them a picture of a crowd scene from the movie, with a big arrow pointing to Willow."

Derek laughed. "So we know she does her own website."

"Can't Mildred figure out that this woman just wants some free publicity?" Sammie asked.

I shrugged. "Like I said, I don't have a lot of confidence in Mildred."

Sammie abruptly got up. "I really need a break," she said, handing the baby to me. "You two fight over Isabelle or solve a murder or whatever. Just let me close my eyes for five minutes. Or cry."

We nodded. She looked exhausted. So did Isabelle.

I burped Isabelle again while Derek continued looking at Willow's website on his own phone, snickering occasionally. Snuggling Izzie-Bee close, I sang "Bye-Baby Bunting" over and over until she was out cold. It's my technique— boring her to sleep. When I put her carefully in the bassinet in the bedroom, I found Sammie passed out on the bed. I decided she needed more than five minutes and left her alone.

In the living room, I called Dan. "That blonde who accused Sammie—who is she visiting in town? Do you know?"

"Ella, you know I couldn't tell you that even if I knew."

"But I'm not asking you about the case. I'm just asking who someone is visiting."

"You *are* aware that the interview was not with the police department? It was with a gossipy entertainment TV channel."

"I'm aware. But does it really matter? The lie is out there, and we need to reveal that woman for what she is."

"*We* don't need to do anything. Mildred is leading this investigation and will handle things. Not you. Not me."

I didn't say anything. I knew that Mildred needed help, whether he knew it or not.

He sighed. "I'll see you about midnight. You're not staying alone tonight."

CHAPTER ELEVEN

"Are we going to have class tomorrow night?" I asked Sammie, calling the next morning before I went to work. Thursday nights were our normal meeting time; last Saturday night had been a make-up class.

"Who's going to want to come to a tap class where a murder took place? Especially when I'm supposedly the murderer? I should just give everybody a refund."

Where was her enthusiasm for her classes, her studio, her dream of running the most popular dance studio in northern Colorado? "They'll want to come," I said. "They must be dying to share what they know and find out what everybody else knows. And we really, really need to talk to them."

"I can't see poor Nell barreling through a sea of reporters." At 80, Nell was taking her first dance class in 65 years.

"She's tough. She'll want to come. Everybody will. Just tell them to keep their heads down and refuse to comment."

Sammie was silent, so I went on. "Remember, we *know* these women. Surely we can find out something Mildred can't. Talking to them may give us a chance to figure out who did this."

"Do you think they would actually come back?"

"Of course. If you were in their shoes, wouldn't you?"

"Let me think about it."

I was just parking my car at school when I got a text, to all the tappers:

Class will resume at regular time tomorrow. If reporters bug you, say NO COMMENT.

The parking lot was empty of reporters, and none were waiting at the school doors, not even the Redhead. Maybe they were finished with me at last and pursuing Willow Wisteria.

At recess, I stood in the warm May sunshine talking to Amelia, my fellow kindergarten teacher while we supervised the kids outside.

"A day and a half left," she sighed. "They're bouncing off the walls."

I rushed to stop Victoria, who was standing backwards at the top of the ladder to the slide, ready to leap to the ground. "Victoria! Turn around. Go down the regular way," I said in my "Don't mess with me" voice.

She turned around.

Then we saw Henry holding his arms across a section of the play structure, refusing to let Claire pass on the walkway. I stepped forward to intervene, but Amelia took my arm. "Wait a minute," she said. "Listen."

Claire had both hands on her hips and was standing tall, head high. "Stop it, Henry. Let me by."

Henry took one hand and began flapping it on her shoulder, not quite hitting her but annoying her just the same.

"Stop!" Claire said again, holding her hands before her in a "Stop!" gesture. "Stop it now, or I'm telling!"

Evidently, the thought of a recess spent sitting along the fence or in the office didn't appeal to him. He stopped flapping and let her pass.

Amelia and I smiled at each other. Maybe our

anti-bullying techniques were working. We had taught the kids not to cower if someone was bothering them, but to hold their heads high and stand up tall. We had been teaching them a list of steps: *Tell them firmly to stop. If they don't stop, hold both hands in front of you if you can, and tell them again. If that doesn't work, get help.* Claire was one of the meekest kids in my class and Henry one of the most aggressive. I was thrilled to see her stand up for herself.

That afternoon I decided to model my own advice. When I got home from work, the Redhead and her photographer buddy were sitting on my front steps waiting for me. I stayed in the car for a few moments, getting into my stand-tall-and-be-powerful mindset while they walked towards me. Then I opened the door.

"What do you make of the latest news?" the Redhead asked, thrusting a microphone in my face. I assumed she was referring to Willow Wisteria's accusation about Sammie.

I got out and locked my car.

"So did you know your best friend evidently did it, according to the witness?"

I stood tall and held my head high. "Move!" I said. "Let me pass."

"We will, after we get a comment from you," the Redhead said.

"You need to leave, now."

"Come on, Kendall," the photographer said.

She ignored him. "What are your thoughts about the boyfriend, Sam Quillan, now that a witness has identified him as probably the one who helped Sammie move the body?"

I pulled my attention back to the Redhead—Kendall,

evidently—and called the police station. "This is Ella Polansky. I'd like to report two people trespassing on my property and blocking entrance to my own home." I glanced at the red car. "License plate FNN …"

"We're leaving," the Redhead said.

I continued, finishing the license plate number and giving my address. "They have threatened me, refusing to move unless I talk to them."

"Get over it already!" the Redhead said, moving more quickly. "God only knows what kind of backwards sheriff they'd send in this town," she said to the photographer. They left.

I knew I hadn't heard the last of them, but I was proud of myself for standing up to bullies.

After they left, little Skyden came out of the duplex next door and sat down on his Paw Patrol 6V Quad. His mother followed with the new baby, Amaryllis. I was hoping Maria and Foster would come up with a nickname soon so that whenever I said the baby's name, I didn't think of the Christmas plants my aunt sent to the whole family every December.

"Mama made me play inside," Skyden said, frowning at the injustice. "Because of those reporters."

"I'm sorry. Can I make it up to you?" I was hoping he wanted a big hug. I certainly wanted one.

"Chutes and Ladders!" he said.

I'd made a tactical error. Skyden's love of the Chutes and Ladders game knows no bounds. I wanted to come up with an excuse, but I didn't have the energy just then to handle that crushed look he gets on his face. It's devastating.

"Okay, let's get you washed up first," I said. I glanced at Maria, and she nodded, giving me permission to take him inside. "Looks like you had PBJ. Grape jelly, I'd say."

As I held him up to wash at my bathroom sink, I admired his reflection in the mirror. His almost black eyes, his thick lashes, his flawless skin—so perfect, even with a little grape jelly.

Then I accidentally glanced at myself. It is never a good idea to look at the perfect face of a three-year-old next to your own, even if you're looking your best, and I wasn't. The murder and my late nights were taking a toll on me. The curls in my long hair had a limp, dispirited look, and dark shadows lay under my eyes. I'd skipped the mascara that morning—kindergartners think I'm beautiful, no matter what—but I wasn't sure Dan would feel the same. I made a mental note to add some makeup before I saw Dan.

I eased Skyden to the floor. He scrunched his perfect face into a scowl as I used a washcloth to wipe off the jelly. Then I squared my shoulders and followed him to the hall closet, where he knew I kept Chutes and Ladders.

Two games later, I begged for mercy. "I have to go over to Detective Dan's house for a while."

"Can I go, too? He likes Chutes and Ladders."

Actually, he does not, largely because Skyden has destroyed any residual fondness from Cassie's childhood. "I'm sorry," I said, giving his sweet face another kiss.

He took it well, if I ignore the stink eye he shot me as I returned him to his mother.

Dan had invited me over to take a walk with him and Cassie. Schools were already out in Harper Springs, where Cassie went to high school, and she was spending the afternoon. The May weather was warm, so she had worn shorts. Her long hair was pulled up into a ponytail and folded over on itself into a messy bun.

When we were on the neighborhood walking path, Cassie said, "I saw Donald Sanders, like, flirting with the receptionist the night of the murder. Do you think maybe she left to meet him at the dance studio when we were at the lecture? And, like, maybe murdered him? And then came back? Or maybe the lady from the tap dance class did. Affinity. Affinity was flirting with Donald, too."

Dan just walked on. "Not on the case, remember."

She continued. "And what about this Willow Wisteria?"

I was surprised that Cassie was following the case. Then I thought of all the semi-salacious details and wasn't surprised. I would have followed it at her age, too, even though I'd never paid much attention to the news otherwise.

"Willow's a fake," I said.

"What do you think, Dad?"

"I think I don't want to discuss it. It's a beautiful day. Let's talk about something else."

We walked a bit. Then Cassie said, "It seems pretty weird that this lady didn't report what she supposedly saw right away. I mean, like, if you saw a person hit someone and then drag the body off, wouldn't you call in and report it right away?"

"I would," I said. "I'd call it in immediately."

"So don't you think something is weird here?" Cassie asked.

"I told you I don't want to talk about it," Dan said. "I'm off work. Surely you can find another topic." He pointed to the Rocky Mountains looming to the west of us. "Look at those beautiful mountains." He burst into song. "The hills are alive, with the sound of music." I joined in.

Cassie groaned. "Dad! People are looking at us!" She stalked ahead, pretending not to know us.

We finished the song and Dan said, "Ella, you choose next."

I picked the first thing that popped into my head, "You're the One That I Want," from *Grease*. *Subtle*, I thought. *Real subtle*.

Dan chimed right in with the *ooh, ooh, oohs* as I sang. Then he called, "Cassie, your turn."

"Like that's going to happen," she said, waiting for us to catch up.

"So didn't you ever think of getting involved in musical theater like your dad did in high school?" I asked.

"As if," she said.

Her dad gave her a warning look. She added with ever-so-slightly exaggerated politeness, "No, I'm not interested in theater. I do *sports*. Volleyball. Softball. Soccer."

"Got it," I said.

She looked at her dad. She seemed hesitant about something. "And now I want to sign up for pole dancing. Not at school. At a gym."

"What?" Dan stopped abruptly and stared at her. I tried hard not to laugh.

"It's not like pole dance *stripping*, Dad. It's kind of like dancing, but on a pole. It takes a lot of strength. A *lot.*"

"No," he said.

"What do you mean, 'No'? You don't even know anything about it."

"I know it involves hanging on a pole in skimpy costumes and looking sexy. You are too young to look sexy."

"I am not too young to look sexy! Tell him, Ella."

Now she wanted me on her side? I decided to ignore the issue of her sexiness, pretty sure Dan wasn't ready for that. "I have heard about pole dancing," I said carefully. "It's a thing. An exercise thing. It's not necessarily a bar or stripper thing."

She wasn't letting the sexy thing go. "Sometimes guys say I look sexy."

"*What* guys??" Dan wasn't liking this at all.

"You know, guys."

"If guys are talking to you about sexiness, they are the wrong guys." He looked at her short shorts. "And don't wear shorts like that again!"

Wrong thing to say.

"Like what?"

"Like so *short!*"

"These are perfectly ordinary shorts. Mom has no problem with them."

"I didn't either until you started talking about guys saying you are sexy. You are my *child*, not a *femme fatale*."

"What's a *femme fatale?*"

"Never mind. You aren't taking pole dancing lessons. Jesus! Pole dancing!"

"Um ..." I hesitated. "I have a friend who takes pole dancing."

Cassie looked at me gratefully. "See, Dad? And Ella wouldn't have any slutty friends. Right?"

Actually, I did have one kind of slutty friend, but she wasn't the pole dancer. I decided not to mention that. "My friend Sydney has been pole dancing for a couple of years.

She loves it. Says it's really good exercise, with really cool, supportive women. I went to one of their open house exhibitions once, and it was pretty incredible."

"Did the men put dollar bills in their G-strings?" Dan's face was reddish and his kind brown eyes now looked only brown.

A couple of the women had worn G-strings, but I decided I wouldn't tell him that part. "There were girls and women of all ages at the show. Some 12-year-olds used the big aerial hoop thing. A Lyra, I think it's called. There was even a lady who was seven months pregnant. It was kind of like a gymnastics event, but with everyone using the poles. Or the hoop things."

"Come on, Dad. I want to do it, and Mom says I can if you say it's okay. She came to the studio and looked into it."

"No," he said.

My, my. I was seeing another side of Dan. His little girl was turning into a young woman, but he was having none of it.

"You never let me do anything!" she said. I have to say she looked more like a petulant toddler than a sexy young woman at the moment.

He ignored her.

"I'm going back to the house." She stomped away.

"I don't know what's gotten in to her," Dan muttered.

I did, but I don't think he was ready to accept it. His little girl was growing up. *And* sexy.

I thought it best I change the subject. "Cassie had a good point about the receptionist, whose name I now know is Mariah because Mildred told me." I could have chosen more wisely when it came to subject matter, but the murder was never far from my thoughts.

He scowled. Finally, he said, "Mariah seems to have disappeared."

That was certainly interesting.

He stopped and faced me. "And that is all I am going to say on the matter. Period. Do you understand?"

I nodded, trying to think of a safe topic to defuse the situation. Faking a swagger, I said, "So … how 'bout them Broncos?"

He couldn't help it. He laughed. "*Them* Broncos aren't playing in May. Not football season. Try again."

I was glad to see his smile. I grabbed his hand and said, "Let's just walk."

CHAPTER TWELVE

That evening was my regular rehearsal night with the Streusals. At the end of our walk, I kissed Dan and went home to get my accordion—the smaller one I call Frankie after the late Frankie Yankovich, America's Polka King.

I was relieved to see there wasn't another "Slut" sign on the front lawn, but when I got to the front door I found an envelope taped to the front. I opened it and read *Your best friend is a murderer. Repent!*

As I unlocked the door, I thought, *Why should I be the one to repent if my best friend is the murderer?* It made no sense. Then I realized I was arguing, mentally, with an anonymous note. I wadded it up and threw it away.

Frankie, my accordion, lives in the bedroom closet, so I pulled out the case and sat it by the front door, then grabbed my music stand and music bag. Before I could leave, though, I got a text from Otto. He had to cancel rehearsal because of an emergency babysitting gig with his granddaughter. Grandchildren take precedence over pretty much everything else with this group.

I decided to go visit Baba. As I unlocked my car, I noticed the Redhead sitting in her red car about half a block away. Was she ever going to give up? I pretended I hadn't seen her and started driving.

I was feeling, as Baba would put it, "contrary," and decided to mess with her a little. As I drove to Baba's, I hurried through a yellow light, but the Redhead followed. I took a right turn without signaling. She followed. I took a left turn onto a busy road without signaling. She followed.

As I half-seriously contemplated flipping a U-turn in front of a truck, I heard a siren and in my rear view mirror saw spiraling red lights and the Nissan pulling over to the curb. Smiling, I drove on, taking more evasive actions just in case. I turned into a subdivision and drove around the lake (probably an artificial one created by Harvey Klump's development company) and then followed a meandering route to Baba's. I needed a break from reporters. Her house would be a safe haven.

In Baba's driveway, I texted her.

Open your garage door. Fast.

Baba peered out the front window. The garage door opened, and I drove in, squeezing in next to her Buick Lucerne. Baba stood in the doorway to the laundry room, holding up her can of pepper spray.

"Are they after you?" she asked.

"They are. All the time. But a cop pulled over the one who was on my tail this time."

"Detective Dan!" she breathed. She adored Detective Dan.

"I saw the policeman get out of his car. No, it wasn't Dan."

Baba's shoulders drooped in disappointment, but she quickly rallied. "You're staying the night. You're safe here," she said, hugging me. "I've got my pepper spray."

She ushered me into the living room, where the television

blasted. "All the shows are loving this story." On the screen, Donald and Sammie danced a sexy tango, Sammie with a plunging neckline and a slit in her dress up to mid-thigh. "She looks like a movie star."

"She always looks like a movie star."

"So where did they get those pictures?" Baba asked.

"Probably from the insurance company she used to work for in Denver. They had a 'Dancing with the Stars' kind of contest a couple of years ago to raise money for a food bank. Sammie asked Donald to be her partner."

"Oh, I remember now. You danced something with her brother ... was it a polka?"

"No, Baba. Just because I play the accordion doesn't mean the polka is the only dance I know." I noticed her grinning and saw that she was kidding me. "Funny. No, we did a country-western thing. We came in fifth."

"Where did Sammie and Donald come in?"

"What do you think?" I didn't bother answering. When I sat down on the sofa, the afghan fell off the back, as usual. I folded it and put it beside me.

"You wouldn't believe the stuff they're saying," Baba said, settling into her recliner and looking at the television again. She pointed at a man with hair that didn't move. "That guy's talking about Sammie and Donald's dance partnership like it was a torrid affair."

I shook my head. "Let's hope they never figure out that Donald's name is on Isabelle's birth certificate. It should be okay, though. Vital records are supposed to be confidential in Colorado, unless you fit eligibility requirements. I checked."

Baba yanked the lever at the side of the recliner, and her

legs shot up. "By the way, why didn't *Sam* just sign the birth certificate? No one would have known the difference."

"Sammie wanted to be honest. She wasn't about to start her daughter's life with a lie. She has pretty rigid views on right and wrong sometimes."

When Baba raised her eyebrows, I continued. "Sammie is a good Catholic girl, Baba."

"*He that committeth fornication sinneth against his own body.*" Every now and then Baba showed signs that her Catholic schooling had been a lot more rigorous than mine. She continued, "I'm just saying ..."

"You're 'just saying' *what?* Of course you're 'saying' if you are the one talking. I hate that phrase. It's like 'It is what it is.' Stupid. Of course it is what it is. If it wasn't ..."

Baba interrupted. "Technically, *I'm just saying* is a sentence, not a phrase, honey."

"Okay, I hate vague sentences like *I'm just saying,* and I hate…"

"Let it go," she said, clicking off the television. "You don't have to get hung up on such little things when there are so many bigger things to worry about. Climate change, for example." She moved the lever again and lurched forward. "Let me get you something to drink."

I got up and followed her into the kitchen, wondering when Baba had started worrying about climate change. She poured half a can of Pepsi into a glass, just as she had when I was a child, covered the can with aluminum foil, and put it in the refrigerator. "I have some nice pork chops," she said, handing me the glass. "Your mom's off work in a bit. I'll call her and we'll have dinner."

"Ask her to bring wine."

Baba opened the refrigerator. "Ta-da!" It was a bottle of Smoking Loon Chardonnay, my favorite." I bought it just for you."

"You went into a liquor store?" I was shocked. In Colorado, you can't buy wine at the supermarket. Baba had always made my brothers buy wine and beer for her when she needed it. She thinks a woman going into a liquor store looks cheap.

"Times change," she said.

I smiled. "Pour."

"After you finish your Pepsi and ask properly."

I finished my Pepsi and asked properly. "May I have some wine, please?"

When Mom knocked fifteen minutes later, I went to the front door to let her in and stopped in the foyer, startled—to say the least—to see a five-foot tall statue of the Virgin Mary standing beside the coat rack. "Holy smoke," I said, looking it up and down. Mary's bare foot was standing on a plaster snake.

Mom used her key and let herself in. "I knocked for a *reason*," she said. "Why didn't you open the door?" Then she saw me staring and sighed. "Mrs. Mascari rescued that a long time ago from Holy Name when they renovated the school. They were going to throw it away, but Mrs. Mascari thought all six of her kids would fight to inherit it one day. It sat in her living room for 30 years."

"Okay. So what's it doing in Baba's entryway now?"

"Mrs. Mascari died last month. Guess what?"

"Her kids don't want the statue."

"Bingo."

Baba joined us. "You can't throw away the Virgin Mary. I'm housing it temporarily, until we can find it a home."

"I hope you find one soon. It's creepy."

"Ella, the Blessed Virgin is not creepy."

"Okay, *very* startling and inappropriate as a greeter in a home."

Baba led us into the kitchen to make dinner.

Forty-five minutes later, Mom added a bowl of mashed potatoes to the pork chops, salad, and peas already on the table. I sighed happily. I love mashed potatoes, especially whipped smoothly the way Mom makes them.

Then Mom set out a cube of real butter instead of Baba's tub of I Can't Believe It's Not Butter. "Don't start," she said. I suspected she didn't want to hear my rant about how I, for one, *can* believe it's not butter and how a little bit of something real and delicious like butter is much better than a whole lot of something processed that includes a lot of weird sounding chemicals.

I sliced off a big hunk of butter and put it on the mound of potatoes on my plate, allowing it time to melt, then poured wine for all of us (a second glass for me) as Baba shook up the bottle of ranch dressing. Her dressing must be ranch, her mustard must be bright yellow, and her "mayonnaise" must be Miracle Whip.

Baba started right in. "So what do you think happened that night?"

I knew what night she meant. "Donald was murdered," I said.

She put down her fork and gave me her "Get on with it" look. She waited.

"I don't know what happened, Baba."

"What do you *think* happened? What *might* have happened? Speculate."

"Okay, okay." I thought quickly. She loved this sort of thing. "Sammie gave Donald permission to use the studio from 8:00 to 9:00 that night so he could practice for an audition, and he invited someone in to practice with him." I thought again. "Or to whatever. But the woman got mad at Donald for some reason when she was there. Maybe he tried to seduce her, and she was insulted because she thought they were just there to dance. Or maybe she got sick of hearing stories about his red Mercedes. Or his front-row tickets to Hamilton. Or the importance of hydration for your skin. Whatever it was, the woman decided she'd had it with him and started telling him off."

Baba waited for me to continue. Mom just kept chewing a bite of pork chop. And chewing. As usual, Baba had overcooked the meat.

I thought quickly. "So Donald reached out to calm her down, and she took it wrong." I let my imagination go. "Her self-defense training kicked in. She didn't stop to think, just whipped around and swung the bag she was carrying, and bam! She hit him in the temple. A blow to the temple can kill a person, you know."

"She had self-defense training?" Mom couldn't help herself. "And you know that *how?*"

"Remember, I'm speculating."

"But I heard Donald died because someone hit him with a tap shoe," Baba said.

"No. That's ridiculous. But a blow from a *bag* of tap shoes. That's plausible. Yes, that's probably it. The dance they were rehearsing was a tap dance, so she had a bag of tap shoes with her."

Baba nodded, as if that made perfect sense. I helped myself to more mashed potatoes and went on. "He went down. Crash. The blow from the bag of tap shoes killed him."

"And then?" Baba asked. She was listening intently, though I suspected part of her focus was coming up with improvements to my story.

"And then she took the bag of tap shoes with her and got out of there." I decided to make up some more details, just for Baba. "It was the bag her sister had made for her. A special bag out of a fabric with little dancing ballerinas all over it."

"Not little tap dancers?"

"No one makes fabric with little tap dancers on it, just ballerinas." I went on, my mind filling in details quickly. "Her sister had embroidered her name at the top of the bag in pink letters, so leaving the bag in the studio would not have been wise. She remembered to take it with her, even though she was pretty shaken up. She didn't want to be charged with murder. Accidental murder."

"Or maybe your entire scenario is ridiculous," said Mom.

"Okay, come up with a better one," I said.

Mom set her fork down. "How about this one? Harvey Klump saw Donald sneak into the studio, so he went in after him and bonked him on the head with one of his campaign signs."

"I like it," Baba smiled.

I wasn't going to let Mom off that easily. "*Why* would Harvey kill Donald?"

"Donald was in Sammie's studio. He hoped to implicate

her and have her charged with murder, thus devastating Geraldine and causing her to drop out of the race."

I gave up. "You win. Let's go with Harvey Klump and the yard sign. Guilty!" We all toasted, and Baba passed me the bowl of mashed potatoes.

I changed the subject, remembering what I'd seen in the foyer. "So who's the guy you have keeping the Virgin Mary company?" I asked Baba. "There's a man's hat on the coat tree."

"That's her boyfriend's," Mom said.

"Gentleman friend's," corrected Baba. "You can't call an 85-year-old a boyfriend."

"Since when do you have a gentleman friend?" I asked.

"Since about three months ago. I met him bowling."

"Nobody tells me anything. This is big news. What's his name?"

"Lester."

"I only found out last week," Mom said. "I came over early to give her half the big bag of almonds I bought at Costco. Anyway, no one answered, so I came on in. A barefoot man came out of the guest bathroom." She looked at me. "It was almost exactly what happened when I discovered Detective Dan at your house at 7:30 in the morning."

"Not the same thing at all," said Baba, shuddering a little, probably at the thought of Detective Dan staying the night with me. "Lester slept on the couch. He'd had a tad too much wine and couldn't drive."

I thought of saying something about fornication again, but I didn't know any Bible verses. Or if fornication applies to people in their 80s. So I just said, "So he bowls."

"Well, no, not really. He had to drive his friend Isaac that night because Isaac's car was in the garage. It's Isaac who bowls."

"Got it."

She smiled. "While Lester was waiting for Isaac's league to finish, he came over to me, complimented my T-shirt, and that was that."

"Must have been some T-shirt."

"I'll show you." She hurried into the bedroom.

Mom didn't say anything, but she gave the same "What're you gonna do?" shrug she had used when my brothers were middle schoolers and tried to snort Smarties in the backyard or filled their Super Soakers with red Kool-Aid to make their battles more interesting.

Grandma came back with a purple T-shirt with pink letters that read, "Three Gals and a Chick." The frame around the words was highlighted in silver sequins.

"Cool, huh?" Baba said. Her bowling team is made up of three women her age and the twenty-something granddaughter of one of them.

"Very."

"Myrna designed them, but they needed a little something. I'm the one who came up with the sequins. It adds so much, don't you think?"

"Sparkle always does." I wasn't letting go of the boyfriend news. "So tell me about Lester."

"Okay. He's a nice man, bicycles a lot. He's very health conscious," she said.

"Very," Mom added.

"He lives in an independent living facility, but he has a whole garden on his second floor deck. Herbs. Tomatoes.

Arugula. Greens, greens, greens. He makes his own salad. A *lot* of salad." She stopped and seemed to be about to say more, but didn't.

"Health conscious is good," I said.

"He eats only steel-cut oatmeal. Nothing with chemical preservatives."

"Gluten free, I presume?" Mom asked.

"Isn't everyone these days?" Baba said. "I remember back when everyone was hypoglycemic."

She passed me the plate with two remaining pork chops. I declined. My teeth were tired.

"Your mom's already met Lester, and you'll meet him soon," Baba said. She hesitated, then continued. "When you do, change the subject if he starts talking about Big Pharma and political power and patented drugs. He gives ... well, more details than you might want to hear."

"A lot more," Mom said.

I was confused by all the health details. "But wine is okay with him?"

Baba shrugged. "Wine is okay. Go figure. He just likes wine."

Now I knew why she was suddenly willing to look cheap and go into a liquor store. I raised a glass. "So do we. So do we."

Baba put me up in the room she had decorated just for me when I was seven. It's still lavender, with a purple flowered quilt and ruffled pillow shams on the bed. I always feel strangely safe in that room. (My two rambunctious brothers, when they stayed over as kids, were relegated to beds in the unfinished basement. "They can do less damage down there," Baba said.)

As I lay in bed, I found myself wondering if old people have sex. If Baba wasn't such a staunch Catholic, would she be sleeping with Lester? I pulled my mind away from that thought, shuddering.

Then I wondered why I shuddered. Was imagining Baba and Lester in bed any weirder than imagining, say, Sammie and Sam in bed?

Yes, it was.

I needed to move my thoughts firmly and quickly to something else. I tried yoga breathing again and finally drifted off to sleep.

At 1:00 a.m., my phone vibrated. I saw it was Derek and answered.

"There's a guy who works at the Saturn who comes into Whitney's after work, so I asked him about Willow Wisteria," he said. "He remembers Willow being at the Saturn, but he doesn't remember when. He remembers her because, well, you can guess why he remembers her. Anyway, meet Eric. I'm handing him the phone."

"Hi, Eric. I'm Ella," I said. "What can you tell me?"

"Willow's lying."

"We *know* that. But how can we prove it?"

"Customers do not go out back of the restaurant to smoke. They'd have to go through the kitchen and stand out on the cement pad out back. Only staff do that."

"Maybe she had an 'in' with someone there."

He snorted. "A babe like that standing out there with the sweaty dishwasher taking a break? Stepping over rotten lettuce that has fallen out of bags on the way to the Dumpster? Trust me. She was *not* smoking out back. If she was smoking at all, she smoked out front with all the other addicts."

"*If* she was smoking?"

"Did you smell her?" he asked.

"I've never met her."

"Someone should. Smell her, that is. She doesn't look like a smoker to me."

I called Dan and told him what Eric had said. He was quiet for a while, as if figuring out what to say—or maybe just trying to wake up. Finally, he said, "I'll tell Mildred. Now, can I go back to sleep?"

"Absolutely."

"By the way," he added. "Has it ever occurred to you that the police department might already have *known* all that?"

Actually, it had not. But I noticed he hadn't said they *had* known all that. He'd said *might have* known. I wondered which it was.

CHAPTER THIRTEEN

The next day, the last morning of school, was a busy one. The kids collected papers to take home, cleaned cubbies, and shared summer plans. As I said goodbye to my 23 munchkins, I marveled at how much they had changed in our short nine months together. As always, I felt sad to see them go. Some would return as first graders next year, so I would be able to keep track of them. Others, though, would move, and I might never see them again. I knew from past experience that I would often find myself wondering—or worrying—about them.

When I checked in at the office at the end of the day, a couple of teachers seemed to be avoiding me, and the PE teacher was definitely undressing me with his eyes. I wanted to make an announcement over the intercom: *In case you missed it, the police have cleared Ella Polansky of showing up naked on a murdered man's phone.*

I held my head high as I walked to my car.

Sammie texted me:

Come over early before class?

I didn't bother answering, just drove.

Only one news van and the Redhead's car were parked in the alley. I wasn't surprised. Most reporters were still probably off hounding Willow Wisteria for more details.

Only with Willow, it wouldn't be hounding. It was exactly what she wanted.

I pulled in beside the Redhead, who was parked in Sam's parking spot, no one with her. She didn't bother getting out, just watched me, looking up now and then from thumbing something into her smart phone. I tried to imagine what she could be writing. *Ella Polansky parks car? Ella gets out of car? Ella locks car?*

I used the key pad to let myself into the building. "Coming up!" I called as I unlocked Sammie's door and started up the stairs.

"Here," Sammie said when I entered. She thrust a crying Isabelle at me. "I have to pee."

"Hello to you, too," I called as she left the room.

I heard the toilet flush and then the sound of the shower running. "Okay, Izzie-Bee. I guess it's just you and me. Mommy needs a break." I walked with her until she calmed down and stopped crying, then sat down and rested her on my legs, facing me. When I held out my finger, she latched on to it. I tickled the area above her lip with my other finger, and she smiled.

I sang to her—the Isabella-Boo song I'd made up.

Isabelle, Isabelle, Isabella Boo.
Isabelle, Isabelle, I love you.

She looked interested, so I continued.

Isabelle, Isabelle, Isabella Bug.
Isabelle, Isabelle, here's a hug.

I picked her up and snuggled her. She started to fuss, so I rested her against my thighs and sang again.

Isabelle, Isabelle. Isabella Beep.
Isabelle, Isabelle, time to sleep.

She loved it.

I'm pretty sure she loved it.

I repeated my "boring her to sleep" technique, singing that verse over and over. As her eyes drifted closed, then open, then half-closed, fighting sleep, I sang more and more softly, winding down, and finally her eyes stayed closed.

Sammie emerged from the bedroom, hair still damp but combed. "I needed that," she said.

I spoke softly, so as not to wake Isabelle. "An emergency pee and shower?"

"Both." She sat down beside me, smiling at her sleeping baby. She gave Isabelle's little arm a tender pat, then looked at me. "No, I don't have postpartum depression, which I know is what you were thinking. I just needed to pee and take a shower. And think on my own for 15 minutes."

I waited, holding still so as not to disturb Isabelle. I knew something else was up.

She stretched her feet out and wiggled her toes. Then she blew out a little puff of air. "There is no way on God's green earth that I can prove I was really up here with Isabelle when Donald was murdered. No way. No one saw me. I didn't call anyone. Isabelle can't talk. I'm screwed."

"But no one can prove *otherwise,* either. There is that."

"Like that gives me much hope," she commented. "And you heard the worst, right? Thanks to 'Parnella Tonight,' they're saying I had a ten year affair with Donald. So now I look like a slut, Sam looks like a cuckolded wimp, and any fool can see that we'd both be better off if Donald disappeared from our lives."

"*Cuckolded*. Not a word you hear everyday."

"Ella! Focus."

"Okay, okay. So things don't look real good right now. But you haven't been arrested. Remember, that's something."

"There's more bad news."

"More?"

"Well, sort of bad. Maybe not bad. I don't know yet." She looked down at her lap. "Donald's mother called me today," she said.

That couldn't be good.

"She was a mess, of course. She wants me to come to the memorial service next week. I warned her about the paparazzi, but she's already dealing with them and they're going to be there whether I come or not."

I waited.

"And she knows about Isabelle. Donald told her about two weeks before he came to see me."

I winced. What could that mean?

"She wants to meet her."

I raised my eyebrows. Was that a good idea?

"And she wants to stay in Isabelle's life."

I didn't have any idea what to say, but my thoughts were racing. How was *that* going to work? Sammie had wanted Donald out of her life after she found she was pregnant. She knew he was not father material. Should his parents be involved now? Were they *entitled* to be in Isabelle's life? After all, Donald was listed on the birth certificate as the father, and the adoption hadn't taken place yet. Would they have some kind of inherited right to stop the adoption? I had no idea.

And how would Isabelle cope with a ridiculous number of grandparents. I counted: Sammie's mother and stepfather, Sammie's father and stepmother, Sam's mother and stepfather, Sam's father and stepmother, Donald's mother and father.

I thought of my students. One of them talked about Nana and Gramps and Grandma Ruth and Grandpa Earl and Grancie and G-pop and someone called Grandy-pa. He seemed to navigate all those grandparents just fine. Maybe Isabelle could, too.

"I've always liked them, and they *are* his parents," Sammie said. "They often said they wished I was more than a friend to Donald."

"I guess they got their wish."

"She said to bring Sam and Isabelle to the service, so I told her I'd come. I had to. Isabelle is all they have left of their son." Sammie started crying. "I feel so bad for them."

Maybe it was sympathy, but Isabelle started crying, too. Sammie reached for her, and they cried together.

After half a sandwich, a glass of water, and a cool washcloth over her face, Sammie pulled herself together. As soon as Sam came home and could take over with Isabelle, we went downstairs for tap class.

"You need to dance," I said. "Right now." Dancing has always been Sammie's route to happiness.

She hesitated.

"Do it," I said. "Put on your shoes while I pull up Beyonce."

The thought of "Run the World (Girls)" must have done it. In nothing flat, she had her tap shoes on and was stretching. I started the music, and Sammie took off. She was dancing.

My, but she was dancing. The aggressive beat allowed her to vent all her frustrations, and she was in her element, owning the floor. As students from class trickled in, they stood and watched, mouths open. Sammie's feet flew, and she had the same presence she always has on the dance floor, no matter the kind of dance. Something about her demands your attention, and it's almost impossible to look anywhere else. At the end of the song, Sammie stood, legs apart, one fist in the air as if she really *did* run the world.

There was a moment of silence, and then the group burst into cheers and applause. Sammie smiled, looking like her old happy self.

"Wow," said Nell. "Those are nothing like the steps we're learning. What do you call some of them?"

Sammie was breathing hard, but she answered. "Let me think. There were double-triple time steps, pullbacks, wings, a Broadway. Truthfully, I can't remember everything. I choreographed the dance and taught it to some advanced level teenagers a few years ago, and it's just kind of *in* me now. Muscle memory. I don't have to think about it."

"We have a goal now," one of the students said. "To be able to look like that for even ten seconds when we're on stage."

"Great goal," I said. "Now while Sammie winds down, let's talk about what happened here last Saturday. If you're willing."

Oh, they were willing. "It was scary to be questioned

about what I'd seen after class," said one of my teacher friends who was learning to tap. "Especially since I didn't see anything. I felt like I was failing some kind of test."

"Detective Kendrick wanted to know if I had any connection to Donald Sanders," said Nell. "I'm old enough to be his great-grandmother, so, no, we didn't exactly hang out." She looked around the room. "What about the rest of you?"

I explained how Sammie had been Donald's longtime dance partner until the baby came, and I knew him through Sammie.

"I knew him a little," Affinity said. "His parents live next door to me."

"I met him once," said Serenity. "Through Affinity."

Aunt Ruth looked at her twin nieces. "I guess that's a connection then. But I never even heard of him before he died."

"You never saw the commercial with the little girl and the pony?" another woman asked, amazed. "Look it up on YouTube. It's worth it. For *reals.*"

"Sammie, were you *ever* his girlfriend?" someone asked.

Sammie shook her head. "Absolutely not. I was his dance partner for over ten years, and that was it. As a person, he was not at all like that sweet dad in the cowboy hat. He was more ... let's just say *self-absorbed.* Definitely not my boyfriend. And, in case your wondering, I definitely didn't kill him."

"So we know Sammie didn't murder Donald, but we need to figure out who did," I said. "Did anyone see anything suspicious in the alley that night? Or anywhere? Anything even slightly unusual?"

Again, they shook their heads.

Sammie sighed. "Anything at all anyone can add?"

They all shook their heads.

Everyone was silent. Then Sammie said, "Okay then. If we can't solve a murder, let's dance."

We were learning a routine for the annual "Tap, Rattle, and Roll" show sponsored by the Colorado Tap Association and featuring performances by adult tap dancers from all over northern Colorado.

"This show doesn't sound like a great idea," I'd said to Sammie when she first told me she had signed up our group. "Who wants to see amateur adult tap dancers?"

"No one," she answered. "That's why they put on the show every year. Dancers need an audience, and the show gives them one. Everyone in the show gets to watch the other dancers when it's not their turn on stage."

"But we're so new at this. How are we going to get through a whole dance?"

"Trust me. You will."

So I trusted her.

We had now learned all the sections of the dance she had choreographed to "Big, Blonde, and Beautiful" from the musical *Hairspray*. We certainly hadn't mastered anything, though. One problem was getting from one sequence to another. We'd finish *step, shuffle, hop, step, around-the-world, stomp, clap,* for example, and then freeze, our faces telegraphing a panicked "What comes next?" When we were supposed to have our weight on the left foot so that the right foot was free to flap, we would have our weight on the wrong foot. When we were supposed to flap-heel left for four measures, someone would inevitably flap-heel right. Stomps came just a hair too late. Turns were forgotten entirely.

But we were improving. We could feel it. Muscle memory was starting to kick in, and we were getting more and more things right. Sometimes, when I did a whole section of the dance correctly, I even felt just a little bit like a real dancer.

When Sammie called it a night, Nell collapsed in a chair and bent over to wipe her face with the bottom of her tunic T-shirt, leaving a smudge of foundation on the white fabric. "I'm beat," she said.

"I feel like I've lost five pounds," Aunt Ruth said.

But we were all smiling as we stretched and took off our shoes. "Big, Blonde, and Beautiful" was starting to feel like a real dance, a real dance that we might actually be able to pull off.

CHAPTER FOURTEEN

The next morning Dan brought me a cup of coffee in bed before he left to pick up Cassie. He had slipped in the night before, but I knew there would be no more staying over while Cassie was around for the weekend.

School was out for the summer, but I had to go back sometime that day to finish putting things away so that the custodians could paint. It didn't have to be right away, though, so I sat in bed doodling.

It was murder doodling. I wrote names, drawing little lines between any of connections I saw, making squiggly lines for tenuous connections and bold lines for strong connections. I added question marks and exclamation points and random notes, as appropriate, as well as a few flowers. I just like drawing flowers.

Then I looked at the page. The name that stood out to me was Mariah, the receptionist. She'd *said* she was upstairs at the reception desk all evening—except for her little photo shoot with Donald—but maybe she'd managed to run over to the dance studio for a few minutes before the lecture was over, to kill him. After all, she was prone to violence, what with the nose flute whacking and all. I should have talked to her a long time ago.

Dan said she had disappeared, though. Why? Very suspicious.

A text from Dan interrupted my analysis:

Bringing Cassie over. U have to hear this.

I was puzzled. **Here what?** Darned auto-correct. I re-texted. **Hear what?**

Tell U later. Leaving her mom's house now.

I had no idea what was up.

Fifteen minutes later, I heard a knock at the door. Why wasn't Dan using his key? Then I remembered. Cassie. It wouldn't do to have it look like he was that familiar with my place.

I let them in. Dan kissed me quickly, and Cassie rushed to the kitchen table.

"Sit down! Sit down!" she said. I saw more enthusiasm in her face than I'd seen since, well, ever.

I shrugged my shoulders and said, "Okay. Coffee, Dan?" He nodded.

"I drink coffee too now," said Cassie.

"Okay. Coffee, Cassie?"

"Yes, please."

"So I found out Willow Wisteria is a fake," she announced.

"Of course she is." This is what Dan brought Cassie over to tell me?

"I *proved* she is a fake!" Cassie smiled at her dad, her face glowing. He put his arm around her and kissed the top of her head, then sat down.

"This, I have to hear," I said. I poured everyone some coffee.

Cassie took a sip and grimaced. Guessing she didn't take it straight, I took the sugar bowl out of the cupboard, sat it in front of her, and watched her stir three teaspoons into her coffee. My teeth hurt just watching.

Cassie talked as she sipped. "So this guy I know at school had to watch some movie with his parents. They, like, have this family night thing they do every Monday. He thinks it's lame, but anyway, they watched some old movie called *Six Degrees of Separation.*"

I nodded. "I watched it with Baba a long time ago."

"Supposedly, we are all only six people away from finding anyone. Is that cool, or what?"

I nodded. "Amazing." I hoped she would get on with the story now, but, no. She had to describe the Kevin Bacon game where people guess the number of connections between any actor and Kevin Bacon.

"There's even a website and everything on this," she said. "The Oracle of Bacon."

"I'm familiar with it," I said.

"Really?" She looked impressed.

"Cassie, cut to the story of what *you* did," Dan said. He took the sting out of his words by adding, "It's pretty amazing."

"Okay." She took a sip of coffee. "So I decided to do six degrees of separation on Willow Wisteria. And you know how many people I had to ask before I found someone who actually knows her?" She waited.

"Six?" I guessed.

"Four!!"

"You actually found someone who knows her?"

"Not *know* knows. But someone who's met her."

"Who?"

She wasn't going to let go of her information that easily. "I figured Willow had to be an actress. You know, looking like she does and all? So I looked her up. Have you seen her website? It's, like, so lame!"

"I've seen it. It's, like, so lame," I agreed.

"So I asked my friend Annalise if she knew her because she's in plays and stuff. Annalise had never heard of Willow, but she asked her mother because she used to live in California."

"What does living in California have to do with it?" I wasn't keeping up.

She gave me a "duh" look. "Willow's website says she's a California actress."

California is a big state. That seemed like a pretty random way to go about things, but I kept quiet, just nodded.

"Can you condense a little, honey?" Dan asked. "Speed it up some?"

Cassie sighed but did speed up a bit. "Annalise's mother doesn't know anyone in California anymore because she's been gone, like, 20 years or something. So Annalise asked her sister, who didn't know Willow, but her sister's friend Kylie knew the name. Kylie was in a Harper Springs Community Theater production a couple of years ago. *The Addams Family.* This girl who was in the show—Halo Felker—brought her cousin from California to a rehearsal. Her cousin was an actress, so she was giving her acting tips. And the cousin was ... Ta-da! Willow Wisteria. Kylie actually met her!"

"That's impressive." I wasn't sure I followed it all, but it was impressive. "But I don't see how this will help Sammie."

Cassie grinned. "Get this. Kylie and Halo Felker are in another community theater show right now. *Shrek.* And Willow is in town again to see Halo in it!"

"Really?" That *was* interesting.

Cassie was not finished. "So I have a friend who's in *Shrek.*" She looked at her dad. "Trevor." She blushed slightly but hurried on. "He's a *drummer*, not an actor." I guess she didn't want Trevor tainted with a *drama nerd* label. "Trevor and I, like, had coffee, and I told him my amazing four step discovery. And then he said he sort of met her, too! And that's why he's coming over—to tell you what he told me. Before he goes to the police station. Because I wanted you to hear it first!" She smiled. She actually smiled at me.

My mind was struggling a bit. Did she want me to hear whatever Trevor had to say because she wanted to impress me? Or for some other reason?

The doorbell rang. Soon Trevor was sitting at my table beside Cassie, drinking coffee. He wore a T-shirt with some band's name that I didn't recognize, stylishly ripped jeans, a baseball cap worn backwards, and what had to be expensive sneakers. He had that cocky kind of confidence girls are drawn to, and he was handsome, alarmingly so, if you buy into Sammie's theory that extremely good-looking men are terrible lovers. I stopped myself. But of course Cassie was too young for that kind of thing.

Or was she? I thought back to making out with Oscar Baldridge at a high school kegger. Are they still called keggers? I wondered. Do they even have them these days? If they do and Cassie went to one, would she make out with Trevor?

I looked at him. Of course she would.

Trevor brought me back to the present. It was his turn now. "So I was staying with my dad, and this girl named Halo Felker asked if I could pick her up before play rehearsal for *Shrek*. She needed a ride."

I'll bet she did, I thought, looking at Cassie, who frowned.

"It was her *and* some other girl in the show," he said to Cassie.

They were both probably hot for him was my thought, but I kept it to myself. Instead I asked, "Was Halo playing Fiona, the lead?" I asked for Cassie's sake. We needed a better sense of her competition.

Trevor laughed. "Nope. She can't sing. I saw her when her high school did some musical … I can't remember what it was … maybe *Hairspray?* Or *Bye, Bye Birdie?* One of those, like, 1950s deals. She started singing a song and, like, *croaked* it out."

"Like Lee Marvin in *Paint Your Wagon*!" I started singing "Wand'rin' Star" from the show, growling out the words in a mumbling voice the way Lee Marvin had, but without the choral background attempting to drown him out. Dan cracked up, but Trevor just looked puzzled. Cassie, to my surprise, smiled, her braces flashing. I knew she must have seen the movie, too. Geraldine had made Sammie and me watch it when we were kids, just for that scene. Maybe Dan had done the same with Cassie. "Google the scene on YouTube," I said. "It's really worth seeing. You know, for it's complete badness."

"Let's move on," said Dan. "Trevor?

"Okay, so when I got to Halo's house to pick her up,

she was, like, all upset because she had to leave for play practice. Willow had just got there, and they were still, like, unpacking stuff from the car. Halo made Willow come to the car so I could meet her. I guess she wanted to impress me or something." He imitated her. "'This is Willow Wisteria, my *actress* cousin from California.' She acted like Willow was a movie star or something." He paused. "She kind of looked like one. A movie star, I mean."

Cassie frowned and interrupted. "Tell them what day this was."

"It was Monday night."

"This past Monday night?" I asked. "You're sure?"

"Yep. I'd stayed with Dad in Juniper for the weekend. Normally, I'd be back with Mom in Harper Springs on Monday, but she's at a conference all week, so I drive back and forth from Dad's to school."

He had a car. I was pretty sure Dan wasn't pleased about that, but I focused on what Trevor was saying. "You couldn't be mixed up on the day?"

"Nope. It was the first night the whole band was rehearsing with the cast. A big night."

Cassie was triumphant. "So do you get it? Willow wasn't even in town the night that Donald was murdered. He was murdered Saturday, but she didn't even get here until Monday night. So much for not coming forward as a witness because she was embarrassed!"

"So, *so* embarrassed," I added.

She smiled. "So, *so* embarrassed. But really, the reason she didn't come forward was because she so, so wasn't there at all. She was just making up all that stuff up for publicity. For herself."

"We don't *know* that it was for publicity," said her father. She frowned at him, and he went on. "We're assuming it, though. Or she was making it up for some other reason."

I thought of mentioning that Harvey Klump might have had something to do with it, but I let it go and said, "This sure puts a hole in Willow's eye-witness account. Good job!" I reached out and gave her a high-five. Cassie grinned.

Dan turned to Trevor. "Thank you so much for coming forward. Now let's go talk to Detective Kendrick."

"Doesn't he need a parent with him when he's interviewed?" I asked.

"He's 18," Dan said. He didn't sound pleased about it. "We wanted you to hear this first."

"You know, because you're so worried and stuff," Cassie said.

I smiled. "Thanks, Cassie."

They went to their cars, but Dan came back quickly and grinned at me. "Just for the record, Mildred knows all this. We're not idiots at the police department."

"What? Then why go through this charade?"

"I was glad Cassie was taking an interest in my work. She is so *proud* and wanted to tell you about it. Mildred's going to play along."

"But mainly you wanted to get a look at Trevor, right?"

"Right."

After a couple of hours of clean-up at school, I was finished for the summer. I stopped off at Mom's house on the way home to help her sand a dresser she was going to paint.

Afterward, as I stood at her kitchen counter finishing a glass of iced tea, she took out a business card and handed it to me.

Nicole Pettigrew, LPC

Mom pinned me with one of her "Don't even think of messing with me" looks and said, "You promised."

I wanted to cry. "I know."

"I haven't mentioned it again for months, hoping you were going to follow through. School's out. It's time."

"I will, Mom. I will." I put my empty glass by the sink.

"Ella, I've heard great things about this doctor. You can do this."

"I'll call," I said. "Really, I'll call."

And I did *mean* to call. Several months before, after I'd passed out during a different murder investigation, I had promised my mother and Baba that I would make an appointment with a therapist to deal with my problem—an irrational fear of needles. My *trypanophobia* had worsened over the years, and even the thought of a needle was sometimes enough to make me faint. My mother, a nurse, said that my fear was more of my *vasovagel syncope reaction* to the needle, rather than the needle itself. I just knew that needles made me sweat, feel nauseated, and fear that a panic attack was coming on. And most of the time, one did.

The problem with therapy was that I had read about the *systematic desensitization* I'd be asked to do. The therapist would guide me to think about needles and then imagine them in more and more intimate circumstances, increasing exposure gradually in my imagination. Then I'd graduate to seeing and touching the real deal. I was terrified that by the end there would be a test—like actually getting a flu shot with a hypodermic needle.

Just the thought of going through the therapy terrified me in a way that I knew no one would understand. So I put off calling again. I *would* do it. Sometime. Just not now.

CHAPTER FIFTEEN

Dan had promised me that Mildred was going to make an announcement about Willow Wisteria the next morning, so I tuned in to the local radio station and listened while I fed Fluffles. Sure enough, an announcer said, "There is new development in the murder of Donald Sanders. We are going, live, to a press conference with Mildred Kendrick, lead detective in the investigation."

I heard Mildred's voice:

I would like to make three announcements concerning the murder of Donald Sanders. First, the supposed eye-witness account of someone striking Donald Sanders and dragging his body into Russo Dance studio is false. The supposed witness was not even in town the night of the murder, and her widely circulated account has no basis at all in fact. None. The police department is considering charges.

Second, the autopsy report on Donald Sanders has revealed further information. First, Mr. Sanders received one very minor blow and cut to one side of his head the evening of the murder, but that blow was not, as some false media reports have indicated, a blow from a tap dancing shoe. Instead, we have determined that he was struck in the Juniper Museum by a musical instrument on display there—a double-pipe Taiwanese nose flute. However—and this is important—his death did not result from that minor blow.

It resulted from cardiac arrhythmia and seizure, due to the ingestion of a toxic amount of caffeine powder.

Caffeine occurs in coffee, of course. But it is also an ingredient in dietary supplements like No-Doz. Only qualified commercial and scientific establishments can legally purchase caffeine in its pure form, which is quite powerful. According to the Food and Drug Administration, one teaspoon of powder packs the same amount as 28 cups of coffee. One tablespoon can be lethal. Autopsy results indicate that Mr. Sanders ingested a toxic amount of caffeine, causing his death.

I would like to stress that official information about this case comes always from the police department and not from blogs or social media, whether local, state, or national. Thank you.

Fluffles meowed with the urgency I had come to expect if I took the can of Fancy Feast out of the refrigerator and did not immediately put some in her dish. Taking pity on her, I scooped her teaspoon of Fancy Feast on top of her dry food and set it down. Then I sat down with my coffee. Donald had been killed by *caffeine?*

He did drink a lot of coffee, I remembered. Could the poisoning have been accidental? I opened the calculator on my phone and did quick calculations. If one teaspoon packs the same punch as 28 cups of coffee, the lethal dose in a tablespoon would be three times that, as a tablespoon is the equivalent of three teaspoons. So was someone supposed to have given him 84 cups of coffee? That was ridiculous, of course.

I googled *caffeine poisoning.* According to a 2018 study

of scientific journal articles, there had been 92 deaths from caffeine poisoning over the years. I read about a 19-year-old young man in Connecticut who died after ingesting two dozen NoDoz capsules. A 26 year-old woman from the UK committed suicide by ingesting 50-100 pills that contained caffeine. A 28-year-old man in Australia drank seven or eight cans of an unnamed energy drink and later collapsed, suffering a fatal cardiac arrest.

I read on. Deaths are most likely to come from dietary supplements or caffeine tablets, not coffee, and they are extremely rare. Still, there had been enough cases of caffeine poisoning that in 2018 the FDA banned some forms of caffeine, mostly liquids and powders containing pure and highly concentrated form of caffeine.

It was clear that caffeine is nothing to fool with, especially in pure powder form. Where would a person get it? I went to Amazon.com and searched for caffeine supplements. I found a lot of supplements, but none with more than 200 milligrams of caffeine. I'd read that a lethal dose is 10 grams—or about 10,000 milligrams. These pills would not be lethal unless you chewed about 50 of them.

I googled "caffeine powder for sale" and found sites with this warning: *Pure caffeine powder sales are limited to qualified commercial, scientific and business buyers only.* What makes a buyer qualified? I tried placing a container of powder in my shopping cart, but a message said I needed to create an account first. How hard would be to create a fake account for a fake business?

I wanted to try it, but common sense told me it wouldn't be a good idea right now to go on record anywhere as ordering caffeine powder.

With the announcement that caffeine had killed Donald, the paparazzi multiplied, crowding Juniper's downtown once again. Sammie was going stir-crazy. She wanted to be able to take Izzie-Bee to the grocery store, take a walk, do *anything* without being surrounded by reporters and photographers.

"I need to get out of here," she said.

I agreed that she needed to get away. But how? Where?

Two hours later I had a plan—an escape to the mountains for Sammie, Isabelle, and me. Sam's parents had a vacation home in a remote area near Estes Park, and they agreed to let us borrow it. Sam had taken us to there once for a long weekend in February. The road was impassable in winter, so we had to ski in, pulling sleds with supplies. But at this time of year, we could drive in. If we played our cards right, no one would be able to find us or bother us there. It was just what we needed.

Unfortunately, Sammie mentioned our plan to her step-father, Jake, and he suggested that we take Geraldine along. "He sounded kind of desperate," Sammie told me. "He said that Mom really, *really* needs to chill out for a while and forget about Harvey Klump. So I said yes."

When I told Dan I'd be gone for a few days, he sounded a little too happy about it. I suspected he liked the thought of me being far away from the murder investigation. Little did he know that one of my projects in the mountains was to do some serious Internet sleuthing and probably make a number of murder-related phone calls. I remembered that the place had Wi-Fi.

"Maybe you could take Cassie, too?" he asked.

That was the last thing I wanted, but I didn't say so. I hesitated.

"She's out of school now," he said. "Her mom's working. I'm working. She's not old enough to work. That kid Trevor is always hanging around. If she was with you for several days, I could relax a little."

I couldn't resist. "Maybe it would help if she developed a real interest in something that could occupy a lot of her time—maybe pole dancing?"

He didn't respond, so I moved on. "Are you sure you want her so far from home? No other kids around? She'll hate the idea."

"Maybe, but I love it. And it could be a great way for the two of you to get to know each other better."

What else could I say? I caved. "Of course I'll invite her."

I decided to invite Baba along, too. Maybe she and Geraldine could help me deal with Cassie. They had a lot more experience than I did with teenagers. So did Mom, but I knew she had to work.

Baba, however, was a little reluctant to leave Lester. "He's having issues with plantar fasciitis," she said. "I help him stay positive."

"Can't he try a kale foot rub or something?"

"Not funny. And you just want me so I can cook."

I hadn't thought of that. "Good idea. Are you volunteering?"

She smiled.

"Really, Baba. You can get to know Cassie and maybe give me tips for getting along with her. And *Isabelle* will be there."

Oh, Isabelle! Her face took on that dreamy, mystical look it always does when I mention the baby. She sighed. "Someday I hope to hold a little baby of *yours.*" Then the dreamy look was replaced with one of perceptiveness. "How are things with Detective Dan?"

"Good, Baba." *Good* if I ignored the unwelcome presence of a teenage girl in our relationship. *Good* if I ignored the fact that I wanted to share the thrill of bringing a new life into the world someday with someone who had not already experienced it all before. "So will you come?"

"I'll come, sweetheart. Of course I'll come."

Geraldine, to my surprise, agreed quite readily. She needed quiet, she said, time to strategize without reporters hounding her. "Harvey Klump is going *down.*" She did have a practical question, though: "How are we going to get away without reporters following us? They are everywhere again."

"I'm working on it," I said. I had a plan in mind.

Before I told anyone the rest of my plan, I had a stop to make. Even though Dan said they couldn't prove it, I was pretty sure that Evelyn's brother-in-law was the source of leaks in the police department. I stopped by school, where Evelyn was still working. Secretaries, principals, and librarians in the district work a couple of weeks longer than teachers.

"Hi, Evelyn," I said. "I forgot to grab some papers I need from my file cabinet. How are things going without all of us running around and bugging you?"

"You don't bug me," she said, her tone prim. "I do my work happily."

"Of course you do," I smiled. "It's good you'll have time to relax after all this end of school work is done."

I checked my mailbox and then turned, casually tossing out my lie. "I know I'm going to enjoy relaxing. My best friend and I are escaping to Santa Barbara this weekend. I can't wait! A bit of sunshine and lying on the beach will do us both some good. Have a great summer, Evelyn!"

Next I needed to stop at Mom's. Even though she wouldn't be going on the retreat, I needed her help.

I was reluctant to talk to her again before I'd made an appointment with the therapist, but to her credit, she didn't mention the therapist again. She listened to my plan and agreed to help, then said. "But if you do manage to get out of town without being followed, do you really think you'll manage to relax with this particular set of people in one place?" I could hear the skepticism in her voice.

I followed her into the kitchen, telling her how Dan had come up with the idea of inviting Cassie, not me.

"You could have said no." Mom poured herself a cup of cold coffee and warmed it in the microwave.

"She's his daughter. I couldn't say she drives me crazy. I'm hoping Geraldine and Baba can help deal with her. They're used to teenagers." I poured myself some water using the tap in the refrigerator door. As usual, a trickle of water dripped down the front of the refrigerator into a small puddle. I grabbed a paper towel. "The girl is impossible. Really."

"She's a teenager. They're all impossible."

We took our drinks into the living room, and Mom sank into the couch. She leaned back with her "resigned to listening to something I don't really want to hear" look on her face.

"How am I going to survive four days with her?" I asked. "She barely talks to me. Or she's sarcastic."

"Oh no, not *sarcastic,*" Mom said. Sarcastically.

"I'm worried that this is going to be a deal breaker with Dan. Like, what if we lived together … Or, you know …" I didn't want to say it.

"Got married?"

"Not that we're talking about it."

"But you're thinking about it."

"Maybe. But I can't see a life of having her around so much. I never imagined a *teenager* in my future, unless it was my own teenager."

"Oh, just stop it, Ella." Mom had kicked off her sneakers and put her feet up on the coffee table. She still wore her hospital scrubs, which I thought, not for the first time, couldn't possibly be any uglier. "You think I don't know about impossible teenagers? You think I sometimes didn't wish I'd never even met you and your brothers, let alone given birth to you?"

"That's a little harsh. But still, we were *your* teenagers."

"Sammie wasn't. And she was around here half the time, too. Making out with Jeremy Wilson in the basement. Smoking joints behind the garage."

I didn't think she'd known about the joints.

She wasn't finished. "Rolling her eyes at Jell-O with bananas for dessert and telling me how *Geraldine* made homemade pies and cookies. And I wanted to tell her *Geraldine* didn't have a full-time job, and she could eat our damn Jell-O with bananas or go home." Mom took a sip and continued. She was on a roll. "And I *wanted* to tell her to scrape all that makeup off her face and find someone better than Jeremy Wilson and stop pretending she hadn't been drinking when she could barely stand up and I knew you were suddenly having a sleepover because she knew Geraldine would kill her if she went home. And sometimes when you were practicing for ballet downstairs, I'd hear her telling you how to do things better, raise your head more, turn your leg *this* way, blah, blah, blah, like *she* was the teacher, and I wanted to tell her to leave you alone, that she wasn't the boss of you, and you were doing just fine."

"She *was* a better dancer than me, Mom."

"That's not the point."

This was taking a different turn than I expected. I leaned back and put my own "resigned to listening to something I don't really want to hear" face on.

"And then there were your brothers driving off to Lord only knows where, no matter what they told me. Alex getting arrested for driving while impaired when—surprise— he didn't even have a driver's license. *That* was fun."

I decided not to interrupt. She's a little scary when she goes on a rant. "And Christopher? Jesus. All those years of him wearing black and not talking except in grunts and spending most of his time in his room at the computer with headphones on."

Then I had no choice but to interrupt. She could go on for half an hour about Christopher. "But *I* was pretty easy. At least you had that."

"Oh, 'Miss I Hate This Family?' The girl who would sneak out through the laundry room in the middle of the night to go God only knows where?"

"It was just the once." Actually, it wasn't. But it was just the once that she had caught me.

"Do you know I started getting a knot in my stomach every time I saw you wear a baggy sweatshirt? I'd try to figure out if you were gaining weight and could be pregnant."

"Mom!"

"Well, you weren't sneaking out the laundry room door to go play dominoes."

"Okay, well." I didn't want to dwell on this. "So I wasn't perfect."

"Your dad and I learned to cope by reminding ourselves that the right stuff was there. Somewhere. Our motto was, 'They're going to be fine, *if*—and it was a big if—*if* we can keep from strangling them before they grow up.'"

"We weren't that bad, really."

She raised her eyebrows.

Maybe this wasn't the day to vent. I went on. "Okay, teenagers are difficult. I get that. And I guess it's normal for Cassie to be difficult." I hesitated. "But the truth is, I just don't *like* Cassie very much."

"Oh, for heavens' sake, stop it! You think Cassie doesn't *feel* that? Where's the smart young woman I know who's told me how she handles difficult students?"

"My kids are five, Mom. Cassie is 15."

"And so are teenagers, really. Deep down. Heck, deep down we're *all* five." She set her cup down and grabbed a pillow and put it under her feet on the table. "So tell me again what you do when you have a little kid who is so awful in class that you find you're starting to hate him."

Man, I hadn't asked for this. Her "resigned to listening to something I don't really want to hear" look changed to her "Do it now or else" look, so I answered. "I find a way not to hate them because if you don't like a child, they know it. They just *know.* And you can't fake it and just pretend to like them. You have to find a way to *actually* like them."

"And how do you do that?" She wasn't giving up. She waited, looking at me over the top of her glasses. I noticed a tiny gold safety pin holding one arm onto the main frame.

"You need to take those glasses in. They'll put a screw in for free."

"Don't change the subject. How do you find a way to actually like them?"

"Okay." I thought carefully about my words before speaking. "You try to look at them through their mother's eyes. You try to see the baby the mother rocked in her arms, the child she now kisses good night."

"Good. And?"

"And you try to find things to like about them by looking outside the classroom. Like one time I heard this kid Raylen talking about this awful horror flick his dad had taken him to see. So I asked him about it and listened while he told me how cool it was. In great detail. And I saw a different side of the kid. I mean, I couldn't imagine what his dad was thinking taking a five-year-old to that movie, but I did relate to Raylen's enthusiasm. I liked the way he got all bubbly and excited."

"And what about that kid who screamed when anyone touched him?"

"I thought about his mother. How hard it must be to love him and not be able to take him in her arms. And I thought about how hard it must be for *him* to be that way."

"And what happens when you do this kind of thing?"

"I'm able to stop myself from not liking a kid. "

"Always?"

"So far."

"Except for Cassie."

"But she's …"

"Treat her like a five-year-old. You're a good teacher. Apply some of what you know as a teacher."

I thought about it. She had a point. But I *had* tried. I'd asked her about school and other things, and she always cut me off.

"Dan's a keeper, honey." Mom said.

"But he comes with baggage."

"Everyone comes with baggage. You take the baggage with the good stuff and learn to live with it. Think of Cassie as an opportunity, not baggage."

I was quiet for a while. "You know, I never knew that Sammie bothered you so much."

"That's because I looked at her through Geraldine's eyes. And at the same time that she annoyed the hell out of me, I loved her."

"Geraldine sometimes wanted to kill her, too."

"I know. But we didn't kill her, and she turned out fine, just like you did. And Alex did. And Christopher … Well, the jury's still out on Christopher." She smiled. "It's hard to tell."

Christopher still pretty much lives with his headphones on, sitting at a computer or playing video games. He's not exactly gregarious.

"Christopher is just Christopher," she added. "Underneath, he's still the little boy who loved 'Elvira.'"

"Elvira." Our grandfather had played the song once for Christopher when he was little, and Christopher had fallen in love. For years, he threw a fit if we didn't want to listen to "Elvira" when we got in the car. The whole family learned to hate the song and, by extension, anything to do with the Oak Ridge Boys. Even today, when Christopher is coaxed into coming to a family dinner, he will start humming "Elvira" as we carry the dishes into the kitchen, just to drive us crazy.

CHAPTER SIXTEEN

I mulled over what Mom has said on the way home. My mulling had to be brief, though, as I still needed to swing by Derek's apartment to enlist his help.

"Look at this," he said when I came in. He showed me the headline on his phone from an entertainment website: *Birth certificate reveals Donald Sanders as father of Sammie Russo's baby.*

"Holy cow," I said. "Sammie's going to go off the deep end now. How did they get access to the birth certificate?"

"Who knows? Does it really matter? The damage is done."

"Even more reason for Sammie to get out of town." I told him my plan.

"I'm in," he said. "What do you think about *buff jogger* as a look for this encounter?"

"What would you do about the buff part?"

He ignored me. "Where were you all day? I came over to tell you about some developments. I called, too."

I looked at my phone. I'd missed two calls and a text. Oops. I'd put the phone on mute earlier when I was talking to Mom. She hates cell phone interruptions.

"I found out something interesting while I was eavesdropping at work," he said.

"So no one has identified you as Sammie's brother yet?"

"If they have, it hasn't made a difference. Anyway, this is about staff, not what reporters said. One of the waitresses was talking last night about how she saw Donald at Whitney's the night of the murder."

"Really? And you didn't?"

"I saw him come in but didn't pay any attention. It was really busy that night, and Clay was there." Clay was the high school chemistry teacher he was dating.

"Got it." I sang, "And I only have eyes for you…"

"Yeah, yeah. So I was a little focused. But I guess the waitress, Nadia, was pretty focused on Donald's table."

"On Donald, you mean."

"Most likely."

"Who was with him? I can't see Donald sitting alone for long."

"Nadia said it was three girls from Cheyenne."

"Girls or women?"

"Okay, young women. Just for you, I quizzed Nadia a little. The girls—young women—had an early flight to New Zealand the next day, so they were on their way to DIA. They were planning to hang out at the airport all night and then sleep on the plane."

I knew exactly where this was going. "I assume they were cute?"

"Nadia seemed jealous, so I'd guess so."

"Let me guess. Donald suggested they go dancing."

He nodded.

"And they decided—at his suggestion—to meet him at the Yellow Rose. He probably thought that if they were from Cheyenne, they'd like country-western dancing. Am I right?"

"You're right."

I smiled. My excellent instincts again.

Derek continued. "Nadia heard them agree to meet him later, and after he left they got all giggly and excited, accordion to her."

"Hmmm. I wonder how long they planned to be in New Zealand."

Derek shrugged and got up. "Don't know, but I have to go to work. Good luck tracking down three unknown females who might or might not still be in New Zealand and who might or might not know something relevant."

I followed him out and drove to Otto and Moriko's house. I had called a special meeting of the Streusals to enlist their help, and Moriko had invited the whole band to come early for krautburgers, or as Otto calls them, *bierock*. Though Moriko is Japanese-American, she has learned to cook all of Otto's favorite German dishes.

"So what are we going to do about you?" Otto asked as we sat down. "First the accordion murder. Now a tap dance murder. What's next? A polka murder? A trumpet murder?"

"I didn't have anything to do with the murder."

"Of course you didn't," said Moriko. "But who did?"

I started to take a bite out of my krautburger, then put it back on my plate. "I really don't know. All I know is that Donald was at the museum reception for a while, and then he turned up in Sammie's studio at around 8:40. Dead."

"You and Derek didn't get sick of going out dancing with him and knock him off?" Alan asked. The Streusals had heard me complaining often enough about my occasional evenings with Sammie and Donald.

"We did not."

"You must have a theory then."

"I'm working on one."

"Harvey Klump has had some pretty interesting accusations in his blog," Carl said.

I looked around the room at all the men, one at a time, my eyes daring them to say anything. "I did not pose nude with a glockenspiel. Or a Sousaphone."

"We never believed it for a second," Moriko said. The men all nodded in agreement, but I caught Otto trying to conceal just a hint of a smile on his face.

"So whodunit? However they dunit? Do you have suspects?" Otto asked.

"Maybe the receptionist at the museum. Maybe a museum volunteer. Maybe a jealous boyfriend or husband. Maybe an unknown woman, undoubtedly good-looking, that Donald might have met. It could be anyone. Just not Sammie Russo."

Carl said, "If you're looking at good-looking women for the murder, maybe we can help. We all had dinner downtown before the museum reception." He looked around. "Did any of you see any good-looking women that night? Good looking women who might be murderers?" He helped himself to more potato salad, and Moriko moved the bowl away from him. She wasn't his wife, but she had taken it upon herself to look out for him. Carl really did eat too much.

"Joan Mascari's daughter was eating at Whitney's. She's a looker," said Otto.

"Joan Mascari," Carl mused. He looked at Otto. "Isn't she a Whalen now? Married Art Whalen?" He looked around at the guys. Otto nodded. Like Carl and Henry, he had grown up in Juniper.

I decided to focus on my food. I knew they would be taking a circuitous ramble through their many Juniper connections.

Henry started laughing. "Remember the scandal? Mrs. Mascari was mortified about the Blessed Virgin's bouquet at Joan and Art's wedding."

"Virgin bouquet?" Moriko said, a baffled look on her face.

I'd heard the story before and smiled.

"You know how the bride in a Catholic wedding needs two bouquets?" Henry asked. "Or at least she used to."

"No," said Moriko. "I was raised Presbyterian."

"I'm no longer Catholic, but in my day, brides placed a bouquet on the Blessed Virgin's altar." He looked at me. I shrugged my shoulders. I didn't know if that was still the case. He continued. "Sex before marriage was a mortal sin on your soul, of course. So the bouquet signified that the bride was a virgin."

"Only Joan didn't present a bouquet," Moriko guessed.

"She did not. She was four months pregnant." He smiled. "I guess no amount of confessing could turn her into a virgin."

"This stuff is so weird," Moriko said. "It's a wonder you turned out halfway normal. Halfway."

"Ella is Catholic, too," he said.

"Just sort of," I said. "Mom and Dad sent us to Catholic school because they thought discipline would be good for us." I grabbed another krautburger. "Oh, and because of the grammar. There was one really old nun teaching English at Holy Name, and Mom had her when ..."

Carl set down his fork. "Sister Dalmatia was still there when you were???"

I nodded."You knew her?"

"Hoo-boy. She was a stickler."

"I know! She was so tough I thought I'd lose my mind sometimes. She must have been about a hundred years old."

Allan was looking up at the ceiling, doing the math in his head. He had been an engineer before retirement. "More likely in her late seventies, early eighties. Say she was 20 when Carl was 14, then ..."

"Doesn't matter. She was really old to still be teaching," Moriko said. "So why are you only sort of a Catholic, Ella?" She is always fascinated by stories of growing up Catholic.

"Because Mom is only sort of Catholic. She likes the ritual, the music, the good works that some of the organizations and committees do. But she told me she'd had it when she was a teenager and confessed to a priest that she was having impure thoughts. He asked her, "What thoughts, exactly?"

"Creepy!" said Moriko.

"Very creepy. There were always rumors about priests and little boys. Well, little girls, too. Mom told us we were never to confess to a priest or be alone with one. That was a little hard to pull off sometimes," I remembered.

"How did she explain such a thing to a kid?"

"Dad helped. He told us that priests were only men. Some were good, some were not. Some were good with bad parts, and some were bad with good parts, just like people. And you know Sammie's mom, the Pickle Queen?" They nodded. Everyone knew the Pickle Queen. "She was more direct. She told all of us—her kids and my brothers and me—that if we ever found ourselves in a situation where a priest wanted us to be alone with him, we were to, and I quote, 'Run like hell.'"

"Good advice. Now let's get back to Joan Mascari, I mean Whalen." Allan said. He always stuck to the subject better than the rest of us. "Her daughter was at the bar at Whitney's. No date. She's a looker. Maybe she met Donald and got involved with him."

This was beyond grasping at straws, but I let them go on. A good detective pays attention, open to all ideas, no matter how absurd.

"And she's into acting stuff. Colleen, I think is her name. I saw her in *Brigadoon*."

"What does acting have to do with being involved with Donald?" I asked.

"Acting—modeling. Kind of similar areas. Maybe she and Donald knew each other."

"A Juniper actress. A New York City model. Oh, sure, they probably ran in the same circles," I said.

"It could happen," he said. "Keep an open mind."

"I'll poke around, see what I can find out about her," said Moriko. "Just in case." Moriko is a docent at the Juniper Theater. A real docent, with training. A *decent* docent, too.

"Great. Anyone see any other good-looking women downtown?"

"That woman who volunteers everywhere since she moved to town," Moriko said. "Affinity Knowles. She collects tickets at the theater sometimes, when she gets there on time." She exhaled in a puff of disgust. "I saw her walking into Starbucks. If she wants to embrace this town like she says, she ought to support local business. Mocha Bean—not Starbucks."

"I went to school with Affinity's grandmother," said Otto. "And Affinity's got an aunt who lives in town. Can't think of her name right now."

"Ruth," I said. "We call her Aunt Ruth. She's in my tap dance class with Affinity." Oh, small town connections. They're everywhere. "I don't think this avenue is going to be productive. We can't possibly know all the good-looking women who were downtown Saturday night."

"I'm pretty observant," said Carl.

"Maybe so, but just picking out random women …"

"Random good-*looking* women.*"*

"Okay," I said. "We need something *more*. Something to connect them to the case." I pushed my plate back a little. "Enough. This whole thing is making my brain hurt. Besides, I need to ask your help on something."

"First, dessert," said Carl, his mind on food again.

"Deal," said Moriko, and she passed a plate of brownies.

Henry watched Carl take three brownies. "You're not going to fit into your damn lederhosen," he said. "Which is not a bad thing."

Carl insists on wearing lederhosen when we perform. "I have an extra pair."

"Wonderful. I guess we'll always be five normal guys, a babe, and an old fart wearing leather shorts."

I decided to interrupt. "I have a hypothetical question. Let's say that nobody wore lederhosen and you all wore a jacket and tie when we performed. If you had a choice between a plain red tie and a red sequined tie that sparkled, which would you choose?"

"The sparkle," they answered, almost all at once.

"Really?" I was a bit surprised.

"That's because you said *when you're performing*," Moriko said. "They wouldn't choose sequins if they were going to a funeral."

"No," said Otto. "But I'd *want* to."

"Society would pressure me to be more modest," said Henry. "Why do you ask?"

"I've just been wondering if it's a female thing or if it applies to men, too. Love of sparkle, I mean."

"Hoo-boy," said Carl, the bass player. "Her feminist side is coming out."

"It's never been hidden."

"Fair enough. But I don't get why 'sparkle' is relevant."

"Girls in my class are obsessed with wearing sparkling Elsa dresses from the *Frozen* movies. And Baba put sequins on her bowling shirt to jazz it up. So I just wonder if guys ever want sparkle, too." I thought of mentioning Donald's red sparkled bow tie but remembered, just in time, that I wasn't supposed to share that information.

"Sure they want it," Moriko said. She looked at her husband. "Who spent Saturday waxing his little Corvette until it sparkled?"

"So what does this have to do with anything?" Otto asked.

"Nothing at all. I just wonder about things sometimes."

Carl gave an exaggerated sigh. "Lord, we know."

"Forget sparkle for now," said Moriko. "You called us here for a reason, and we need to get to it. What is it you need help with?"

I told them about the ladies' retreat and the problem getting away without being followed. Reporters were bound to follow if they saw Sammie leaving with a baby carrier and all the baby paraphernalia required. "So I think what we need to do is stage a major distraction in the alley, one that is loud enough to make any stray reporters out front come to the alley to see what is going on. When they do, Sammie will slip out the front with Isabelle, where her brother Derek will have parked his car, complete with baby seat and baby supplies from Geraldine's house loaded up." Moriko gave me a questioning look, so I added, "Geraldine wants to be prepared for when she gets to babysit at her house, so she has bought *everything*. The house looks like a nursery. Anyway, Derek will put the car there after he gets off work at 2:00 a.m., so there should be a space right out front. His boyfriend Clay will take him home."

"Why not have Sammie and the baby slip out then, too? At 2:00 a.m.?" Allan, the engineer, asked.

I frowned. "Good question. I probably should have thought of that ... Maybe we should go with that idea."

Moriko shook her head. "You can't send a new mom out at 2:00 a.m. with her baby and then have her drive to Estes Park. She doesn't get enough sleep as it is."

"All right, all right," Allan agreed. "So let's get to the good part. We create a distraction, and I'll bet I know what it will be." He smiled.

I smiled back. "Yes, a little polka concert. With all those paparazzi around, we might even wind up on TV."

"I'm in," said Otto. The others agreed.

"But how are we going to do this?" Allan asked, ever the practical one. "What's our motivation?"

"We'll play doddering old fools," said Henry.

"We *are* doddering old fools," said Carl.

"We'll play doddering old fools who have no idea how to change a flat tire. We'll be on our way to a gig when we'll discover the flat tire, right at the entrance to the alley."

"I don't want you to ruin anyone's tire," I said, thinking they'd have to slice into one.

"We'll just let the air out a block away," Henry said. "Then, when we discover the flat, we'll have to unload all our gear in the alley in order to get to the jack."

"Allan can drive over with all his drums and double-park in front of the alley entrance to Sammie's apartment, where you will be waiting," Otto said. "When the doddering guys discover they have no jack, Allan will have to unload all his drum stuff, so he can get to *his* jack."

I was liking this. "Then Moriko can come down the alley to see what's going on, and she'll see our sign, which I will have removed from the car while Allan was unloading the drums." Our sign said *The Streusals—A Polka Band with Punch*! "Moriko can pretend to be a polka fan and say, 'How about a polka?'"

"I *am* a polka fan," Moriko said.

"And then Derek will happen by and offer to change the tire if we play a song. So we will. And any reporters out in front of Second Chance will hear us and come around to the alley see what's going on, right?"

"Right!" said Leroy, finally speaking up. "And Sammie can escape while everyone's looking at us."

"And filming us, I hope," added Otto. "I'll bet we make it on Channel Nine News!"

And that is, more or less, exactly how it happened. The reporters at first snickered at the doddering guys, confirming to me that kindness is not a quality required for their jobs. They snickered some more as we unloaded a trumpet, bass, clarinet, saxophone, accordion, music stands, and all the many sections of a drum kit all over the alley.

But when Moriko said, "How about a polka?" they stopped snickering and started to pay attention, sensing a visual moment.

Derek arrived at the scene, opting for a punk rocker rather than buff jogger look. It involved a lot of leather, chains and fake tattoos. He said, "Hey, I'll change the tire if you guys will play for us."

And so we did. While I played the accordion, the guys played and sang one of our original polkas:

Some say we're geezers
So out of touch.
Just a bunch of old farts
Who don't know much.
Polkas may seem ancient,
Relics of the past.
But add a little beatbox,
And polkas kick ass!

Then I pulled out the cheap karaoke microphone Leroy had bought at WalMart and held it close to my mouth. Allan froze his drumsticks in mid-air, and I put my mouth near the microphone and provided all the percussive sound we needed while the others continued playing. Beatboxing kind of baffles the older people in most of our audiences—and let's face it, they are usually older people—but this crowd seemed to get a kick out of it.

We ended the number to wild applause. After we took a bow, someone yelled, "Now play the 'Beer Barrel Polka!'"

Someone *always* says, "Play the 'Beer Barrel Polka.'"

We played the "Beer Barrel Polka."

Then we loaded all our instruments and equipment back into the vehicles and carefully edged through the crowd. By then, I'd received a thumbs up emoji from Mom in front of Second Chance. She'd been the lookout out front, making sure any likely witnesses were at the polka concert before Sammie slipped out and drove away with Isabelle.

After we loaded his van again, Allan drove me to Baba's house via a wandering route through the suburbs, just in case anyone followed us. He dropped me off, and I hurried into the house, where Dan, Cassie, Sammie, Isabelle, and Baba waited.

"I think it worked!" I said. Sammie smiled and gave me a high five.

Cassie sat, sullen, beside her backpack. She had pitched a fit about going along, but something—I wasn't sure what—had made her stop complaining, eventually. She still didn't look happy, though.

"Woo-hoo!" said Baba from the kitchen, where she and Geraldine were packing coolers.

"Let's get out of here quickly," I said. "I don't think anyone knows Baba's connection to me, but you never know. Reporters might show up." Geraldine would drive Derek's car with the baby equipment and Sammie. I would drive

Dan's car with Baba and Cassie. We definitely didn't want anyone to recognize the vehicles we usually drove.

Dan kissed Cassie and me goodbye, and I said, "Let's get this show on the road!"

CHAPTER SEVENTEEN

The drive to Estes Park was long—or, rather, felt long. Baba was strangely quiet and turned in her seat several times to look behind us. "Are you looking for something?" I asked.

"No, no," she said. "Just admiring the view."

"The view ahead of us is pretty nice, too," I pointed out.

Cassie sat in the back seat, ear-buds in her ears, eyes on her phone. The only time she looked up was when we joined other cars stopped at the side of the road to admire some big-horn sheep munching on grass, twigs, leaves, and probably salt from winter road treatment. When they'd had enough of being watched, the sheep nimbly danced up the rocks to a higher perch where it seemed they were posing just for us. Even Cassie watched that.

We crawled through Estes Park, gateway to Rocky Mountain National Park. Tourist season had begun, and cars inched through the town. It was slow going, but eventually the Google Maps voice told me to turn and led us up a winding road for many miles, finally guiding us onto an unpaved road. Peeping through the aspen and spruce ahead, we could see Sam's family's beautiful mountain lodge. We were there, paparazzi-free, for four days.

I relaxed. This was just what we all needed—a little retreat. We could hike, read, cook, relax, try to solve a murder, and—I looked over at Cassie—look at our cell phones.

It would be healing.

It would be relaxing.

It would be fun.

It was not. Right away there was tension between Geraldine and Sammie. She thought that swaddling Isabelle for a nap was barbaric. "She can't move her arms. She must feel claustrophobic."

"Just because *you* are claustrophobic, don't assume Isabelle is," Sammie said. "Swaddling makes her feel safe."

Geraldine followed Sammie to the Pack 'N Play. "At least put the blanket over her. A draft could give her a cold."

"It won't. Research shows that being cold does not give anyone a cold. It's a myth."

"I don't care if you think it's a myth. That baby ..."

Baba interrupted. "Geraldine, can you help me in the kitchen? We need to get the chili going."

"I can help," I said.

"I want Geraldine." Her tone told us there was to be no arguing with her.

Interesting. Baba can be a little bossy.

I followed them into the kitchen and pulled up a stool at the kitchen island.

Baba handed Geraldine an onion and said, "Chop, please."

Even more interesting. People don't give Geraldine orders. Geraldine *gives* them. She's the Pickle Queen, after all. I definitely wanted to see how this played out.

Geraldine shot Baba a suspicious look but started peeling the onion. "Why me?"

"You know why."

She didn't say anything.

"*I* don't know why," I said.

"Then listen. Geraldine, tell Ella about your mother-in-law," Baba said, plopping hamburger into a large pot.

"Ex-mother-in-law. And I'm nothing like her."

"Did I say you were?" Baba said, her face telling me she was pretending innocence. "Tell her."

"My ex-mother-in-law was Sylvia Russo. Italian. A real piece of work. And, oh, how she babied her 'Alfie.'"

I frowned. "Alfie?"

"My ex," she explained. "Sammie's dad. Al or Alfred to everyone else. Alfie to her."

"I remember Sylvia well," Baba said. "She was a woman of exacting standards."

Geraldine sniffed. I don't think it was because of the onion.

Baba continued. "I ran into her mostly when we brought food to the church for funerals. One time she gave us all suggestions for improving the presentation of the dishes we'd made."

"She made suggestions about everything," Geraldine said, whacking the onion in half. "I know what you are suggesting, but there is no parallel between how Sylvia treated me and how I treat Sammie."

Baba remained silent, breaking up hunks of hamburger in the pot with a wooden spoon.

Her silence egged Geraldine on. "For heavens' sake, one of Sylvia's suggestions was that I stop nursing at two months because I was spoiling the baby!" She chopped vigorously. "And when she bought the baby an outfit, she would complain when I washed the clothes before letting him wear them. She said I was *way* too fussy about cleanliness and chemicals and all that nonsense."

"Hmmmm," Baba murmured. "I hear you. She definitely thought she knew best."

Geraldine got it. "But this is different. I'm not a mother-in-law. I am Sammie's *mother*."

Baba said, "I know how you feel. Daughters can be slow learners. Ella, when your brother was born, your mom fussed way too much about stuff that wasn't important. And, believe me, I told her so. Moms do that. They don't want their children to go wrong."

Geraldine nodded. "And your help must have worked. Alex turned out just fine."

"No. I mean he turned out fine, but my help didn't work out. Pretty soon I noticed I was seeing my grandson less and less. Finally, my husband told me I needed to learn how to shut up." She opened a can of beans with the electric opener. "Brutal, but the best advice I ever got."

Geraldine started to say something, but then didn't. Maybe she was taking the "Learn to shut up" advice to heart.

"Let me have that onion," Baba said. She must have decided she had pushed enough and abruptly changed the subject. "Did you hear about my Virgin Mary?"

"I did," Geraldine smiled. "Did you ever have dinner at Mrs. Mascari's house? The Virgin sat in the corner of the dining room and peered at you while you were having your spaghetti and meatballs."

"Remember when Mrs. Mascari was president of Christian Mothers?" Baba asked. "I think you had joined by then."

"It was hell," Geraldine said. She turned to me. "Mrs.

Mascari gave a talk at every meeting about a different saint. She had a little traveling cosmetics case—one of those old-fashioned squarish ones—and she turned it on its side and put a doily on it. Then she sat a statuette of whatever saint she was talking about on top, so we could look at it while she spoke."

Baba laughed. "For inspiration, she said."

"And her rosary! My god, how I got sick of hearing about that rosary."

"It was blessed by the pope," Baba explained to me. She dumped beans and canned tomatoes in with the beef and onions.

They chattered on and on. They had both worked on church committees together, even though they are of different generations, and knew a story or two about nearly every Catholic in town. I sat listening and smiling at the stories.

After a bit, I noticed that Cassie had slipped in and was listening as well.

We left the chili to simmer, and Baba and I stepped outside to cool off after cleaning up the hot kitchen. I said, "You must have been pretty awful when Alex was born for Mom to shut you out like that."

Baba had filled a large watering can and was giving the roses next to the door a drink. "Oh, I was never awful at all. Nobody had to tell me to learn to shut up. I *knew*." She filled the can again with the nearby hose and left the can beside the door.

"So all that stuff you told Geraldine …?"

"She needed a story, so I gave her one."

I smiled.

"Sometimes people just need a story," Baba said and went back inside. I followed.

We found Sammie on the floor, changing cloth spread out, and Isabelle wiggling her naked legs. Geraldine silently handed Sammie a Huggies. Not a word about how cloth was better for the baby's skin. Not a word about landfills and diapers and damage to the environment. Maybe, just maybe, Geraldine was learning to shut up.

I was heading upstairs to my room when I heard her say, "So you're not using any diaper cream?"

There were limits to how much Geraldine could learn in one afternoon.

While we were enjoying our chili that evening, there was a knock at the door.

"I've got it," Baba said, winking at Cassie. "Coming!"

What was that wink all about? I wondered. Baba got up and strolled slowly, very slowly, to the door, a tea towel still draped over one shoulder. I followed and watched as she opened the door.

There stood the Redhead. She held up a cell phone and quickly took a picture.

How had she found us? We had been so careful. It didn't seem possible that she was standing there in front of us.

And then, out of the blue, a gush of water came from overhead, and the Redhead was drenched.

And then another gush.

She moved aside, sputtering and looking confused. I was confused, too.

Baba looked up at the window above, remaining calm. "Oh dear. Kids!" she said. She called upstairs. "Cassie, shame on you!" Then she took her tea towel and started mopping at the woman, who was uttering words I knew Baba hated. Baba kept mopping. "My goodness," she said. "I hope that lovely blouse is washable."

As she dried the woman's hands, Baba somehow managed to get a hold of the Redhead's cell phone. With an "Oopsy daisy," she dropped the phone into the plant watering can she had left by the front door.

The expletives became much worse.

Baba quickly picked up the watering can and clutched it to her chest. "There is no need for that sort of language."

The Redhead reached out. "My cell phone!"

Baba backed up. "It's right here. Newer phones like yours are supposed to be water resistant, but for how long, I wonder. Do you want to test that?"

"Get it out of there!" the Redhead cried, panicking.

Baba continued, unperturbed. "Here's the deal. I could take your cell phone out and put it in a bowl of rice. I hear that, with some time, that's supposed to fix a wet phone if there is damage. Or I could leave it where it is, in the water. Up to you. If you agree not to bother us for the next three days, at all, we'll keep the phone in rice and give it back in three days, hopefully as good as new. But if anyone at all bothers us, I'm afraid the phone will immediately go back in the water."

"You have no right!"

Baba shrugged.

The Redhead started toward Baba, then stopped. I was relieved to see that even she had her limits. She wasn't going to wrestle an 80-year-old woman. Instead she just yelled, "Take it out! Hurry!"

"Do you promise to stay away from here?"

"I promise, I promise. I won't bother you."

"Swear to God? Cross your heart and hope to die?"

"I swear!"

"And you won't tell anyone else where we are?"

"I won't!"

Baba held the watering can out to me, and I reached in and pulled out the phone.

The Redhead was shivering. Evenings can get cold in the mountains, and she was wet.

"You'd best get in your car now and leave," Baba said. "If you hurry, we'll forget about pressing charges. It's nice that those pictures I took from the kitchen window this afternoon turned out so well—the ones of you prying that window open and breaking into the garage."

The Redhead uttered a "Shit!" and hurried off to her car.

"You need to watch your language, hon!" Baba called. "See you Thursday!" She shut the door.

Cassie bounded down the stairs, laughing. "OMG, Baba! We did it!"

Baba? What was Cassie doing conspiring with *my* Baba? When had they set this up? "How did you know she was coming?"

"When we were driving up here, I noticed her car at that cherry cider place on the way up the canyon," Baba said.

"You knew it was her?"

She shrugged. "I saw a redhead standing beside a red car. She was watching traffic, which was kind of strange. When we passed, she got in her car and backed out. I just had a feeling it might be her and she'd find us. "

I was still a little confused. "Why would she have been waiting there? How could she have known we were heading this direction?"

"No idea," Baba said, "but she must be pretty resourceful. I didn't want to worry you, so I hatched a plan with Cassie while you were hauling in baby stuff and making beds. I had a hunch the Redhead would show up at the front door, eventually. Which she did."

Maybe I'd inherited my good instincts from Baba.

Baba continued. "So I had Cassie take a couple of pots of water upstairs and put them in her room, which is right above the front door."

"I took the window screen off and left the window unlatched," Cassie said. "All I had to do was pop it open, and bam! Pour the pot of water out the window."

"Two pots of water," Baba smiled.

"Amazing," I said, and meant it.

After helping with the dishes, I announced that I was exhausted and going to go to my room to read. What I was really going to do was research the Redhead. She had an interest in this murder that seemed almost personal. Why? Maybe I could find out more online.

I opened my laptop and logged on to the Wi-Fi with a password Sam had provided. An email from Otto announced, "We're famous!" I clicked on the link he had included, and there we were on Channel Nine News.

I was glad I'd been careful about my hair that morning. I looked pretty good—or maybe it was just in comparison to six guys over 70. As I was playing the clip for the third time and laughing, Dan texted me:

I am humbled to be dating such a star.

I sent back three smiling emojis and decided to wait until the next day to share with everyone else at the cabin. I needed to get on with my research.

I'd heard the photographer call the woman "Kendall" when I asked them to leave my house that day, so at least I had a first name. Using my developing powers as a sleuth, I determined that the Redhead was probably from Colorado. She never showed up in a labeled news van, so I suspected she worked for a smaller, low budget organization located somewhere close. She was almost always around, even when not much was happening, so I figured she must drive to Juniper each day.

I began googling.

Sure enough, I found a Kendall who worked at a free Boulder newspaper that featured local stories, often about the arts community. She was listed on the website as Kendall Whitehead.

I googled "Kendall Whitehead" images. It was her.

Why did her interest in this case seem so extreme? Was it personal to her? Could she actually have known Donald? I spent an hour learning what I could.

She had two brothers. She graduated from Littleton High School and attended the University of Colorado in Boulder. She was around twenty-nine. She'd been in a sorority. Her dad was a dentist. Her mom was a Realtor. She was maid of honor in her friend Candace Gallegos' wedding.

Nothing connected her to Donald.

I kept "next paging" in Google. Much of the material was a repeat of previous information. Finally, though, I found a mention of Kendall Whitehead in a ballet recital from about ten years ago. Maybe that was the connection—dance. I started googling "Kendall Whitehead" plus "dance" plus "Donald Sanders." Nothing, except for that recital program someone had posted.

Maybe Sammie would know something.

I found Sammie where I often found her—on the floor with Isabelle and a diaper bag. "Do you know if Donald ever took ballet lessons?" I asked.

"Wouldn't surprise me. That's where girls are."

"Could you call his mother and ask?"

"Come on, Ella. I can't bother a grieving mother with that."

"You could tell her it would help the police with a line of inquiry."

"Would it?"

"Maybe." I explained my theory about a Redhead connection while Isabelle wiggled and kicked her legs and Sammie rummaged in the diaper bag.

"So what if there is a connection? What does that tell us?"

"I don't know. That's the thing about murder investigations. You don't know what will be helpful."

"Oh, you're an investigator now?"

"Unofficially, yes."

"Oh, all right. You change Isabelle. I'll call." She smiled and got up. "She's poopy."

I gritted my teeth. I wasn't fond of poopy diapers, even

newborn poop, which I knew from my brother's two boys was a whole lot less offensive than toddler poop. I could never get through any kind of poop without gagging.

And I didn't this time, either. Isabelle's poop had leaked through her onesie. Trying to breathe through my mouth and not my nose, I had to do a major clean-up involving a startling number of baby wipes. When I had finally disposed of everything and cleaned my hands, I sat down with a happy baby—clean and dry and gazing up at Auntie Bellella. I hugged her to me and kissed her forehead.

"Poor Cecilia," Sammie said when she joined us again. "She's a mess. Of course."

I tried to imagine what she was going through, but when I thought of losing my nephews or Isabelle, even though they weren't my own children, my brain froze. I couldn't go there, not even in my imagination.

Sammie went on. "It seems Donald did start ballet lessons when he was about 15. He loved dancing, and he loved girls, Cecilia said, so he signed up and took lessons for a couple of years. She said he was good."

No surprise there.

"But he had to quit when he was about 17. I asked Cecilia about that 'had to quit,' and she said the owner of the studio kicked him out for doing something inappropriate. She said she thought that was harsh, that boys *will* take any opportunity to make out with girls."

"Make out only?"

"It sounded like that was her take on 'something inappropriate.'" She twisted her lips to the side a little. "You know I like Cecilia, but she may have gone a little easy on her son sometimes. Ignored things she shouldn't have ignored. Assumed the best when she maybe should have assumed the worst."

"Something inappropriate involved Kendall Whitehead. I'd bet money on it." I thrust a sweet-smelling Isabelle toward Sammie. "Here. I'm going to do a little more research."

Despite further searching online, I couldn't find any more information about Kendall Whitehead that might indicate a connection to Donald. I gave up, opened the window, and went to bed.

I lay there listening to the quiet of the night. A cricket. A rustle in the tree next to the window. That was about it. Instead of calming me, the silence left me a little on edge as I found myself straining to hear something else, anything else. It took a while, but I finally fell asleep.

CHAPTER EIGHTEEN

The next morning I couldn't help myself. I checked Harvey Klump's blog.

This is just a brief update on speculation surrounding the murder of Donald Sanders. Why would a person known to have met with Sanders before his death by poisoning be allowed to leave the state??? Reliable sources report that Sammie Russo, murder suspect and daughter of my opponent Geraldine Betz, has fled to Santa Barbara with her best friend!!! Why would a murder suspect be allowed to do that, if not for her connections to people with power? Some say it is because Sammie Russo's best friend is dating a police officer.

This situation smells!!! That's the only way to put it. It smells!!!

So I was right. Evelyn did indeed have a big mouth. But did she pass on my fake news to her sister, her sister's husband, or someone else? Could she herself have passed it on to Harvey? Or was there another route to Harvey?

Late that morning, I decided to take a walk. I do my best thinking while walking, and I hoped that I'd come up with an idea for how to move my unauthorized murder investigation forward. I walked down a path that led to a trail looping around a beautiful little lake.

As I neared the trail head, I noticed, through the trees, a

car parked along the road that ran parallel to the path, almost hidden by foliage. I wouldn't have seen it if I hadn't happened to glance that direction when a flock of Canada geese went honking by overhead, forming a perfect "V."

Had another reporter found us somehow? Alarmed, I walked quietly through the trees, approaching the car. No one was sitting there with binoculars. Did that mean he or she was somewhere around the house spying on us?

Then I heard groans coming from the car—not groans of misery, groans of pleasure. I couldn't help myself. I stepped closer and looked inside.

Oh, lord. In the backseat, two bodies lay intertwined. They were clothed, mostly. I stepped back quickly, recognizing the shirt flung over the front seat. Cassie's.

I wished I hadn't chosen to investigate. Quickly, I walked away. Cassie would never forgive me if I confronted them, and, besides, I wasn't her parent. Who was I to confront her?

But Cassie had invited Trevor—I assumed it was Trevor—even though we had gone to such lengths to keep our destination a secret. That *was* my business, and I was angry that she had betrayed us.

Really angry. Making out, I could understand. Betraying those close to you—that was another matter. When I got back to the cabin I sat on the porch out of the sunlight and texted Cassie, writing the words I had composed carefully on the walk back:

I see Trevor is here. Must stay for lunch. If he leaves w/out coming back with you, who knows consequences?

I thought that was sufficient—vague but suggesting that I knew more. She would know I saw something, and she would wonder how much. I hoped she was worried, really worried. She had blabbed our location.

Baba sat down beside me in the porch swing, and I quickly explained the situation.

"Lordy, that girl is headed for trouble," she said.

In just a few minutes, Cassie and Trevor came walking up the path to the house. We nodded as they approached, careful not to smile and allow them to relax. "So is this your young man?" Baba asked.

Cassie didn't look at me. "Baba, this is Trevor. Trevor Girard."

Baba held out her hand. He hesitated and then shook it. She didn't smile, and her eyes drilled into his.

"So surprised to see you up here, Trevor," I said, my voice cold. "We went to so much trouble to keep our location a secret."

"A *lot* of trouble," Baba added.

"Okay, I invited him," Cassie said. "I didn't think it would matter. He won't tell anyone."

We waited.

Trevor finally got the message. "I won't tell anyone," he said. "Like, why would I?" He shrugged, clearly not as worried about the situation as Cassie was.

"Don't tell Dad," Cassie begged. "Please."

"I can't have secrets from your dad," I said. "I have to tell him—at *least*—that I discovered you invited Trevor." The "at least" would remind her that maybe, just maybe, I had discovered a lot more.

"You two set the table for lunch in the dining room,"

Baba said, nodding at Cassie and Trevor. The tone of her voice told them there would be no arguing.

I took Geraldine and Sammie aside and filled them in as we made grilled cheese sandwiches. They were just as mad as I was. Who knows who Trevor might tell about our location? Or might already have told? No one smiled at the teenagers as we sat down at the kitchen table.

"Take off your hat, please," Baba said. Trevor looked at her as though she had asked him to take off all his clothes. "Gentlemen don't wear hats at a table. It's not polite."

Trevor took off his hat.

Baba dished up tomato soup, and I passed a plate of sandwiches. Before anyone could even take a bite, Geraldine looked at Cassie and Trevor and said, "So how much did they teach you two in school about birth control?"

Covering a smile with my napkin, I looked down at my soup. I knew where this was going, as I had experienced the Pickle Queen's blunt interrogations myself. She goes bravely where others fear to tread.

Trevor managed to dribble tomato soup down his front. Cassie choked on a bite of her grilled cheese sandwich.

"Well?" Geraldine demanded. "Don't you have sex ed in school?"

"Yes," muttered Cassie, and Trevor nodded.

"Okay then, I'm sure they have given you the mechanics of it all, and I'm sure they talked about how it's an emotional investment as well as a physical one, right?"

Looking miserable, Trevor and Cassie both nodded.

"So how much do you know about the stuff they probably *didn't* teach you?"

"I don't know what you mean," Cassie said.

"I assume they did the condom on a banana thing, or is that too controversial these days?"

"Zucchini," Trevor said. He looked down at his soup.

Cassie sat, head bent, arms folded and hands holding her elbows. I'm sure the two kids wished they were anywhere else on earth. In the middle of the Sahara. Riding in a car across the boring stretch of Wyoming. Attending a senior center square dance. Still, Geraldine continued. Sometimes her ability to ignore all social cues cracks me up. I'm never sure if she doesn't see them or if she is perfectly aware of what she is doing and just ignores them.

"Great. I'm sure the zucchini worked well. And I'm sure they must have told you always to use a condom, at least until you're in a committed relationship with someone who is clear of all disease, right?" She didn't wait for a nod. "Otherwise, condoms. Always."

The two just sat there.

"But what's the thing I'll bet they *didn't* tell you? Cassie?"

"I don't know because they didn't tell me?" She looked at Sammie and me for help. Sammie looked down at Isabelle, resting in the crook of one arm, and tried to hide her smile.

I wasn't sure where Geraldine was going with this, but I ventured a guess. "They didn't tell them that condoms break?"

Geraldine sniffed. "Of course they told them that. Right?"

They nodded.

"Anything else?"

Nothing.

"Okay then I'll tell you. This is especially important for girls. What they don't tell you is that men don't *like* to use condoms. They hate it. They will try to talk you out of it. They will tell you how it doesn't feel as good for them. They will insist it will be okay this once, or they say they will pull out, and you will *want* them to keep going and you will want to make them happy, and putting on a condom sure does interrupt the flow of things. You will want more than anything in the world just to forget about the condom because *you're* different, and it will be safe, and *your* relationship is different." She finally took a breath. "But it's not."

She took a bite of sandwich and looked at Cassie and Trevor. They weren't eating. Cassie was stirring her soup, pointlessly. Trevor was just sitting there, turning a deeper and deeper shade of red. He looked vulnerable, somehow, without his hat.

Geraldine swallowed. She wasn't finished. "And it only takes once. Once to give you a baby … Or HIV … Or an STD."

Baba looked up and frowned. I'm not completely sure she knew what an STD was, but I wasn't about to check.

Geraldine took another bite. The table was silent. If she had been talking to her own kids, they would have argued, "Mom! We know all that!" or "Stop!" Or they would have stomped off, refusing to hear anymore. But Cassie and Trevor didn't know her that well, and they were already on shaky ground.

Geraldine swallowed, then continued. "And what else makes it harder to be sensible? Sammie, field this one."

Sammie sighed. "Wine. Definitely wine."

"Ella, other ideas?"

"Weed. Smoked or ingested. Drugs."

"Okay, so we've got that covered. They probably told you that in school, too, right?"

Cassie nodded, almost imperceptibly.

Geraldine chewed thoughtfully. She still wasn't finished. "Anybody who is smart should learn about *all* the methods of birth control, not just condoms. Boys *and* girls. And figure out what's safe for them."

Sammie couldn't resist saying, "Unless you're Catholic. Then you're not supposed to use birth control at all."

Geraldine shot her a "Don't start with me" look and said, "Sometimes we have to ignore rules that are wrongheaded and hurt people."

Baba calmly looked up from her soup and said, "There's a reason I have only three children and not fifteen."

I stared. Were we really discussing contraception with my grandmother?

Suddenly, Geraldine switched gears. "Enough sex talk. Eat your lunch." I was familiar with Geraldine's quick changes of direction. When we were kids, she would be giving Sammie and me hell about something and going on and on until we felt we were shrinking into nothing, and then, suddenly, she'd be done. She'd say, "Okay, let's go watch TV. I'll make popcorn," or, "Want to go with me to the mall?"

We all ate in silence for a bit. Then I said, "We could talk politics, I guess, or religion."

Cassie and Trevor looked at me, puzzled.

"Kidding. You're not supposed to talk religion or politics at a meal," I said.

"Probably not sex, either," Sammie said.

Baba must have decided we had tortured the kids enough. "Finish up, everyone. I've got a treat for dessert."

Cassie kept stirring her soup and staring into it, now and then taking a half-hearted spoonful. Trevor, head down, kept eating. Birth control talk had not hurt his appetite once he got started. He ate all of his soup, all of his sandwich, half of Cassie's, and three helpings of potato chips. We all waited. I'd forgotten how much teenage boys can eat.

"Now for dessert," Baba said. "I made Yum Cake."

I love, love, *love* Baba's Yum Cake. Everyone does.

"Yum Cake?" Trevor asked.

"It's really a chocolate fudge cake with filling between the layers and a caramel cream topping," Baba explained. "We call it Yum Cake because when Ella's older brother Alex was about five, he would say 'Yum!' after every bite." She cut a huge slice for Trevor and smaller slices for the rest of us.

We dug in, and there were sighs and "Yums!" all around. That's one of our traditions with Yum cake. You have to say "Yum" a lot, just like Alex did.

Suddenly Trevor wasn't saying "Yum" or anything else. His face was turning red, and he was clutching his throat. "What's in the filling?" he choked.

"It's a hazelnut caramel cream," Baba said, "My own special recipe with Nutella."

"I'm allergic!"

"To what?"

"Hazelnuts!"

I leapt up. "Oh my god. You must have an Epi-pen? Where is it?"

"In the car."

"Go, Cassie. You're the runner, and you know where the car is."

"Glove compartment," Trevor choked.

"Why in the world don't you have it on you?" Geraldine asked.

"It's not the time for criticism," I said. Trevor was turning redder and redder and gasping. "Google *allergy treatment.*"

Sammie called 9-1-1 while I helped Trevor to the floor and Geraldine grabbed her phone.

"Allergy emergency treatment," Geraldine said into her phone's microphone. Then, "No, allergy. *Allergy.*" She started typing in the words instead.

Sammie was on the line with the 9-1-1 operator. "Yes, someone went to get the Epi-pen …" She turned to all of us. "What's the address, someone?"

I didn't know. "Wait … I put it into Google Maps when we were driving up here. Let me see if it's still up on my phone." I wasn't very good about taking down pages after I'd opened them. Here!" I handed her the phone.

Sammie read the address aloud. "Yes, I'll stay on the line … No, not yet." She looked at Trevor. "An ambulance is on the way."

Cassie burst in, breathing hard, holding the Epi-pen.

"Can you do it yourself?" Geraldine asked Trevor. He nodded and struggled to sit up. He pulled one leg of his shorts up and placed the Epi-pen on his thigh. Geraldine held his leg steady.

Sammie said, "Ella, don't …" She had realized, a little too late, that I was in danger. She was right. As Trevor aimed the Epi-pen, I suddenly grasped what it really was. He was shooting himself with a needle. A needle. In the thigh. *A needle.* The room began to swim.

I passed out.

When I regained consciousness, I noticed two things. First, my arm ached where I must have hit the corner of the table going down. Second, Cassie was holding my hand, her face full of concern. "Come on, Ella. Wake up, Ella!"

"Whoa …" I said. I was groggy. I liked the feeling of Cassie holding my hand. I didn't like the pain in my arm. Then I remembered Trevor and tried to sit up. "Is it working? The pen?"

"Yeah," Trevor mumbled. He wasn't gasping as much, but he didn't look good.

"The ambulance will be here soon," Sammie said. "Baba went down to the end of the lane to make sure they see the place. She'll wave them in."

When we heard sirens, I breathed a sigh of relief. Sammie helped me up and guided me to the bathroom. "Stay there," she said. "We don't need you passing out again." She closed the door, and I waited, listening to all the action. Soon Trevor was being loaded into an ambulance.

I heard Baba say, "Someone needs to go with them."

"I'll go," Geraldine said. "I'll contact his parents, too. Whoever they are. I hope he didn't leave his cell phone in the glove compartment, too."

"No kid leaves their cell phone in the glove compartment," Sammie said. "Life-saving Epi-pen, yes. Cell phone, no."

When I heard sirens again, Sammie let me out of the bathroom.

I insisted Cassie call her dad to tell him what had been going on. I stayed in the room to make sure she told him *why* Trevor was here in the first place.

It was a blubbery confession that, darn it, included the fact that I had passed out. After a lot of tears and "I'm sorry, Dad," she handed her phone to me.

"Unfricking believable," were his first words. "You can't keep doing this, Ella."

I hoped to lighten the mood. "Hosting getaways?"

"Passing out."

"I can't help it."

"You *can* help it. You promised to get therapy six months ago and haven't done it."

"I'm going to call."

"You're so lucky there were other people around when Trevor had his attack. What if it had been only you around to administer the pen, and you couldn't stay conscious long enough to save someone's life? What if you had really hurt *yourself* when you passed out and fell?"

I didn't know what to say.

He waited a moment, then said, "You know, I can't talk to you any more right now." His voice was icy, and he hung up.

I sat quietly, trying not to cry. "He hung up on me. Dan hung up on me."

"He's *so* mad at me," Cassie said, tears streaming down her face. "I think he hates me."

"He doesn't hate you. He might hate me, though."

"He doesn't hate you."

"Does he stay mad long?" I asked her. "He hasn't been really mad at me before."

"Not usually. But he's pretty mad." Her sobs increased. "What's he mad at you about?"

"He wants me to see a therapist about my needle problem."

She slowly got hold of herself and turned her attention to me. "Maybe you should. Really. I mean nobody likes to get a shot, but normal people don't pass out just looking at an Epi-pen."

I told her how it had started when I was a teenager and passed out getting a flu shot. The incident seemed to come out of the blue and shocked me, but then I became more and more terrified of it happening again. And it did. "And now … well, it just keeps getting worse and worse. I'm afraid I'm going to have a panic attack if I even think about getting a shot. Which I don't get. Not any kind of shot."

She looked sympathetic. Were we finally bonding? "What about the dentist?" she asked.

"I take *really* good care of my teeth, and I haven't had a cavity. Luckily, I had all my childhood shots before this needle thing started."

"You really are a wimp," she said.

So much for bonding. "At least I don't betray friends who ask you to keep a secret," I said. *Real mature, Ella,* I told myself.

"You are not my *friends.* Dad made me come."

"Fine. You still knew you weren't supposed to tell anyone."

"And you knew you were supposed to get therapy. And not just for my dad. For *you.* " She stomped off.

She had a point. I considered the possibility, really considered the possibility, that Cassie could be right.

I went upstairs and made an appointment with the therapist.

Geraldine came back several hours later, looking drained. "Guess who Trevor's mother is."

"Not a clue," Sammie said.

"Lauren Rose, the lawyer. Guess who her father is."

"I have a bad feeling about this," I said.

"Harvey Klump," Geraldine said. "Guess who showed up at the hospital."

"Harvey Klump," Sammie said.

"Harvey Klump *and* Lauren Rose *and* her current husband *and* Trevor's father. We all groaned.

"Guess who got blamed for almost killing Trevor."

"You. Us. Baba."

"Got it." Geraldine looked at all of us. Sammie looked okay, but my eyes were swollen and red, and so were Cassie's. Baba's eyes looked the worst.

"I didn't *know,* " Baba said, for about the millionth time. "I'll never make Yum Cake again."

Geraldine lost her drained look and snapped into Pickle Queen mode. "You absolutely *will* make Yum Cake again. Life will go on."

Baba sat up a little straighter. Maybe she was surprised to be yelled at.

"Listen," Geraldine said. "Trevor knew he was allergic to hazelnuts. We didn't. He should have asked what was in the cake, and he should have had the Epi-pen with him."

"But I told him it was a chocolate fudge cake, not a hazelnut cake," Baba said.

"It *is* a chocolate fudge cake. A chocolate fudge cake

with hazelnut filling and caramel whipped cream topping. He would have known that if he had asked some questions. He is 18. He has a life-threatening allergy. Sorry Cassie, but he is simply an irresponsible boy who needs to learn that *he* is responsible for his own health."

Geraldine stomped to the kitchen, strangely angry, and came back with a bottle of chardonnay and a can of Coke. We all sat quietly, wondering what was next.

"Now," she continued, "All of us—except you, Cassie—are going to have a glass of wine. Even a teeny bit for you, Sammie. Get glasses, Ella."

I got glasses.

Geraldine poured wine for us and Coke into a wine glass for Cassie. Then she held up her glass. "Now a toast—to Trevor, who is going to be fine. And to Cassie, for saving his life. That was a sprint that should go down in record books, Cassie."

Cassie smiled.

Geraldine continued. "To Baba, for making the most delicious cake in the world, and one we are going to enjoy again and again and again in the future—*after* pointing out that the filling is made of Nutella, which is, of course, made with hazelnuts."

We toasted and then drank our wine.

"You want to grab that big Costco jug of nuts?" I asked Cassie. "I think we need some snacks to go with this."

She rolled her eyes and sighed as if I'd asked her to whip up a meal. She slouched to the kitchen, sighing.

"Just when I thought things were getting better," I said softly. "She was holding my hand and everything when I passed out. Like she might even like me a little."

"Get used to it, sweetie," said Geraldine."

"To what?"

"The whiplash. You're cool—you suck. I love you—I hate you. All stepparents go through it."

"All *parents* go through it," Baba added.

"Yes, but it's worse with stepparents. Not that you're a stepparent. Yet."

I swallowed. What if I became one? Could I handle it?

Geraldine continued, quietly, so that Cassie couldn't hear us. "Jake went through it, too. The kids get close and realize they like you—even love you—and then they feel disloyal to their real mom or dad, and they distance themselves. It's a push-pull thing. And it will go on, probably until she grows up. If you're around that long." She gave me a pat on the back and we drank in silence.

Cassie was taking a long time with those nuts. Finally she returned. She had brought the nuts, poured them into a nice bowl, centered it on a platter, and surrounded it with crackers and some carrots. Was this part of the push-pull thing? Moaning about being sent to the kitchen, then doing it up right?

I thanked her nicely, and we ate.

CHAPTER NINETEEN

The next morning. Geraldine showed us Harvey's latest blog. She was not happy.

Yesterday Geraldine Betz's irresponsibility almost killed my grandson!!!!!
I'm not exagerating!!!!!

He spelled *exaggerating* wrong, I noticed, reading over her shoulder. Looking at Geraldine's angry face, I decided this wasn't the time to point it out.

As I reported earlier, Betz and her daughter, along with Ella Polansky, have escaped from Juniper and are hiding out. However, it is not in Santa Barbara after all. It's in the Estes Park area.
With them is Detective Dan Sherman's daughter. My grandson, in his innocence, allowed the daughter to lure him to the retreat, where—instead of sending him immediately home—Betz and the others allowed him to stay and have lunch. Who in this day and age doesn't ask about allergies????? Kids drop dead from even peanut butter sandwiches, so the group certainly should have asked my grandson about allergies before feeding him cake with a filling made of hazelnuts. He is violently allergic to hazelnuts.

Of course, he went into anaphylactic shock!!!!! He could have died before they had the sense to call an ambulance!!!!

In the ambulance, Betz finally acted. She called my grandson's mother, and we all raced to Estes Park to be with him.

I am so relieved my grandson survived!!! However, his life would never even have been in danger if Geraldine Betz had acted appropriately. She should have sent my grandson home instead of allowing him to eat lunch with a suspected murderer—and then almost kill him by feeding him hazelnut cake!!!!!!!!

I ask you, is this the kind of woman we want as mayor of our fair city??????

And why is she hiding out????? And where??????

Some Juniper residents want to know.

None of us said anything. Cassie looked pale, probably realizing how serious the ramifications of her actions had been.

I filled the silence. "Harvey sure does like his punctuation marks."

Geraldine didn't respond, just closed the laptop. "What we can say, in our defense, is that we had no idea who this boy was," she said.

Cassie looked at her lap.

I actually felt sorry for her. "Remember, Cassie did manage to save Trevor's life," I reminded everyone. She smiled at me, looking grateful.

"So what do we do now?" Baba asked. "Should you resign, Geraldine?"

"Of course I shouldn't resign! In the first place, his

accusations are way over the line. *Way* over. In the second place, this has nothing to do with being mayor. And we don't want *him* as mayor. He'd be terrible—probably pave over all the parks so he could build condos. We need to let things calm down, see what plays out in the next couple of days."

"She's right," Sammie said. "Just leave it alone until we get back."

The next two days passed uneventfully, and we all actually did relax, more or less. Trevor evidently had the good sense not to rat out our location, and Kendall must have kept quiet about it, too. I joined the others hiking, reading, and just talking, but in the back of my mind, always, was the murder. At night I stayed up late playing with ideas and typing them up on my laptop. When I reread my notes, though, they didn't lead anywhere that made sense to me.

Dan didn't call, though he sent a couple of cryptic texts asking if we were okay.

On Thursday, right on schedule, Kendall arrived and knocked on the door. "I kept my part of the deal," she said. "I'd like my phone back."

"It's been resting in rice the whole time," I said. "That's supposed to work."

I invited her in and pointed to the box of rice on the bureau. "Be my guest."

She fished the phone out and took a charger out of her purse. "Can I test it?"

"Sure."

She plugged it in. The charging icon flashed, and her face softened in relief.

"Let it charge a bit," I said, "while we take a short walk. We need to talk."

She stood there, unconvinced.

"You're a reporter, aren't you? Maybe we can help each other out, even get you a good story, eventually." I hadn't ruled her out as a murder suspect herself, but I thought it best not to mention that.

"I'm listening."

"I know you studied ballet when you were a teenager," I began. She looked surprised. "And I know Donald did, too. Did you know him?

She hesitated. "Yes," she said, her voice tight.

"Did you know him *well?*"

"Not as well as I thought," she said. "Asshole."

I assumed she meant Donald, not me. "So is that your interest in this case? That you're still mad about something he did? You seem a lot more invested in this than the other reporters."

"I could tell you, but what do you have for *me?* "

I had given the subject some thought. "I've known Donald for ten years and Sammie for most of my life. If I figure out who the murderer is, I'll give you an exclusive interview and persuade Sammie to join me."

She was thinking.

"With pictures," I added.

That did it. Sammie takes great pictures. "Okay," she said. "Let's go then."

We headed toward the lake, walking in silence for a few minutes. Then I said, "I assume you must have had a relationship with Donald at some point."

"As much as anyone can have a relationship with

Donald," she said. "But at the time I thought I was special. I was in *love*. I was fifteen."

The same age as Cassie.

She continued. "Everyone at the dance studio had a crush on him. I mean, boys in ballet are few and far between, and straight boys—well, I'd never met one. And then he came along. Wow."

"Yes, wow," I agreed.

"Our teacher was having Donald and me dance a *pas de deux*—a duet—in a recital, and we practiced together. A lot." She picked up a fallen tree branch and began snapping into pieces as she walked.

"And you did more than practice, right?"

"Of course. I was 15. He was gorgeous. The other girls were so envious." She smiled, remembering. "Pretty heady stuff." The smile disappeared. "Little did I know that I was just his *ballet* girlfriend. I later found out he had a tap dance girlfriend, a drama class girlfriend, a cross-country girl-friend … well, you get the picture."

"Got it. So what happened?"

"So our teacher was letting us use the studio to prac-tice one night after class while she caught up on her books. She got a call from her babysitter and had to go home, but Donald asked if we could stay and practice and then lock the door behind us when we left. He'd bring the extra key back the next day. She was in a hurry, and she was friends with both our moms, so she said yes. The second she was out of there, the practicing went out the window, and he was all over me."

"Right there on the dance floor?"

"Yeah. We didn't care. We'd never had the opportunity

to go all the way before. Now we were alone. So what if the floor was hard?" She stopped. Something she was remembering bothered her. "He was good at making out, not so good when he got to the real deal. The floor was hard, and the fluorescent lights too bright, but he couldn't be interrupted to go into the office and find the switch. Or maybe he thought he had to act quickly or I'd back out."

"But you didn't."

"I already told you I didn't," she snapped. She walked on. "Afterward he had this 'great' idea. He wanted us to dance naked together. I refused, but he kept telling me I was beautiful and to imagine how beautiful the two of us would look together. So, finally, I agreed. I was in love, remember?" She stopped walking again and gazed off at the heron standing on top of one of the pines across the lake. "It was the 'Coppelia Waltz.' Beautiful. It's not so easy to dance with boobs flopping, but I admit the whole thing was kind of a turn-on. In case you should ever want to try it." She looked at me.

"I think I'll pass."

She continued. "And when the song was over, he said, 'Can you do an arabesque there at the bar?' And I went over, and when I posed, he grabbed his cell phone and snapped a picture."

"Oh, no."

"It gets worse. Then Mrs. Wright opened the door. She'd decided to come back and check on things after she got her babysitter emergency straightened out."

I put myself in Kendall's shoes—ballet shoes—and imagined being discovered like that as a teenager. It was beyond painful.

I could also imagine what else likely happened. "He shared the photo," I said.

"Of course he did. The good news is that it could have been worse. He couldn't forward it to his female friends because he wouldn't want them to know, and he had only one real guy friend. A guy named Bucky. Bucky was my friend, too."

"So he sent Bucky a copy?"

"Yes, and Bucky was absolutely outraged. He told me how he grabbed the phone from Donald and deleted the photo. He was so furious with Donald that he stopped being friends with him."

"Wow. Pretty extreme reaction."

"Truthfully, I knew Bucky had a crush on me, so maybe that entered into it. I guess he felt duty-bound to defend me." She sighed and shook her head. "But then it got worse. I turned out to be pregnant. Bucky was the only one who knew the story, so he was my rock—at least until I talked about getting an abortion, which he was very much against. He really laid a guilt trip on me and insisted I could just give the baby up for adoption. I was leaning that direction, but then I had to tell my parents, and they insisted that an abortion was the only sensible solution. Bucky never got over that, really. Said it was a terrible sin. He stopped being my friend, too."

Bucky moved to my list of suspects.

Kendall was on a roll. "When I heard Donald had been found dead in a dance studio, I wondered if maybe he had been repeating his old tricks. Was he naked when you found him? I mean, I know from good authority that you looked in when the police opened the door."

"That's the kind of information I can't divulge," I said, surprised to hear a certain primness in my voice. I softened my tone. "Really. I can't. My boyfriend is a cop, and it would be a violation he would never get over."

"Hmmmm. I have a hunch Donald was naked at some point and that at some point there was a naked woman there, too." She looked at me hard. "Like Sammie Russo."

I just laughed. "You obviously don't know Sammie."

"So tell me about her."

I told her how Sammie was my best friend, how she loved dancing, how she'd put up with Donald's annoying personality traits because no one else made her feel the way he did when they were dancing. "She felt beautiful when she danced with him."

"She *is* beautiful."

"But normally it's no big deal for her. She just accepts it as a fact of life. But when she dances with Donald—I mean *danced* with Donald—she said she felt beautiful in a different way. She described it as like floating on sunshine. I'm not exactly sure what that means, but she used that term a lot. Floating on sunshine."

"I know what she means. I felt like that dancing with him. Like we weren't part of the earth and the normal world. We were more than that."

"I don't get it, but whatever. Sammie made me go dancing with them sometimes—me and her brother—so she'd have someone to talk to. Donald could be pretty boring."

"I never got to experience the boring part. We were too busy making out. But don't you think Sammie might have wanted to feel what floating on sunshine *naked* was like? Maybe she danced naked with him, too."

"Not a chance. Sammie kept him firmly in place—a dance partner, nothing else. A *clothed* dance partner."

She wasn't buying it. "You're forgetting we know about the birth certificate. Are you saying she lied on the birth certificate and said Donald was the father when he wasn't? That makes no sense."

"That's something you'll have to ask Sammie about," I said. "In your interview."

"But …"

"Really. I'm not saying any more about that."

She switched gears. "So who killed him?"

"I wish I knew. I can tell you for sure, though, that it wasn't Sammie or her fiancé or me."

"Or maybe you're trying to throw me off."

"Or maybe you're feeding me a crazy naked dancing story."

We stopped walking and assessed one another. I believed her. I think she believed me.

"It would be one hell of a story if we figure out who did this," I said.

She nodded.

We walked back to the house, and she unplugged her phone and turned it on. It worked.

"Thank God," she said. She started out the door, checking messages on her way. No goodbye.

I stood in the doorway and watched. She actually gave me a wave as she drove off. I was happy to discover a reason that Kendall was so interested in the murder. It might or might not be relevant, but I had a hunch it was. Maybe Donald had been meeting someone in Sammie's studio for more naked dancing. If so, who was it?

Or maybe someone had been meeting him for another reason. I added Kendall to my list of suspects. She certainly had reason to seek revenge.

And maybe the guy named Bucky did, as well.

Isabelle was taking a nap, so Sammie and I sat on the front porch swing while I told her what Kendall had said. "Have you ever heard anything about him having some kind of naked dancing fetish?"

"Not exactly." We rocked for a while, silent. Finally she gave a deep sigh. "I need to tell you something. But don't get mad."

Whenever someone says "Don't get mad," I know I'm going to get mad. I looked at her, feeling nervous.

"Just remember you're my best friend," she said.

Now I was really freaking out. "Did you sleep with Detective Dan or something?"

"Of course not. But …" She took a deep breath. "Okay, here's the deal. It's not true that I slept with Donald only that one time. There was another time—just twice total. Honest."

"What?" I couldn't believe it. "When?"

"The first time was when I was about 19. In college. And it was pretty awful. And that's the only other time. Really."

I couldn't think what to say, angry and hurt that she'd kept such a thing from me. Finally, I said, "You've been lying to me for ten years?"

"I know. I feel awful. I was embarrassed."

"So, so embarrassed? Like that's a reason?"

"I'm sorry, Bellella. I know it's no excuse, but it was right after the Wyatt thing."

I remembered the Wyatt thing. He was a fraternity guy, and anyone could see he was a jerk. Sammie was temporarily and uncharacteristically blinded by his looks and confidence. It took a couple of weeks before she realized I was right. He was a jerk.

"It was all so stupid. Donald and I were at his parents' golf club for a dance, and it was late. He wanted some air, and he led me out onto the golf course. I maybe had a bit too much wine."

"A theme with you and Donald." Yes, I was sarcastic. Being mad can do that to a person.

She started to respond, then let it go. She looked down, picking the fingernail of her thumb as she continued. "First we danced. Then he wanted to do more than dance. He seemed really into the danger of doing it where someone might catch us. Finally I just went along with him. It *was* kind of exciting."

Sammie did have a daredevil streak. I remembered an incident involving the boys' locker room in high school. "Doing it on a golf course was exciting?"

"The idea of doing it out in the open was. The actual *doing,* though? Not good. Not good at all. And then the sprinklers went off, and we were soaked. He had to call his parents and tell them I was suddenly feeling sick and he was taking me home." She finally looked at me. "Why do you think I keep telling you that good-looking guys make god-awful lovers? There was the football jock in high school, then Wyatt. Then Donald. He was the final confirmation of my theory."

"So why would you ever do it *again* with Donald? I mean, besides the too-much-to-drink influence?"

"Like I've said before, I don't really know. Maybe I just temporarily lost my mind. Or maybe I wanted to see if he had learned anything in ten years." She shook her head. "He hadn't. So my theory stands." She grabbed my hand. "At first I didn't tell you because I was embarrassed. And then as time went on, it didn't seem that important. It was an irrelevant blip in my life."

"Until you did it again. You could have told me about the first time *then.*"

"It was bad enough that I had to tell you I was pregnant. Why would I want to tell you about something ten years in the past?"

"Why are you telling me now?"

"Because I want to confirm that Donald had kind of a kinky side. It might be important. The whole golf course thing was his idea. Another time he wanted to take nude pictures of me in my kitchen. Like standing naked by a KitchenAid would turn him on or something. I didn't do it, of course"

I didn't know what to say. But I kind of understood. It's not like I had never made a bad decision. Or told her absolutely everything. She didn't know, for example, that I'd once overheard Baba telling Mom she'd seen Geraldine get into a car with Jake, Sammie's future stepfather, long before she and her husband were divorced. Baba had thought they had looked "a little too chummy."

I weighed my options for a few moments. Sammie wasn't perfect, but she was still the best friend I'd ever had. I had to forgive her. "Okay. This is between us," I said.

"And Sam. I did tell Sam the truth right away."

That didn't help at all.

When we got home, Dan grounded Cassie for a week, with a reminder about how he and her mother were not the kind of parents who ground their kids and then forget about it. "It will be a week, firm," he said in my kitchen when he came over to pick up Cassie. "You're not going anywhere except with an adult. You're not having anyone over."

She started to protest, but he held up a hand in a "Stop!" gesture and said, "I don't want to hear it. I thought about taking your cell phone, too."

She paled.

"I decided you should have it, for safety reasons. Now get your stuff, and I'll take you home."

He gave me only a perfunctory kiss on the cheek as they were leaving. He closed the door so firmly that Fluffles looked up, startled, from her nest on one of the sofa pillows.

I looked at the clock. I was supposed to go to tap class at 5:30, but I was too depressed. Things weren't looking great in my life. Dan was mad, I had an appointment with a therapist, and I wasn't making much progress on the murder front. Would Mildred be arresting Sammie soon?

I texted Sammie:

Have to miss class. Need to mope.

Mope later, she answered. **Get your butt to class.**

So I got.

CHAPTER TWENTY

I managed to find some energy for tap dancing, but I wasn't at my best. Sammie gave me a couple of frustrated looks, and I know she was thinking of the "Tap, Rattle, and Roll" show coming up, but she didn't say anything.

After class when everyone had gone, she opened the door cautiously and looked out. "No reporters. Must be chasing some part of the story we haven't even heard about yet. So let's go have a drink. Or, rather, you have a drink and I'll watch." She wasn't enjoying her nursing sobriety.

She texted Sam quickly to make sure all was okay with Isabelle, and we grabbed our purses. We were going out the door when Aunt Ruth showed up. "Forgot my sweater," she said, taking it from a peg.

I had an idea. "Hey, Sammie and I were about to go to Whitney's for a drink. Why don't you join us?" Then I remembered that Serenity drove up from Denver for class, partly to spend time with her sister and aunt. "Bring Serenity and Affinity, too."

She looked surprised, but pleased. She hesitated, then said, "That would be great. Serenity and Affinity already left, though. They're going out to the Yellow Rose. If I was twenty years younger, I'd be right there with them." She smiled. "A drink sounds good."

I crossed my fingers and hoped she would reveal something helpful about the twins. I knew they had an alibi but had a feeling they were somehow connected to the murder, even if indirectly. Maybe the fact that Affinity lived next to Donald's parents was relevant. Why had she been late getting to the museum the night of the murder? Why, *really,* had Serenity been absent from class that night? I was reaching, but who knew what might be relevant?

If I didn't find out anything useful, that would be fine. I just liked Aunt Ruth.

Sammie gave me a nod as we left. She was on board with having company. She liked Aunt Ruth, too.

I gave Derek a thumbs up as we walked in, liking his look of the day—funky red glasses, spiked hair, and one dangly skeleton earring.

I wondered if the waitress taking our orders was Nadia, the one so interested in Donald the night of the murder. I decided it didn't matter and turned my attention to Ruth. "So we know you're Affinity and Serenity's aunt. Mom or Dad's side?"

"Their mom is my sister. Bossy older sister. I think Serenity may have inherited some of that," she smiled. "Likes being in charge. A go-getter."

"What does she do?"

"Runs her own business. A corporate gift company she started years ago. She does *very* well. Seems like a weird business, but what do I know? I work at Verizon."

"Can you get me a deal on a new iPhone?" I was only half kidding.

"I wish."

Aunt Ruth was a talker, one of those people without a filter. Sister Dalmatia would criticize me for saying she was an open book—such a cliché—but she was an open book. My friend Libby is a lot like her, so I recognized the traits. Open book people don't keep secrets, not because they aren't trustworthy but because they have an inability to hide anything. What you see is what you get. Libby will share the most intimate details about her marriage or her gynecologist appointment without even blushing. Information is information is information to her.

Aunt Ruth told us more about Serenity's business, how she'd started it with a $5,000 loan from her mother, repaid the money with interest in just two years, and now had a business reportedly worth, well, she wasn't sure, but a *lot*.

"Is Affinity a go-getter, too?" Sammie asked.

"Lord no. She only works part-time at the Kut 'n Kurl." She lowered her voice to a whisper. "Serenity helps her out a lot."

"And you? Are you a go-getter?"

"I do okay, but I had the sense to have my kids when my eggs were perky and my husband was horny, so that set me back in the career department."

I smiled at the thought of eggs being perky, then asked, "How many kids?"

"Three kids, four grandkids. No horny husband now, though—or any husband, actually." She paused. "You're young. Enjoy men at least long enough to have kids. Then if it doesn't work out, you still have them. The kids, I mean"

Sammie raised her glass in a toast. "Here's to babies."

I raised my glass, too, but I was a tad slower, worrying. *Would I have babies?*

We clicked glasses and Aunt Ruth continued. "If you're lucky, you'll both have kids *and* your man. Lots of people do." She drank. "My ex was perfectly normal for a long time."

She stopped and didn't say more, but I couldn't let a vague statement like that stand. "Then he stopped being normal?"

"He got into body building. Entered competitions all the time, even Mr. America contests."

"Wow. You were married to a Mr. America contestant?" We were both looking at her carefully. Aunt Ruth was pretty ordinary looking to have landed a Mr. America type for a husband.

She sniffed. "It's not what you think. The guy's face doesn't have much to do with that kind of competition. It's all about half-naked bodies posing with overgrown pecs and biceps. Freaky."

We nodded. We'd seen half-naked bodies posing with overgrown pecs and biceps on TV. It wasn't a pleasant sight.

Aunt Ruth continued. "Anyway, he started working out all the time. Got a personal coach who told him what to eat and when. What supplements to take. What exercises to do and for how long. He had charts all over the house, and he was at the gym all the time. Drove me nuts."

"So that's why you broke up?"

"Oh, no. Turns out he was boinking the receptionist at the gym. But, honestly, by then she was kind of welcome to him. I didn't find his cartoon muscles attractive at all."

Cartoon muscles. I smiled, imagining them—dispropor-tionately huge. I waited for more, but it seemed she was fin-ished with Mr. America. I tried a new angle.

"Do Affinity and Serenity have kids?"

"Not yet. I mean Affinity doesn't want them, and Serenity can't have them. But she will soon. She's got a sperm donor lined up." She smiled. "I hear it's some genius professor who doesn't want kids but doesn't want his brilliant genes left out of the gene pool, either. You know, for humanity's sake." She caught our puzzled looks. "Affinity is going to be a surrogate mother for Serenity."

"Really?" Sammie said. "That's some great sister!"

"Yeah. Serenity wants a baby *so* bad. The two of them have pretty much the same DNA—maybe exactly the same? I'm not clear on all that. But as soon as Affinity loses some more weight, those genius little spermies are going to be doing their job." She toasted again. "To sperm."

"What does losing weight have to do with being a surrogate?" Sammie asked.

"Nothing. It's stupid. Affinity wants to lose ten pounds before the insemination. She figures that way, when she gains weight in pregnancy, she'll wind up about the same size she is now after the baby is born." She shook her head. "What an idiot. You think baby weight behaves in predictable ways?" She patted her abdomen. "I used to have an actual waist."

Sammie patted her own waist. "I hear you."

Ruth drank again and rubbed her finger around the rim of the glass. "No one's ever been able to talk sense into Affinity. Waiting any longer is just plain dumb. She's 38, so I don't imagine her eggs are real perky, and the longer she waits, the more unlikely the insemination will work."

I began worrying about my own eggs, which weren't getting any younger, either. *Are there exercises or foods you can eat for healthy eggs?* I wondered silently.

"Ella, your eggs are fine," Sammie said. "You're barely 30." She looked at Ruth. "She obsesses about things. I know she's worrying about her eggs."

"So you want kids. Smart," said Ruth. "They'll drive you crazy, but they'll also be the biggest joy of your life."

Sammie and I smiled. I knew we were both thinking of sweet Isabelle.

"But Affinity? She'd rather have a car than a kid." Ruth shook her head. "I just don't get it."

"A car instead of a kid?" I prompted.

"Oh, Serenity promised Affinity a car as a thank-you for doing this. A car for a baby—can you imagine? I guess there's some ethical or legal thing about paying her outright, but Affinity has always wanted some fancy Mercedes that costs a fortune. Donald Sanders evidently went with them to look at one recently, so maybe it's a done deal." She frowned. "I don't know why they didn't mention that when you were asking about things in class. Anyway, I guess he owned a Mercedes and that made him a good judge or something."

"He had two of them."

"I hope it works out for Serenity," Sammie said.

"Me, too," said Aunt Ruth. "She really wants a baby."

We went on to talk of other things—Verizon, the international pottery festival coming to Juniper in July, cats, the unseasonably hot weather, the best place for a pedicure, whether the Impossible Burger really tastes like a burger, chocolate vs. caramel, and Wayfair. Then Ruth got a text and said she had to leave. "A crisis with my thirteen-year-old grandson. Something about Cocoa Puffs and his science fair project." She gave Sammie a warning look. "You will grow to loathe science fairs one day. Mark my words." She threw some money for her drink on the table and left.

"I kind of regret knowing about this surrogacy plan," I said.

"Because?"

"Because I don't know if we should tell Mildred. Ruth told it like it's no big secret, but it seems awfully personal. But maybe it could be relevant to the murder somehow."

"How?"

"I have no idea."

"We don't tell Mildred," Sammie said, sounding exactly like Geraldine when she is unwilling to bend. "Maybe my opinion is influenced by how I feel having people poke around in my life, but if Serenity wants a baby, I think how she goes about it should be *her* business." She looked at me with a Geraldine-like "I mean business" look in her eyes. "Leave it alone. Telling Mildred—or Dan—feels like a betrayal."

"Okay then," I said. She was clearly not in a mood for any kind of discussion about the issue. I wasn't sure that was the right decision, in light of Dan's often stated opinion that in an investigation everything matters. Still, I would keep my mouth shut. At least for now.

She changed the subject. "So I take it Detective Dan is not so happy with you?"

"It all goes back to Cassie," I said. "Anything involving her goes sideways."

"Are you going to be an evil stepmother and send her off to boarding school?"

"Like that's an option. Dan loves Cassie."

"He loves you, too."

"He says he does. But I get confused about love."

She groaned. "Not the cell phone thing again. Have another drink."

"I have to drive home, so no. And I *worry* about the cell phone thing." I had long ago noticed how many people never, *never* end a phone conversation with "goodbye." It's always, "I love you," no matter how short the conversion. It seems weird to me. Could frequency cheapen the words "I love you" and make them meaningless? Does "I love you" have the same meaning for everyone?

"Let me take a guess at your logic," Sammie said. "You're dad almost never said he loved you, but you know he did. So your twisted mind worries that because Dan *does* say he loves you, that might mean he *doesn't*. That it's just words. Is that what you're thinking?"

"Not exactly," I said slowly. "But sort of. Love is confusing. There are just so many kinds."

"There are not."

"Of course there are. The love I feel for anchovy pizza is not the same as the love I feel for Dan."

"Really? I've seen the look on your face when you bite into a slice of anchovy pizza. It's the same look you get when you talk about Detective Dan." She looked at me over the rim of her glass as she took a drink. "Not the same look a *normal* person gets biting into anchovy pizza, but love nonetheless." Like everyone else I know, except Dan, she shudders at the thought of anchovy pizza.

I smiled. "I do love Detective Dan."

"He loves you *and* anchovy pizza. So what in God's name is your problem?"

I didn't want to say it, but I finally did. "I think if he

really loved me, he'd ask me to marry him. I think maybe he loves Cassie so much he can't see fitting me into his life."

"He *is* fitting you into his life. Maybe he's smart enough to give you and Cassie time to work things out."

I nodded. "Maybe."

"Try harder," Sammie said. "Maybe invite Cassie to lunch. Spend some time with her, just the two of you."

I nodded again. "Maybe."

Sammie got up. "And here's the last thing I'm saying on this subject. Dan is not in charge of your relationship. You are perfectly capable of bringing up marriage yourself. Who says he's the one who has to do the proposing?"

I must have looked terrified.

"Okay, not immediately. Work some more on the Cassie thing." She grabbed my shoulders. "Things will be fine. Trust me. Now I've got to go."

I wasn't ready to call it a night, so I moved to the bar, where I could talk to Derek. He was busy, so I pulled my laptop out of my tote and opened it. I wrote a title:

Questions That Must Be Answered. I capitalized the first, last and all important words in the title, just as sister Dalmatia had taught me. I hesitated over the word *that,* though. Was it important enough for an uppercase letter? I decided it was and started my list:

1. *Who gave Donald caffeine?*

2. *How was it administered?*

3. *How can we blame Harvey Klump?*

As I sat thinking, Derek finished wiping the counter and turned the screen towards him. He saw it had gone into sleep mode.

"My code is …" I began.

"I know your code." He typed it in and looked up after he read my last question. "Seriously? Blame Harvey? Good luck pulling that one off."

"It feels good to imagine it."

"Revenge. It's so mature of you." He left to pour a customer a beer, then came back to me. "I found out something about caffeine today, googling," he said. "Caffeine powder tastes really, really bad. How could someone get Donald to swallow some if it tastes terrible?"

"Pot brownie," I said immediately, surprising him. "Warn him that it's got such a potent grade of marijuana in it that it might not taste as good as usual. Add chocolate chunks and nuts. Provide milk on the side."

"That's very specific."

I shrugged. College had taught me a thing or two not in the curriculum. Also, I'd been thinking about how I would poison someone if I wanted to.

"You might be right," Derek said. "I remember that Donald didn't want to damage his lungs or get wrinkles from sucking on joints, so he stuck to edibles."

"Whoever gave him a poisoned pot brownie had to be a true monster," I said. "What if he decided to share it? They'd have to know they might kill someone else, too."

"I'm not sure someone intent on poisoning has stellar ethical standards," he said.

"True." I stared at the giant bottles of liquor on display on the wall over the bar and thought about ethical standards. *Who the heck was capable of killing Donald Sanders?*

CHAPTER TWENTY-ONE

The memorial service for Donald was to be held at a mega church just north of Jupiter. The plan was for Sam and Sammie to meet Donald's parents in their home. I would stay there with Isabelle while they attended the service.

On the short trip to the Sanders home, Sammie sat in the backseat next to Isabelle, hoping to be able to soothe her if necessary. Isabelle was not one of those babies who falls asleep as soon as the car starts moving. Sam turned into a subdivision where news vans and reporters dotted the street. As planned, Sammie texted Mrs. Sanders, who opened the garage door so we could pull in. The door closed immediately behind us, and Sammie took a deep breath.

"You can do this, babe. I'm with you," Sam said, looking back at her in the rear view mirror. She nodded and got out, going to the other side of the car to unbuckle the baby carrier.

Mr. and Mrs. Sanders stood in the open doorway to the garage, a laundry room visible behind them.

Sam thrust out his hand. "I'm Sam," he said. "Sammie's fiancé. This is our friend Ella."

I shook hands and offered the usual entirely inadequate words, "I'm so sorry for your loss."

Mrs. Sanders somehow managed to hug Sammie and, at the same time, take the baby carrier from her. She set it down on top of the washing machine and managed a long, "Ohhhhh," her tense face softening as Isabelle stopped crying and stared at her. "May I?" Mrs. Sanders asked Sammie.

Sammie nodded and unbuckled the straps. When Mrs. Sanders took Isabelle from the basket, Isabelle didn't fuss at all.

We followed Mrs. Sanders into the kitchen/family room, which was empty of mourners. I was surprised, remembering that before my father's funeral, family members were everywhere.

"We told people to meet us at the church," Mrs. Sanders explained. Her voice broke. "They're sending a car for us in 45 minutes."

Isabelle began squirming in her arms and started what I think of as her soft Phase One Wind-Up Cry. Sammie said, "I'm sorry, but I need to nurse her again before we go." She quickly took Isabelle in her arms, sat down on the couch, and began the complicated process of covering up, unbuttoning, and sliding a fussing baby underneath her clothes. Mr. Sanders tactfully looked away.

Mrs. Sanders sat down on a bar stool at the kitchen island, then stood up again, looking lost, as if she couldn't figure out why she had stood up.

Sam held up a refrigerated bag that he'd carried in. "Could we put this in the fridge? Breast milk?"

She started. "Of course." She took the bag, then swayed a bit. Sam grabbed her arm and led her to the sofa, seating her beside Sammie and Isabelle and then putting the breast milk in the refrigerator himself.

Mr. Sanders had been standing, rigid, but his manners kicked in. "Coffee?" he offered. Knowing it can help to have something to do with your hands in awkward situations, I nodded. While he poured, I looked around the living room, where walls held picture hangers but no pictures. Photos of Donald had probably been taken down to be displayed at the service, I realized.

I sat down at the counter, overcome with sadness. These poor people. Their son. Their only child. I looked around the room and saw a picture remaining on the mantle of Donald as a little boy, teeth missing. They had tucked that little boy into bed at night, read him stories, pushed him in playground swings, watched him in school plays and recitals, picked out birthday presents for him, decorated Christmas trees with him. I tried not to cry.

Mr. Sanders sat down next to his wife, but Sam remained standing. "May I say something?" They nodded. "This is a terrible, terrible day for you, and our hearts ache," he said.

"Thank you," Mr. Sanders murmured.

Sam continued. "Nothing will take away your pain, but one thing may bring a speck of light into your life. Sammie asked me to announce this, as it comes from both of us." He paused. "We would welcome having you be part of Isabelle's life. You are her biological grandparents, and in our opinion, a child can't have too many grandparents to love her."

Mrs. Sanders stared for just a moment taking in what he said, then buried her face in a pillow, crying in gulping sobs. Mr. Sanders put his arm around her, hiding his face. In a few moments, he got up and shook Sam's hand, then reached around him in a man hug.

I sat, frankly bawling.

Sammie pulled Isabelle out from under the nursing

cover and turned to Mrs. Sanders. "Would you like to burp your grandbaby?"

Mrs. Sanders smiled through her tears and pulled herself together. She took Isabelle from Sammie's arms and cradled her. "She has Donald's eyes," she said. "So blue."

Sammie smiled through her tears, nodding.

Mrs. Sanders put Isabelle over her shoulder and began patting her back while Sam rummaged in the giant diaper bag. Isabelle let loose an enormous belch just as Sam was about to hand her a burp cloth.

"Your dress," said Sammie, frowning.

Mrs. Sanders held Isabelle close. "Screw my dress."

Sammie smiled and nevertheless helped her mop up.

Mrs. Sanders got up and walked Isabelle around and around the room, talking to her the whole time. In the kitchen, she told her, "Someday your pictures are going to be on this refrigerator." In the living room area, she pointed to the picture of Donald on the mantle. "When you lose your first tooth, I'll bet you look just like your … just like Donald." She stood at the sliding glass patio door. "Someday you'll play in this back yard."

"I hate to interrupt, but I think she needs to nurse a little more," Sammie said.

Mrs. Sanders nodded. She held Isabelle out to Sam. "Here, Isabelle. Your daddy will take you to your mom."

I completely lost it then and had to leave the room to compose myself and find some tissues. When I came back, carrying the box of tissues with me for everyone, the mortuary car was pulling into the driveway.

"Do you have everything you need?" Mrs. Sanders asked me.

"Izzie-Bee and I will be fine. We're old friends."

"Izzie-Bee. I love it!"

I was liking Mrs. Sanders more and more. She gave me some instructions for the caterers, who would arrive later. Then Sammie took her hand and squeezed it. "We can do this," she said. "For Donald."

Mrs. Sanders nodded. She opened the door, and she and Sammie stepped out into a sea of flashing cameras and reporters.

I watched as the limousine backed out of the driveway, followed by all the reporters and news vans. Exhausted from emotion, I sat down with Isabelle in my lap and looked down at her sweet face.

She was wide awake. "Listen, munchkin, you need your beauty rest," I said. She stared as if she was expecting something more original from me. "Really," I said.

She continued to stare.

I picked her up and kissed her, then stood up and looked outside again. It was a beautiful May day. Why not get some fresh air? I put Isabelle in the baby carrier and moved to the front porch, sitting down on a bench there with Isabelle at my feet. Absently, I rocked the carrier and gazed at the mountains in the distance.

"Come on, Sophie," I heard someone say. Turning to look, I saw a young woman take a stroller from the porch next door and then help a small girl take uncertain steps down the front steps. The woman appeared to be in her early twenties and wore brightly patterned leggings, sneakers, and a stretch top that did her no favors, highlighting rolls of fat around her middle. The top was sleeveless, showing off elaborate tattoos down each arm and across the top of the low-cut back. She had multiple ear piercings, and her hair was lavender, shaved off on one side. Was she the mother or the babysitter? I watched as she started to lift the child into the stroller, then saw me. "Let's go say hi next door," she said to the little girl.

"Si! Si!" the little girl said happily.

Spanish? I wondered at her blond curls.

"She loves CeeCee," the young woman called. "Cecilia." I realized she must be referring to Donald's mother. She bent to talk to the child. "CeeCee is not at home, but a *baby* is visiting. Shall we so go say hi to the baby?"

The child started a jerky run toward us. "Hi," said the young woman, following. "I'm Taylor, Sophie's nanny."

I introduced myself as a friend of a friend of the family. Sophie leaned over, staring into the carrier. "Bay-bee," she said.

"Yes, *baby*. Careful. Don't touch. Just look," said Taylor. She sat down beside me on the steps. "I feel awful for Cecilia and her husband," she said. "Such a terrible thing. Did you know Donald?"

"A bit. Through my friend. You?"

"A bit. Through Cecilia."

We were both quiet for a moment, waiting for the other to say more. Then Taylor spoke up. "Sorry, but I didn't like him much."

I nodded. "Me neither."

Sophie lost interest in the baby and plopped down on the lawn. She patted the grass, then looked at her hand, then patted the grass again. She peered at the blades and tried to pull up a handful.

"How did such nice people wind up with such a loser son?" Taylor asked.

I half-heartedly defended him. "He *was* very successful. You know, in his field."

"I mean loser in the sense of decent human being, at least when it came to women."

"There is that," I said. "It happens sometimes. Awful parents sometimes wind up with wonderful kids. Wonderful parents sometimes wind up with jerks."

"Personally, I think it had more to do with his weird Uncle Bart, CeeCee's sister's husband. He could be the poster child for how not to treat women. Definitely a bad influence."

That was interesting, though I wondered how much influence an uncle could have. I heard a garage door open on the other side of us and idly watched a car back out. Affinity Knowles sat in the passenger side of the car, a man in the driver's seat. I remembered then that Donald had said Affinity lived next door to his parents.

Taylor nodded toward the car. "I bet her boyfriend doesn't know she was screwing Donald."

"Affinity was?"

"You know her?"

"She's been showing up all over town. Volunteering. Taking classes. She's in a tap dance class I'm taking."

"Small world. Yes, she was sleeping with him. After Cecilia and Frank moved in last fall, they invited everyone in the neighborhood over for a party. Any fool could see that Affinity was really into Donald."

"He was pretty spectacular looking."

"Duh. But then he talked."

Someone understood! "Right. Didn't you hate how he said *have ran* and *supposebly* and *flustrate?*"

She looked puzzled. "I meant that he was unbelievably boring."

"Oh." I looked at Taylor while she took a tissue and wiped green snot coming from Sophie's nose. Sophie squirmed and protested, then went back to playing with the grass. "So are you a live-in nanny?" I asked.

"Yes. I'm not welcome in my own family's house."

I felt alarm. What kind of person was she? And yet the people next door were entrusting her with their child?

The alarm must have shown on my face. "Don't freak. It's not like I'm a criminal. Just, you know, someone who doesn't fit in real well with church people who think I'm going to hell because I like women. Plus, you know, the tattoos and hair and all."

Taylor certainly was the chatty sort.

Sophie had lost interest in the grass and was standing up, looking around. "Want to take her out in the back yard where she can run around?" I asked. "I think the back is fenced."

"Of course it is. CeeCee fenced it just for Sophie. Got a little jungle gym for her, too. Let's go."

We went through the Sanders' house to the back yard and settled in lawn chairs while Sophie played with a red wagon. Isabelle quietly looked around, lying comfortably in her carrier.

"So you're pretty sure Affinity was sleeping with Donald?" I asked. Taylor seemed like a person who could handle bluntness.

"She wound up taking a 'walk' with him after that party

last fall, but Donald didn't come back home until after 2:00 a.m. I know. I was up with Sophie."

"Don't her folks get up with her at night?" I wasn't really familiar with nanny responsibilities, but it seemed that a child would want her mommy or daddy in the middle of the night.

"Not usually. They, like, have to be fresh for work and all. I don't mind. Sophie responds better to me anyway."

I decided never to have a nanny, not if it meant my child would grow to respond better to the nanny than to me. There wasn't much chance of a nanny on a teacher's salary, though.

Sophie pulled the wagon to the edge of a dry creek that ran through the yard and began putting rocks in the wagon. Taylor continued. "So Donald visited his folks several times over the next few months, and I noticed a *lot* of late night visits to Affinity—usually when he got home from dancing. Without her, of course. She's a little too old for his image."

"You know about his dancing?"

"Oh, sure. His mom talks about it all the time, how we ought to see him on the dance floor. She said he ought to be in movies. I mean, honestly, she's a good mom, but I'd say she taught her boy to be a little too full of himself."

"Hmmmm," I said, deciding to keep quiet and just see what else she would tell me.

Sophie pulled the wagon over to us and gravely handed me a rock.

"Thank you," I said.

She handed Taylor a rock, then turned the wagon over, dumping the rest of the rocks beside us. Then she started filling the wagon again.

Taylor continued. "Donald didn't take Affinity out or anything, like on dates. Just slept with her. But she put up with it, so I don't feel sorry for her." She accepted another rock from Sophie. "The guy you saw driving her car is her boyfriend, Knox. What a piece of work."

"Oh?"

"He's a flat earther. You know, one of those people who think that the world is flat, with, like, a dome fitting over it. I got the whole story a couple of weeks ago at a barbecue at CeeCee's." She shook her head. "It's scary. He really believes that shit."

"So Affinity is juggling both of them?"

"Probably not too hard. She knows from CeeCee when Donald is going to be in town, so she just doesn't make plans with Knox on those dates. Shouldn't be too hard to fool him. He's a guy who thinks we're living on a cake plate under a big dome. Jesus." She looked at Sophie. "Oops. I try to watch my language around her."

I changed the subject. "So who do you think murdered Donald?"

"No idea. You?"

"No idea, but I'm trying to find out. Kind of investigating on my own. I think the police woman in charge is looking in all the wrong places."

"Yeah? Are you making any progress?"

"Not yet. But this information about Donald's affair with Affinity could be important. Who knows? I don't know what's important yet. Could I have your number, in case I think of any questions?"

"Sure. Hang on." She pulled her phone from the waist of her leggings, and we exchanged information. "I need to take the stroller and go for our walk now. Sophie's parents will ask about her exercise."

I wondered how riding in a stroller qualified as exercise. Taylor must have read my mind. "She doesn't ride the *whole* way." She turned to Sophie. "It's time to put all these rocks back where you got them. Shall we help?"

Sophie nodded, and we finished filling the wagon, then emptied the rocks back into the dry creek.

Isabelle had fallen asleep, so I carried the baby carrier carefully as we walked through the house to the front porch, where Taylor bent to pick up Sophie and put her in the stroller. Sophie grabbed a yellow toy duck and tossed it on the ground. It immediately lit up and began blaring "Three Little Ducks." Taylor grabbed it and shut it off.

Alarmed at the noise, I looked down at Isabelle.

Taylor looked, too, and then said, "Don't worry. She's out—the *out* out kind, not the "I'm just faking you out kind."

"You know a lot about babies."

Her whole being transformed. She glowed. "I *love* babies."

A catering van pulled into the driveway, and Taylor said, "Come on, Sophie. We'll be back later to pay our respects."

I went inside and put Isabelle's carrier safely on the floor in the bedroom. It was warm outside, so no one would be coming in with coats and wake her. Then I tried to stay out of the caterers' way, playing Words with Friends on my phone until I was caught up, then opening my news feed. But instead of clicking on an actual news item like "US Senate: Recent Floor Activity," I chose items like, "Ten Great Curly Hair Tips and Tricks" and "Dip is Dumb. Have Seasoned Crudités Instead." My brain wasn't up for anything difficult.

Eventually, the streets outside filled with cars, and people started coming into the house. Both the memorial and the reception afterward were by invitation only, so two off-duty policemen were stationed at the door. Through the front window, I saw Kendall try to scam them with a tearful face, a black dress, and a big hat, but these guys were tough. She didn't have an invitation, so she didn't get in.

Most people who did get in appeared to be around the age of Mr. And Mrs. Sanders—friends and relatives, I assumed. A couple of models—or at least I assumed they were models, since they were tall and ridiculously thin—hung out far away from the food. Another guy about my age hovered by the bar. He made up for his ordinary looks with impeccable taste, wearing an expensive looking suit.

"Rich guy," Taylor said, joining me. "Started that huge medical marijuana company. He was born the same day in the same hospital as Donald. *Bucky* somebody or other."

Bucky? I wondered about Kendall's story. If this was the same Bucky who stopped having anything to do with Donald, why was he here?

"Bucky's here with his Mom," Taylor said. "His mother is CeeCee's good friend."

Maybe that would explain it.

Affinity nodded at me once but kept to her side of the room, the man I assumed was Flat Earther Knox never leaving her side. Sophie's young parents stood in the corner of the living room with glasses of white wine, letting Taylor tend to their daughter.

Mr. and Mrs. Sanders introduced Sammie again and again as Donald's long-time dance partner. Somehow, Sammie managed to find kind words to say about him. I heard a lot of, "Those eyes of his—so powerful in photographs, weren't they?" and "I've never known anyone who could jitterbug like Donald. Or salsa. Oh, man, he could do a wicked salsa. I loved dancing with him." Then she would smile. "But I also love dancing with my fiancé. This is Sam."

She even managed a few graceful tears. I marveled at her poise.

Sam told me that Mr. Sanders had spoken at the memorial. "It was kind of surprising," he said. "He sounded really pissed off and said that he didn't want to hear one more person tell him that 'Things happen for a reason.' He didn't find it comforting to think of a god who would kill a loved one as part of some big plan. 'Sometimes things happen for *no* reason,' he said, 'so please don't try to comfort me by saying they do.'"

"That was kind of gutsy of him. People always say that at funerals."

"They didn't after that."

Sammie brought Isabelle into the room after her long nap and sat down with her on the sofa. Across the room Mrs. Sanders reached down and took little Sophie's hand. "Let's go see the baby."

"Bay-bee."

"This is Isabelle," she said to Sophie. She addressed Sammie then. "Can Isabelle come to CeeCee?"

"Of course she can go to CeeCee."

And with that, her name was decided. Donald's mother would be CeeCee to Isabelle."

Sam backed carefully through the mob as we left, letting them know with his slow but steady progress that he wasn't stopping for anyone. One reporter leaped back just before a wheel rolled over his foot, yelling at Sam as if it were his fault.

Sam ignored him, and soon we were on our way. I looked back at Sammie, whose eyes were closed.

"You okay, honey?" Sam asked, glancing in the rear-view mirror.

"As okay as you can be after watching people's souls ripped out."

We drove home in silence.

I closed my own eyes and reviewed what I'd learned from Taylor. I had a hunch I'd discovered the murderer.

As soon as Sammie and Sam dropped me off, I called Dan, who was still at work. He was still pretty mad at me, but maybe this would help.

"I think I've got it," I said.

"Got what?" He sounded distracted.

"Who murdered Donald. I mean, I've had a bit of suspicion for a while, but now I know."

"I told you to stay out of this. I mean, *asked* you to stay out of this."

"It was Affinity Knowles. She was having an affair with Donald, and I think she left the museum to meet him at the dance studio. She'd probably gotten sick of him because he was just using her, so she offed him."

"Donald was murdered sometime between 8:15 and 8:30."

"So? Affinity left the museum shortly after the lecture started. Probably about 7:40. That gave her plenty of time."

"We have a picture of Affinity and her twin sister at an

ATM in north Denver at 8:45. They were apparently a little tipsy and joking around for the camera. How could Affinity have killed Donald between 8:15 and 8:30 and appeared in Denver 15 minutes later? Or even 30 minutes later? It's over an hour drive, even if traffic is decent."

He had me there. I was quiet, thinking.

"Ella?"

"I get it." I waited a moment. "Maybe we should look at Knox, the boyfriend. Do you know about Knox?"

"It's Mildred's investigation." His voice was sharp.

"You're sounding frustrated with me."

"That's because I *am* frustrated with you."

Was he going to be mad at me forever?

Then his voice softened. "But I'm not too frustrated to come over later."

"Good. I need comforting after my emotionally exhausting day."

"I'll come after work. Probably about 9:00 tonight." There was a smile in his voice. "But I'm not coming to comfort you for your emotionally exhausting day. I'm coming over to comfort you for being *wrong* about Affinity."

He hung up.

CHAPTER TWENTY-TWO

My first appointment with the therapist was the next morning, and it started out fine. Dr. Rodriguez explained what I already knew about systematic desensitization. I'd be guided to imagine needles in more and more intimate circumstances, increasing my "exposure" gradually until I would eventually be able to handle having an actual needle in my presence. We talked about my fear, and she led me through my first exercise.

In seconds, I was gripping the arms of the chair and starting to sway.

"Open your eyes," she said. "You are safe."

I breathed through the dizziness as her soothing voice calmed me.

Then she said, "Let's try it again."

I did not like systematic desensitization therapy. At all. The exercise in the therapist's office had been bad enough, but my homework was to lie on the floor at least once a day and imagine a needle, any kind of needle, as I breathed deeply and calmly, knowing that my imagination couldn't hurt me.

Saturday afternoon, I opened the front door for air and nudged the coffee table close to the sofa for extra room. I took several deep breaths and stretched out on the floor. Closing my eyes, I started by imagining a tiny embroidery needle with pink thread hanging from it. Pink seemed friendly. I imagined Baba's hand holding it as she cross-stitched *I love you* on a sweet lavender baby blanket. I felt a bit vertigo but got through it. Then I made the needle bigger in my mind, without pink thread or Baba's hand. The room started getting a bit wavy, and I felt sick.

That was enough visualization for the day, I decided. Or maybe for many days.

I heard something at the screen door. Skyden. He had been watching. "Can you play?" he asked.

"Sorry, sweetie. I have to go." I mashed my face against the screen door and said, "Give me a kiss," which made him laugh. He kissed me through the screen. Then I closed the door, which didn't please him at all.

I knew from experience that nothing less than a firmly closed door will deter Skyden.

To make more of an effort with Cassie, I had invited her out for ice cream. I figured she would be pleased to go anywhere, even with me, since she was grounded and couldn't do anything without adult accompaniment. Dan had even granted his permission for the outing, happy that I was reaching out to her.

When I walked into Dan's house to pick her up, the first indications that something was wrong were the indentations in the carpet. The sofa and a chair in Dan's living room had been moved but not placed back precisely where they had been. There were also lines in the carpet left by a vacuum cleaner.

Cassie was not the kind of girl to surprise Dad by cleaning the house, so something was up. I recognized the damning details from an incident with my brothers when they were in high school. They'd had a party when Mom and Dad took me to Denver to see *Chicago* for my birthday, and we stayed overnight at a hotel. The boys had been smart—beer cans carted to someone else's recycle bin and the kitchen left just a teeny bit messy, but teenage-boy messy, not party messy. Still, Mom noticed the carpet indentations immediately and said, "You guys are grounded and if there is one bit of damage, large or small, from your party, you're paying for it." The boys were mystified about what had given them away, and so was my dad. But I knew. If the boys had done more vacuuming in their lives, they would have realized their mistake.

Cassie was not supposed to have anyone over while she was grounded, but she had obviously broken that rule. Who had come? How many people? Male or female? I decided to learn more before—or if—I acted. "Want me to help you put the furniture back where it was?" I asked, gesturing toward the carpet impressions.

She gave me an alarmed glance and nodded. We scooted the furniture over an inch.

"What gives?" I said. Then I waited. I'd learned in teaching that sometimes it's smart to just shut up and let the kids hang themselves.

Cassie seemed to know the technique. She sat waiting, too. Finally, though, she broke. "I didn't mean to have any-one over. Really! My friend Lacey was in town to buy some pottery for her mom's birthday. That little Almost Heaven store downtown? Her mom loves stuff from there. You know, like those cheesy pots with the hearts on the bottom?"

The details were good. Either she'd thought things through, in case she was busted, or she was telling the truth.

I nodded. "Was she alone?"

"She was alone. I swear." She hesitated. "But then, as long as she was here, we decided to make popcorn and watch a movie."

I glanced toward the kitchen and saw two bowls in the drain. I was sure she would be putting one of them away before her dad got home. "What did you watch?

"An old version of *Ghostbusters.*"

"Male or female?"

"Female. Leslie Jones was in it. And we spilled some popcorn, so I vacuumed."

"Would you have vacuumed if you'd spilled it and Lacey wasn't here?"

"Um, no."

"That was your mistake. Was Trevor here?"

"No!"

"Beer? Alcohol? Pot?"

"I'm a runner!" she said with disdain.

"Okay. I'll keep it to myself. For now."

"Thank you," she breathed. "Let me grab my phone. It's charging."

As I waited for her at the door, I saw a car I recognized doing a U-turn and heading away from the cul-de-sac. Trevor's car.

Maybe she had been telling the truth about Lacey. Maybe. But I'll bet Trevor had been planning to stop in, if he hadn't been here already.

I took Cassie to a little cookie and ice cream shop downtown, and she ordered a triple scoop in a cup while I ordered a single. "How are you handling being grounded?" I asked as we sat down.

"It sucks."

"Have you tried reading? I know some really good mysteries."

She looked at me as though I'd suggested she watch *PBS NewsHour*, but she limited her answer to "No." The top scoop of her ice cream was leaning precariously, so she balanced it with her spoon, then circled the mound with several circles of her tongue.

Silence.

Finally, desperate, I decided to try talking to her about the only thing we seemed to have in common—Donald's murder. She perked right up when I asked her opinion about the most likely suspects. After we tossed around ideas, she said, "I think we need to look more at those ladies in your tap class. There's something we're missing. I could come visit again, but I think it would be better if I actually signed up for the class."

"Really? You actually want to tap dance?"

"It's not pole dancing, but I think I can live through it."

Since murder was going so well as a method of bonding, we decided to stop for a few minutes at Derek's apartment and talk murder with him, too. I wanted to pick his brain some more about the Cheyenne women. They were a possible source of information I had not been able to explore yet.

I began by giving Cassie a little background. "Derek talked to the waitress at Whitney's who waited on Donald. Some young women recognized him and asked for autographs, then asked him to join them at their table."

"So maybe *they* poisoned Donald?" Cassie suggested.

"I doubt they carried around poison on the off-chance they would meet someone they wanted to kill," Derek said.

I continued explaining. "Nadia, the waitress, found out they were from Cheyenne and going to New Zealand for a vacation. They were going to spend the night at the airport and catch an early morning flight."

"Nadia found all this out by just waiting on them?" Cassie asked.

"I'm told she hung around the table *a lot*," Derek said. "You've actually seen Donald, right?"

She nodded, understanding. "Oh. Got it."

"According to Nadia, Donald suggested that they meet later at the Yellow Rose," I said. "That's a country-western bar."

"I *know,*" Cassie said.

"So here's what we need to do—find out who those women were," I said.

"Why?"

"I don't know why until I talk to them."

"This will be a challenge," Derek said. "I never even saw them."

"He was busy waiting on his boyfriend," I explained to Cassie.

"Oh, you're gay?"

"I'm gay."

"Got it. So, like, you wouldn't have noticed them even if your boyfriend wasn't there."

"I'm gay, Cassie, not blind. I notice and appreciate nice-looking men *and* women. I didn't happen to see these partic-ular women, but I'm sure they were good-looking. Donald wouldn't have joined them otherwise.

"So how do we find them?" I needed to get Derek and Cassie back on track. "Can't you look at credit card receipts or something?"

"No. I don't own Whitney's."

"Okay, could you ask Nadia if she remembers their names or how long they were going to be in New Zealand or *anything* else?"

He sighed. "I'll ask. I'll ask everyone who works there if they remember anything, but it's such a long shot, Ella."

"I know it's a long shot. But it's worth a try."

"If were going to the Yellow Rose to meet Donald, maybe someone there remembers them," Cassie suggested.

"Good point," I said, wondering how to find out.

"No, we're not going dancing," Derek said, anticipating my next thought. "It's not feasible to interview people who were drinking and dancing that night, at least with no more information than 'They were from Cheyenne.' Probably a quarter of the people at the Rose are from Cheyenne."

He was right.

"Do you remember anyone else who was at Whitney's that night?" Cassie asked. "Like, you know, other than your boyfriend? Like a customer? Someone who might have paid attention to what was going on at Donald's table?"

Derek thought. "I do remember this guy Leo was there. His wife left him, and he comes in a lot looking for women and hoping to pick up someone. He's not a bad-looking guy, just comes off as a little desperate sometimes."

"Maybe you should give Leo some pick-up pointers," I said.

"Off the subject," Cassie said. "Besides, Derek probably

wouldn't be all that believable. You know—a gay guy giving pick-up advice."

Derek raised one of his eyebrows and looked at her. Before he could start a lecture about pick-ups applying to both sexes, Cassie started making odd faces.

I knew exactly what she was doing. "I can't do it either," I said. "The eyebrow thing."

"It's amazing. It shoots up right above your green eye," she told Derek. "And you've got different colored eyes. One is brown, and one is green."

"I'm aware of that," he said. "And I can do it with my other eye, too." He raised the eyebrow over his brown eye. "You wouldn't believe how helpful this is with *pickups*."

She smiled. She got the message.

"Let's get back to the subject," I said. "Maybe Leo heard something or tried to pick up one of the Cheyenne girls."

"Women," Derek said, grinning to have caught me. "Young women."

"Okay, right. Young women. Can you talk to Leo next time he comes in?"

"Yes. But what do you hope to find out?"

"I don't know, but any little piece of information might help break the case," I said.

"You sound like a detective," Cassie said.

"Don't tell your dad," I said.

"I thought we weren't supposed to have secrets from my dad," she said. Her eyes were wide and innocent.

Derek laughed.

Cassie was allowed out again that night to attend the next lecture at the museum with Dan and me. Looking at the huge number of people in the museum reception area when we arrived, Cassie said, "Is the theremin, like, some kind of cult instrument in Juniper? Like, they love it?"

"No. It's gossip people are looking for tonight," I said. I was glad Dan was with me.

The museum board members had decided, in light of the recent "ugliness," that Geraldine, Affinity, and I should not act in an official capacity that evening. As one of the people initially accused of posing naked with a glockenspiel, that was fine with me. I hadn't wanted to go at all and have people looking at me and whispering, but Geraldine had said, "We have to go as regular members of the public, hold our heads high, and show that we have nothing at all to be ashamed of." At her insistence, all of us tainted ladies attended, except for Mariah, the receptionist who actually had posed for the nude pictures. According to Geraldine, Mariah was no longer working at the museum.

"Did she really disappear?" I asked.

Geraldine shrugged.

The new receptionist was not anyone Donald or any other young man was likely to hit on. She reminded me of my soft, plump great Aunt Hope.

Wisely, the museum board had placed a docent—a fully trained docent, Geraldine pointed out—beside the display of the double-piped Taiwanese nose flute, which was the highlight of the exhibit. Everyone wanted to see what someone had used to hit Donald Sanders, and everyone wanted to see where he had snapped naked pictures of someone who was *not,* I hoped they remembered, Affinity Knowles, Geraldine, or me.

While Cassie sat with her phone on the same bench she'd used the night of the murder, Dan and I circulated, greeting people we knew. All of the Streusals were there, of course. "We'll be keeping an eye out for good-looking women as suspects," Carl winked.

I talked briefly with Serenity, who had driven up from Denver to go out with Affinity after the lecture. Later I watched her and her sister mingle with the crowd. *How can two people look and dress so much alike, yet make such different impressions?* I wondered. Both wore knit tops with skirts that hit above the knee, but Affinity paired hers with high platform sandals, while Serenity wore flats. Their hair was about the same length, highlighted in about the same way, and both wore large gold hoops in their ears. They were so similar, yet Serenity somehow came off looking like one of those people always chosen to chair a committee because everyone knows, just *knows*, she'll get the job done and do it right. Affinity, on the other hand, looked like the person you'd never, ever put in charge of even bringing donuts to a meeting because she'd almost certainly forget. Somehow, Affinity just looked less respectable.

Maybe it was the push-up bra.

The theremin lecture was a hit. The speaker, who had come up from Colorado Springs, told us how in 2002 she had heard a National Public Radio piece about a theremin concert at the American Museum of Natural History. She was curious, and since she happened to be in New York at a conference, she went. "A woman named Pamelia Kurstin played the theremin at the concert, and it was beautiful," she said. "Theremins were available at the concert for attendees to experiment with, and I was hooked. That was the most important thing that I learned as a result of my first job out of college—that I wanted to learn to play the theremin."

So she did. She loved how the instrument, one of the first electronic instruments, is played without touching it. Antennas generate an electromagnetic field, and the distance of the hands from the antennas controls pitch and volume. "It's best known for creating a spooky sound, but it doesn't have to sound spooky at all," she said, and then she demonstrated. The music was eerily lovely.

It was a fascinating evening. As Dan drove us back to my place, I thought about how things are not always as they appear. The theremin doesn't even look like a musical instrument, yet it is, and in the right hands, it can surprise you with haunting, beautiful sounds.

I wondered what was not as it appeared in the murder of Donald Sanders. Would anything surprise us when we finally got to the truth?

CHAPTER TWENTY-THREE

The next morning I woke up at 6:00 and decided to drop by Baba's for coffee, knowing she would be up. I needed advice.

"Did you ever keep stuff from Jaja?" I asked, as we sat down with our coffees. "Is it okay for a wife not to tell her husband something about their kids?"

Baba laughed. "Lordy, honey, a lot of kids owe their lives to mothers not telling their husbands something about their kids."

"You lied to Jaja sometimes?"

"No, no. I selectively edited." She thought back, shaking her head as she remembered. "One time Jaja had to go to Kansas City for something. Your Uncle Bob was a real handful then and had been giving us fits. Hard to believe now, isn't it?"

It was. He's now some kind of insurance adjuster in Laramie, and on the rare occasions he joins us for family events, I sometimes have to remind myself who he is.

"Anyway, Bob left a six-pack of beer in the Chevy pickup while Jaja was gone and then managed to lock himself out. He knew there would be hell to pay if he got caught with beer—he was only 16. So with his not-fully-cranking-on-all-cylinders brain, he decided to knock out the back window to get the beer out." She shook her head, remembering. "His dad was already so dang mad at him that I couldn't deal with him finding out Bob had broken the window himself. So I helped him get the window fixed before Jaja got home."

"Wow. You were easy."

"No. I got a *lot* of uncomplaining assistance with the dishes for an entire month. Jaja knew something was up, but he just didn't want to know."

"Do you think Jaja ever selectively edited stuff for you?"

"Of course he did. I didn't find out until years later that the reason your Uncle Paul suddenly couldn't sleep at night was because he had watched *The Exorcist* with his father— after I had forbidden it. I knew the kid's nature couldn't take that kind of thing. He was only seven."

I thought back to that time I had come home late from a date and was surprised to find my parents up having cocoa. Dad probably never knew that when I took off my sweater, my bra fell out of a pocket and onto the floor. Mom quietly picked it up and slipped it to me.

I decided to keep Cassie's "no visitors" violation to myself, for now.

Things were awfully quiet on the murder front. No one had been arrested. Harvey Klump hadn't come up with any recent speculation on his blog. The paparazzi had largely disappeared. Could the murder be settling into old news? I was worried because the case hadn't been solved. Until it was, a cloud of suspicion would be hanging over Sammie. And me.

Sam announced that it was time we all resumed being the people we were before the murder and return to normal. "Screw the gossip," he said. "Screw the paparazzi. Screw the world. We're getting a babysitter and going out for a nice dinner at the Saturn. We're going back to real life. Our new real life."

I was so glad Sammie had found Sam. She could wrap most men around her little finger or, worse, use them. (No, she wasn't above that. I remember the guy with the Super Bowl tickets.) But Sam was not a man who would let her run roughshod over him. Anyone could tell they were a match.

When Dan and I walked into the apartment for our date night, Geraldine was gumming Isabelle's tummy and making her laugh. We watched for a bit, smiling.

"Get going," Geraldine said. "Izzie-Bee and I are fine."

"The breast milk …"

"I know where it is."

"And if she needs a clean sleep sack …"

"I know where it is. Go."

We went.

"Wine!" Sammie said as we walked down the block to the restaurant. "I can't wait." She looked at me. "Don't worry. I already pumped enough milk for tomorrow. Isabelle won't get drunk." She looked at Dan. "Bellella is a worrier."

"Really? I had no idea." I elbowed him. "We can really celebrate," he said. No paparazzi around."

"And not one of us is in jail," I said.

"Yet," said Sammie.

"A positive attitude, please," Dan said. He bent and held his hand out, as if we were royalty. "Miladies."

We stepped inside the restaurant.

"Reservations for four. Quillan," Sam said. While the host marked our table on his board and gathered napkins rolled with silverware, I looked at the nook to the side of the host/hostess desk. A low wall with plants separated the table from the vestibule. At that table sat Harvey Klump, the woman I assumed was his wife, Police Chief Mendocito, and his lawyer wife, Lauren Rose, all looking down at their menus. "Danger!" I whispered. "Harvey Klump."

"Really?" said Sam. He peered through the plants. "Hang on a minute." While we watched, he walked around the ledge and approached Harvey's table, beaming. "Excuse me for interrupting," he said, "but aren't you the guy running for mayor?"

Harvey beamed back at him and got up, holding out his hand like a good politician.

Sam shook it. "I read your blog every day!"

"Wonderful!" said Harvey.

"I'm Sam Quillan, and I'm engaged to Sammie Russo. You know, the woman you keep writing about? And there she is with other people you keep writing about—Ella Polansky and Officer Dan Sherman." We took our cue and smiled, so happy with each other, so not bothered by silly Harvey.

Harvey paled. Those at his table looked down in embarrassment. "Just wanted to meet you," Sam said. "See what a guy like you looks like." Somehow, Sam infused the words "a guy like you" with shade. He held up his hand in a wave, and we followed our waiter to the table on the other side of the room.

"As long as we're having fun here, shouldn't you stop before we sit down and give me a passionate kiss?" Sammie murmured.

"No," he said. "I'm not a restaurant kisser."

"But you're a pretend-to-be-thrilled-at-meeting-a-jerk kind of guy?" I asked.

"I wasn't pretending. I *was* glad to meet him. Glad to show him I'm a nice guy who isn't even a little bit afraid of him."

"He may not be a restaurant kisser, but I am," said Dan, bending me over in a Hollywood style kiss. People at the next table applauded.

At that, we heard a disturbance at the door. A photographer with a Denver television station logo on his camera approached us, taping as he walked, while a woman I assumed was a reporter stayed at his side. The restaurant host hurried behind them, saying, "Ma'am! Sir!"

"So much for no paparazzi," I muttered. I decided to continue acting as if we didn't have a care in the world. "Oh, let us help you," I said. "We'll pose." I moved behind Sam and Sammie, who were already seated, and Dan joined me.

"You should wait until we order our wine, and we can toast," Sammie said to the photographer. "It will make even better footage."

The host and the photographer looked confused at our willingness to cooperate, but the reporter looked thrilled. "What are you celebrating?" she asked.

"Love!" said Sam.

"I must ask you to leave," the host insisted. "I have called security."

"Like this place has a security team," the reporter sniffed.

At that, one of the cooks came from the kitchen drying his hands. He was enormous, with beefy arms.

"Nunzio," the host said, "please escort this couple out."

Nunzio took an arm from each of the intruders and "guided" them to the front door.

"My apologies," the host said. "I will send a complimentary bottle of wine to your table."

People throughout the restaurant were staring. *In real life, what would we do in such a situation?* I wondered. It was hard to tell. Our real lives, in the past, had not included paparazzi.

I opted for grace and dignity. I smiled and nodded, and Dan and I sat down.

"A toast to us," Sam said cheerfully. "We're together. We're happy. We have wine. We have a would-be mayor feeling uncomfortable and wondering what we've got up our sleeves. We've got the best baby in the world and wonderful friends."

"And we haven't been arrested," Sammie added.

We toasted with our water glasses. When the waiter came and poured a sample of the complimentary wine, Sammie tasted it and sighed. "Ah. It's wine."

"She likes it," Sam said, nodding at the waiter to pour for all of us.

We toasted again.

When it came time to order, I chose the mussels. Not at all to my surprise, the waiter said. "Perfect."

Dan hesitated and said, "Really? I was going to order the seafood linguini, but if the mussels ..."

"Don't start," I warned him. He smiled and ordered the seafood linguini.

We ate. We drank. We laughed. It was a normal evening—if you didn't count the visit by paparazzi. Or the presence of the mayoral candidate who had made borderline libelous suggestions about us, or the police chief who had allowed the ludicrous accusations by an actress to go on too long, or the lawyer who thought we had almost killed her son by feeding him hazelnuts. If you ignored all that, it *was* a normal evening.

Our new normal.

CHAPTER TWENTY-FOUR

Monday afternoon, I had to take a class for recertification. I needed two more credit hours to advance to the next pay step, and I'd signed up for "Fundamentals of Blended Learning." I wasn't looking forward to it. The course description said it involved "rethinking time allocation of resources" and "fostering engagement" and finding ways "to combine technology-driven learning in an optimized educational environment." I strongly questioned the expertise of anyone who couldn't come up with a more appealing description than that. Would he be able to foster *my* engagement?

As it turns out, he couldn't. The first afternoon was deadly dull, and I had two more afternoons to go, plus a technology-driven project to come up with. Venting afterward with three friends over a glass of wine was a lot more engaging than the class had been.

One friend came home with me for more venting on a different subject. Ainsley was not happy that her divorced boyfriend was having dinner, again, with his ex-wife, who wanted to discuss a problem with their son. "I mean, it's like they might as well still be married," Ainsley complained. "They talk all the time. She even called him to come over and fix a problem with her automatic sprinkler system. And of course he goes over there every other day to pick up Franklin. Are they connected for *life*?"

I didn't like discussing this topic with her. Dan had been divorced for 13 years, and I'd already figured out that he *was* connected to his ex for life, through Cassie. What I hadn't figured out was how I was going to learn to deal with that.

The only comfort I could give Ainsley was popcorn, Lindor chocolates, another glass of wine, and a comfortable place to watch three taped episodes of *Jane the Virgin*. (I had decided that the Hallmark Channel wasn't right for her. It was pretty clear to me that things were not going to work out with her boyfriend, so why rub her face in the perfection of the Hallmark world?)

When she left, I picked up the murder mystery I'd been reading, hoping that reading about a detective would give me some ideas, but I fell asleep.

At midnight, Derek woke me with a phone call. "That guy Leo came into the bar tonight, and I talked to him. He was a success, sort of, in the hitting-on department the night of the murder. He got a phone number for one of the Cheyenne ladies."

"Wow! Great!" I waited.

Nothing.

"Can I *have* the number?" Sometimes he really tried to annoy me.

"It was fake."

I groaned.

Derek had mercy on me. "I did find someone else who got her name. Clay."

I was puzzled. "Is Clay bi?"

He ignored me and continued. "I finally got a chance to talk to him to see if he remembered anything from that night.

He's been in Iowa, you know, visiting his folks. Anyway, he said he was standing near the table with Donald and the girls, waiting for a seat at the bar."

"Young women."

"Yeah, yeah. Young women. Anyway, he heard one of them say something like, "Partridge, Peacock, Parrot, what difference does it make if you didn't want to go out with him anyway?' and then she said, 'Because I'm a Partridge! If he can't even get my name right, I'm not interested.' Then the first one said to Donald, 'Jasmine gets pretty picky.' So he knew her name was Jasmine Partridge."

"He remembered all that from chance eavesdropping?" I was skeptical.

'Jasmine' stuck, he said, because he thought it was kind of different and he remembered it was a flower. He was pretty bored waiting for a table, so he started thinking that it was a good thing her parents didn't name her Motherwort."

"What?"

"It's a flowering plant. His mother's into gardening. Clay thinks a lot like you."

I could see how that might be true. I definitely needed to get to know this guy. "So how did he remember the last name?"

"He got the line 'and a partridge in a pear tree' stuck in his head and couldn't sleep that night. 'The Twelve Days of Christmas' kept looping through his brain."

It made sense. "Jasmine Partridge. Thank you! And thank Clay."

"He's not bi," Derek said. He hung up.

I sat in bed thinking and petting Fluffles, who had decided to curl in my lap. Then I texted Cassie:

You up?

Yes.

Cheyenne woman is Jasmine Partridge. 6 degrees?

She texted back. **On it.**

CHAPTER TWENTY-FIVE

I was soaking in the tub after another dismal afternoon with "Fundamentals of Blended Learning" when the phone rang. Drying my hands, I grabbed the phone, careful not to drop it in the tub.

It was Cassie. "I found her! Jasmine. Six degrees worked again."

"Really? Did you get a phone number or address?"

"Let me tell you what I did."

I didn't really care about the six steps, but I knew I'd have to hear the whole story.

"So my friend Skye moved here from Wyoming last year, so I asked her if she knew anyone named Jasmine Partridge. She didn't, so I called this goat roper in my class."

"That's not very nice, Cassie."

"Oh, that's, like, just what we call cowboy kids. It doesn't mean anything."

"Oh? Like some people call black people or Hispanic people names like … well, you know. It's just what we *call* them?"

She sighed. "Okay, you're right. I asked a kid I know who wears cowboy boots and blue jeans and western shirts and a big CASE belt buckle if he knew anyone named Jasmine Partridge. I figured, like, Cheyenne is cowboy country. Maybe he'd know someone."

"A stretch. But did he?"

"He didn't. But he has relatives who live in Cheyenne, so he said he'd ask his aunt."

"Nice guy." I wondered if he was another one of Cassie's admirers.

"His aunt had heard of some Partridges in the area, so she asked her sister, who's a UPS driver, and her sister said there were some Partridges on Foothills Road."

I wondered if UPS drivers were allowed to divulge information like that. I doubted it, but I sure wasn't going to rat on her.

Cassie continued. "So my friend—Gary—told them about the six degree thing, and they, like, kind of got into it. The aunt had to deliver a package on Foothills Road this afternoon, and she asked the kid who answered the door at the cul-de-sac if he knew a Jasmine Partridge in the area. He nodded at a place a couple of houses away. Said it was his friend's big sister, but she was probably sleeping. Jet lag."

"Has to be her! Did you get the address?"

"I did."

"Wow. All we need now is her phone number."

"Got it."

"How the heck did you get that?"

"Okay, like, I figured a girl from Cheyenne going to New Zealand with friends had to be at least college age. And she might be going to the University of Wyoming. I have a friend who has a sister I know is going to school in Laramie so I, like, thought maybe she might know Jasmine. Or maybe be able to look at, like, a school directory or something. And his sister did. Looked. Some kind of sorority thing."

Another "his" I noted. She sure had a lot of male friends willing to help her.

"Anyway, she gave Greg the cell phone number of Jasmine Partridge, a senior at the University of Wyoming!"

"You are amazing!" I said, and meant it.

She gave me the number. "So when are we going to talk to her?"

"You can't go along. You're grounded, remember?"

"This sucks!" She hung up.

I decided to call Sammie and tell her about Jasmine. But before I could, she texted me:

Read Harvey.

What now? I wondered as I opened my laptop. On Harvey's website an animated cartoon of a naked man, head not showing, danced across the top of the page in tap shoes. A "Censored" label fell across his significant parts. *Who is doing Harvey's animation?* I wondered. *And why is the dancing man naked?* I read:

Confidential sources indicate that there is more to the story of model Donald Sanders' death in Russo Tap Studio. I have it on good authority that he was entirely nude, except for a pair of pink-laced tap shoes!!! Why? Why pink? Could Sanders have been gay????

Or was he dancing nude with one of the tap students, Ella Polansky? And, if so, why???? Some say that Sanders had a kinky side, and Russo walked in and found the two of them. That may have caused Russo to fly into a jealous rage and kill Sanders. Of course, no one can say for sure, but many believe that this is a likely scenario.

Again, some say critical information has not been revealed because of the influence of the prominent (and wealthy) mayoral candidate Geraldine Betz, mother of Sammie Russo. Others say it is because of Ella Polansky's connection to the police department. As I have mentioned before, her boyfriend is Detective Dan Sherman.

But there is good news!!!! "Juniper Today" has it on good authority that the police have their ducks in order and are finally getting ready to arrest either Sammie Russo or Ella Polansky for the murder of Donald Sanders. Time will tell if my information is correct.

As for why Donald Sanders was naked, that is beyond the imagination of this blogger. Or maybe beyond the imagination of anyone who doesn't have a streak of perversion in their soul!!!!!

My shoulders sank. I was a marked woman. I called Sammie, who uttered a string of words I was very glad Baba wasn't around to hear.

"Do you think Harvey's connection at the police department knows something Dan isn't telling us?" Sammie asked. "Are the police really going to be knocking at one of our doors any second now?"

"His source obviously isn't entirely reliable. Donald wasn't naked. I saw him."

"So maybe his source is also wrong about this, too."

"Not entirely wrong. Donald *was* naked from the waist up. Except for a bow tie. Mildred told me not to tell."

Sammie sighed.

"Remember," I told her, trying to be optimistic. "They have to have evidence to arrest us, and there *is* no evidence."

After I hung up, I got out a bag of Lindor chocolates. They would give me strength as I scanned the Juniper Times online to see if a more legitimate news source was reporting anything Harvey had written.

I saw nothing about an imminent arrest or naked dancing. I did see something else that concerned me, though, and called Derek.

"What?" he asked. I could hear bar noise in the background.

"There's a headline in the paper that says, 'Local man pens book about miniature horses.'"

"So? I'm working, Ella."

"When you get your book published, are they going to say, 'Local bartender pens novel?'"

"Uh … maybe? What are you all overwrought about?"

"When someone writes a book, why do the headlines never, never, *never* say that they *wrote* a book. They always say they *penned* a book. Even though nobody in real life ever says *pens*. They say *writes.*"

"Maybe it's because *pens* is shorter, fits better in a headline."

"Two letters shorter. And if length was a problem, why not say *tiny* horse instead of *miniature* horse? That would save a lot more letters."

"Good point. It's weird. I don't know why. But I promise, when I'm published and reporters are beating a path to my door, I will beg them to say *writes* instead of *pens.*"

"Thank you." I hung up, feeling better having vented to someone who would understand.

I was depressed, and when I'm depressed, I wallow. I need comfort food, wine, and my softest pajamas. It was only 6:30, but I decided to get on with the wallowing.

Sadly, my softest pajamas are flannel, but it was 85 degrees outside. I turned on the air-conditioner and let the house cool down. Then I put on the pajamas and crawled into bed with a tray full of treats. Fluffles nosed the covers until she could crawl under them, then snuggled up under my bent legs.

When we were both comfortable, I turned on the Hallmark channel to a movie already in progress. It was at the point of the almost-kiss between the lead characters. (There is always an almost-kiss between the lead characters. Then everything falls apart.)

I settled down to watch the rest and smiled at the happy ending when the heroine finally received a chaste kiss from the too-pretty hero I suspected might be gay.

I watched a second episode about a city girl moving temporarily to an adorable small town and basking in the warmth of the friendly townspeople. I fell asleep before I could witness the almost-kiss between the city girl and a handsome firefighter I was pretty sure was *not* gay.

Dan turned off the television at 12:30 and slipped into bed with me. Happily, I turned to him; Dan beats the Hallmark Channel any day.

I snuggled up next to him. "So are you going to arrest Sammie? Or me?"

He didn't answer, just kissed me and said, "I love you, Bellella Polansky."

And then he started doing more than kissing me.

I was getting distracted, but I tried to stay focused. "You didn't answer my question. Are you going to arrest us?"

No answer. More kissing. "And will you still love me if I wind up in prison?" I asked.

He stopped doing more than kissing me and sat up. "Okay, I give up. What are you going on about? Why do you think I'm going to arrest you?

"Harvey Klump's blog." I had the page ready on my laptop and reached over him to grab it.

He read it. "Naked, huh? Must have missed that part." He kissed me again. "Were you naked tap dancing with Donald Sanders?"

"Be serious. He says the police are going to arrest one of us. His sources have been right about *some* things. How about this one?"

"Seriously, no. Mildred hasn't arrested you or Sammie because she doesn't have evidence that you killed Donald. Because you didn't. You aren't going to prison."

"That's a relief," I smiled. "Now I can love you properly." I kissed him. "But, seriously, is Mildred close to charging anyone?"

"It's a tough case."

"Does that mean 'No, she isn't?'"

"Could we go back to the kissing and loving stuff, please?" He pulled me close.

"You're not answering the question."

He started kissing my ear. He knows I can't concentrate when he kisses my ear. "Could we please move on from this subject?" he asked. "Maybe find a better activity?"

I couldn't speak. The ear kissing paralyzed my tongue. But when he moved on to kissing my neck, I was able to say, "I love you, Detective Dan Sherman."

And then all talk of the murder was over for the night.

CHAPTER TWENTY-SIX

After Dan left the next morning, I called Derek. "I need you."

"Of course you do. What's up?"

"I need a ride to Cheyenne. I don't want to take my car because it needs an oil change."

"Your car won't explode if you put off an oil change for another 150 miles. Or, you know, you could actually go *get* the oil change."

"No time. And I also need backup."

"Should I bring my gun?"

"Not that kind of backup. Just another ear to listen to an interview. I found Jasmine Partridge. Or, rather, Cassie did."

"I'll be over."

After handing him a cup of coffee, I offered Derek a Pop-Tart (Little Skyden next door loves them), but Derek doesn't do processed sugar. "Give me some fruit," he said.

Before I could remind him, again, that sugar is sugar, chemically, he cut me off. "I don't want to have this discussion again. Fruit. Now."

So I gave him an orange.

"Let me see if I have this right," he said, peeling the orange. "You want me to drive to Cheyenne with you to ask this Jasmine Partridge—a complete stranger—questions that may or may not apply to a murder that you are not officially supposed to be investigating."

"Yes."

"And you think she'll be happy to answer these questions."

"I do."

"And why do you think that?"

"Because of a shared disdain for self-absorbed men."

He raised the eyebrow over his green eye. "More information, please."

"I called Miss Jasmine Partridge this morning and talked to her. We bonded. We have an appointment with her in an hour and a half."

Derek sat quietly eating the segments of his orange, saying nothing, but I'm pretty sure I detected a look on his face that said, "Okay, I'm impressed."

As Derek was washing his hands after the last segment of orange, Dan called. "Lunch?" he asked. "I could meet you at El Burrito at 1:00."

I hesitated, then said, "I'd love to, but I have to go to Cheyenne."

"What's in Cheyenne?"

I didn't really want to tell him, but what was I to do? "I'm going to talk to Jasmine Partridge. She's one of the young women who sat at the table with Donald at Whitney's the night he was murdered."

He didn't say anything. I had the feeling he was weighing whether to be impressed by my ingenuity or annoyed by my interference.

He finally asked, "So how did you get this Jasmine's name?"

"Kind of a long story. But Cassie actually used six degrees again."

He was silent again.

"She likes this stuff," I said.

"It's not a game."

I bristled. "If there's anyone who knows that, it's me! I'm the one whose name is being dragged through the mud. Half the town thinks my best friend did it. Or me."

"Okay, okay. But you need to tell Mildred about this.

"I will. But she doesn't take me seriously. I'll find out what I can from Jasmine first, and maybe then she'll pay attention."

He sighed. "Be careful. And you *will* talk to Mildred when you get back?"

"I promise."

"And you *will* be home tonight so I can take you out to dinner? And maybe have another sleepover?"

"Absolutely."

Jasmine said she was jet-lagged. If that's what jet-lagged looks like, I'd like some. The young woman could have stepped out of a Sahalie or Title Nine catalog. Healthy tan. Strong legs and arms, shown off in one of those athletic skorts and a cross-back tank top. She wore Tevas on her feet, and her blonde hair was knotted in a messy ponytail with strands loose around her face. Not a speck of make-up but gorgeous in a healthy, wholesome way that made me re-think my lukewarm commitment to exercise.

I gave Jasmine more background than I had on the phone and explained how we were trying to learn anything at all that might remove my friend and me from suspicion. I told her how I didn't trust that the detective in charge was pursuing the right angles, and Derek explained how he had heard about her and her friends from the waitress who had waited on them at Whitney's.

"That waitress! What a Nosy Nellie!" she said.

Nosy Nellie? Was Wyoming a little behind the times in the slang department?

She continued. "She kept butting in, just so she could flirt with Donald. He was getting enough flirting from my friends. They were all gaga about him sitting with us. Puh-lease!"

"You didn't think so much of him?" Derek asked.

"He was all about himself. My friends didn't care. They were all, 'Oh, I love you in that commercial with the little girl and the pony!' Gag. And he looked all fake modest and said, 'Have you seen my perfume commercial, too?'"

"Sounds like Donald," I said. "Just curious. Did he eat anything?"

"Oh, no." She began imitating him. "'No burger for me. I've got a shoot tomorrow.' She patted her flat stomach, imitating him. "'Gotta look good in my shorts.' He was in the area to shoot some sportswear stuff for The North Face or Patagonia—one of those places. Then Nosy Nellie asked if he'd like a beer or a glass of wine." She resumed imitating him. 'Just coffee. I don't drink—bad for the face, you know.' Then he winked and told us he does do a little weed now and then."

"It's legal in Colorado," Derek said.

"Do you think I don't know that? I live in Wyoming, like *next door?*" She was a little snippy. Maybe it was the jet lag. "Anyway, when he got his coffee he pulled out this Altoids tin with his own special 'healthy' creamer in it."

Healthy creamer? I glanced at Derek. Could this be the source of the poisonous caffeine dose?

Jasmine continued. "When he brought it out, I thought, 'Good Lord, this guy is carrying cocaine!' But he said it was just some kind of 'healthy' creamer with 'functional mushrooms' that he orders special from some place. What the heck are *non*-functional mushrooms? He insisted we should try it instead of using those artificial little plastic creamer cups on the table. Well, I was drinking beer, so I wasn't about to switch to coffee, but Gracie immediately ordered coffee so she could endear herself to Donald and use his precious creamer."

"Did Gracie use it?" I asked, worried about poison.

"She *loved* it and was *so* grateful to him for telling her about it." She sniffed. "Functional mushrooms. Give me a break." She sighed. "Sorry if I'm being a little snotty. I had a little too much of Gracie on this trip."

"Was she okay the rest of the night?" I pressed.

"Okay how? She was still all stupid and giggly around Donald. I didn't think that was okay."

"I mean, did she act sick or anything?"

She frowned, puzzled. "No. But she was wide awake. Didn't sleep at all at the airport or on the flight. Too much coffee."

Derek and I exchanged glances. So the poison couldn't have been in the Altoids tin.

"This is really helpful," I said. "Please go on. What happened after the coffee?"

"Let's see ... Donald suggested we meet him later at the Yellow Rose for some dancing." She imitated him again. "'Let me show you Wyoming gals some *real* two-stepping.'

My friends were falling all over themselves making plans to meet him. Disgusting."

"Was he there when you got there? To the Rose?"

"Didn't show. Jerk."

"He did have a good excuse," I said. "You know, being dead and all."

"Right. Sorry."

"So that was pretty much it?" Derek asked.

"Pretty much. Oh, that waitress. She would *not* leave us alone." She reached over and touched Derek's shoulder. "'Oh, are you sure there's nothing I can bring you? Water, maybe?' And then, 'Let me freshen that coffee,' even though he'd taken about three sips. She would freshen our water about every two minutes just so she'd have an excuse to come to the table. She just couldn't keep her eyes off Mr. Big Head."

"When did you hear about the murder?" I asked.

"Just as we were about to leave on this three-day hiking trip on the south island. My friends fell apart, like he'd been our best buddy or something. One even wanted to cancel the trip. 'We've suffered a loss,' she said. Heavens to Murgatroyd. We met him once."

Heavens to Murgatroyd? Maybe Wyoming really was a little behind the times in the slang department. "Anything else you can tell us about that evening in the bar?" I asked. "Anything at all?"

She thought a moment. "I hated Donald's shirt."

"Why?"

"It was plaid."

"And that's a problem because ...?"

"I just hate plaid. Too down-home, sit-on-a-hay-bale,

give-me-a-straw-to-suck-on. Looks stupid on city types. Real plaid should be flannel or on a cowboy shirt, preferably on a real cowboy."

"I see," I said, and I sort of did.

On the drive back to Juniper, I asked Derek, "Did you know about the creamer in an Altoids tin thing? Did you ever seen him pull that out?"

"Nope. Never saw it."

I called Sammie and asked her if she'd ever seen it.

"He brought it out once. I thought it was cocaine. Or, if it wasn't, that people would *think* it was cocaine. I told him I didn't ever want to see it again if he wanted to go out with me."

"I guess he did listen to you if you never saw it again."

"He always listened to me." Pretty much everyone listens to Sammie. She does take after her mother in that respect.

"Did he happen to have coffee that night he came to see you?"

"Donald *always* had coffee."

"So he didn't use special creamer then?"

"No. He put milk in it. Some of our two per-cent."

I hung up and talked to Derek. "No Altoids with functional mushrooms at Sammie's. Only at Whitney's."

"Where someone else used it, too. So it wasn't poisoned."

"Could someone have doctored his 'special mix' later?" I wondered.

"I suppose the girls from Cheyenne maybe could have slipped some poison in it," Derek said. "But why would one of them be carrying caffeine powder?"

"They wouldn't. They had opportunity, but no means and no motive. You need all of them."

I really was becoming a detective.

CHAPTER TWENTY-SEVEN

"Maybe this is a stretch, but I might have found something that could be important," Sammie said when I came up to the apartment for Isabelle cuddling before tap class that evening. "I was catching up on bookwork for the store this morning while Isabelle slept, and I saw we sold a Coach purse."

"So? Don't you sell a lot of them?" I knew her online business had really done well over the last year.

"Yes, but this one was sold right in the store. That's really unusual. In fact, I've never had a local sale of one of these bags, only online. The date of the sale was the day of the murder. That afternoon, in fact. Maybe that's important somehow. Donald knew people with money to spend on stuff like that."

"Who bought it?"

"The name on the receipt isn't one I recognize. Buckminster Bagwell."

"Buckminster ..." Something was clicking, but I couldn't quite grab it. "Wait. The nickname is probably Bucky. Maybe it was Donald's friend at the funeral—the one who stopped being his friend. The one who got rich starting an edible marijuana business."

I googled him. "Buckminster Bagwell. Marijuana maven. Yep. It's him. I'm going downstairs to talk to Bianca and see if she remembers him."

Bianca was going through some new consignment pieces. An aqua cashmere sweater caught my eye, but I made myself focus on Bianca.

She remembered Buckminster. "Really well-dressed guy. Excellent taste. He wasn't handsome, but his clothes made him look good. And he had a good-looking woman with him." She smiled. "Clothes can do so much."

"So can money. It was Buckminster Bagwell, a Denver guy who's made a fortune selling marijuana. Did he ask questions or look around or anything?"

"Yes, actually." She looked up, head tilting to one side as she thought. "He asked if I owned the store. I explained that I was running it for my sister-in-law, who was on maternity leave." She thought a minute. "He and the redhead with him smiled when I said Sammie was the one with the good taste, not me."

"Redhead? She was a redhead?"

"Yes. Pretty. Probably late twenties."

Aha! Kendall had lied to me about not being in contact with Bucky. I was sure of it. "What else can you remember?"

"Let's see. The guy asked for Sammie's card, so I gave him one. When he looked at the name, he commented that Russo Dance studio next door must be hers, too. And I said that Sammie had many talents, and good taste and dancing were two of them ... Did I do something wrong?"

"No, no. But those two may have. I'm going to look into it."

I ran back upstairs.

Derek was now there having his daily dose of Isabelle time. "Listen to this," I said. "Buckminster Bagwell, the guy who stopped being friends with Donald, was downstairs the day of the murder, in Sammie's store, and asking questions about Sammie. And he was with a redhead. It had to be the redheaded reporter, Kendall Whitehead. The one I talked to up in the mountains."

"There are other redheads in the world besides Kendall," Derek said.

"She was good-looking."

"There are other good-looking redheads in the world besides Kendall."

"It's her. I feel it in my bones." Before Derek could comment on my bones, Sammie interrupted.

"Kendall told you Bucky hadn't been in touch since he got mad at her for having an abortion. Right?" I nodded. "So if it *was* her, you have caught her in a lie."

"And a lie is something to investigate. Could she and Bucky be in cahoots?" I frowned. "Lord, I sounded like Baba. *Cahoots.* Where does that word come from? Google *cahoots,* Derek."

"You can delve into *cahoots* later," Sammie said. "Concentrate on Bucky. Do we tell Dan about him?"

"We're supposed to tell Mildred. And I will after tap class when I tell her about Jasmine."

"If Bucky was checking out Sammie's store and bought a purse, the purse was probably for Kendall herself. If it was Kendall," Sammie said.

"Which means he's probably dating her again. Which means her lie was a whopper. We need to know more about this guy."

Derek was already on it. Isabelle was now resting on his legs, facing him, as he tapped on his phone. "Oh, this is interesting. Google images. There are pictures of him at the International Church of Cannabis. He's on the board or something."

"What the heck is the International Church of Cannabis?"

"It's a church in Denver. Really. I remember a couple of years ago it had quite a bit of media attention. Some legal issues, maybe? I can't remember the details."

I took my laptop out of my bag and typed in the name. I stared at the vivid images that popped up. The International Church of Cannabis looked like a normal church on the outside but *nothing* like an ordinary church on the inside. Brilliant colors covered almost every square inch.

Derek read excerpts from the website. "The religion is Elevationism. That's the belief that 'weed can accelerate and deepen a person's individual spiritual journey, whatever it happens to be.' It says THC 'magnifies sensory perception, which heightens the spiritual experience.'" He was quiet, reading some more, then continued. "You bring your own pot to services. It's a private organization, but it's easy to join."

"So let's join and go. Maybe we can find Bucky and Kendall there together and confront them," I said.

"We don't even know if Kendall is a member," Sammie said.

"We don't know that she isn't."

Geraldine arrived then for *her* turn at Isabelle cuddling. "What's up?" she asked, taking Isabelle from Derek's lap and kissing her.

We brought her up to speed. "I think Ella's right," she said. It's not like we can call Kendall and say, 'Is it true you're seeing Bucky again? Is it true you lied? We need to go to church and see if we can maybe catch them together to *talk* to them."

I nodded. "We can observe Bucky if he's there. Maybe find out more about him somehow. It's worth a chance," I said.

Derek was scouring the website. "Services are on Friday night. Tomorrow. All we have to do to join is fill out an online application. Let's do it."

I entered my name and address on the application, then read aloud the next item. *"Do you affirm that cannabis is a spiritual sacrament in your life?"* I looked up from my laptop. "I can't affirm that."

"Jesus, Ella, You aren't in Catholic school anymore," Derek said. "Just say *yes*."

"But it's a *church*. I can't lie to a church. I don't believe cannabis is a sacrament."

"You could be helping clear your best friend of suspicion in a murder case," Sammie pointed out. "I'd go myself, but Sam is working Friday night. Imagine if I took a baby with me to a pot church and *Parnella Tonight* got a hold of *that*."

"You're not committing a crime by saying pot is important in your life, Bellella. Right now it *is* important," Geraldine said.

"It's important but it isn't a spiritual sacrament," I insisted.

Geraldine sighed. "Well, I'm going."

"Really, Mom? To a pot church?" Derek said. "If you're going, I'm going."

"But neither one of us knows what Kendall or Bucky looks like," she said. "Wish us luck with *that*."

"Okay, okay. I'm in," I said. "But I'll cancel my membership when we're done."

"Fine. And cross your fingers when you affirm, to show you didn't mean it. I'm sure that will help," Derek said.

He was kidding, but I did cross my fingers.

When Sammie and I went downstairs for class, Dan was dropping Cassie off. He had been reluctant to let her come at first, given the reason for her interest, but he finally agreed, happy that the two of us were doing something together.

Cassie found a perfect pair of shoes in the Borrow Box and then strutted around the floor like a little kid, thrilled at the sounds she could make with her taps. I smiled. I'd done the same thing when I first put on tap shoes.

While the rest of us stretched and practiced steps individually, Sammie gave Cassie some quick instruction on a few tap basics. Cassie picked it all up quickly.

"I think she's been paying more attention than she let on when she was here before," Sammie told us. "Or else we have a real natural here."

Cassie flushed with pleasure. She admitted, "I did take some lessons when I was eight."

We continued working on our dance number for the "Tap, Rattle, and Roll" show. "I know this is hard," Sammie told us, "but you're going to feel so proud of yourselves after you have your moment on stage." We humored her, though we were pretty skeptical about feeling proud of ourselves. I, for one, was more focused on hoping not to make a fool of myself.

Before we started our first run-through, Sammie told us that one of the most important things for us to learn was attitude. "Even when you're just walking or swaying in time to the music, do it with style," she said. "Don't look at your feet. Relax. Feel the music."

We tried. Several times. Sammie would start the music, and we'd walk in from either side of the room, holding our heads high and smiling. We could *step, shuffle, hop, step, around-the-world, stomp, clap* pretty successfully now. We could manage a single Buffalo and a shuffle-ball-change. But when we flap-heeled around in a circle, someone would mess up and go the wrong direction, or just stand there, frustrated. When those on either side of her looked to see what was wrong, they would lose their focus and fall out of step, too.

Sammie remained calm. "You can't expect to do things perfectly right off. This time through, pretend you are on stage, and people are watching you. No matter what, you have to get through the dance. You can't just run off or stand there looking baffled. If you screw up, don't announce it by frowning or wincing or looking frustrated. You'll just draw attention to yourself. Instead, just keep smiling and try to get back in sync with everyone as soon as you can."

We did better.

Then she added another layer of difficulty. She had us turn around so that we weren't facing the mirror across the front of the room.

The group fell apart.

Some women froze, panicked because they could no longer see themselves or others in the mirror. Those who were supposed to stand in the second row became disoriented and stood in the first row. Some moved left when they were supposed to move right. Others forgot whole chunks of the routine, as well as the advice not to call attention to themselves by looking frustrated.

"Can't we turn around and face the mirror again?" Aunt Joan begged after our first mirrorless run-through.

"You aren't going to be able to see yourself when you're on stage," Sammie explained, "so you need to practice. It will get easier."

And it did. Eventually. Once we finally got used to it, it actually helped not to see ourselves in the mirror. Maybe it was because we couldn't witness our own screw-ups.

"I kinda-sorta felt like I was actually dancing that time," said Nell, looking proud of herself after one of our more successful run-throughs.

"That's because you kinda-sorta were," Sammie smiled.

At the end of class Cassie said, "Let me take a class photo of all of you. I can send it to Sammie to share with everyone."

"I'll take it" Sammie said, reaching for Cassie's phone. "So you can be in it."

We all lined up and posed, and Sammie snapped the photos.

Dan was home from work and drinking a beer when we walked in after class. I kissed him and sat down next to him. Cassie sat down on the floor and started doing yoga stretches.

"So did you figure out who did it?" he smiled at Cassie. He knew she was more interested in finding a clue than in learning to tap dance.

"Not yet," she said bending forward, legs wide, and grabbing each foot. Her body was almost flat against the floor. I didn't think I'd ever been able to do that, even when I was 15.

We watched her sit back up, then hoist up into a runner's lunge. "So when's Affinity due?" she asked.

"What???" She definitely had our attention.

"I just wonder if all that tap dance bouncing around is good for a baby."

"You think Affinity is pregnant?" I asked.

She nodded.

"Why?"

"Because she's acting like Mom." She switched to a lunge with her other leg.

Dan and I sat with that sentence for a moment, processing it. Then Dan finally found his voice. "Your mom is *pregnant?*"

"Yep. I'm going to have a baby brother or sister. Probably a stepdad, too."

I decided it was a good time for me to keep quiet.

Dan said, "Well, *that's* some news. Vern, I assume?"

"Of course Vern."

I knew her mother had been dating Vern for a long time.

"How do you feel about all that?" Dan asked. Looking at his face, I suspected he didn't know how to feel about it himself.

She shrugged. "Okay, I guess. A baby is nice. I mean if she's like Isabelle. Or he."

"And a stepdad?"

"Probably won't be that different. He's there most of the time already. Too bad he's such a cheesehead." She looked at me, knowing I wouldn't understand. "A person who cheers for the Green Bay Packers."

"Vern is from Wisconsin," Dan said.

"He wore a cheese hat when we played the Packers,"

she said. By "we" I knew she meant the Denver Broncos. "He lives in Colorado now. He should get over the Packers."

"I wonder when your mother was going to mention this," Dan said. He didn't sound mad exactly, but not happy, either. "I need to know if a stepdad is going to be in your life. And a baby."

"What will the baby be to you?" Cassie wondered. "I'll be a half-sister. You'll be a what?"

"I don't think the mother's ex-husband is anything to her new husband's baby," Dan said. "Kind of sad, in a way."

"Hmmm," she said, then moved into downward-facing dog.

I wanted to get back to Affinity. "So how was Affinity acting like your mother?"

In her upside down position, Cassie said, "For one thing, she went to the bathroom twice during class, and once after."

I thought about that. "True."

"Then there was her sister. I've noticed how Serenity and her pretty much dress the same but, like, somehow look different?" She walked her feet to her hands, then rolled to a standing position. "They're both, like, pretty proud of their bodies. Usually Lycra leggings and a tight top or sports bra, both of them. But tonight Affinity had a loose, sleeveless top over her sports bra. It just doesn't seem like Affinity's style." She reached for her phone. "Look at the pictures Sammie sent us. I think there's a baby bump under there."

We looked. I couldn't see a baby bump, but maybe Cassie was onto something.

"What if she *is* pregnant." I asked. "What does it mean if it's true?"

"Oh, it's true," said Cassie. "I have good instincts."

CHAPTER TWENTY-EIGHT

As I tried to decide what to wear to an Elevationist church service, I remembered my promise to Dan and called the police station. I asked for Mildred, explaining that I had information relating to the Sanders case. She was out for the rest of the day, but I made an appointment for 8:00 the next morning.

Then Dan called. "Want to get pizza and watch a movie with Cassie and me tonight?"

"I can't." I hesitated, knowing I couldn't leave it at that. Why did he always call at the wrong time? "Derek and Geraldine and I are doing some investigating. Nothing that will interfere with the police."

I could tell he didn't like the sound of that. "Where?"

"Denver."

"Where exactly?"

"A church." He mulled that over. I knew he wanted to ask me more. "I guess it's better I don't know whatever the hell you guys have planned, but be careful."

I think the word "church" must have reassured him.

When I arrived at Geraldine's house, she looked me over. "Interesting outfit choice for the kind of church we're going to."

I was wearing a knee-length skirt in a muted floral, a navy blue knit top with a matching cardigan sweater, and sandals with a heel. "Baba and Mom always insist we look nice in the Lord's house," I said.

"This church may be just a tad more open-minded in the appropriate dress category." She wore a purple tank top, a mid-calf length skirt covered in purple and orange flowers, pink flip-flops, and a red sequined baseball cap. "Hats show respect, don't you think?"

"You'll be a star in the respect department then," Derek said. He wore beige cargo shorts, flip-flops, and a gray T-shirt that nearly reached his knees.

"Going for a stoner look?" I asked.

"I want to fade into the background. People will be eyeing you two—uptight girl and hippie mama."

"I am not looking uptight," I said. "Just respectful."

"I'm sure the Lord will appreciate it," Geraldine said, patting my arm. "Now let's go."

She insisted on driving, at least one way. "You can drive back, Ella. I know you'll be too uptight to partake of any offerings the worshipers might choose to share."

"I'm not uptight!"

We found a parking place in the residential area where the Church of Cannabis is located. It looks like a perfectly ordinary church and clearly had been at one time.

Someone was checking names at the door. As I fidgeted in line, Derek leaned toward me and whispered, "Cut out the blushing. You look guilty of a whole lot more than lying on an application."

A smiling woman in her sixties said hello as we walked in. With her long gray braids and Birkenstocks, she had a look Baba would have described as "Woodstocky." We slipped into a pew in back where a couple of young men dressed pretty much like Derek were leaning back, inhaling deeply, and passing a joint. Derek slid close to them, and they passed the joint to him. He took a hit and turned to Geraldine. "I stick to edibles," she said as she pulled some wrapped candies from her purse. "She does, too," she said before he could pass it on to me.

"Whatever," said one guy.

"Cool," said the other.

A couple sat down next to me. In athleisure tracksuits, they looked ready to go to the gym after church. "First time?" the woman asked, looking at me and smiling.

So maybe I did look uptight. I nodded.

They began swaying to music from the band on the stage, so I did, too. I felt awkward.

"You look awkward," Derek whispered, leaning over Geraldine. "Chill out."

I decided to lean back and admire the vivid colors covering almost every surface. Kaleidoscope-like patterns looped over the arched ceilings and down the walls. Bright pink carpet covered the floor. At either side of the podium in front were blue velvet chairs. A giant bull—at least I thought it was a bull—looked down from one area, its eyes glittering. Two giant figures with cone noses looked at each other on the wall behind us. It was a dizzying display, even for someone who wasn't high, which of course I wasn't.

A man went to the podium and talked about spiritual discovery, pathways to self-discovery, states of consciousness and community. It reminded me a little of Seraphina's lectures at school, so I tuned him out. My surroundings were much more interesting.

The band played again, and we were encouraged to talk to one other. Like the couple beside me, Geraldine got up and began circulating, introducing herself. Derek stayed with the stoners, and I sat alone, searching the crowd for Buckminster Bagwell or Kendall. Smoke hung in the air.

A young woman sat down beside me. "Welcome. First time?"

I might as well have had a neon sign on my head flashing *Does not belong! Does not belong!*

She talked to me about pot and how her migraines had improved since she started using regularly. "And the church, well, it just adds a new dimension to my life. I'm sure it will to yours, too."

I was pretty sure it wouldn't, but I smiled and tried to look stoned.

And then, finally, I saw Buckminster Bagwell. He was at the front of the room with a woman by his side. Kendall. I watched them circulate, chatting with several small groups. Twice, Bucky put his arm around her and gave her a hug. Once he even kissed her.

I wanted to get up and confront Kendall about lying to me, but even though I've made great strides in this area, I am not by nature a confronter. I tend to freeze up, thinking murderous thoughts without being able to articulate any of them.

But then I thought of Sammie. I could do this. For her. For me. For all of us. I got up and walked toward them. Kendall saw me approaching and whispered to Bucky, who looked my way.

"So you haven't seen Bucky since high school," I said

to Kendall. I tried to make icicles drip from my voice. It was hard surrounded by peace, love, and music.

"Okay, I lied," Kendall said.

"Interesting," I said, trying to sound like a hardboiled detective holding back details that would condemn them. "So why were the two of you at Second Chance in downtown Juniper the day of the murder?"

"We were buying a purse," Kendall said. She turned to Bucky, who looked puzzled. Then he recognized me.

"You were at Donald's memorial. We didn't meet, though. Buckminster Bagwell." He held out his hand.

Reluctantly, I shook it. His was a just-right handshake—firm, but not too firm. I liked that. I have a thing about handshakes and once declined a date with a really cute guy because his handshake felt squishy. I knew I couldn't trust him.

"Why were you asking about Sammie Russo at her store?" I asked.

"We'd heard she had a baby," Bucky said. "We were just confirming that."

"Why?" I demanded.

"Why are you here?" Kendall asked. I noticed that Geraldine and Derek were standing behind me protectively.

"To see if you were lying, and it turns out you were. You two have clearly made up since high school. Now I have to wonder why."

"Not your business," Kendall said.

"Maybe it's because you had something to do with Donald's murder. Maybe it wasn't *reporting* you were interested in. Maybe you just wanted to keep a close eye on things and see who knew what."

"How much pot have you had?" Kendall asked. "You're being ridiculous."

Bucky gave me a firm and level look that matched his handshake. "I think you need to be careful about jumping to unwarranted conclusions."

"Chill out, dudes," a stoner said, sensing the tension in the air.

"Let's go," I said. I'd had all the confrontation I could handle. The three of us headed toward the entrance.

"Peace," Geraldine said, turning back as we went down the aisle and flashing two fingers up with her right hand.

"Later," Derek said to the stoners. It seems they had bonded.

"So she lied," I said as we got in the car.

"You've established that," Derek said.

"*Why* did she lie? Why were they checking out Sammie that day and asking about the tap studio? Could they have been planning the murder? That's first-degree."

No answer. Geraldine and Derek were focusing on the bag of Doritos and a package of Oreos they'd had the foresight to bring.

I drove.

They fell asleep.

At home later, I opened my computer and typed an old-fashioned letter:

Dear International Church of Cannabis:

This is to notify you that I am canceling my membership to your organization. I admit that I lied to get in, and I apologize for that. However, it was for a good and worthy cause.

I do not believe that weed can accelerate and deepen a person's individual spiritual journey, whatever it happens to be. I think it just, mainly, makes you hungry.

Sincerely,
Ella Polansky

I printed the letter, signed it, and put it in an old-fashioned envelope with an old-fashioned stamp. I would mail it in the morning.

CHAPTER TWENTY-NINE

I was feeling a little guilty about my recent interactions with Mom and Baba. I had been stopping by because I wanted something—advice, an ear to listen to my problems, a place to hide from reporters, help with an impromptu polka concert. As I drove home from my therapy session on Saturday, I decided to go see them both for no reason other than that I loved them. When I stopped at an intersection, I texted Mom:

Dropping by. OK?

I knew she'd be off work by now. Dan had to work late, so maybe I'd take her to dinner.

She sent a thumbs up emoji.

"Come in," Mom yelled when I knocked. I found her standing in the kitchen looking into the refrigerator. "I keep hoping something good will materialize, but it's not happening."

"That's okay. Let me take you and Baba out for dinner. My treat."

She nodded. "I could go for that." She paused. "Any particular reason?"

"Just 'cuz. Let's go surprise Baba." I drove us the few blocks to Baba's house, where we found a strange car in the driveway.

"Lester's?" I asked.

"I imagine so. It's a Prius. Check out the bumper sticker."

It read *EAT ORGANIC*. The "C" was an apple with a bite out of it.

"Great. I haven't met Lester yet. I'll treat him, too." I rang the doorbell.

And then things happened fast. I don't remember a lot, but I remember that Baba opened the door, holding what appeared to be a hypodermic needle. My thoughts in the next second or so were these, in this order: *What is Baba doing with a hypodermic needle? She is not going to give me a shot. She's not a doctor. There's no need to panic, though. I have been practicing exposure therapy. I can hold it together. Breathe. Breathe. Breathe. I am NOT going to faint.*

And then I fainted.

Unfortunately, as I found out later, I fell forward into the statue of the Virgin Mary in Baba's entryway. Baba stepped back as I fell, and the statue fell against her, knocking her to the floor.

I awoke to a strange man hovering over Baba and Mom on her cell phone talking with a 9-1-1 dispatcher. Baba was moaning.

I rose to my elbows and looked at the fallen Virgin. Then I remembered the hypodermic needle and started to get dizzy again.

"Are you okay, Ella?" Baba managed to ask.

"She's fine," Mom said. "You're not. Don't move. Your arm is broken."

"I think I'm going to throw up," Baba said. The man—I assumed it was Lester—jumped back.

"Breathe," Mom said. "Breathe. An ambulance is coming." Baba's legs were shaking, and she looked so pale.

"We don't need an ambulance," Baba said. "Just load me in the car and take me to the hospital like we used to do with your boys."

"The boys were kids. You're an 80-year-old woman, and we're taking no chances. Live with it."

I was slowly coming up to speed. "You broke your arm?" I asked Baba.

"It appears so," Mom answered for her. "On the other hand, it doesn't appear that you broke anything, except maybe the Virgin Mary's toe when you knocked it over. So get out of the way." She gestured toward the man. "And this is Lester."

Mom was never one of those mothers who passes out Band-Aids and frozen boo-boo cold packs and comforting hugs. She was more of the "You're okay. Get up" school of thought when we were kids. We would fall off the swings or our bikes and come running to her. She'd check us over briefly, wash off any blood, and tell us to go back and play. It was the rare injury that merited a Band-aid, and we cherished those Band-aids as marks of the suffering we had endured.

Mom continued. "Lester, get a bag of ice. A bag of frozen peas. Corn. Anything. The arm is swelling."

Baba moaned again.

Slowly realizing that this scenario was my fault, I managed to sit up and, not very helpfully, started crying. "Baba. I'm sorry! I'm sorry!"

"It's okay, honey." She smiled through her pain. "You didn't mean to. And I didn't realize it looked like ..."

"It's in my purse," Mom interrupted. "It will remain there."

I was afraid I knew exactly what "it" was.

Lester handed Mom a frozen block of hamburger. "Honestly, Lester. No. Ella, get it together and go look for peas. You know where she keeps them."

Lester helped me up and I got the peas, which Mom applied to Baba's forearm. She winced. Then Mom turned to Lester. "Help Ella take that damned statue out of here. We'll need room for the EMTs."

We put the Virgin Mary on the bed in the guest bedroom. Lester questioned my decision to put her there, suggesting, instead, the back porch, but I was firm.

"No, Baba would want it this way." I put a pillow under the Blessed Virgin's head.

Mom's next order was, "Ella, go in the kitchen and stay there, and keep your back to this door. You are not to be looking anywhere in this area when the ambulance arrives." We could hear the sirens getting close. "Go!"

I sat in the kitchen, staring down at the table, thinking of Baba, and leaking tears. I was a little vague on the details, but I knew I must have passed out and, as a result, hurt Baba. But why on earth had Baba been holding a hypodermic needle?

I listened as the EMTs asked Baba her date of birth. "What do you care?" she snapped.

"They're checking you for a concussion," Mom said. "Just answer their questions."

As they were getting ready to leave, Mom hurried into the kitchen with Lester. "Sit right beside Ella when you talk about what happened, in case she needs help."

And then they were off.

As ordered, Lester sat down beside me. "Are you hurt somewhere? Could I get you some frozen peas?"

"I'm not hurt." My elbow was throbbing a little, but that was nothing. It was my heart that hurt. There was no way around it; it was my fault that Baba was suffering.

"Have you tried meditation?" he asked. Lester was trying to help. I'll give him that.

"I don't need meditation," I said. "I need some Kleenex."

He looked around.

"By the toaster," I said. Baba had boxes everywhere in the house. Couldn't he see that?

He stood up and grimaced, waited a moment, then walked carefully to the Kleenex box. His plantar fasciitis, I assumed. He brought me the box and sat down again, sliding his chair even closer.

"I'm not sure what happened back there," he said. "Do you have epilepsy or something? If so, I was reading about some recent homeopathic treatment advances that ..."

"I don't have epilepsy. I have *trypanophobia*."

His eyes widened. "Oh. That sounds serious."

"It's just a fancy name for fear of needles."

"A phobia," he nodded. "I get it. Phobias can be quite debilitating. My late wife had a phobia about bridges. She made me drive miles out of our way to avoid them. Sometimes you just can't get where you're going without going across a bridge, though, and then she would lie down in the back seat and pray until we made it to the other side. I told her she was in more danger from lying there without a seat belt than from a bridge collapsing, but logic was pointless. There's no logic involved with a phobia."

He understood.

Finally, my thoughts were clearing. "What happened? I can think of no logical reason for Baba to be answering the door with a hypodermic needle."

He frowned. "What?"

Was he dense? "She was holding one up like she was ready to plunge it into an arm."

"Oh, that wasn't a hypodermic needle. It was a syringe. I guess it looks a lot like a hypodermic needle, though, with the plunger and all. But there was no needle."

"You're kidding me. Why did you have a syringe?"

"CBD oil. Your grandmother and I went to a medical marijuana store yesterday. My plantar fasciitis bothers me, and also Vera doesn't sleep well, so we thought we'd try something new. Marijuana products are legal in Colorado now, you know."

Why did everyone keep mentioning that? "I know."

"The kind we got came in a syringe, so you can get exactly the right amount." He thought a minute. "Vera was holding it and trying to figure out how to work it when the doorbell rang. You came in, saw it, fell onto the statue, and the statue fell on her and knocked her over. Poor Vera."

I nodded, blowing my nose yet again.

"Do you think they'll keep her overnight?" he asked.

"I doubt it. It's only a broken arm. Oh, I don't mean *only* like it's not a big deal. It is a big deal, but broken arms ..."

He interrupted. "Got it. I think I'll wait in the den then, watch a little TV."

"Go," I said. "I'm calling my boyfriend." Lester patted my shoulder as he limped past.

I texted Dan:

Baba hurt. My fault. Please come.

Where?

Baba's house.

On my way.

He was there in ten minutes. I opened the door, and he pulled me into his arms. As I blubbered away, trying to tell him what happened, he led me to the sofa, grabbing a box of Kleenex from the entryway table on the way. He pulled me down on the sofa, letting me cry into his shoulder. I cried and cried, and he listened and listened, never once saying, "I told you that you needed to get serious about therapy." He didn't say, "It was an accident," or, "You didn't mean to," or, "Don't beat yourself up." He didn't say anything at all, just held me.

And when I had told him all about what had happened and noticed that I was repeating myself, I stopped crying. I pulled myself away and looked at him through the remaining slits in my swollen eyes.

"I will work even harder with the therapist. I promise. More appointments—once a week now until I get this licked, even if insurance won't pay for it all."

He finally spoke. "Good decision."

I fell asleep curled up next to Dan on the sofa. I had no idea what time it was when Mom texted me:

Come get us. No car.

Why hadn't I realized that? I'd been so full of my own guilt that I hadn't taken the sensible step of following the ambulance to the hospital. "I'm an idiot," I said, tears forming again as I rummaged in my purse for my car keys. I had forgotten, again, to put them in the pocket I'd designated for car keys. As I started to turn the bag upside down and dump everything on the coffee table, Dan took my arm.

"I'll drive you. You're in no shape."

I nodded and went to tell Lester where we were going. He was snoring loudly while a *Frasier* rerun blared. I decided to leave him alone.

As we pulled up to the emergency room, a nurse rolled Baba out in a wheelchair, Mom beside her. Baba drooped to one side a little, but when she saw me she held up her left arm. It was in a pink fiberglass cast.

"I can still bowl!" she said. She was right-handed.

When Baba was safely in bed at home, Mom insisted that she should be the one to stay with her. "I am a nurse, after all." Lester, we knew, would be useless. He was snoring on the Barcalounger. Reluctantly, I agreed. Dan and I drove to my place to sleep what remained of the night.

When Dan walked out of the bathroom in the morning with a towel around his waist, his hair wet from the shower, I sat up in bed. "You look pretty good for not having much sleep."

He smiled and kissed me. "You look pretty good for someone who needs ice packs on her eyes."

Crying can make anyone's eyes puffy, but mine always swell to a ridiculous degree. Mom calls it *periorbital puffiness.*

"But you're still beautiful," Dan said. "Puffy eyes and all. I'd show you how beautiful I think you are, but I have to go to work."

I looked at the time. "Yikes. I've got to get up, too. Appointment with Mildred this morning. We've been trying to connect for a couple of days."

His eyes narrowed.

"Important information I discovered in Cheyenne and at the church. I'm *telling* her, as promised," I said.

"What information?"

"But you're not the lead investigator," I said, tilting my head to one side and trying to look innocent.

His eyes narrowed more.

"Okay, I guess I can trust you." I put a pillow in my lap and patted the bed beside me.

He sat.

"Donald carried around a special concoction of creamer for his coffee, in an Altoids container. It had something called functional mushrooms in it." In case he didn't get it, I added, "A possible source of poisoning."

"Got it."

"But one of the Wyoming girls—women, I mean—put it in her coffee to see how it tasted. And she didn't die."

"Good to know," he nodded. "More relevant if the Wyoming girl—woman—had died."

My eyes narrowed back at him.

"It could be important information," he acknowledged.

"Information I uncovered in my sleuthing. Which I'm not supposed to be doing." Before he could say anything, I kissed him and headed for the shower. "I've got an 8:00 o'clock with the lead detective."

CHAPTER THIRTY

"Do you have allergies?" Mildred asked.

I assumed she we was looking at my swollen face. I was not looking my best. "No. It's periorbital puffiness."

"Oh, I'm sorry. Is it serious?"

"I'll get over it."

"Okay, what is this important news you discovered?"

"Two things, actually. First, I found one of the women who met with Donald at Whitney's the night of the murder. Her name is Jasmine Partridge. You know, like the pear tree."

She frowned. Briefly, I thought of singing, "…and a partridge in a pear tree" but decided to move on. Mildred obviously wasn't good at musical references. "Jasmine lives in Wyoming, and I talked to her. She said that at Whitney's the night of the murder, Donald pulled out an Altoids tin with a special creamer in it, something with 'functional mushrooms.'"

Now she looked *really* interested, in spite of herself, but I hurried on. "Don't get excited. It wasn't the poison because another woman at the table named Gracie tried it herself. And she's not dead. But it might be relevant."

"Can you give me this woman's phone number?" I nodded and pulled it up on my phone for her to write down.

"But that's not all I discovered." Then I remembered that Sammie had insisted that the we keep the surrogacy information to ourselves. I wasn't sure that was the right course—at least for now—but we had agreed. Then I realized I had painted myself into a corner. What else could I tell her I'd discovered?

Mildred was waiting.

Finally, after wrestling with it a bit, I decided I needed to follow the *You don't know what might be relevant* theory I'd been promoting. Surely Sammie would understand. "Affinity Knowles has agreed to be a surrogate mother for her sister Serenity as soon as she—Affinity—loses ten pounds."

"What does ten pounds have to do with it?"

I wanted to say, "You're missing the point," but I held my tongue. I explained about Affinity's plan to remain svelte by losing extra weight *before* pregnancy. "Anyway, I don't know what the surrogacy thing has to do with the murder. Maybe nothing. But it might be relevant." I gave her an earnest look. "And I know how *anything* can be relevant in a murder investigation."

She appeared to be thinking, so I plunged ahead. "And I found out that Serenity is giving Affinity a Mercedes to thank her for having her baby. They had Donald come check out one they found to see it was a good buy. He owned two Mercedes, you know. And his parents live next door to Affinity, in case you didn't know."

She couldn't help it. "I know," she snapped. "So where are you going with this?"

"I have a theory that caffeine powder was given to Donald in the form of a marijuana brownie. Maybe Serenity or Affinity gave it to him, supposedly to thank him for looking at the Mercedes. He would expect it to taste bad if she told him there was a lot of pot in it."

"Why do you think he used pot?"

"Because he was a young rich guy under 30 who came to Colorado a lot more than necessary to see his parents. Marijuana is legal in Colorado."

"I *know* that."

"And I used to go dancing with Donald and Sammie. I never saw him smoke pot, but I know he sometimes stepped outside for some air and came back high. Edibles, he said."

She looked thoughtful. "Why would Serenity and/or Affinity want to kill Donald?"

"That I don't know. But I have some ideas. Would you like to hear them?"

"Okay. Lay it on me." Her arms were folded across her chest, and she was leaning back in her chair. She didn't look very professional. I didn't think she was taking me seriously, but I went on, doing my duty.

"Maybe Serenity thought getting Donald out of the way would make Affinity concentrate more on losing the weight so she could get inseminated by the smart professor she had lined up. I mean, it sounds like Donald *was* a distraction for her. You know about the affair, of course?"

She raised her eyebrows. I wasn't sure what she meant by that but guessed it was, "Yes, of course I know."

"So if Serenity gave Affinity something poisonous to pass on to Donald, she would know Affinity wouldn't be tempted to have any herself. The munchies, you know. Not good for weight loss."

Mildred's face remained impassive, so I went on. "Another possibility is that Affinity got sick of being used— he never took her out, just came over after going out dancing. She was a little too old to be seen with him. Donald is—was—*very* conscious of his image. Anyway, maybe resentment built up, and she decided on revenge. Or maybe the boyfriend, who is no genius, finally figured out that Affinity was screwing around. Or maybe Knox, the boyfriend, saw Affinity heading towards the studio that night to meet Donald for a quickie, and he put two and two together. He was crazy with jealousy, so he killed Donald."

"He just happened to be carrying a killer dose of caffeine with him?"

I realized there was a serious flaw in that theory. "Okay, no."

"Anything else you want to tell me?"

"I think Affinity might be pregnant."

"And this is relevant how?"

"I'm not sure."

"And how do you know?"

I decided not to mention Cassie. "Her clothes are a little less form-fitting than before. And she goes to the bathroom a lot."

"Anything else?"

"Well, yes. There is the kinky dancing thing."

"The what?"

I told her everything I knew about Donald and Kendall and the naked ballet dancing incident, but I didn't use Kendall's name. I explained that I'd promised not to reveal the name unless it became absolutely necessary. Even though I was mad at Kendall, I did appreciate the sensitivity of what she had told me about her past relationship with Donald.

When I had finished, Mildred said that I had damn well better tell her the name, or it wasn't going to look good for

Detective Dan Sherman when his girlfriend refused to cooperate with the police, and it wasn't going to look good for Sammie when her best friend refused to cooperate with the police, and ... well, you get the picture.

I gave her Kendall's name.

I didn't think Mildred seemed very grateful for my work.

I went to Sammie's apartment to tell her about the possible pregnancy and found her sitting on the couch looking at magazines.

"You look calm for someone reportedly about to be arrested."

"Every day I'm not in jail is a good day," she said. She paused mid-page turn, glancing at my face. "You look like hell, though."

I told her about Baba. "And don't even start about the therapy. I've doubled up on therapy appointments, and I'm doing my exercises twice a day, religiously. I *promise* to get over this."

"It's about time," she said. I was hearing that a lot.

I noticed her open magazine. "*Brides*?"

"I'm going to need a dress."

Sammie and Sam were getting married in August. They would have been happy just to go to the courthouse, but, as Sammie put it, "Mom would never get over it." So they had compromised. Instead of a ceremony in the Catholic Church, Sammie would have a small, simple wedding hosted by Geraldine and Jake in their large back yard. Geraldine would plan the decorations and the reception, but Sammie would have complete control over the ceremony itself.

Sadly, from Geraldine's point of view, Sammie was not to be budged about certain details: me as maid of honor, carrying Isabelle. Sam's brother as best man. All eight parents and stepparents walking in together as a group. ("Nobody's going to be giving me away, like a donation to Goodwill," Sammie insisted.) Derek officiating. ("He's a writer. He'll come up with something good.")

Geraldine was especially unhappy with the idea of all the parents walking in together. "Like we're equals!" she said. Sammie had told her to get over it. It was happening. There was a lot of Geraldine in Sammie.

Sammie turned a page, and her face lit up in a smile. "Look at this. I *love* this."

Of course she did. The bodice was covered in sparkly beads. "I've heard you're supposed to order a dress six months to a year in advance," I said. "You've got less than two months."

"I know. I can't order this one, but we can find something similar in a bridal shop. In stock," she said. "Trip to Denver shopping soon?"

"Absolutely."

" And what are you thinking *you'd* like to wear?"

"I don't know. What are your colors?"

"Mom's department. She's decided on white. White flowers. White tablecloths. White arch. That's because she figures Elva won't pay attention to the colors I'd pick anyway." Elva is Sammie's stepmother, and she and Geraldine don't always see eye to eye. Or, actually, ever. "Mom figures she might as well use white as a palette and let us all wear whatever the hell we like."

"Makes sense to me." I pictured the perfect dress in

my mind. "I'm thinking I'd like a sundress since it will be August and probably hot as hell. Something form-fitting, short or tea length. It just needs to knock Dan's socks off. Maybe in teal? Strappy heels?"

"Sounds good. And strappy heels will help aerate the lawn."

When I stopped in to check on Baba, Lester was sitting at the kitchen table with the newspapers. "Lester stay over?" I asked Mom.

"Barcalounger. I used your room." We always refer to the guest room as *my* room. "I had to put the Blessed Virgin on the floor, though," she added.

Baba frowned at her. She looked pale and small, sitting on the sofa with a blanket pulled up around her and her feet up on the coffee table, a pillow underneath them and another pillow under her arm. Easing onto the sofa next to her, I kissed her cheek. "I hope you know how awful I feel, Baba. I'm so sorry."

"I know, honey. I know."

"I'm going to show you how sorry I am." I took out my therapist's business card. "See this? I moved up my appointments with the therapist to once a week now, and I'm doing my exercises twice a day, every day. I'm going to lick this."

"Finally," Mom said.

CHAPTER THIRTY-ONE

Monday morning I was supposed to work on my class project, but I could muster no enthusiasm for it. I had no enthusiasm for my *trypanophobia* exercises, either, but I did them. I even successfully imagined a hypodermic needle, ever so briefly, and didn't faint. I'd made it a lavender plastic needle from a child's doctor play kit, but I still thought that qualified as progress.

Lying on the floor after my exercises, my thoughts turned once again to murder. I had been googling motives for murder, and found that they generally fall into four categories: greed, love, pride, and gluttony. "Gluttony" surprised me, but it turns out it usually means "being drunk."

Other sites listed the motives as *lust, love, loathing,* and *loot.* I liked that list best, probably, to be honest, because of the alliteration.

Lust I could understand. It would be easy to be attracted to Donald if you didn't know him. Falling in love with him, though, would be harder. Still, maybe someone had. Maybe she'd been rejected. Maybe she couldn't handle rejection and decided, "If I can't have him, no one will."

Maybe.

Or could *loathing* be a factor? That seemed more likely, though too extreme. People might dislike Donald or be annoyed by him, but they didn't *loathe* him. I thought a minute. But maybe Bucky was an exception. Cutting off a lifelong friendship was pretty extreme. I definitely needed to look more into Bucky.

Finally, there was *loot.* Donald did have money, but I couldn't see who would have gained by killing him, except for his parents, and they certainly didn't do it. Mildred knew about the trust fund Geraldine had set up to take care of Isabelle until she was 21. Surely she could see that, rich as Geraldine was, money couldn't have been a motive for Sammie to murder Donald.

Fluffles interrupted my thoughts by crawling onto my chest, settling with her head on my neck, and purring in my ear. I knew I had to move or her purring would lull me to sleep. I petted her an apology, then sat up and texted Sammie.

Can I host a meeting at your place?

I'm here. Always here. I could almost hear a sigh in her words.

I texted Derek.

Brainstorming 11:00 at Sammie's?

He sent a thumbs-up emoji. I hesitated, then decided to text Cassie. She had good ideas and had finished her week of being grounded. I decided to include her.

Brainstorming 11:00 at Sammie's? Pick you up.

Another thumbs-up emoji.

I was surprised to see Sam at home when Cassie and I arrived. "Took off work as soon as I heard you were coming," he said. "Had to keep an eye on things."

Was he turning into one of those controlling guys who has to approve everything his wife does? My face must have reflected my thoughts. "He's kidding," Sammie said. "Don't let your imagination get away from you."

I was relieved.

Derek arrived, wearing a straw bowler hat, a crisp white shirt, and khaki pants. "Off for tea later?" I asked. He looked as though he could walk into the Brown Palace Hotel in Denver and fit right in.

"A late lunch with Clay," he said. "Harper Springs."

I couldn't even think of a place in Harper Springs that would require dressing up. "Just want to look your best?" I asked.

"Oh, this is not even close to my best," he said. "Wait until you see me at the wedding."

"I don't even want to know," said Sammie. "Whatever you decide to wear, just don't tell Mom. It's better that she's surprised."

"So what is our plan?" Sam said. As so often happens in meetings, a man was taking the lead. I decided not to let that happen.

"I have decided that we need a time line," I said, emphasizing the "I" ever so slightly. "Donald left your apartment at about 4:30 the afternoon of the murder. He turned up at Whitney's at around 6:00. Where was he before that?

"Maybe he was meeting someone somewhere downtown," Cassie said.

"Who would he be meeting?" Derek asked.

"Buckminster," I said. "We know he was in town that afternoon because he bought a purse at Second Chance. I think maybe he made arrangements to meet Donald."

"Why? After he hadn't spoken to him in 10 years?" Sammie asked.

"Here's my theory," I said. "He found out from his Mom that you had a baby. Remember, Donald told Cecelia a couple of weeks before the murder, and Cecelia probably told Bucky's mother. So Bucky knew Donald was the sperm donor."

"As does the world now," Sam sighed.

"So maybe Bucky was meeting Donald to applaud his growth," I continued, "or even to forgive him. After all, Donald didn't allow *this* baby to be aborted, so maybe that meant he had grown, in Bucky's eyes."

"That wasn't Donald's decision," Sammie said. "He wasn't the one who decided to have the baby."

"I know, but he didn't encourage you to have an abortion, either."

"Bucky doesn't know that," she said. "And how come he's dating Kendall, someone he knows *did* have an abortion?"

Derek looked thoughtful. "Maybe he forgave her."

"Hmmmm." I wondered how hard it would be to forgive someone for having an abortion if you felt as strongly as Bucky obviously did. But maybe it was possible. "Let's just assume that maybe it *was* Bucky that Donald met somewhere. We know Bucky was in town, and we know Donald seems to have disappeared for about an hour and a half. Since his car was still in the museum parking lot when the reception started, he must have stayed downtown. Where would he have gone?"

"Somewhere no one would recognize him and, to quote Jasmine, 'go all gaga.' Derek thought a moment and continued. "A dive. Some crummy hole in the wall where guys sit all day nursing beers or bourbon or whatever and wouldn't recognize Donald."

"But Donald doesn't drink. *Didn't* drink."

"They have coffee in dives."

"Okay, maybe it was a dive."

"Lucky's," Derek said. "It's downtown. It's crummy. Let's check it out."

I hesitated. Lucky's was not the kind of place I was eager to experience.

Derek raised one of his eyebrows at me. "And you call yourself an amateur detective?"

"Okay. Let's go," I said. "After we have some lunch."

"I'll come, too," Cassie said.

"Like that's going to happen," I said. "No. You're pushing your luck even being here at this meeting."

She glared at me, but didn't pursue it. She knew I was right.

Sam and Derek made tuna sandwiches for all of us, and then Derek ran across the street to pick up two orders of Whitney's giant brownie sundaes for us to share. Sam offered to take Cassie home, but she suggested staying and waiting for us to come back from Lucky's. "I can play with Isabelle," she said. "I need baby practice. My mom's having a baby."

"Then by all means, stay," Sam said. "You can practice all you want with Isabelle."

"Especially changing diapers," Sammie added.

"First we will check with Detective Dan to make sure that's okay," I said. I was getting pretty good at remembering to do the responsible thing with a teenager.

CHAPTER THIRTY-TWO

Lucky's was about as bad as I had imagined. Dark. Smelled funny—what was it? Maybe a combination of beer, urine, and microwave popcorn. Two guys sat at one end of the bar drooping into their drinks. They didn't even look up when Derek and I sat down at the other end.

I wanted a chardonnay, but I was pretty sure any white wine would be from a $4.00 bottle opened a year or so ago and kept in the refrigerator with a cork that fell out periodically. I ordered beer.

"So what do you want?" the bartender asked, even though we had already ordered.

Derek raised an eyebrow.

"Hey, you and your little girlfriend didn't choose this place for the ambiance."

Derek showed him a picture of Donald. "Has this guy ever been in here?"

"Why should I tell you?"

"Because it might help solve a murder investigation," I said.

"Are you with the police?"

"No," I said. "But the police aren't solving it, and they think my best friend might have done it, or me, just because it's my friend's studio, and I'm sick of everybody acting like we might be criminals when we're not, and I think the police woman in charge is barking up the wrong tree, going about everything wrong and choosing to pursue paths that don't show our innocence, and Harvey Klump is making all kinds of stupid accusations and accusing of us all sorts of things." Here I conjured up a few tears. "We are innocent!"

"Okay, okay, lady. Calm down. No, I haven't seen this guy."

I pulled out a picture of Bucky. "How about him?"

"Yeah, I've seen him. Came in the day the toilet backed up—couple of weeks ago. Cost me a fortune."

"Thank you," I tried to smile sweetly. Maybe he had a daughter and would feel protective. "Are you Lucky?"

"Yeah. But a backed up toilet wasn't so lucky."

"Did the guy come in with someone?"

"No. Came in and looked around and sat down towards the back. Then he ordered coffee. Jesus. Coffee. I had a clogged toilet on my hands, but I had to make coffee. While I was plunging, some other guy came in, but I didn't really get a look at him. The first guy came up to the counter and asked for a refill and a second cup of coffee. What am I, Starbucks?" He paused. "I thought something was a little weird about the whole deal."

"Weird? Why?

"Because the guy I did get a look at—he pointed to the picture—sure has hell didn't look like he belonged here. Dressed real well—even had on a sports jacket in this heat." He took a drink of whatever was in a short glass beside him. "All that plunging and it didn't work. Had to call the god- dam plumber anyway."

"Do you remember anything else about the two guys?"

"Nope. I was on the phone with the plumber when they

left, so one of them threw down a twenty-dollar bill on their way out."

"Did you tell the police all this?"

"Not my business. Why would I tell the police about two guys having coffee? And nobody asked me about them anyway."

"One of them got murdered an hour or so later," Derek said.

"No shit? Was one of them that tap-dancing guy?"

I nodded and sipped my beer.

"Do you think the fancy jacket guy did it?"

"I don't know yet. But this may help us figure it out. Thank you." I smiled at him in what I hoped was a charming manner. I fished in my pocket and found a twenty. We had to do as well as Bucky. No, we had to do *better* than Bucky. I fished out another ten. "Thanks again." I pushed the rest of my beer away, and Derek drained his.

"Good luck, lady," Lucky said.

"Wait. I almost forgot the most important part. When did this happen?"

"I got the plumber's bill right here." He reached into a drawer behind the bar and read the date on a receipt stapled to the bill. "It was May 18. The plumber came about 5:30, so I'd say these guys were here from about 5:00-6:00. Quite a while for just drinking coffee."

"Thank you so, so much!" I was starting to sound like Willow Wisteria.

Derek and I high-fived when we got out on the street. "Maybe Bucky is our guy," Derek said. "And, hey, the tears were a nice touch. You're quite the actress."

"Have you forgotten my breakout performance in *Oklahoma!* my senior year?"

"Ado Annie doesn't exactly reveal depth."

"I was pretty good in *Grease,* too."

"You did the hand jive in the chorus." He moved us back on track. "Where does this information from Lucky's get us?"

"For one thing, Bucky could have given Donald a caffeinated, marijuana brownie—or some other special toxic edible he made. He definitely had opportunity and probably means. He could have accessed caffeine powder through his business."

"But what about motive? Why was he meeting Donald after crossing him off his friend list ten years ago?"

"That's the question of the day."

CHAPTER THIRTY-THREE

I was stuck. I didn't know where to go with any of the information I'd uncovered. I sat in bed with Fluffles and my morning coffee, looking over my list of suspects again. Who did I know the *least* about?

Mariah and Knox. According to Geraldine, Mariah had disappeared, so that didn't seem a fruitful route to pursue. Besides, Geraldine was convinced she was guilty only of being naive. I trusted Geraldine's instincts.

So that left Knox. I decided that maybe Taylor, the nanny, could tell me more about him. If Cecilia was at home, she probably could, too, but I didn't want to bother a grieving woman. I was pretty sure Taylor would be happy to tell me anything she knew, though. I texted her.

Can i come pick your brain?

Sure. Pick away! Noonish.

I glanced at Cecilia's house as I pulled up later and parked. The draperies were all drawn. The lawn was about two inches longer than neighboring lawns. The hanging plant by the door needed deadheading, and if there had been an Amazon package by the front door, I'd have thought Cecilia and her husband were away. I suspected, though, that they were just having trouble coping with the demands of ordinary life since their world had fallen apart.

I rang the doorbell at Taylor's house. "Hang on," she said when she opened the door. "I'm not supposed to let friends come in the house. I'll get Sophie, and we'll sit on the porch."

She came out in a moment with Sophie and a tub full of Duplo blocks. "You remember Ella, Sophie?" she asked.

Sophie just looked at me.

"Hi, Sophie," I said.

She ignored me, sat down, and began pulling blocks out of the tub.

"They have a nanny cam," Taylor said. "They trust me with their *child*, but they can't possibly trust my judgment when it comes to other people. A friend might swipe some coasters or, god forbid, eat one of their bagels. We are restricted to the front porch."

"Geez. What do you do in winter?"

"Sophie spends a lot of time with me in coffee shops. Or next door. CeeCee lets us come over and have guests. She'll even run errands to give me privacy with friends sometimes. *She* has good sense."

Taylor reached over and helped Sophie fit a Duplo palm tree onto the top of a block. "So what's up, Agatha?" she asked me. "Or are you channeling Angela Lansbury today?"

"I'm searching for information anywhere I can, anything that might help. Right now I'm interested in Affinity's boyfriend."

"What about Affinity herself?"

"She has an airtight alibi that I'm not supposed to know

about. So Knox seems worth looking at more closely. What do you know about him?"

"Honestly, he seems like a nice guy. He's what, maybe 33 or 34? Seems to really care about Affinity, though who knows why? She's about as deep as … oh, a Ritz cracker." She thought a moment. "But I guess Knox isn't exactly an intellectual heavyweight."

I nodded in agreement, thinking about his belief in the Flat Earth Society, which I'd been reading more about. I wondered if he was one of the members who think the "disc" of Earth is surrounded by a wall of ice and guarded by NASA employees who keep people from climbing the wall and falling off.

Taylor continued. "Knox loves kids. He adores Sophie and told me he can't wait to have kids of his own. He'll be good at being a dad. Maybe not helping with science home-work, but, you know, otherwise. At gatherings, kids flock to him. They love him."

"And it's not, you know, creepy?"

"No, no. I don't get creepy vibes at all. Deluded vibes, definitely, but not creepy. Affinity doesn't look it, but she's no spring chicken. She's not likely to be popping a kid or two out. Knox needs to focus elsewhere, but he wants her." She shook her head. "Not sure why. Idiot."

"No accounting for tastes. What does he do for a living?"

"He's a puppy sitter. Runs that doggie daycare on the edge of town—Happy Puppy Haven."

That gave me just what I needed—a way to meet Knox. I'd figure out the details later, but a visit to Happy Puppy Haven was in my very near future. I changed the subject. "So what else do you know about Bucky, Donald's ex-friend?"

"Not much. You saw him at the funeral. Spiffy dresser. I've met him at a couple of Cecilia's parties. Always comes with his mother, but I've never seen him hang out with Donald. Just Cecilia. Calls her Aunt CeeCee."

"Bay-bee?" Sophie was standing in front of me. She'd evidently had enough of the Duplos. "Bay-bee?"

"I don't have the baby with me today, sweetie," I said.

"Bay-bee!" In a millisecond, Sophie went from calm, happy toddler to scary maniac, throwing herself on the lawn and screaming bloody murder. "Come here, snickerdoodle," Taylor said. She picked Sophie up and walked around the yard with her. "You're okay, honey. Shhhh ... shhh ... Ella doesn't have Baby Isabelle with her today."

Sophie wanted what she wanted, and logic had nothing to do with it. The fact that I didn't have a baby with me was completely irrelevant. "Bay-bee! Bay-bee!" she screamed.

Next door, Cecilia must have heard the ruckus. She walked out onto her porch and called,"Taylor, come on over. I'll help." Her hair was blown dry and styled, and she was neatly dressed in cropped pants and a tunic.

Sophie continued to scream as we walked across the lawn. Cecilia held out her arms, and Sophie went to her. "Coffee's on," she said to Taylor, nodding at me. We all went inside.

"I've got a banana, Sophie," she said. "Want a banana?" Sophie paused for just a second, looking interested. Cecilia quickly added, "I could put peanut butter on it."

Sophie managed to sputter, "Nana!" She started gulping

more slowly, her screams fading. Cecilia handed her to Taylor. "Let me get the peanut butter."

"Do you have an Epi-pen?" I asked.

"Peanut butter is okay for babies now," Taylor said. "Doctors say they *need* to eat it to avoid allergies later on."

"Good to know."

Taylor bounced Sophie gently in her arms while Cecilia cut up half a banana and put peanut butter on the slices. She held up the jar. "All natural. No sugar."

Taylor nodded. "God help us if they found out we gave her sugar." She looked at me. "Sometimes we actually let her have a little jelly with the peanut butter. So far God hasn't told on us."

I sat down on a bar stool at the counter. Up close, I could see that although Cecilia was put together on the outside, something was broken on the inside. She wore no make-up, and her eyes had the swollen, puffy look of someone who has spent a lot of time crying.

"So what brings you here?" Cecelia asked me, surprising me with her bluntness. She grabbed a monkey-covered bib that was hanging from a refrigerator magnet hook and deftly slipped it on Sophie.

I decided to be honest with her. She deserved that. "I came to talk to Taylor about people who knew your son. The police—and the rumor mill—seem to be focusing on Sammie and, well, me. I was hoping to learn something, anything, that might point them in a different direction." I paused, thinking that maybe it needed to be said. "We didn't do it."

"Of course not. I'm happy to help if I can. She looked at Sophie. Milk?" Sophie nodded, and Cecelia took a sippy cup from a drawer and opened the refrigerator.

"Ella wants to know about Bucky," Taylor said.

Cecilia frowned. "Why?"

"Because he knew Donald," I said. "I'm not looking to accuse people, just trying to make connections and find something—anything—to tell Mildred. *Detective* Mildred. She's barking up the wrong tree, in my opinion."

Cecelia handed Sophie the sippy cup of milk, then pulled a chair to the other side of the counter so she could face us. "Bucky used to be Donald's friend. His mom and I met in the hospital when the boys were born and have been good friends ever since. The boys played together, went to school together, took Taekwondo lessons together, played soccer together." She smiled, remembering.

After a moment she continued. "Then in high school, suddenly Bucky changed. He completely stopped hanging out with Donald, ever. Oh, he usually came over with his mom when we had get-togethers, but I think that was for his mom's sake. I never saw him even talk to Donald again." She sighed, remembering. "I don't know what happened between Bucky and Donald, and his mom couldn't figure it out, either. Both boys just shrugged it off, like it was no big deal. But it *was* a big deal. I could tell Donald was really hurt." She sighed. "I just had to accept it and hope it would change."

"Down," Sophie said, finished with her bananas. Cecelia was right there with a wet washcloth.

"Let's get the toy box," Taylor said. She and Sophie headed for a living room closet, leaving me with Cecelia.

"Who else do you want to know about?" Cecelia asked.

"Maybe Donald's friends? Like the models at the service?"

"The ones there were the only friends I knew at all. Kayla, the pregnant one, is the one I've talked to the most. She came to our big Christmas party last year."

"One of the models was *pregnant?*" I asked.

"Hard to believe, I know. Six months."

"Where was she hiding the baby?" I shook my head.

She shrugged. "Kayla is sweet. She told me Donald was the most professional model she ever worked with. He always made everyone look good." She smiled again. "And she said she loved how he came to Colorado to see his parents so often. He loved his mom and dad, she said." Tears welled in her eyes. "And he did. He wasn't like other kids who get so busy with their lives that they forget their parents. He even visited my father in the nursing home every single time he was here—and not just for a perfunctory hello. He'd stay and talk and then be sure to go back at least one more time before he left. When Dad died, he cried like a baby."

Donald had a side I've never seen. A caring side. I wished I had known that side.

"Kayla just went on and on about what she'd learned from Donald about honoring your roots, and she told me that's why she moved back to Colorado with her husband after she was pregnant. She wanted her children to know her parents and cousins." She got up and wiped the counter, as well as her tears. "But I'll bet you want to know what was going on with Affinity," she said.

She kept surprising me. I nodded.

"They were having an affair. He thought he was hiding it, but I knew. It was not a good thing. She was too old for him, and she had a boyfriend. He was using her." She looked at me. "He was a grown man. I had to stay out of it."

I nodded.

"The woman doesn't have enough to do. I think all the volunteering is mostly to keep her busy. She doesn't work that much at the hair salon, either."

"I heard her sister helps support her. What do you know about her? Serenity?"

"She's misnamed, for one thing. She's about as Serene as—oh, I can't think these days. What's not serene?"

I thought a moment. "A mother who finds out her daughter went to bed with bubblegum the day before she was going to be a flower girl for her aunt's wedding."

Cecilia smiled. "Oh dear. Personal experience?"

"Mom was beside herself. She finally had to cut most of it out, and I'm pretty sure no one said I was adorable when I went down the aisle."

She smiled again, then got back to the subject at hand. "Serenity has a hard time letting people run their own lives. Always has something to point out. Did I know those cords on my kitchen window could strangle a child? Have I ever tried shining the leaves on my plants? Did I know that the meat at Costco is better than the meat at Sam's Club?"

I looked at the cord on the kitchen window shades. "There's no loop on your shade."

"I know. She was right. I replaced the shade."

"Is she married?"

"Divorced. No kids. She owns a company that does corporate gifts. *Very* used to being in control."

"And Affinity?"

"She lets Serenity be in control when she wants. But she's pretty good at looking out for herself. Then there's Divinity."

"What?"

"The other sister."

"There's another sister, besides the twins?"

"Didn't you know? Affinity, Serenity, and little sister Divinity."

"Divinity? Like the candy?"

"What candy?" Taylor said. She had left Sophie with her toys and sat down beside me.

"The white stuff, shaped like fat teardrops. My grandma makes it at Christmas," I said.

"I don't know anything about white candy. I just know that Divinity married a Mormon, and I think she's having enough kids for all three sisters," Taylor said.

"Three sisters. Affinity, Serenity, Divinity." I had a hard time wrapping my mind around those names.

"Get your brain in gear, honey. Three sisters with weird names. It happens. You'd be surprised if you saw Divinity, though. None of the glam of her sisters. Never any make-up, hair wadded up in a scrunchie, giant T-shirts that probably belong to her husband. Probably worn to a frazzle with all those kids."

"How many kids does she have?"

"At least five, maybe more. I'm not sure," Cecilia said. "I met one of them once. A little girl named Tuppence."

I winced. "So Divinity's got the family gene for coming up with weird names."

"Evidently," Cecilia said. Then she added, "I think she's got brothers named Quid and Shilling,"

"You're kidding!"

She smiled. "I'm kidding."

I loved the way this woman thought. "So a new question.

You must know Affinity's boyfriend Knox. What do you think of him?"

"Aside from the Flat Earth Society nonsense? I assume Taylor told you about that."

I nodded. "How does he treat her? Is he good to her? Kind?"

"As far as I can tell, he's better to her than she deserves, sneaking around the way she was with Donald." She shook her head in disapproval. "It's all very hard for me to watch." She started crying. "Or *was.*"

I didn't know what to say. I didn't know her well enough to hug her. Finally, I just reached over and put my hand on her arm, letting her know I was there.

CHAPTER THIRTY-FOUR

When I got home, I took a few notes about what I'd learned, adding them to the file on my laptop. Then I made a list of suspects and looked it over:

- Serenity
- Affinity
- Kendall
- Bucky
- Knox
- Mariah
- Unknown female who was fed up with Donald (probably many possibilities across the country)
- Unknown jealous male (probably many possibilities across the country)
- Unknown others

Then to be fair, I added Sammie, Sam, Geraldine, Derek, Jake, and me to the list, just to have an accurate record. We all had motives.

Then I crossed Sammie, Sam, Geraldine, Derek, Jake, and me off the list, just to have an even more accurate record. None of us did it.

What I needed was another brain or two to help me think. Luckily Mom had invited Baba and me for dinner. She suggested bringing Cassie, too. "I didn't get to spend time with her in the mountains like the rest of you. I'd like to get to know her better."

"And ask that adorable Derek, too," Baba said. "We can talk about the murder. I know he's good at murders."

Before dinner, I had work to do. I finished my paper for the "Fundamentals of Blended Learning" class and gave a sigh of relief. Then, instead of celebrating, I headed to my next appointment with Doctor Rodriguez.

I was dreading it, as usual, and she probably wasn't looking forward to it all that much, either. She hid any impatience she felt, though, and praised my efforts. She had the most soothing voice I've ever heard, and I often found myself wishing I could record it and play it back at night when I had trouble sleeping.

I had a breakthrough during this session. I actually picked up and held a real hypodermic needle for 20 seconds or so. I was focusing on the plunger part and not the needle, but still I did it, and with only minor dizziness. Dr. Rodriguez was proud of me.

"But you were right here to catch me if I keeled over," I told her. "What if you were a nurse aiming for my arm?"

"We'll get there," she said. "You're going to be able to get a flu shot someday soon. Or a tetanus shot. Or a shot of Novocaine at the dentist's."

I shuddered.

"Trust me. You're going to be fine."

I felt hopeful, in spite of myself, as I drove to Mom's. Maybe I *would* overcome this needle phobia some day. I didn't let Cassie's terse "Hey" bring me down when I picked her up and she immediately turned to her phone. I didn't even let it bother me when she put the phone away and began chatting amiably with Derek when he got in the car.

"Burgers in the back yard," Mom said when we arrived. I eyed the wine she poured for Baba and Derek but knew I needed to be a good role model. I'd be driving Cassie home, so I had iced tea.

Baba was definitely getting back to her old self; she'd even been bowling, she said. She was still seeing Lester but hadn't invited him to dinner. "Sometimes a person just wants to eat their potato salad without hearing about the health impacts of mayonnaise," she said.

"Are you having a good summer?" Mom asked Cassie, opening the table umbrella as we settled in chairs on the deck. It was a lame question, and I tried to imagine how Cassie would have answered me if I'd asked it. Certainly, it wouldn't have been the polite way she answered Mom.

"Yes, thank you," she said. "That murder has really, like, spiced things up around here."

"Murders will do that," Mom said mildly.

"Do you know I've been helping?" Cassie added. "I found out that stupid Willow lady was a fake. And I tracked down another lady who had been with Donald before the murder. Well, actually, her and several other girls."

"Young women," I said.

She sighed. "So when exactly does a girl change over to being a woman?"

"Ooh, there are many theories about that," Baba said.

"I just don't think it's right to refer to females over eighteen as *girls,*" I said. "We don't refer to young men as *boys.*"

"Unless they're drinking and being stupid," Mom said.

"Boys will be boys," Baba added.

"Okay, we *usually* don't refer to men as boys. But people call grown-up women *girls* all the time."

"Has Ella always had this thing about words?" Cassie asked. "I mean, like, she has this stupid thing going with dad about *perfect.*"

"Oh, that's just the tip of the iceberg," Baba said.

"She hates how writers always have people *padding* into the kitchen," said Derek. "She insists people don't *pad* in real life, just in books."

"And she doesn't like *It is what it is,*" said Baba.

"Lately she's been complaining that experts being interviewed on NPR or CNN always, at some point, say 'Great question,'" Mom said.

"Not all questions are great," I said. "And half the time they don't even answer the 'great' question at all."

"I don't get it," Cassie said. "Who cares?"

"Not most of the world, obviously," I said. "Now let's move on. Since you're so interested in the murder, let's talk murder."

"Always a good dinner topic," Mom said.

"Who do you think did it?" Baba asked. "How about if Ella tells us everything she knows, and then we each say who we think the murderer is."

"Yes!" said Cassie.

Why not? It might help. I outlined everything I knew. Well, almost everything. I did not tell about Affinity and Serenity at the ATM shortly after the time of the murder. That was police information that pretty much eliminated them as suspects, but who knows? There might be some explanation I couldn't imagine. At any rate, I kept it to myself because

Dan had told me to. But I did tell them about what Donald had been wearing when he was found, even though Mildred had asked Cassie and me not to share that information. I didn't feel the same loyalty to Mildred.

I even betrayed Sammie, a little, by sharing Serenity's surrogacy plans, which I had said I would keep to myself. I'd already broken that promise and told Mildred, so it seemed only fair to share it with the people helping me. I thought Sammie would understand.

When I finished, Derek said, "We need to finish your time line." I pulled my laptop out of my tote bag and handed it to him.

Cassie watched him log in. "Ella has no secrets from me," he winked, with his brown eye. Tonight he wore a preppie outfit I didn't like—plaid shorts, sneakers and a polo shirt. A pale sweater knotted over his shoulders would have completed the look, but, luckily, Derek knew where to draw the line.

"So we know Donald was with Sammie, meeting Isabelle, until about 4:30," I said. "Then he disappears from our radar for about half an hour and shows up at Lucky's at around 5:00."

"Slow down," said Derek, typing quickly.

"He stays there until around 6:00. Then he goes to Whitney's for an hour or so and walks into the Juniper Museum at about 7:15."

"When does he leave there?" asked Baba.

"Not sure. Affinity leaves at about 7:40, but Donald either stays or leaves briefly and comes back to do his naked pictures thing with Mariah. He leaves her around 8:00. The next thing we know, he's found dead at about 8:40."

"Okay, time line is done," Mom said, getting to her feet. "I'm putting the burgers on, and no more murder talk until after we eat. I mean it."

"Lester would probably tell us murder is bad for the digestion," Baba said. "He always says *the* digestion. And *the* Facebook. And *the* Google."

"So maybe Ella gets her word hang-up from you," Cassie suggested.

"Is Lester getting on your nerves a little, Baba?" I asked.

She hesitated. "Okay, a little. But that's normal. People who care about each other *do* get on each other's nerves sometimes."

"Tell me about it," Mom said. She scooted the mustard and ketchup bottles over to make room for an enormous green salad. Maybe she hadn't known Lester wasn't coming.

After we had eaten and taken the dishes to the kitchen, Baba said, "*Now* we can talk murder."

"I need a little more wine first," Mom said. I don't think she had as much interest in speculating as the rest of us.

We settled back around the table, and Derek opened my laptop again to record our theories.

"I'll go first," Baba said. "I think it was Knox. It's always the boyfriend or the husband who does it." She thought a minute. "Or it could be a gay lover."

"*Whose* gay lover?" I asked.

"Donald's. He was awfully pretty. He took ballet lessons. Maybe he was gay."

"Stereotypes, Baba," Derek said. "Some of us don't even like ballet."

"Sorry."

"But we're all devastatingly handsome."

"That you are," Baba smiled. "I'll stick with the boy-friend, not a gay lover. Knox did it."

"One vote for Knox then. Mom?"

"Do we really need to do this?" We all waited. Finally she said, "I'll vote for the receptionist. She went to the dance studio while everyone was at the heckelphone lecture."

"Hurdy-gurdy," I said.

"Okay, hurdy-gurdy lecture. Mariah is my vote."

I saw many problems with this scenario but moved on. "Derek?"

"I think it might have been Bucky and Kendall, working together for revenge." He typed in his vote, then said, "But it could also have been Serenity. She knocked off Donald so that Affinity would get on with getting inseminated while she was still young enough for it to work."

"Or maybe it was Affinity," Baba said. "She finally got sick of Donald using her."

"You already voted," I said.

"Just throwing out another idea."

"And not a bad idea," Derek said. "Either Affinity *or* Serenity could have given Donald something with poison in it. Affinity could have done it anytime, or Serenity could have given it to Affinity to pass on. I think Ella's right about it probably being a marijuana brownie. Donald would expect a brownie with a lot of pot in it not to taste that great."

"Maybe I'll make a marijuana brownie for Lester," Baba said. "He has a high tolerance for things that don't taste great."

"You're straying off the subject, Baba," I said. "Cassie, what's your vote?"

"I think it was Serenity, but she was dressed up and pretending to be Affinity."

"Like in *Parent Trap!*" Baba said, excited.

"Exactly. Donald thought he was meeting Affinity for, like, a quickie in the studio, but it was really Serenity with a poisoned brownie. Affinity and Serenity switched places!"

"Maybe," I said, mentally rolling my eyes. But I'd often wondered if a twins actually ever do trade places. If one went out with her sister's boyfriend and he kissed her, would he be able to tell he wasn't kissing who he thought he was? Is there that much difference in how people kiss?

I remembered Brantley Aversham and his kiss from several years ago—a kiss so bad that I wanted to kiss him again, just to study its badness. Wisely, I'd refrained.

Then I thought of Dan and smiled. Now *there* was a man who could kiss.

"Earth to Ella. Where *are* you?" Derek asked.

"Sorry. Just thinking." I gave Cassie my attention. "So I know you've kissed Trevor, right?"

"What does that have to do with ..."

"Just answer. I'm going somewhere with this."

"Okay, yes," she said, looking away. She knew I knew she'd done more than kiss him.

"And have you kissed other boys?"

"I *am* 15, you know."

"So, yes?"

"Yes."

"Name one."

"A guy named Landry."

"Okay. If your eyes were closed, would you ever mistake a kiss from Landry for a kiss from Trevor?"

"As if!" She started to laugh, then didn't. "Okay, I see what you mean. But maybe Serenity didn't kiss him."

"In your scenario, she was planning to do *more* than kiss him. Do you really think she could have pulled that off?"

"Maybe she knew he'd be dead before they got to that. Because she brought him a poisoned whatever."

"Maybe. Or maybe it wasn't Serenity dressed up like Affinity who killed him," I said.

"It's a theory," she said, lifting her chin stubbornly. "All of us are trying out *theories.*"

"You're right," Baba said. "We're talking theories, and mine is still 'The boyfriend did it.' I think we should pay a visit to Happy Puppy Haven."

"Yes!" said Cassie. "We can pretend to be checking out the place for our dog."

"We don't have a dog," I said.

Everyone looked at me as if I was an idiot. "Okay," I said, "What will our pretend dog's name be?"

"Max," Derek said.

"No, it's a girl dog," said Cassie. "Marilyn."

"For a *dog?*" He shook his head in disgust.

"It's my dog!"

The girl could be difficult even playing pretend. "Okay, fine. So Marilyn is your dog. What kinds of things do we want to know about Knox?"

"Does he have a short temper? I could bring up something controversial, see if he gets a little hot," Baba said.

"They're considering a ban on pit bulls in town," Mom said. "There's been a lot in the paper from dog owners complaining about it. Maybe you could mention that." She was getting interested, in spite of herself.

I nodded, taking out my phone. "Good ideas. I'll call and make an appointment for tomorrow."

"Two o'clock," I said when I hung up. "Who's in?"

"Me!" said Baba.

"Sadly, gotta work," said Derek.

"Me, too," said Mom.

"Pick me up?" Cassie asked.

I knew I was going to be in trouble. "No. I can't get you involved in going to see someone who might turn out to be a murderer. Your dad would kill me."

"But you're okay with getting your grandmother involved?" Mom asked. Sometimes she really annoys me.

"Baba is an adult!" I snapped.

"And I'm fifteen. And it's *my* dog!"

"I'm sorry. Really. I can't do it."

She pouted the rest of the evening. She talked to Baba and Mom and Derek, but she only glared at me.

CHAPTER THIRTY-FIVE

Baba and I pulled into the Puppy Haven parking lot at 2:00 and went in to the lobby. Just as the door closed behind us, the little bell over the door rang again as it opened. In came Cassie.

She gave an exasperated sigh and said, "Mo-om!" turning the word into two syllables. "You might have waited twenty seconds for me!"

I frowned, momentarily confused, then realized she was playing "surly teenager." I turned around and saw Trevor's car driving out of the parking lot. What was I going to do? I had to play along.

Baba was hiding a smile by holding her cast in front of her face, trying to scratch inside.

A nice-looking man about six feet tall came out of an office near the reception desk. He wore a Happy Puppy Haven T-shirt and a friendly smile. "How can I help you?" he asked.

I smiled back. "Hi. I'm Cindy Newberry, and this is my daughter …"

"Rachel," Cassie said.

"… and my grandmother, Vera. We're looking for a good place to leave my daughter—Rachel's—dog during the day. Someone I met at my neighbor's house the other day said I should come here. Are you Knox?"

"I am. Who was it who recommended us?"

Oops. I hesitated, but Cassie jumped right in. "I think her name was Lisa," she said. "It was at a friend's barbecue."

I tried not to look surprised.

"Oh, sure," he nodded. "Lisa Langston, probably. Her little Lionel stays here most week days. Cute dog. What's your dog's name?"

"Marilyn." Cassie smiled sweetly. "She's adorable. Nana used to take care of her during the day, but Nana's going into assisted living now." Cassie cast her eyes downward, putting her arm around Baba. I looked away.

"I'll *so* miss Marilyn," said Baba sadly. Cassie patted her cast.

"I'm sorry. I'm sure Marilyn would be happy here, though." Knox said. "It's not home, but it's the next best thing. Can I show you around?"

"That would be great," I said.

"Are you okay to walk, ma'am?" he asked Baba.

Her voice turned weak. "Yes, with just a little help. Rachel?"

Cassie took her arm.

"First let me tell you a little bit about our facility." He began talking about the dog runs, training areas, even a doggie spa. "Our counselors are trained in dog behavior, pet CPR, and pet first aid."

"Wow," I said approvingly. Happy Puppy Haven was quite the operation.

As we passed the open door of what appeared to be his office, Cassie nudged me. A sign over the desk read, *The only thing that stops a bad guy with a gun is a good guy with a gun.*

Knox led us to a large indoor dog run, where a variety of dogs played. "Oh, Marilyn will love this!" Cassie said.

"The dogs get outdoor potty breaks and walks, and you can see the dog tread mill and the elevated canine cot. We have three dog rooms—one for high energy, small dogs, and one for dogs that are a little suspicious of other dogs. Then one mixed room for all kinds of dogs who love other dogs. People from miles around bring their dogs here, just because of our careful attention to their pets' needs. What kind of dog is your Marilyn?"

"A whoodle," Cassie answered.

What the heck is a whoodle? I wondered.

Cassie continued, "We were going to get a pit bull when we were looking around. Mom loves pit bulls." She smiled at me and I nodded, gritting my teeth. Pit bulls give me the creeps. "Then we heard they were maybe going to ban pit bulls in town. Don't you think that's the *stupidest* thing?"

"Actually, no," Knox said. "Pit bulls can be pretty dangerous unless they're raised right."

"We would have raised it right," Cassie said.

"Of course you would have. But some people don't. I sure wouldn't want a little kid hurt by a pit bull who hadn't been raised right."

Baba decided to take a more active role and asked about rates and references. Cassie gave an exaggerated yawn when Knox's back was turned.

As we passed by the office again on the way back to the reception area, Cassie pointed to the gun sign and said, "My dad has that sign, too." She shook her head. "He gets pretty mad about all those checks he has to go through when he buys a gun. Like he's a criminal or something."

She is awfully good at this, I thought, a little concerned.

"Oh, I don't mind them" Knox said. "They take just a

few minutes, and it's worth it. We don't want criminals to buy guns."

"I agree with you," I said. I was not going to be a meek little gun nut wife. "So what if Daddy has to spend a few extra minutes waiting to buy something? I think it's a good safety feature."

"You're a wise woman," Knox said. "I'm a big supporter of our second amendment rights, but I'm not one of those gun nuts who thinks anything goes when it comes to guns." I suspect he realized that he might have insulted my fake husband, so he added, "Not that your husband is a gun nut, ma'am."

"No offense taken."

"And he *is* a little bit of a gun nut," Cassie added.

I decided it was time to change the subject. "Knox, thank you so much for showing us around. Happy Puppy Haven looks like a wonderful place. I'm sure Marilyn would be happy here, but I need to discuss it with my husband first. I'll get back to you."

"Just call if you have any questions, any questions at all," Knox said, handing me his card.

Knox Varner. Adorable puppies frolicked along both sides of the card. I wondered if one of them was a whoodle.

"I assume I'm taking you home," I said as we walked to the car. "Does your dad know you're seeing Trevor?"

She didn't say, just shrugged.

"Where did you come up with the name Lisa?" Baba asked.

"Lisa's are everywhere. I figured it was a safe bet."

"Seriously, are you *sure* acting isn't in your future? The drama club would be lucky to have you."

I helped Baba into the front seat. With her cast, she always had a little trouble with the seatbelt. Cassie climbed in the back. "So what do you think?" I asked.

"I don't think he could have done it," Cassie said. Neither did I, but I was interested in her reasoning. She continued. "He just seems too calm. Like what he said about the pit bulls. And the guns. Didn't get, like, all riled up that I disagreed."

"But we were being potential customers. Maybe all that was just for show."

"But you could see how much he loves dogs. I don't think someone who loves dogs that much could murder someone. Even if it was someone sleeping with his girl-friend. He just seems too nice."

So I told her the story of Ted Bundy, the handsome, charming serial killer executed in 1989. Geraldine had made Sammie and me watch a 2002 film about him when we were about 13. Cassie was quiet, listening. I hoped she was taking what I said to heart.

Maybe not. I had barely finished speaking and started the car when she changed the subject. "You know, when we were guessing about the murderer last night …"

"Speculating," Baba said.

"Okay, speculating. We didn't really talk about what if Affinity *is* pregnant. Like, if she is, does Knox know? I think we need to go back in and talk to him some more, see if we can, like, find out."

I was skeptical. "We can't exactly say, 'Hey, do you know your girlfriend might be pregnant?'"

"Cassie might get him *talking* about his girlfriend," Baba said. "If anybody can do it, Cassie can. Something might come up."

When I didn't say anything, Cassie assumed I was wavering. "So what's our story?" she asked.

I thought a minute as I drove around the block and headed back to Puppy Haven. It was worth a shot, and Cassie had been good at getting Knox to talk. "Marilyn doesn't get along with standard poodles. We need to check on how Knox would handle that."

"Got it."

"Having a plan of action for difficult problems is very important with dogs and children," Baba said.

I looked at her. "Since when have you ever had a dog? You sound like a public service announcement."

"I'm in character," she said. "Serious grandmother looking out for the needs of her loved ones."

Back at Puppy Haven with Knox, I started to outline our problem—well, Marilyn's problem. "We think she must have been traumatized by a standard poodle when she was a puppy. That's the only thing we can think of. We wouldn't want her to stay here if there are standard poodles who might scare her."

"I understand your concern. We do have one standard poodle, Cocoa. But she's such a gentle thing I can't imagine Marilyn would be afraid of her. Would you like to meet her and see for yourself?"

"Could we? Please?"

As we headed to the doggie play area, Knox nodded at another man in a Puppy Haven shirt. Muscles bulged under his short sleeves. "See you at the gym tonight?" the man asked Knox.

"You bet. Deb's got night duty. I'm free."

Cassie pounced. "Is Deb your girlfriend?"

"No, no. Just an employee. She'll be in charge here tonight."

"Do you have a girlfriend?"

"Rachel! You shouldn't ask such personal questions," I said.

Knox smiled. "It's okay. I do have a girlfriend."

"Are you going to marry her?"

"Rachel!"

"I sure hope so."

"I bet you work out just to look good for her."

"That's one reason, for sure."

"That other guy—the one you're going to meet at the gym. Is he a boxer or something? His arms are like tree trunks."

"Not a boxer, no. He's into weight lifting."

"My stepbrother is into that," Cassie said. "Does some kind of competitions."

"Johnny is, too. What's your stepbrother's name?"

"Desmond. From my dad's first marriage to Corrine."

Now I wondered if Cassie had ever considered a career as a writer.

We arrived at a puppy area surrounded by a plastic fence, and Knox stepped inside. "Cocoa!" he called. "Cocoa, come." Cocoa just looked at him.

Knox turned slightly toward us and said, "Sometimes she doesn't listen, and ..." Before he could finish, the huge chocolate brown poodle suddenly streaked toward him and jumped up, paws on his chest. That's when Knox let out a startled yip. "You surprised me there, Cocoa," he said to the dog. To us, he said, "She's just being friendly. She doesn't do that to other dogs. Just to me." He petted Cocoa's ears while inviting Cassie to do the same.

I wasn't listening. Knox had yipped. *Yipped.* That was the word that came to mind when he let out that squeaky cry of surprise. I remembered hearing the word recently. Where?

Pizza guy. Blake. He'd said the man he'd seen hurrying away from the murder scene had *yipped,* that it was a squeaky little sound for a big guy. Could Knox have been there that night? Could he be the murderer?

We needed to get out. Now.

I pretended my phone had vibrated and answered. "Oh no! … Yes, yes. Are you sure … Okay, honey. We're on our way." I ended the call and turned to Cassie. "We have to go. Dad's been in a an accident."

Cassie looked frightened, for real. "Oh, no!"

Baba gasped.

"He's cut up and bruised, but he says he's all right. The car's totaled, though. We have to get to the emergency room." I saw a nearby exit and turned to Knox. "Can we go out that door? It's closer to the parking lot."

"Sure, of course. I'm so sorry about your husband."

I tried to act like a distraught wife and didn't thank him for the dog information. As we hurried out, I put one arm around Cassie and the other around Baba. "It's okay," I whispered. "No accident. Look upset."

Cassie fell into character and raced to the car. "Hurry, Mom!" Baba dabbed pretend tears with the tissue she always kept slipped under the cuff of her cardigan.

We got in the car, and I peeled out of there.

"What's going on?" Cassie demanded.

"He yipped." I told them about Blake using the same word. "Big guy, weird little squeak. I think Knox was there that night. What if he caught on that we were feeding him a bunch of crap? What if he's the murderer?"

"But ..."

"I'm responsible for you, so better to be safe than sorry. And now we've got to find Blake. I need to ask him something."

"This is so exciting!" Baba gushed.

We went to Blackjack Pizza. I didn't know Blake's last name, but the woman at the desk knew him. He wasn't working that day.

"Could you give me his phone number?" I asked. "I really need to reach him."

"I can't give out personal information," she said.

I sighed and left the lobby. As we were buckling our seat belts, a girl with a Blackjack Pizza flag on her antenna drove up. "Hang on," Cassie said, getting out of the car. Soon she was back. "Got it," she said. She waved to the girl as we drove off.

"So aren't you going to call him?" Baba asked me.

"Not now." I didn't have a whole lot of time before our tap class, and I needed to clear up several things, then call Mildred. I'd promised Detective Dan.

"Hold on," Cassie said. "We want to hear what you say to Blake. Call him now."

"I'm driving.

"So pull over," Baba said, clearly on Cassie's side.

I sighed and pulled over. "Put your phone on speaker," Cassie said.

I put it on speaker and called. "Blake? This is Ella Polansky. I talked to you at the gas pump the other day."

"Yeah, I remember. You were right. They came after me."

"I knew they would. Sorry. I need to ask you something really important," I said. "It's about the night of the murder. Remember how you told me the man you saw in the alley that night 'yipped' as they left the tap studio? That's the word you used—yipped. Like something hurt him."

"Yeah, I said that. That's because it was such a squeaky sound for a guy his size."

"But *why* did he yip? Could he have yipped because the woman stepped on his toe or maybe spilled something on him?"

"Sure. Probably spilled coffee on him. The lady was holding two big cups, now that I think of it. Coffee cups."

"Couldn't they have been cups of lemonade or something?"

"Nah ... they were coffee cups. I remember now thinking that it was too hot for coffee. They had those white plastic lids, not straws like cold drinks."

"Thanks, Blake. You've been a big help!"

I hung up and twisted in my seat to talk to both of them. "Let's say you murdered someone with a poisoned cup of coffee," I said. "What would you be sure to take with you when you fled the scene?"

"Duh. The poisoned cup of coffee," Cassie said.

I gave her a thumbs up. Then she took the wind out of my sails. "But what if I didn't do it and was just trying to avoid anybody *thinking* I did?" she asked. "Like, I'd still take the coffee because I wouldn't want my DNA left on anything at the scene."

"But your DNA wouldn't be on the *victim's* cup."

"It would be if I was the one who brought him the coffee. So I'd still take both cups."

"She's right," Baba said. "But the yipping is still an important clue. I don't know why he was there, but I'll bet it was Knox."

Cassie looked at me, scrunching her eyes and thinking. "Do we tell Dad about this?"

"I'm supposed to talk to Mildred, not your dad. But, yes, I need to tell her about the yipping and the coffee. And maybe a couple of other things." I shook my head. "And eventually, we'll have to tell your dad. He is *so* not going to like this."

I dropped off Baba, then pulled up in front of Dan's house. "See you at class at 5:30," I told Cassie.

She didn't get out of the car. "I know you're going home to do something else about the murder. *What?*"

"I need to go," I said. She was right, but I wasn't going to tell her about it now.

Reluctantly, she unbuckled. "I'm glad Dad is dropping me off at class. That way I don't have to ride with *you* again," she said. She slammed the door.

Do parents ever feel like giving up? I wondered. and how about stepparents?

Sitting down at home with my laptop, I reviewed my notes and put my thoughts in order, then pulled up Harvey Klump's blog to see if whatever he had to say today had any actual relevance to the murder.

Not a good idea. He ranted as usual about the fact that neither Sammie nor I had been arrested, but this time he even included pictures of both of us. Sammie's photo was a glamorous publicity shot from the insurance company's "Dancing with the Stars" benefit of several years ago. Red lipstick, low-cut dress, black hair cascading over one shoulder. Mine was last year's school photo. Collar crooked, eyes half-closed, mouth open. Even Baba still laughed at that picture. Trying to put the image out of my mind, I opened Google Images and began my last task—searching for photos of a different kind. After twenty minutes, I finally found what I was looking for.

I called Mildred but got her voice mail. As instructed, I left a detailed message. Maybe too detailed.

And I asked her to call me back.

CHAPTER THIRTY-SIX

Mildred hadn't called by the time I got to the studio for tap class. She probably wasn't exactly impressed by "yipping" as a pivotal clue. I vowed to call Dan after class and explain everything to him instead.

The "Tap, Rattle, and Roll" show was coming right up, so after warm-ups, Sammie had us run through the routine twice. Then she had a surprise for us. "Costumes!" She opened two large cardboard boxes at the front of the room. From one she took out a glittered boa and threw it around her neck. From the other, she pulled a blonde wig. She put it on and struck a pose.

"Ooh, Mama!" Aunt Ruth said. "I want to look like that!" We all gathered around the boxes, grabbing wigs and boas.

It's a wonder what costumes can do. Hidden in wigs and sparkly boas, we were free to act like blonde bombshells in tap shoes. Cassie strutted across the room as if she were at the Academy Awards. "Who am I wearing? Russo Studio Designs," she said in a breathy Marilyn Monroe voice. Aunt Ruth blew kisses to an imaginary audience. Affinity twirled her boa and shimmied suggestively. Everyone took selfies.

After we had vamped enough, Sammie announced, "We're going to do the dance again. This time *show* me that you are 'Big, Blonde, and Beautiful.' Dance like you mean it."

And we did. We flap-heeled onto the imaginary stage with flair. We twirled our boas as we flap-heeled in a circle.

We executed ball changes and Cincinattis and Broadways with, if not perfection, an abundance of attitude. We were *dancing*.

Sammie applauded as we all bowed and curtsied and blew imaginary kisses to our invisible audience at the end.

Then the door opened, and in walked Knox Varner.

"Which one of you is Ella Polansky?" Knox demanded, looking at the sea of blondes.

Eleven blonde heads turned to look at me.

"What do you want with *her?*" Affinity asked, sounding a little pouty.

Knox walked over to me and peered at my face. "You are not Cindy Newberry, and you don't have a daughter *or* a whoodle!"

"What's a whoodle?" I heard Nell ask. Aunt Ruth shushed her.

"Knox, honey," Affinity said, removing her wig and going to his side. "Calm down."

"She's trying to frame you," he said. "Snooping around, asking questions about my girlfriend."

"That was me asking questions, not her," Cassie volunteered.

Even a little bit angry, Knox hardly seemed dangerous. "We weren't trying to frame Affinity," I pointed out. "We were trying to check you out. You know, to see if you are the kind of person who *might* have committed murder."

"And we saw right away that you weren't," Cassie said. Her voice was so comforting that I thought she might walk over and pat his arm. The girl has a dangerous weakness for attractive guys.

"You *lied* to me," he said to Cassie.

"I'm sorry," she said. She sounded so sincere. "Really."

He nodded, maybe forgiving her.

She held his gaze, giving him a look that was both earnest and borderline flirtatious. "But can I ask you a question?"

He nodded again.

"How did you *know* we weren't looking for a place for our dog? I thought we were doing so well."

He reassured her. "Oh, you were. I totally believed you until I read Harvey Klump's blog later." He looked at me then, and it was pretty clear he wasn't even close to forgiving me. "Then I saw your picture. And the name under it was *not* Cindy Newberry."

I was disappointed he'd recognized me so easily from that photo.

"Just let it go, Knox," Affinity said. "All they discovered was a nice guy. They're not accusing you of anything."

Knox put his arm around Affinity and looked into her eyes. "It has gone far enough when *kids* start lying to me and snooping around to see if I might be a murderer. *Me!* I'm sorry, Affinity, but I'm done with this. It's time I told the truth."

"Just hang on," Affinity said. She lowered her voice, speaking to him earnestly. "Let's sort this out privately."

He shook his head. "The truth is going to come out sooner or later, and I'm sick of the lies." He looked at the group. "Serenity did it," he announced. "Serenity murdered Donald Sanders."

A snort came from the back of the room. "Get a grip," Serenity said. "I didn't kill Donald. He was nothing to me. I only met him once." Her voice dripped with sarcasm, and she turned to put one leg up on the ballet bar, then stretched over it, seemingly unconcerned. She turned her head sideways to look at him as she stretched. "As you very well know, I was in Denver getting money from a bank around the time of the murder. Remember that little thing called an ATM camera?"

He ignored her and forged on. "I was there when you gave Affinity one of your gift baskets to give to Donald. You know, to thank him for checking out the Mercedes. I've been thinking hard on all this, and I finally figured out there must have been something edible in that basket—I'm not sure what—that was laced with the caffeine that killed Donald. A cake maybe. Or cookies."

"No, Knox. The basket included a bottle of really nice wine and a selection of imported cheeses. Unpoisoned." She sat down and started taking off her tap shoes. "Why would I want to kill Donald?"

Knox looked stumped. He clearly hadn't thought things through that far. Analysis was probably not his strong suit.

I decided to help him a little. "Serenity could have just wanted to get Donald out of the way. You know, because he was proving a *distraction* to Affinity." I was choosing my words carefully.

Knox didn't read between the lines. He ignored me and continue speaking to Serenity. "I don't know why you wanted to kill him, but I know you had to have done it. The gift basket is the key." He held out his hand toward her. "Come on. I'm taking you to the police station so you can confess and get this over with. A confession will make things go so much easier on you."

"I'm not going anywhere," she said. "This is a cockamamie theory, and nobody's ever going to buy it."

Two thoughts popped into my mind: (1) I loved the word *cockamamie.* (2) I didn't agree that no one in the world would ever buy his theory.

And then I saw something that shook me to my core.

Knox reached under his long shirt tails and pulled a gun from a hidden holster. A 9mm automatic, I knew, because I'd seen the one Derek has for protection when he hikes in back country areas. I couldn't have been more shocked if a Teletubby had suddenly brandished an AK-47.

Everyone froze.

The gun was pointed at Serenity, not the rest of us, but, still, it was a *gun.* "Sorry about this, everyone," Knox apologized, clearly not very good at being a bad guy. "I'm doing my duty and taking Serenity in. It's a citizen's arrest."

I wasn't sure if a citizen's arrest was really a thing. I vowed to look it up later. If there was a later.

Something about the scenario felt off. I was nervous—who knows what could go wrong with a gun around?—but somehow not terrified.

Serenity may have felt the same way. She calmly said, "Listen, Knox, you are wrong, but in the interest of everyone's safety, I'll go with you. We'll go to the police station and straighten this out there. Okay?"

He nodded.

"Let me just grab my purse." She got up and headed for the wall of hooks, where we hung coats and bags.

Cassie couldn't help herself. "But Serenity didn't do it!" she blurted. "We figured it out."

"No, Cassie," I warned. Had she really figured out what I had? Now was not the time to get into it.

"What did you figure out?" He turned to Cassie, and the gun turned along with him, now pointing at Cassie.

Cassie's mouth opened, but nothing came out.

What was he thinking? Or maybe he *wasn't* thinking. I remembered what Taylor had told me about Knox—that he loved children—so I took a chance. "She's a *child*, Knox. You could be traumatizing her for the rest of her life with that gun drawn. Do you really want to do that? She's only 15."

Cassie took her cue and suddenly dissolved into a quivering mass of tears. "I ... I ... I'm so scared," she cried. "I don't want to die." She sank to the floor, head on her knees, sobbing.

At that, Knox noticed where his gun was pointed. "No, no," he said, moving the gun to point back at Serenity. "I didn't mean to do that. Really."

Cassie's kept sobbing. "I h-h-h-ate guns. You never know what they might do. Like Daddy's did that time when he went hunting ... and his friend ... his dead friend ..." Her sobs turned into out-of-control gulping. "

"Rachel! Please! I'll put the gun away. Really!"

Nell opened her mouth, then closed it. She didn't ask about the name Rachel.

Cassie's sobs slowed. She looked up cautiously. "All the way away?"

He pulled up a chair and sat down facing us all. Then he lowered the gun and left it in his lap. "See? It's okay."

She nodded, then spoke in a tiny voice, looking up at him with big eyes. "Could you put it back in your *holster?"*

He sighed and put the gun back in his holster. "Now will you tell me what you and Ella Polansky figured out?"

I hoped Cassie and I were on the same page. Out the

corner of my eye, I could see Sammie holding her phone and pretending not to look at it, her hands blocked from Jax's view by Aunt Ruth's back. Grateful that she always kept her phone on silent mode to avoid waking Isabelle, I fervently hoped she was texting 9-1-1.

I decided to take the lead. "We figured out that *Affinity* is the one who killed Donald," I said.

"Oh, like she really knows," Affinity scoffed. "You're a detective now?"

"We both are," Cassie said. She wiped her eyes with her hand and sniffed. "Does anybody have a Kleenex?" Nell handed her one from her pocket.

Knox frowned. "Okay, yes, she hit him with a tap shoe. But there's more to the story. She *had* to do something. The man had tried to *rape* her!"

The group gasped.

"Rape?" Sammie said. Her voice had an "Are you crazy?" quality, and Affinity didn't like it.

"Nobody ever believes rape victims," she snapped. Knox put an arm around her waist and drew her closer. Her voice quivered. "Donald attacked me, and I hit him. I thought that I'd killed him. Did you know a single blow in just the right place can kill a person?"

I knew.

She continued. "I didn't want to be mixed up in a court case trying to prove self-defense, so we got the hell out of here. We didn't know then that it was caffeine that actually killed him, not the tap shoe."

Knox frowned. "Maybe we should have tried to help Donald in case he wasn't dead yet. But I *did* yell at the pizza guy to call 9-1-1."

"That was kind of you," I said, trying not to sound sarcastic. "Didn't you wonder what Affinity was doing here in the studio, Knox?"

Affinity decided she'd better chime in with some details. "At the museum reception, Donald asked me to meet him here to get my opinion on moves he'd put together for a 'Dancing With the Stars' audition. He was including some tap dancing in it. He loved tap."

"No, he didn't," said Sammie. "He thought tap was kind of dumb. He always said, 'Why tap the rhythm when a drum makes so much more sense?'"

Affinity snapped, "Well, he was tapping *that* night. He had on tap shoes and everything when I got here. So maybe you don't know as much about Donald as you think!"

"I know he liked to take kinky pictures. "Did he want you to put on tap shoes and get naked and pose for him?"

Knox gasped.

I interrupted before she could answer, easing Knox's mind, at least in one respect. "She didn't have to pose naked. He went into convulsions and died first." I nodded my head toward Knox. "And then you showed up."

He choked up. "If only I hadn't stopped to take a phone call, I'd have been a couple of minutes earlier, and none of it would have happened."

Affinity took Knox's arm and rubbed it up and down softly. "Let's just get out of here. Serenity didn't poison Donald, but we can't figure out who did right now. Let's go home, have a drink, get in the hot tub, and think things over."

He was clearly wavering, probably because of the rubbing. Or maybe because of the hot tub. Cassie was having none of it, though. "Affinity is pregnant," she said. "Did you know that?"

Was the girl just begging for trouble?

He laughed. "No, she's not. She can't be." He apparently had a lot of trust in whatever birth control method they used.

"Not by you," Cassie said. "By Donald. They were having an affair."

Affinity shot her a furious glance. "You are crazy, obviously," Affinity said. "Don't listen to her, Knox."

Another man might have said, "Shut up!" at this point, but not a man who yips. "Hush now," he said to Affinity. "Why are you saying such a thing, Rachel?"

"Have you noticed how often she goes to the bathroom lately? She's acting just like my mother, who is also pregnant. And look at what she's wearing—a loose top. Does that look like the kind of thing she usually wears? Where's, like, the sports bra and tight abs she likes to show off ? And I'll bet you anything there's been some recent puking, too."

There must have been some recent puking. For the first time, a look of doubt stole across his face. Knox looked at Affinity closely. "Are you pregnant?" he managed to choke out, the truth perhaps starting to dawn on him.

There was a pause—a pregnant pause, I guess I should say—while Affinity considered her options. She scanned the room, saw my accusing eyes, and then moved on to her sister. Serenity stared open-mouthed, clearly recognizing that Affinity was not going to be getting inseminated by a brilliant professor anytime soon. Finally, Affinity looked at Knox, whose eyes were filling with tears.

She bolted.

Did she panic? Or figure she could hightail it to Mexico with no one catching her? Or decide to run away and jump off the ice rim that supposedly surrounds the earth? Whatever the reason, she headed toward the door.

She didn't make it far. She was still wearing her tap shoes, and when she ran, the metal taps caused her to slip and fall on the floor face first. I ran to her, almost slipping myself, and tried to sit on her to keep her from getting away. She was strong, though, and managed to scramble to her feet. I grabbed the loose top she wore, but in one motion she shrugged out of it, drew her arm back and slugged me, hard, landing a blow on my shoulder, the same shoulder that was still sore from the Virgin Mary incident. I cried out and fell to the floor, my shoulder and upper arm screaming in pain.

I saw the rest through my tears. While we had been grappling, Sammie had rushed forward to block the door. Affinity moved toward her, grabbing her arms to try to move her aside. Quickly, Cassie pulled a tap shoe off her foot, stood, and aimed, hurling the shoe like a softball, right at Affinity's back. It spun through the air and hit her squarely between her shoulder blades. Affinity yelled, paused for just a second, then moved toward the door again, pushing Sammie so that she lost her balance and fell to her knees.

In a flash, Cassie pulled off her other shoe and, with her softball pitching arm, hurled again, even harder, just as the door opened and Mildred entered, gun drawn. Affinity moved to sidestep Mildred, and the shoe sailed right past her, hitting Mildred square in the jaw. She staggered backward, blood pouring from her mouth, and almost dropped the gun. As she tried to regain her balance, Affinity rushed right past her and was gone.

Not for long, though.

Mildred had brought back-up.

And that backup included Detective Dan.

CHAPTER THIRTY-SEVEN

Detective Dan led a squirming Affinity back into the studio, arms handcuffed behind her back. Her eyes found Cassie, then me, and I found myself wondering if looks really *could* kill. Cassie actually took a step backward, as if she could feel the heat of the anger directed our way.

Two more officers immediately handcuffed Knox. Cassie kept her distance but said, "Really, Knox didn't hurt anyone."

"He pulled a gun!" Dan snapped. "Now stay out of this."

An ambulance arrived quickly, and after two EMTs had attended to Mildred and strapped her onto a gurney, one of them checked me over. My upper arm, near the shoulder, was swelling, and my hand felt numb and tingly, but I didn't have trouble reaching over my head and around my back. "Luckily, no dislocation or rotator cuff damage," he said when he was finished examining me. "You're going to have a really bad bruise, though."

As he was closing his bag, I asked, "Could you get out a hypodermic needle?"

"Advil and Tylenol for pain are going to do it," he said.

"No, no. I just want to *see* one. A hypodermic needle."

The man looked puzzled, but Cassie was at my side. "Let her," she said. "Just show her one. You don't have to do anything with it."

"I don't think I should …"

Dan had joined us. "Do it," he said.

So the man did it. Shrugging, he pulled out a hypodermic needle.

I relaxed my shoulders.

I breathed deeply.

I looked at that needle and told myself it was powerless over me.

And then I got dizzy, but it was only a little.

I gave a brief nod. "Advil and Tylenol will be just fine, thank you."

It was a long night. When Dan finally sat down with Cassie and me at the police station, he said, "Now you are going to tell me everything, *everything,* that you have been up to."

"Don't you want to know what we figured out happened the night of the murder?" I asked.

"After you tell me everything you've been up to, then I'll listen to your theories."

So we told him everything we had done to investigate. Dan was very professional. Too professional. No smiles, no loving glances, no forgiving hugs. To be fair, also no comments like, "You did *what?* " or "Are you nuts?"

He worried me.

When I told him my theory about who did it, why, and how, his face remained impassive. He didn't comment until I was finished. "Anything else?" he asked. "Anything else at *all* that you haven't told me? Either of you? Think."

Cassie hesitated, then looked at her lap. "Um, when I was grounded, Trevor came by."

I knew it!

Dan locked her in his gaze. "Anything else?"

She shook her head. "He just showed up. I didn't ask him to. *Honest.* "

"Ella?"

"I've told you everything I can think of."

"Okay. I'm taking you over to Sammie's apartment because I know you'll head over there, regardless. I want you both to stay there until I come back and join you, no matter how late it is."

He was silent as we drove over. When he dropped us off, he said only, "Try, please, to stay out of trouble until I get back."

Cassie and I entered through Second Chance, to avoid the police still in the alley, and we trudged upstairs, exhausted from telling and retelling what we knew. "We'll have to do it again here, you know," I said.

"I know," Cassie said. "It's only fair. They helped."

Inside the apartment, Derek, Jake, and Geraldine waited with Sam and Sammie. "Are you okay?" Sammie said. She'd seen Affinity slug me, of course.

"Sore," I said. "But okay."

"She looked at a hypodermic needle and didn't pass out!" Cassie announced. She actually sounded proud of me.

"That *is* big news," Derek said. "Congratulations. And how's Mildred?"

"Not so good. They took her to the hospital."

"I'm so sorry," Cassie said for the umpteenth time. "I didn't mean to hit *her*!"

"We know, honey," Geraldine said, not really knowing

since she hadn't been there. She put her arm around Cassie and hugged her. Geraldine can be very motherly when she wants to be.

"Now clue us in to what happened, Sherlock," Derek said. He looked at Cassie and added, "And Sherlock assistant. Watson, I guess."

"Okay, here goes." We all settled in chairs around the table with drinks, some alcoholic and some not. Everyone was ready to listen.

I began. "So Donald had already made arrangements with Sammie to use the studio. You know that already. When he ran into Affinity at the museum, he must have got the idea to ask her to join him. He undoubtedly had in mind taking some kinky pictures." I couldn't resist adding, "Probably Affinity naked with a red sparkled bow tie that matched his."

"Speculation," Derek said. "You can't know that."

"But she's probably right," Sammie said. "Go on."

"Affinity was thrilled because she'd been looking for an opportunity to poison Donald." Before anyone could ask *why*, I added, "More on that in a sec. Anyway, after the reception at the museum, she told Mariah that she was headed back to Denver. But she wasn't. She headed to Starbucks and picked up coffee for Donald."

"Something like a white chocolate mocha frappuccino with an extra shot," Cassie said. "Those have so much sugar and junk, he probably wouldn't even notice the bad taste of the poison."

"Right. She added the caffeine to Donald's drink and walked over."

"Knox had got off work early, so—being a nice guy—he

decided to go over to the museum and surprise her," Cassie added.

Was she totally snowed by this guy? "I'm not sure he's *that* nice," I said. "He did help cover up a murder."

"Get on with it," Geraldine demanded.

I got on with it. "Affinity had just left when Knox arrived at the museum. He looked down the alley and saw her go into the dance studio, so he headed over to join her. But then he got a phone call about a problem at work he needed to deal with. While he talked, Donald was probably going into convulsions, and Affinity was just waiting for him to die." I shook my head at the cruelty of it. "By the time Knox walked in, Donald was on the floor, and Affinity was standing over him."

"He must have been shocked out of his gourd," Cassie said. "Knox, I mean. But Affinity made up a story *fast*. She said he tried to rape her."

"Rape??!!" Geraldine said.

"Rape. And she told him she had tried to protect herself by hitting him in the head with her tap shoe."

"Knox believed this?" Derek asked.

"It was Knox. Of course he believed it. He thought that Affinity had killed Donald in self-defense, and he acted to protect her. He got her out of there, and Affinity called her two sisters and told them the same story. She had them go to an ATM and get money out of her account."

"I'm not following," Jake said. "Why?"

"For an *alibi*," Cassie said. "They were pretending to be Affinity and Serenity, acting a little drunk for the camera."

"I nodded. Exactly. There's a third sister—Divinity." Geraldine opened her mouth to comment, but I beat her to it. "Yes, like the candy. Divinity is the little sister, and she looks a lot like the twins, except with no polish."

"You've met her?" Sam asked.

"No, but I finally found a picture of her online at some kind of Mormon picnic with a bunch of kids. Really, same bone structure, strong family resemblance, even in her hassled-mother state. She must have fixed herself up quickly."

"Or Serenity did," Cassie said. "Probably, like, put some lipstick and mascara on her, and earrings and a baseball cap. Then they put on a little act for the ATM camera. Acting drunk."

"You saw the tape?" Sam asked.

"No. Dad told Ella about it. I'm guessing at the lipstick and earrings and stuff."

"I think the sisters believed Affinity really had acted in self-defense, and they were just trying to protect her. Or, even if they didn't believe her, they still wanted to protect her. She was their *sister.*"

"So the big question I have," said Geraldine, "is *why* Affinity wanted to kill Donald. She'd been enjoying her little affair with him."

"Okay, now for that. She was pregnant. Thanks to Cassie for figuring that out."

"Pregnant on *purpose,*" Cassie added.

"Yes, on purpose. Birth control with Knox, no birth control with Donald. She wanted to have Donald's baby."

"But why?" Sammie asked. "She didn't even like kids. She's the only person in the tap class who didn't ooh and ahh over Isabelle when I brought her down to class that time."

"Love, lust, loathing, loot are common motives for murder," Cassie said, sounding as though she was reciting from a textbook. "I've been researching motives. It was the *loot.*"

"It was. If Donald was the father of the baby but he was *dead*, the baby would be one of his heirs. She figured she would keep the money the baby inherited but give the baby to Serenity. Serenity would be happy—well, except for the part about the father being Donald, not the professor she'd lined up. Serenity obviously has money. My guess is she would have been happy to let Affinity keep the inheritance, as long as she got what *she* really wanted—a baby."

"So where did Affinity get the caffeine, Sherlock?" Derek asked.

"I figured that out when we were at Happy Puppy Haven and Cassie and Knox were talking about weight-lifting competitions and her nonexistent stepbrother."

"Desmond," Cassie said.

I saw the questioning looks. "Cassie was making up stuff. She's very good at that. While they were talking about *Desmond* and weight-lifting, I remembered Aunt Ruth telling me about her ex, a body builder who probably has a stock of supplements and everything else under the sun, going way back to his Mr. America competition days. My guess is that Affinity paid her uncle a visit and either talked him into giving her some caffeine powder for extra energy, or stole it."

"So tell them about the yip," Cassie said. "That was the key to everything."

"A yip," Derek said. The eyebrow over his green eye shot up.

"A yip, yes. At Happy Puppy Haven, I heard Knox yip when a dog jumped on him. Big guy, squeaky little yip—and *yip* was the word the pizza guy used when he told me what he had witnessed in the alley. Not many big guys yip. I knew Knox had to have been there."

"Innocently trying to help his girlfriend," Cassie added, still protective of Knox.

I didn't comment, just went on. "Earlier today I talked to Donald's mother and his neighbor, and they happened to mention the third sister. When I got home, I looked up Divinity. The yip and the photo—I put it together and knew that what I'd suspected was right. Affinity did it."

"Did you tell Mildred what you'd learned?"

"I left a message before class."

"And I'll bet that since you mentioned the case turning on a *yip*, she was in no hurry to call you back," Derek said.

"That's my guess," I admitted. "I decided I'd call Dan after class and tell him about it all if she hadn't called back by then."

"This is all a disappointment," Derek said. "I'd kind of hoped that the indecent docent was the one who did it. A great headline."

Geraldine said, "She wasn't a docent."

"We know, we know," I said. "Mariah was definitely on my list of suspects, though. She hit him with a nose flute. She let him take naked pictures of her. She disappeared. I was suspicious about her all along, but I couldn't find out anything."

Jake looked at Geraldine. "Tell them."

"Okay, Mariah had help disappearing. I helped her get a job at a coffee place in Denver and let her rent an apartment in one of my buildings there, cheap. I suggested she go by her middle name, Lorraine, for a while so she'd be harder to track down. I kept Dan informed. He interviewed her, too."

"Why? Why would you help her?" I asked.

"I knew she didn't do it. She's young. She made a dumb mistake. She didn't deserve to have that ruin her life, and she would have been a marked woman here in Juniper." She paused. "I know something about dumb mistakes."

"You posed naked for someone when you were young, Mom?" Derek asked. He tried for an innocent look but wasn't convincing.

"I didn't say *that* was my dumb mistake. And I'm not saying what it was. Period." We didn't even try to pry the truth out of her. When Geraldine says no, she means no.

"How do Bucky and Kendall figure into all this?" Sammie asked.

"I'm still thinking on that," I said. "But I have some ideas."

"How did Dad know to handcuff Serenity when she ran out of the building?" Cassie asked.

"My doing," said Sammie. "I texted Dan. Wrote 'Affinity did it. Tap studio. Knox has gun.' So I helped."

Eventually, we all ran out of energy. No one wanted to go home until we saw Dan, though. Cassie curled up on the couch and fell asleep. Sammie fell asleep nursing Isabelle. Sam took the baby and put her to bed, tucking a blanket over Sammie.

The rest of us were too wound up to sleep. We went into the kitchen and quietly waited for Dan.

He finally came to the apartment at 2:00 a.m. I was nervous, just looking at him. Was he over being mad about Cassie's involvement yet? And mine?

He set my mind at ease. Maybe it was because he was off duty now, or maybe it was because he'd had time to process all we'd told him, but—whatever the reason—he immediately came to me, pulled me to my feet, and took me in his arms. "Thank god you're both okay," he said. Then he gave me a long, lingering kiss in front of everyone. It sure felt like he'd forgiven me.

"Enough already," Cassie said, joining us in the kitchen. Dan turned to her and gave her a long, lingering hug.

"Beer?" Sam asked.

He nodded and sat down.

"You were completely wrong about the coffee," he said, looking at me. "It was a caffeine-laced marijuana brownie that killed Donald, not coffee. Affinity took both cups from the scene because she'd brought along coffee to go *with* the brownie. Knox may have yipped because she spilled on him, but she took the cups because she didn't want to leave anything behind with her DNA on it."

"I suggested that," Cassie said.

"She did," I nodded. "And I believe I was the one who first suggested a pot brownie as a possible murder weapon." Cassie and I grinned and gave each other a high five.

Dan raised his beer in a toast. "I would like to make an announcement for all of you to hear: Ella Polansky *does* have good instincts."

Cassie opened her mouth to speak, but he spoke first. "And so does Miss Cassie Sherman."

CHAPTER THIRTY-EIGHT

Four important things happened after The Night the Murderer Was Revealed.

First, I called Kendall Whitehead to make good on my promise for help with a story, and I arranged a photo session with the very photogenic Sammie Russo. When Kendall asked that Sammie's equally photogenic brother and her handsome fiancé be included in the photo shoot, I was hurt that she didn't ask for me. I knew I was going to be a part of the story, and I was family, too, sort of. Was I not photo-worthy?

Really, I stewed about it. I may not have the star-quality looks of Sammie and her brother, but I'm not going to break a camera. Kindergartners call me their "pretty teacher." Baba calls me her "beautiful granddaughter." Dan calls me—well, he has some very nice things to say, some of which include the words "gorgeous" and "sexy."

As it turned out, Kendall already had the picture of me she wanted to use: me on the front steps of my duplex, looking strong and demanding that she and the photographer leave. I liked it.

It also turned out that Kendall can really write. Her article illustrated how rumor can run wild, affecting a person's life in unexpected ways. People see what they want to see, even if what they see is something based only loosely—or not at all—on fact. It wasn't a revelation that hadn't been made many times before, but she did it in a way that was insightful and moving.

Though she didn't include this information in the story, Kendall even looked into who had leaked information to Harvey Klump. Evelyn, the school secretary, was responsible for at least one piece. She'd told her sister about our supposed plans to go to Santa Barbara, and her sister told her best friend, who told her uncle. Her uncle worked for Harvey Klump.

That didn't explain other leaks that almost certainly came from the police department. My theory was that the chief of police, who was Harvey Klump's son-in-law, probably let information slip after he had a scotch or two.

And Bucky? He learned about Isabelle's birth from his mother, Cecilia's good friend. Bucky was thrilled. "It's almost like he felt this new baby of Donald's was a sign of divine intervention," Kendall told me. "It showed him that maybe Donald had changed and was taking responsibility. No abortion."

"Except he was wrong. Donald was actually giving up his parental rights." I said. "And how is it that you and Bucky started talking again after, like, ten years?"

"We ran into each other at the Church of Cannabis after I joined. We went out for coffee, and I found he had softened his views a little."

"He could forgive you having an abortion?"

"No. But he had learned that sometimes people are pushed into decisions they really don't want to make."

Kendall's story got a lot of attention, both locally and nationally. I was not at all afraid to hold my head high in Juniper or anywhere else.

The part that Kendall did *not* include in the story was the most important part, which she told Sam, Sammie, and me together. When Bucky had reached out to her that day over coffee, she told him the truth: that she had never actually had an abortion at all. She had given birth to a little girl, and her aunt in Oregon had adopted her—an open adoption arranged by her parents. Donald was the biological father of a nine-year-old girl.

After we all let that sink in for a few moments, Kendall said, "Bucky met with Donald that day because he wanted to encourage him to be a part of Isabelle's life, for his mother's sake. Bucky loves CeeCee and didn't want her to miss out on another grandchild."

"But the adoption ..." Sammie said, worried.

"No, no. He didn't suggest Donald actually *be* the father. He knew Donald was too self-absorbed for that. He just wanted to suggest that maybe the adoption could be open, like mine, so that CeeCee could be involved in some way."

"So Isabelle has a half-sister, by one mother," Sammie said, trying to process everything Kendall had said. "And she will have a future half-brother or half-sister by another mother, Affinity, who will likely be in jail. How are we supposed to *deal* with all this?"

"I don't know," Sam said, "but we definitely will." He kissed her. "We definitely will."

The second thing that happened was a trip, finally, to go wedding dress shopping in Denver. I asked Cassie to go along. In case she was ever to become a permanent fixture in my life, I needed to work on my attitude without a murder to bring us close. Dan was pleased I'd invited her and gave me his credit card. "Buy her something beautiful for the wedding. Go all out."

And we did. Sammie found her perfect dress, marked down and a perfect fit. It was starkly simple—no frou-frou to distract from her natural beauty. The only embellishments were a few tiny beads sparkling around the neckline.

I found a filmy aqua dress with spaghetti straps that made my heart beat a little faster. When I came out of the dressing room, Cassie said, "Wow."

"Wow," said Sammie. "You're getting that."

"But it's so fancy," I protested half-heartedly. "It's a backyard wedding. Shouldn't I just wear a sundress, maybe cotton? It will be hot in August."

"You're going to *look* hot. It's my wedding, and I want my maid of honor in that dress."

I nodded, pleased. "Now how about you Cassie?"

She held up a bright red dress. Love lit up her jock-girl eyes.

"Try it on," Sammie ordered.

She did. Dan's little girl glowed, looking a whole lot older than fifteen.

"Wow," I said.

"Wow," said Sammie. "That's it. You're going to do the guest book, and you're going to wear that."

When I saw the price tag, I knew Dan was going to hyperventilate, but I didn't care. She looked beautiful. On the plus side, the dress was modest in length—barely above the knee—and the neckline was not at all low. He couldn't complain.

We put all three dresses in Sammie's SUV. They sparkled in the sunlight through their plastic bags. As I was turning to get into the passenger seat, Cassie reached around me and gave me a big hug. "That was so much fun, Ella."

I smiled. I really was starting to like that girl. And I wasn't pretending.

The third thing that happened was that the woman who owned the quilt shop downtown called Sammie and told her she wanted to deliver a gift. "The day Donald Sanders died, my mother was watching the shop while I went to watch my daughter's softball game in Harper Springs," she explained to both of us later when she brought over a large box. "While I was gone, Mom took an order she wanted to quilt herself. She's a better seamstress than me, so I didn't argue with her. Plus, I was so swamped with graduation celebration plans for my daughter that I didn't really pay any attention."

She handed Sammie the package. "Today, Mom showed me the finished quilt and gave me your name and address. Mom isn't real up on news and hadn't recognized the name on the order. It's from Donald Sanders."

Cautiously, Sammie opened the box. It was a baby quilt, a beautiful quilt with the name "Isabelle" stitched across it in patchwork letters. Tears came to her eyes. Mine, too.

The fourth thing that happened was the "Tap, Rattle, and Roll" show.

We were all absurdly nervous. It's one thing to learn something new. It's quite another to demonstrate what you have learned in front of an audience. I hadn't felt this ter-rified since my first accordion recital when I was six years old.

Sammie gathered us all in our designated spot backstage

for last minute instructions and a pep talk. Affinity, of course, was in jail, and Serenity had never showed up at the studio for class again. Cassie, however, was joining us. Technically, she wasn't an adult, but Sammie had assured us that all was fine because our group was *predominantly* adults.

"You're going to do great," Sammie said. "Just remember, deep breaths. Then dance like you mean it."

"Break a leg everyone!" Nell said. "We're going to kill it!"

"No, no!" Sammie said. "'Break a leg' is for theater. You *never* say that to dancers." I imagined she wasn't too keen on "kill it," either, given recent events.

"Oh. What do you say?"

"*Merde.*"

"What does that mean?"

Sammie looked at Nell's sweet apple-cheeked face and couldn't say it. "It's French. For, um, excrement."

"Excrement?" It wasn't clicking for Nell. I saw Aunt Ruth whisper to her.

"Oh my." Nell's eyes widened. "Can I say 'good luck' instead?"

"No. It's bad luck." Sammie took pity on her. "But I think 'Happy tapping' would be okay."

Nell beamed. "Happy tapping!"

The Dancing Queens from Russo Dance Studio weren't on until after intermission, so Sammie sent us out to find seats and watch the first numbers in the show. Sammie and I slipped into seats beside our fan club—all six of the Streusals, Moriko, Mom, Baba, Geraldine, Sam, and Isabelle. Geraldine sat nearest the door so that she could slip out with Isabelle if she started crying. For now Isabelle rested on her lap, but from the look on Baba's face, I could tell she was itching for a turn.

To my surprise, Dan walked in and joined us. Baba scooted over a seat so he could sit beside me. "I thought you had to work," I said.

"I rearranged some things. Had to do it. How many guys have a girlfriend who plays the accordion *and* tap dances?" he said. "I'm a lucky man."

My stomach had felt queasy before. Now it started churning aggresively.

Dan offered to go in the lobby and get wine, if anyone wanted a glass. "Yes," I said quickly, then retracted. I was going to be dancing.

"Definitely," said Mom, eyeing a group of heavy-set women taking their seats in front of us. They were all wearing gold sequined stretch pants, and gold sequined stretch pants didn't do them any favors. "I may need it," she murmured.

Three women who were probably in their sixties walked past in pink leotards, pink ruffled skirts, and pink tights. Baba slid her eyes to Mom, then to Dan. "I'll take a glass, too."

A group of dancers in their twenties slipped into seats near the front of the auditorium, wearing only black net hose and black leotards. "Now *they* could pull off gold stretch pants," Mom said. Sam nodded, and Sammie elbowed him.

Soon the lights dimmed and the show began. The audience was kind, filled with friends, family, and other tap dancers. We cheered for each group, even the worst ones. After all, it takes a certain kind of bravery to step on stage at all.

The performances varied widely. Some groups did

simple steps—the gold sequined pants ladies, for example— while others did more complex routines, sometimes even featuring soloists. One pink ruffled lady fell down dancing with her group to "Ain't She Sweet," but the audience cheered enthusiastically when she got up. A lady in another group faced the back of the stage for almost 16 measures of "Cups" before she realized everyone else was facing the audience. One of the young women in black leotards dazzled the audience with a professional performance to "Jumpin' Jive."

When it was time for the Russo Studio Dancing Queens to go backstage, we put on our wigs and threw the sparkling boas—red, pink, purple—around our necks. Sammie gave us a thumbs up and we walked carefully backstage, trying not to let our taps make a sound. Taking our places in the wings—five of us on each side—we took deep breaths, as Sammie had instructed.

And then the emcee introduced us. Cheers and whistles came from the side of the audience where our fan club was sitting. The music started and we gulped and took the stage.

The lights were blinding. Sammie had warned us that we wouldn't be able to see much, but it wasn't easy to smile into a brilliant void. Still, we did it. We smiled, and we danced like we meant it.

They loved us. At least it sure *felt* like they loved us. People laughed at our over-the-top boa twirling and our "We are hot, no matter what we look like" attitude. They applauded when we turned, faced the back of the stage, and blew a kiss over our shoulders, all at the same time. When Aunt Ruth entirely forgot one section of the dance, she stood tall and tapped her foot, as if that was part of the routine.

When she figured out where to rejoin us, she flashed a quick thumbs up to the audience, and they applauded again.

When we took our bows at the end, we smiled with relief and joy. There is such a feeling of accomplishment when a diverse group comes together to pull off something difficult, no matter what it is, and we were on a high.

"Great job!!" Sammie whispered to us. We waited back-stage for two more numbers and then joined all the dancers in the show for the finale. It was the "Shim-Sham," the unof-ficial anthem of tap dancers everywhere.

Out in the lobby after the show, Dan presented both Cassie and me with bouquets—roses for Cassie and tulips, my favorite, for me. "You both looked like pros," he lied, but we smiled and pretended he was right.

Baba eyed Nell, who was accepting bouquets from two sets of great-grandchildren. "You know, bowling isn't the challenge it used to be," she said. "Maybe I'll take up tap dancing, too."

Life calmed down. Late one Sunday afternoon in early July, I hosted a gathering in my backyard to thank everyone for their help with my unauthorized murder investigation. To be nice, I'd invited Mildred, but she emailed me a note, politely declining. Her jaw was wired shut, and she said it wasn't much fun to be around others when she couldn't talk or eat. A full recovery was expected, but I really did feel sorry for her. I couldn't imagine not being able to eat or talk.

The Streusals arrived early because Allan is always early, and he had driven everyone over in his van. As I passed out beer, wine, and iced tea, Otto asked me, "Are you prepared for your lecture next week?"

I'd completely forgotten that I was to be the featured speaker in the lecture series, talking about the accordion.

Otto saw it on my face. "You *forgot?*"

"I'll get busy on it tomorrow. It's not like I have to do a lot of research or anything."

"Really? Let's see, do you know that the accordion was inspired by a centuries old Chinese instrument called the *sheng?*"

"Um, no."

"It was. Do you know where 75% of modern acoustic piano accordions are manufactured?"

"No."

"Italy. Can you describe how the free reeds inside …"

"All right, all right. I'll do my research. I'll prepare. And I will choose an appropriately dazzling musical number to demonstrate both the instrument and my expertise."

"And you'll play the 'Beer Barrel Polka,' Carl said.

I sighed. "Of course." I always have to play the "Beer Barrel Polka."

It was a lazy afternoon, the late afternoon sun still bright as we relaxed on the backyard deck. Mom sat at the table with Geraldine putting stamps on campaign postcards because a page with about a hundred names had somehow been left off a bulk mailing. Baba sat drinking a glass of chardonnay, Lester beside her sipping merlot and eating small bites (easier for the digestion) of imported cheese he'd brought with him. They were working a crossword puzzle together, Baba resting her cast on Lester's leg. Every now and then he reached over and patted her hand.

Jake was proofreading Geraldine's latest blog. He looked up at her at one point and said, *"Heartless developers out to destroy our environment with their McMansions*? Is that really what you want to say?"

"Yes," she said.

He half-smiled and went back to proofreading.

"Forty-five minutes," Dan said, after taking down everyone's pizza preferences and calling Blackjack Pizza.

"I hope Blake is the one who delivers," Cassie said. She still hadn't met him. "Who knows? Maybe I'll want to ask for his number for *reals*."

"Don't get your hopes up," I said. I didn't think Blake was probably her type. No bad-boy edge to him.

I sat on a blanket with Isabelle and Cassie while Sammie stretched out on the chaise lounge and closed her eyes. Cassie tried to play peek-a-boo with Isabelle, holding a blanket in front of her own face, then removing it, but Isabelle probably wasn't old enough to respond the way Cassie hoped. Still, she paid attention, watching Cassie with interest.

Derek sat beside Clay, both of them scrolling idly through their phones. Clay, I had already learned, shared Derek's adventurous approach to clothing. He wore neon red shorts and a T-shirt that said *Middle Earth's Annual Mordor Fun Run*. Derek wore equally bright yellow shorts and T-shirt that said *Not all those who wander are lost. J.R.R. Tolkien*. I assumed they had coordinated their looks.

"Interesting headline," Derek said, reading from his phone. "'Scuffle erupts when unauthorized man tries to pre-board airline.'" He looked at me and waited.

I didn't disappoint him. "I don't know why they keep using the term *preboarding*."

Dan smiled. "I get it. Travelers don't *preboard* planes."

"Exactly." I loved this guy.

Cassie frowned. "What's wrong with *preboarding?*"

"It doesn't make sense," I said. "It's like you're saying 'We'll get on the plane *before* we get on the plane.' What you're doing is just boarding first. Not *pre*-boarding. It's like pre-planning. Does that mean you plan before you plan? No. It's a dumb word."

Cassie put down her blanket and gave me a "This is hurting my brain" look. "Why do you make such a big deal about stuff no one cares about, Ella? It's so *stupid.*"

"Cassie," Dan warned.

"It's true, Dad. No one cares about the stuff she cares about. Like words, words, words. It's so *dumb.*"

I felt a prick of annoyance.

Actually, it was more of a stab of annoyance. Words *are* important. But then I told myself that maybe, just maybe, this was all part of the push-pull of stepparenthood that Geraldine had warned me about.

Not that I was a stepparent.

Yet.

I just smiled, picked myself up off the blanket, and went inside to pour another glass of wine.

* * * * *

YUM CAKE
(Try it! It really is delicious.)

Note: Make the caramel topping a day before needed.

INGREDIENTS
Caramel topping
½ cup brown sugar
1½ cups whipping cream

Cake
One chocolate fudge cake mix
(Baba prefers Duncan Hines Dark Chocolate Fudge)

Hazelnut filling
4 ounces mascarpone cheese
½ cup Nutella hazelnut spread
½ cup whipping cream
½ teaspoon vanilla
1½ tablespoons powdered sugar

DIRECTIONS
Make the caramel topping:
1. Heat brown sugar in saucepan over medium low heat, stirring constantly until it is completely melted.
2. Remove from heat and gradually add about half of the cream, being careful about splattering. (The melted brown sugar will likely clump.)
3. Put back on heat and keep stirring, simmering until the caramel is almost completely melted.
4. Add the rest of the cream and bring to a boil.
5. Remove from heat and strain out any caramel bits that haven't melted.
6. Cover and refrigerate for about 8 hours.

(continued)

(continued)

Make the cake:
1.   Follow cake mix directions, using 8 inch pans.
2.   Let cool completely.

Make the hazelnut filling:
1.   Whip the cream.
2.   Add powdered sugar and vanilla.
3.   Beat mascarpone cheese and Nutella until smooth.
4.   Fold the mascarpone/Nutella mixture into the whipped cream.

Whip the chilled caramel topping until stiff peaks form.

Assemble the cake:
1.   Cut one layer of the cake in half horizontally to make two half-layers, slicing carefully.
2.   Place the top half-layer on a plate, rounded top down. Cover it with hazelnut filling.
3.   Place second half-layer over the first and cover with caramel topping. (Note: Don't try to frost the sides of the cake. Let the fillings show.)
4.   Repeat steps with second layer, this time starting with the bottom half-layer, and ending with caramel topping on the rounded top of the cake.
5.   Refrigerate until ready to serve.
6.   Enjoy!

Enjoy another
Ella Polansky mystery!

Ella Polansky is as hip as a kindergarten teacher can be. No apple or alphabet sweaters for her. Ever. And when she plays a gig with her accordion, she steps to the microphone in red boots and tight jeans to add some percussive beatboxing.

But Ella loses her cool when someone pushes her beloved accordion off a balcony and kills the unpopular director of a local musical theater production. Who is the logical suspect? Ella, of course, and she's not happy about it.

Somehow she has to persuade handsome Detective Dan Sherman that she's innocent, get her teaching job back, and rescue her kindergartners from the mean substitute teacher they all hate.

Oh, and she also needs to figure out how to help her best friend, who is accidentally pregnant by a conceited male model with bad grammar and absolutely no potential as a father. Ella enlists the help of friends, family and the doting older men in a polka band (yes, a polka band) to discover the truth and clear her name.

Cheryl Miller Thurston is a Colorado writer, teacher, and musician. She has published articles, books, poetry, plays, musicals, and music on a variety of subjects. She is also the author of *Death By Accordion*, the first book in the Ella Polansky series.

www.CherylMillerThurston.com